The Kill Fee
of Cindy LaCoste

THE
Austin·Stoner
FILES

Book Three

The Kill Fee

of Cindy LaCoste

Stephen Bly

CROSSWAY BOOKS • WHEATON, ILLINOIS
A DIVISION OF GOOD NEWS PUBLISHERS

JM

The Kill Fee of Cindy LaCoste

Copyright © 1997 by Stephen Bly

Published by Crossway Books
    a division of Good News Publishers
    1300 Crescent Street
    Wheaton, Illinois 60187

Cover illustration: Ed Tadiello

Cover design: Cindy Kiple

First printing 1997

Printed in the United States of America

Library of Congress Cataloging-in-Publication Data
Bly, Stephen A., 1944-
 The kill fee of Cindy LaCoste / Stephen Bly.
   p. cm. — (The Austin-Stoner files ; bk. 3.)
 ISBN 0-89107-954-8 (TPB: alk. paper)
 I. Title. II. Series: Bly, Stephen A., 1944- Austin-Stoner files ; bk. 3.
 PS3552.L93K55 1997
813'.54—dc21   97-18925

05		04		03		02		01		00		99		98		97
15	14	13	12	11	10	9	8	7	6	5	4	3	2	1

For
Connie Sue

ONE

It came with a Western twang and the syncopated rhythm of a horse trot.

"I love ya, darlin'."

The voice was low, soft, tender, sincere. Lynda Austin felt a tingle in her throat and a little short of breath.

"Brady, I love you, too. But what do you mean you're 35,000 feet over Detroit on your way to Boston?" She tugged on the carved elk-horn feather earring that dangled beneath her shoulder-length hair. "The big party's tonight! We've got to be out at the Gossmans' place in East Hampton in four hours!"

"Lynda Dawn, you can't blame this one on me or on rodeo. I got up at 4:20 this mornin'. I've been crisscrossin' the country all day long. I was sittin' at Denver for two hours while they repaired the plane." The voice now sounded like a sixteen-year-old trying to explain why he ditched biology. "Then I got to Chicago late, missed my flight. I sat there spinnin' my rowels for an hour and fifteen minutes. And what did they do? They changed gates on me six times and then canceled the flight completely."

She glanced at the picture of a smiling bareback rider in the barnboard-framed picture on her crowded desk. "They what?"

"Don't you just love O'Hare? You know how bizarre it gets on a Friday night. I am surely hopin' this is the last time I ever have to fly to the East Coast."

"But—but why are you going to Boston?" She pushed back from her computer keyboard and stared up at the Navajo-white painted ceiling of her twelfth-floor Madison Avenue office.

"The next flight to La Guardia would get me there at 10:00 P.M. So I told that yella-haired sweetheart at the Service Center she'd have to do better than that 'cause I was missin' my Lynda Dawn. She said I could fly to Boston, and if I hustled my Wranglers, I can catch a flight to New York and be there at 7:05."

Lynda sat up, grabbed a felt tip pen, and doodled the words *yellow hair* on a white note pad. "But the party at the Gossmans' begins at 8:00 P.M. You were supposed to check into your hotel room. Then we'd have a long, slow drive out there. Now we won't have time to—"

"Darlin', you go to the party by yourself. I'll rent a car and be there as quick as I can. I won't be very late. Just tell me how to find the place. It's a little island, right?"

"It's a big, very crowded island." Lynda bit on her bottom lip and ran her left hand through her hair. "But what if you miss the plane in Boston? What if your luggage doesn't get transferred? What if the flight's late getting here? What if there's too much Friday night traffic? Brady, you don't understand! This is the only reception we'll have in New York. This is a big deal to me. With the wedding in Wyoming, this is going to be—"

"Darlin', it's important to me, too! Don't start to cry. I promise I'll—"

"I'm not crying," she sniffled. *I'm crushed . . . but not crying.*

"Lynda Dawn, you've got a cowboy that's so crazy about marryin' you he'll fly to New York City and eat repugnant little green and black slimy things, and visit all night with folks who he has no idea in the world what they're talkin' about. I'm doin' ever'thing I know how to do to get there. I drawed out of two rodeos and got to the airport an hour and fifteen minutes early. What else can I do, babe? You name it, and I'll do it. But don't cry. You'll dilute your perfume. You're not wearing that Prairie Delight, are you?"

Lynda took a deep breath and pressed the Exit button on the computer keyboard. The office suddenly felt stale and stuffy. "Are you changing the subject, Stoner?"

"Yes, ma'am."

His voice revealed the sparkle in his eyes. She felt the muscles in her neck begin to relax. "Actually I'm trying something new."

There was laughter in his voice this time. "You found a perfume you didn't own? What's this one called?"

"First Kiss."

"Really? Whoa, poor thing. I've been away too long."

"Yes, you have, Brady Stoner! And I've had this whole evening planned for weeks. It's already ruined, and you haven't even arrived."

"Wait! Wait! Wait! The evening's not ruined yet. Maybe rearranged, but not ruined. You and me will still be together—hand to hand, toe to toe, buckle to buckle. Darlin', that's all I've been thinkin' about for most of two months."

Lynda whisked back the tears in the corners of her eyes. "Most?" She twisted the solitary diamond engagement ring on her finger.

"Well . . . there was eight seconds last Saturday night in Red Bluff when I forgot about you completely. I was just wonderin' if I'd live until the whistle blew."

"I thought you took first money in Red Bluff."

"I did. Scored an 87. Oh, man, was that a ride! I can't wait to tell you all about it."

"I've got a lot of things to talk to you about, too." She doodled the name Cindy LaCoste on the note pad. "Some really,

really important things. That's the point. We were going to have a slow, leisurely drive out to Long Island and talk and talk and talk." *Am I sounding whiny? I hate it when I whine!*

Brady let out with his deep, hear-it-clear-across-the-room laugh. "It wouldn't have worked anyway."

"Why?"

"'Cause these lips of mine are plumb bored silly of talkin'. They been pinin' and beggin' for a touch of Autumn Rose Blush lipstick."

She swept her fingers along her lips and studied the pink residue on her fingertips. "Oh?"

"I was countin' on Nina or Kelly drivin' us out there while you and me sat in the backseat and necked."

"With Kelly or Nina in the front seat? Yeah, right."

"Eh, excuse me, ma'am." It was his hat-tipping, apologetic voice, aimed away from the telephone.

"Brady?"

"Sorry, darlin', I think I embarrassed the lady sittin' next to me in the plane," he reported in a whisper.

"People are listening to our conversation?"

"Only my end. You can go ahead and say something risque and personal if you want, Miss Lynda Dawn."

"Cool down, cowboy. Listen, I'll have—eh, I'll have Nina wait at the airport and bring you out to Gossmans'. You don't need to rent a car. But you have to promise to behave yourself."

"You got nothin' to worry about. Darlin', you know my heart belongs to you."

"Yeah, and on June 6 I get all the rest, too!" Lynda could feel sweat suddenly pop out on her forehead. *I can't believe I said that.*

"Oooh, wheee! Now you really did embarrass Miss Melinda."

"Who?"

"The redheaded sweetheart sittin' next to me."

"I thought you said she couldn't hear."

"She can't. I was teasin', Lynda Dawn."

She idly spelled "Melinda" on her note pad and then drew a line through it.

"Darlin', I've got a lot to talk to you about, too. I think that's the second thing I'm going to really enjoy about being married. It will be so great to have you right there to talk to."

"Except when you're rodeoing," she reminded him.

"Yeah . . . but I've got a surprise or two to tell you about."

"What?"

"I'll tell ya when I get there."

"Tell me right now."

"No, I've been holding on to this secret for three months, and I'm not going to spill it now."

"Brady, you didn't change our honeymoon plans again, did you?"

"Now don't let it bust your cinch, darlin'. I'd better hang up now. The sound of your sweet voice is breakin' my heart."

"Give me the flight number from Boston."

"United #616."

"La Guardia—not Kennedy?"

"Yep."

"Now you listen to me, cowboy. I want you in East Hampton tonight! Before 9:00 P.M. No excuses. I do not, and I repeat, do not intend to go through another day without seeing you. Have you got that, Stoner?"

"Yes, ma'am."

"Brady, hurry. I really, really miss you!"

"I'll go ask the pilot to kick it into overdrive, darlin'. Listen, I won't have time to change. Will they let me in the door dressed in blue jeans?"

"Brady Stoner, I don't care if your jeans are worn and your boots covered with dried manure. And I couldn't care less what anyone thinks or says about how you are dressed. I want to feel that callused hand in mine and those strong arms wrapped around me. You are mine, cowpuncher, and I'm staking my claim tonight. Is that clear?"

"Yes, ma'am . . . only you embarrassed Miss Melinda again. I reckon she's never seen a man's boots melt like that."

"Well, pack 'em in ice, buckaroo, and I'll see you in East Hampton."

"Yes, ma'am. I think I'll open a window and let in a little fresh air."

"Stoner!"

"Bye, darlin'."

◆ ◆ ◆

One hundred and twenty invited guests swarmed through L. George and Carolyn Gossman's manicured backyard devouring black and green slimy hors d'oeuvres, discussing big city trivialities, and waiting for the arrival of Brady Stoner. Even though the gold engraved invitations suggested casual Western apparel, very few boots and cowboy hats were in sight.

One exception was L. George Gossman, who now sported a wide gray handlebar mustache and chose to wear his black stovepipe-top cowboy boots on the outside of his slightly ill-fitting gray Wranglers. The huge dark gray Tom Mix Stetson and stacked boot heels made him look almost six feet tall.

Many in the crowd were employed by Atlantic-Hampton Publishing Company. Lynda knew most of them but not all. Some were neighbors of the Gossmans, who came just to view the "real" cowboy.

Lynda circled the tiers of cascading fruit, then stopped in front of a table piled high with smartly wrapped presents. "Kelly, how are we going to get all these gifts to Wyoming?"

"We figured it out. Nina and I will rent a van and drive them out to you," she offered. "No! No, we'll rent a pickup and drive out. Can you see that? Nina and me in jeans, boots, and cowboy hats cruising Jackson, Wyoming, in a pickup truck?"

"Jackson Hole is full of tourists. If you're looking for a real cowboy, try Lander, Douglas, Ten Sleep, or Torrington."

"Hey, whatever." Kelly glanced at the crowd hovering around Spunky Hampton. "Terrance O'Brian, Joaquin Estaban, Jack McCrea—don't those famous authors know Spunky's married to T. H. Hampton, Junior?"

Lynda tugged at the tight collar button of her keyhole Western blouse. "Oh, they're just enjoying their own notoriety. They're harmless . . . except perhaps O'Brian. Actually I think marriage has been good for Spunky. She's changed a lot in the last year."

"Yeah." Kelly lifted her eyebrows. "Her tight dress is only slit up to the mid-thigh now."

"But she only has eyes for Junior."

"I'll give her that," Kelly admitted.

"Besides, you can be grateful she's here."

"Why's that?"

"If she weren't, all these men would be hovering around the ravishing Kelly Princeton."

"Oh, yeah, right. As far as they're concerned, I'm just a glo-rified errand girl—an associate editor with sparkling green eyes, gorgeous tumbling dark hair, a dynamite personality, not to mention an hourglass figure. Just a veritable goddess of feminine loveliness waiting patiently for her Lancelot to rescue her from this life of boredom and carry her to a world of conjugal bliss. Of course," she giggled, "I could be wrong about that. Have I been editing romance novels too long, or what?"

"We've all been working in fiction too long. That's what I like about the West—everyone is so real."

Kelly speared two kiwi slices and plopped them on her plate. "Did Brady mention how the house is coming along? I can't believe you two get to build a home right there in Jackson!"

"No, I think he likes keeping it a secret. I presume he's bringing some pictures. This will be the first time I've moved to a place sight unseen. But we picked out the plans last Christmas. I hope we have a view of the Tetons."

"Will your royalties from Grandpa Harrison's books cover all the construction?"

Lynda studied the eight-foot fake saguaro cactus perched behind the buffet table. "That was the plan."

"At least you will have a valuable piece of property even if you two don't live there forever."

Lynda inspected her turquoise stone and silver wristwatch. "Is it almost 8:30? He said he'd be here before nine!" she fussed.

"Oh, you know Nina. She's from Wisconsin. She could get lost and not show up for days. You should have let me bring Brady."

Lynda scowled. "Oh, sure. You'd take a left turn and end up in Montreal—on purpose."

Kelly stuck out her tongue. "Hey, who's the guy over there talking with Julie Quick?"

"That's her fiance."

"No wonder they're huddled in the corner. Did you notice that there aren't many unattached men at this party? Are you sure Brady's not bringing any of his cowboy friends with him?"

Lynda snatched a strawberry, dipped it in a small crystal bowl of powdered sugar, and plopped it in her mouth. "I'm positive," she mumbled.

Kelly raised her eyebrows and studied the buffet table. "Isn't there anything edible here?"

"That's exactly what Brady will say," Lynda reported. "He'll probably want us to go out for Chinese after this is over."

"Oh, look who's finally here!" Kelly cheered.

Lynda whipped her head around. "Brady?"

"No . . . Frank Alverez. This is only the third time I've seen him in six years."

"That's not true. He came out of his office sometime last month," Lynda teased.

"You mean in April when you called the meeting about the LaCoste manuscript. Hey, what did Brady say when you told him you decided not to publish her story?"

Lynda swirled the orange liquid around in her glass cup. "I haven't told him yet."

"What? But that was two months ago!"

"Well . . . I wanted to wait until I see him face to face. I'll tell him this weekend."

L. George Gossman sauntered over to them. "Well, how's Little Miss Sure-Shot? Ms. Princeton, Austin here is the finest I've ever seen at picking out best-selling books. I think maybe it's something a person's born with. Lynda, I'm goin' to get that cowboy of yours to guarantee he'll let you mosey into the city every month and help us evaluate manuscripts!" Gossman tipped his cowboy hat and wandered toward T. H. Hampton, Jr.

"Mosey? Goin'?" Kelly giggled. "Did I hear L. George Gossman drop a *g*?"

"The whole world is changing, girl."

"In L. George's case, I like the changes! But you didn't finish the deal about Cindy LaCoste."

"What's there to say? The book was dated, repetitive, and extremely depressing. The ending just collapsed. We couldn't print it. Especially under the Austin Imprint."

Kelly dug out a slice of something white. "This is cheese, isn't it—not some sort of soy byproduct? Anyway, Cindy's a good friend of Brady's, and so I assumed once the contract was signed, it was a done deal. I figured you'd clean it up."

"That's what I was thinking. But it was just too rough." Lynda picked up a silver butter knife and used it as a mirror to check her mascara and then her teeth. "It's kind of sad, isn't it? Here's a gal who goes through that terrible assault, and the public says, 'Ho, hum, what's new?' We never could find a slant to make it marketable, but I think it was good for her to write it all out. Cindy's a good friend of mine, too, you know."

"Oh, sure." Kelly took a bite of the white sliced food product, coughed, and then swallowed hard. "You're good buddies. That's why she returned the kill-fee check."

"She didn't even look at the check. The envelope said, 'No longer at this address.' I don't think she even knows we've knocked it over yet."

"And I say she's telling you what you can do with Atlantic-Hampton's $5,000."

"I'll find out from Brady where she is now and mail it again. Besides, I told her from the beginning nothing is certain in this business."

"That's not true." Kelly glanced around at the crowd. "Some things are always the same. Take Terrance O'Brian—he's always certain to make a pass at someone. And Spunky will draw a crowd of men. Estaban's westerns will sell over 250,000 on the first printing. Stan will threaten to quit and go to Putnam before the end of the month. Someone will write to claim discovery of a long-lost Martin Taylor Harrison novel . . . and Brady Stoner will look at his Lynda Dawn Darlin' with a sparkle in his eyes like a puppy who's just been plucked out of the pound by a nine-year-old girl."

Lynda spun around to where Kelly was looking. She faced the floor-to-ceiling French provincial doors that led from the Gossmans' sun room to the patio.

Dimpled boyish grin.

Black beaver felt cowboy hat.

Wide shoulders, strong hands.

Long-sleeved shirt.

Slightly shaggy, dark brown hair.

Worn boots.

Wide brown eyes.

Jeans, big silver belt buckle.

Lynda scurried over to the vine-arbored patio. "Brady! You did make it!"

"Darlin', I promised. I wouldn't miss this even if I had to fork a rank bronc clear across the country!"

She threw her arms around his neck, intending to kiss his cheek. But Brady met her lips with his and held her so tight that he lifted her five-foot-ten-inch frame off the ground.

Stoner, save it until later—everyone's watching. That's enough, Brady. You're embarrassing me. I'm a private person.

He eased her down to the ground and started to pull back when she latched onto his neck and jammed her lips back on his. *Oh, no you don't, cowboy. You aren't going to get away with just a little peck. I've been missing you like crazy, and today we start to make up for it.*

The kiss was warm and soft, yet firm with enthusiasm. Brady's hat tumbled to the deck to the cheers and applause of the entire crowd. He finally released her.

Blushing a deep scarlet, Brady turned to the crowd. "Sorry, folks . . . eh, I haven't seen my Lynda Dawn Darlin' in six weeks. And this girl's kiss is sweeter than spring hittin' the Great Divide, if you get my drift."

Spunky Hampton strolled over and snatched up his hat. She plunked it on her head, and it dropped down past her ears and almost covered her eyes. Her long black hair flowed down her back to her waist. "I thought we were going to have to turn the sprinklers on you two," she teased.

Brady snatched his hat back and whispered to Lynda, "We've got to talk, darlin'."

"I know. Why not get some food and we'll—"

Carolyn Gossman in a short red-and-white line-dancing outfit swept between them, clutching their arms and leading them into the crowd. "You'll have a lifetime to whisper and kiss. It's time to meet the guests and open presents!"

"Carrie," Brady insisted, "can Lynda and me have a couple of minutes to—"

"Oh, my heavens, yes! By all means."

"Thanks."

"After you meet the guests, open presents, and enjoy the barbeque."

"Barbeque? You mean there's more food?" Lynda asked.

"Oh, yes. These are just the appetizers. They're for New Yorkers who can't tell the difference between Texas ribs and Tucson chili steaks. The real food comes later, Brady." She squeezed his arm and then pulled them into the waiting crowd. "And this is our—I mean, Lynda's cowboy!"

With Carolyn Gossman on one arm and Lynda Austin on the other, Brady "yes, ma'amed" his way through the Long Island crowd. He sat with what Lynda thought was an apprehensive grin and watched her open present after present. Most of the gifts looked too upscale for newlyweds living in Jackson, Wyoming. She noticed that the only ones that stirred Brady's interest were the eight-place setting of bronc buster designed stoneware from the Gossmans and a beautiful three-foot copy of a Remington bronze bucking horse and panicked rider facing a menacing rattlesnake, given by Mr. and Mrs. T. H. Hampton, Jr.

Kelly boxed up the opened presents, and Nina hurriedly wrote down who gave what. They had just finished when the caterer declared the barbeque ready to serve. Joaquin Estaban blessed the food in Spanish, and then while the haunting sounds of George Strait singing "I Can Still Make Cheyenne" came over the rented sound system, Lynda and Brady led the procession toward the tower of ribs and steaks.

They hardly got to say three words to each other during the mealtime. Brady held most of the audience captive with a buck-by-buck description of his 87-point ride in Red Bluff. This was followed by a round of picture-taking, mainly Long

Island ladies wanting their photo with the professional rodeo cowboy in the black Resistol hat.

Following supper, Carolyn Gossman announced that she and L. George would teach the whole group to line dance. In the laughter and confusion that followed, Brady and Lynda slipped inside the house to the sun room near the patio.

"I can't believe Georgie is out there doin' the 'Boot-Scootin' Boogie,'" Brady roared.

"He's a changed man."

"For the better, I hope."

"Well, at least he's relaxed—not so uptight and formal anymore. Mrs. Gossman says they're having the time of their lives."

"I suppose it was that trip out west they took last fall." Brady stared out the plate glass window at the guests.

"It was you, Brady Stoner—you change people."

"But I don't try to get them to change."

"That's the point. You just ride through life completely enjoying yourself with your boots and your simple life and your 'darlin's,' and it touches a nerve in people. They suddenly remember when their life was less hectic and much more enjoyable. So they say to themselves, 'If Stoner can do it, so can I.'"

Brady stepped beside her and slipped his arm around her waist. The aroma of his aftershave was someplace between sage and pine. "Have I changed you, Miss Lynda Dawn?"

"Changed me? Look at me! Teal blue cowboy boots, Western clothes, squash blossom necklace. In a few weeks I'll be living in Wyoming—Jackson, Wyoming! Changed me? You completely rebuilt me, cowboy!"

"You're built just fine, ma'am. I'm not about to change that. Listen, speakin' of Wyomin', that's a part of what I wanted to tell you." He dropped his arm from her waist and turned to face her.

"About our house? I want to hear everything, but before

you do," Lynda barged on, "I've got something to tell you first. It will just take a minute. Then you can talk house details."

"Darlin', let me finish. This may blow you away." He unfastened the simulated pearl snap on the flap of his shirt pocket and pulled out a photograph. "I took a couple pictures of the place." He beamed.

"Brady, I have to talk to you about Cindy LaCoste." She looked at the picture in his hand. "It's not finished?"

"No, they're still working on it. But it will be done on time. Tip and Ralph Lee Yates are buildin' it, and they gave me their word. But I, eh, made some changes . . . without tellin' you. I was going to wait and just surprise you when we got there, but I couldn't hold it back any longer."

"Changes? We still get three bedrooms and an office and a den, don't we?"

"Oh, sure, darlin'. . . . What did you say about Cindy?"

"Brady, when's the last time you saw her?"

"I suppose it was in February when you were out, when we drove out to L. G. Minor's ranch in Ely and you encouraged her to rewrite the first three chapters of her book." He handed her the photos. "What do you think? Do you like the house?"

"It's larger than I remembered and more, eh, rustic."

"The picture was taken without the roof."

"I'm glad to hear that. It will be like living in a lodge."

"Yeah, isn't it great?"

"I still don't know how we can afford to build that large a house in Jackson."

"Don't worry, darlin'. I figured out a way to cut the costs way down." He didn't look her in the eyes, but gazed up at the ceiling. "How's Cindy's book coming?"

"That's what I'm trying to tell you. I need to talk to Cindy. I wrote her a letter, but it was returned by the post office unopened. Did she move?" She turned the photo over in her hand. "Is our house north of Jackson or toward the airport?"

"It's not in Jackson. Cindy was talkin' about doing some barrel racin', but I haven't seen her on the circuit. Doesn't L. G. know where she's at?"

"No, I called her, and she said Cindy left a couple weeks ago. She's been holding her mail and can't figure out why they sent that one piece back." Lynda cocked her head slightly to the right and squinted her eyes. "What do you mean, it's not in Jackson?"

"If Cindy is rodeoin', she'll check in one of these days. What's the matter? Do you have a question about her book?"

"Where's our house, Stoner?"

"Montana, but what's the fuss about Cindy's book?"

"Montana!" Lynda gasped. "What do you mean, Montana?"

"You didn't finish about Cindy's book."

"Cindy's book? You tell me out of the clear blue sky that we're going to live in Montana instead of Wyoming, and you want me to calmly tell you about how we decided not to publish Cindy's book?"

"You what? You can't be serious." Brady's voice raised to a near shout. "You have a contract! You have to publish the book!"

"It didn't come to us in publishable form! Brady, it just wasn't working," she huffed. "Now what's this joke about us living in Montana?"

"Joke? The only joke around here is this hogwash about not publishing that book. Cindy's whole recovery is contingent on being able to tell her story, and you know it. You can't turn it down. That's—that's incredible!"

"What's incredible is that two weeks before my wedding I have no idea where I'm going to live! Where in Montana?"

"On the ranch, of course. No wonder you can't find Cindy. All she needed was someone else to tell her she's a failure!" Brady yanked off his hat and clutched his forehead in his hand.

"The whole reason I asked you about Cindy is because I can't reach her to tell her about the book. She doesn't know anything yet. And I have no intention of telling her she's a failure." Lynda scooted to the edge of the sofa. "Where is this so-called Montana ranch of ours?"

"The Double Diamond—you knew that. What do you mean, she doesn't know you think her book is horrible?"

"I didn't say it was horrible. We just can't publish it. I explained it all in a letter," Lynda snapped. "I sent her a generous kill fee."

"Talk about kill fee—it will kill her, all right. Lynda Dawn Darlin', you can't do that!"

"I did it. It's done. It's a tough business, and that's the way it works. Did you say the Double Diamond? You don't mean that godforsaken spread out in the blizzards of Judith Gap?"

"Buffalo."

"It has buffalo on it?"

"No, our mailing address is Buffalo, Montana."

Lynda folded her arms. "Not me, buckaroo. I told you I wouldn't live out there. That's the worst place on the face of this earth."

"Well, you're goin' to live there because I already bought the ranch. That's where this house is being built. And not only that, you're goin' to publish that book of Cindy's. No wife of mine is goin' to double-cross our friends!"

"Listen, cowboy, don't you now or ever tell me how to run my business! And there is no way on earth you're going to get me to move out there! You knew that, Brady Stoner!"

"I went in hock up to my withers to buy that ranch. I can't back out," he shouted.

"Well, I can back out of it! Do you hear me? I am not a pioneer woman. I do not intend to live in a place without electricity, indoor plumbing, central air conditioning, or a minimart or mall within walking distance. Do I make myself clear?"

"Excuse me," a feminine voice called out from the door. Kelly and Nina stood in the corner of the sun room. Most of the guests crowded around the sliding glass door peering in.

"It's, ah—time to—you know . . ." Nina cleared her throat. "Cut the cake."

"Well, don't just stand there, Stoner, come on!" Lynda barked.

Kelly handed her a large cake server with a turquoise ribbon tied around it. "Are you sure you want to do this?"

"No, I'm not sure! I'm not sure where I'm going to be living in two weeks. I'm not even sure I'm going to get married," she huffed as she stormed through the crowd.

"Whoa, whoa, whoa!" L. George Gossman blustered his way into the room, his mustache flopping in rhythm with his cowboy hat. "Obviously the honored couple is getting those last-minute jitters. We've all had them, haven't we?" he called out to the others. "Carolyn, teach them how to do the 'Achy-Breaky' while these two settle down a little."

Gossman grabbed Brady by one arm and Lynda by the other and led them over to the white sofa in front of the white brick fireplace. "Now talk through whatever it is that's touched this off. If you need a moderator, I'll be happy to stay . . . but I'd rather go outside and dance. However, I will be watching through the glass door, so don't start throwing lamps and, eh, cake servers."

While George and Carolyn hustled the group out into the backyard, Lynda plopped down on one end of the eight-foot sofa and Brady at the other. She still held the silver server in her hand. Both stared straight ahead at the bricks.

Lynda wiped back the tears from the corner of her eyes. She could feel many eyes watching them through the floor-to-ceiling windows, but she didn't care. The clock on the mantel ticked away, while a distant driving melody of Billy Ray Cyrus rolled in from the backyard.

"I want to go home. I feel rotten," she managed to say in a tone somewhere between panic and pout.

Brady sighed. "I feel like I'm back in that one-room schoolhouse on Reynolds Creek. Whenever we cut up too much, Mrs. Singleton would make us go back and sit in the coat closet with our backs to the class.

"One time in the third grade I teased a girl named Patsy McCalley about how many freckles she had on her nose, and she clobbered me alongside the ear with the B volume of the encyclopedia. I thought my whole head was caved in. Mrs. Singleton made us go sit in the coat closet next to each other until we both apologized. But Patsy was so stubborn she wouldn't talk to me for three hours. 'Course, I didn't talk to her either. Then it was time for lunch, and I knew Mom had packed me a cold liver sandwich . . . so we finally apologized. Well, this feels sort of like you and me sittin' in the coat closet at the Reynolds Creek School."

Lynda shook her head and laid the server on her lap. "I think it's a lot more serious than that. It's more like a car wreck. I mean, you're driving along, everything's going great, and then some guy going the opposite direction swerves across the double yellow line and smashes into you. Suddenly a day, a week, a month, a year, a life that's on even keel is completely altered forever. You never know how close you are to life-changing events."

"Are you sayin' I just wrecked your life—that I'm the one goin' in the wrong direction?"

Nina burst through the door. "Eh, sorry, guys, Mr. Gossman said I should bring you some punch, if you promise not to throw the cups at each other."

Brady took the cup and glanced over at Lynda. "Georgie, the peacemaker? I never figured him for that type."

"Yeah, well, I'm glad you're not yelling at each other anymore," Nina replied as she scampered back out into the backyard.

"And I never thought I'd see George wearing that cowboy getup."

"Yeah," Brady added, "it's like he's suddenly playing frontier marshal."

"We have a problem, Brady."

"Lord, help us—we've got two problems, Lynda Dawn."

Her voice was very quiet. "What are we going to do?"

"Darlin', I don't know. But I have no intention of livin' my life without you."

"You don't?"

"Nope. It's not even an option."

"I feel the same way."

For several more moments they sipped on the orange-colored punch and stared at white bricks.

Brady cleared his throat. "How in the world did two completely different people ever fall in love? We live in opposite worlds, have opposite kinds of friends, use totally different vocabularies, and have jobs totally foreign to the other. Maybe the Lord made a mistake. I mean, maybe He meant it for a joke, and we thought He was serious."

Lynda laid her arm on the back of the sofa and turned toward Brady. "Do you think we can talk about these things without shouting?"

"I really don't know, darlin'. I surely misjudged your reaction to me buyin' the ranch. I thought you'd be as happy as I am."

"I don't know how you could have thought that. I made myself explicitly clear last fall that the Double Diamond would be the last place on earth I would want to live."

"I figured you were just joshin' me."

"Why in heaven's name would I do that?"

"Could you give me three uninterrupted minutes to explain my position?"

"I promise not to interrupt if you give me the same consideration about Cindy's book proposal."

"But I can't believe . . ." Brady put his arm back down and stared at the white sofa. "Yeah, you're right. I'll hush up and listen. You go first."

"No, tell me about the ranch deal."

"It can wait, really. What about the book?"

"Stoner, tell me about the Double Diamond right now! Your three minutes are ticking away."

"Yes, ma'am. Well, this spring I had a long talk with my brother Brock and my dad. Dad's wanting to slow down on the place, which is fine. And Brock's wife wants to quit teachin' in Melba and home-school the girls. That way they could all help Brock with the chores and all."

"What's that have to do with . . . sorry. I didn't mean to interrupt."

"Well, one-fourth of the ranch belongs to Brock and one-fourth to me, and without Lorraine's salary it would be too tough for them to get by, so Brock offered to buy out my quarter."

"But you love that ranch. That's home for you!" she blurted out.

"I know, but it's not big enough for two brothers. Brock's older, and I figured it was his right. Anyway, that meant I was going to have some funds to buy us a place. I checked into Jackson."

"What did you find?"

"A lot 75 x 120 feet facing the Tetons is goin' for a mere $425,000."

"For just a lot?"

"Yep. When I was hitting the spring rodeos in California, I called the insurance company in San Francisco that owned the Double Diamond. They were floored that someone might want the place. Offered me the whole works for $300 an acre, and they'd carry the paper."

"So you bought it?"

"Nope. Told them that was too high. I offered them $200 an acre."

"You can't buy any land in the U.S. for that, can you?"

"Probably not. We settled on $250 an acre if they'd throw the buildings in for free."

"But that house is unlivable!"

"That's what I told them."

"So you spent your inheritance on a down payment on the Double Diamond?"

"Our inheritance—and our children's inheritance."

"What about the log house—how are we paying for that?"

"I used your money to build the house, like we planned. I ran a power line out there and installed a septic tank so we could have indoor plumbing. Even the phone line's in. I had them run three dedicated lines—one for your business, one for a fax, and one for me."

"Brady, it's too isolated. There isn't a neighbor for 100 miles."

"Seven."

"There's no airport."

"It's only 110 miles to Great Falls."

"Over 100 miles to a commuter airport?"

"But there's no speed limit in Montana. I timed it—you can get to the airport in an hour and a half."

"If you drive ninety, have no combines on the road, no snow, no rain, and no ice."

"I'll drive you, darlin'. It's a purdy stretch. You just caught that country on a bad day."

"Brady, I'm a city girl. Jackson, Wyoming, is really roughing it. I don't know if I can even survive there. There's no way—"

"Did I tell you about the hot tub facing the Little Belt Mountains?"

For the first time in an hour a smile broke across Lynda's face. "Indoor or outdoor?"

"Outdoor, in a covered, private patio."

"Are you handing me a line, Stoner?"

"No, ma'am."

"How can you afford all that?"

"I told you, I watched expenses."

The smile dropped off her face. "But it still won't work. I can't live that isolated with you going down the rodeo road. I'm not a loner like you are. I've lived most of my adult life in apartments and condos. I won't be able to sleep. I'll have the doors locked and shades pulled down all the time. Brady, I just can't do it," she sniffed.

"There won't be any rodeo road."

"What?"

"I'm hangin' up my riggin', darlin'."

"You're quitting bareback riding?"

"Yep."

"But—but—the NFR. The World Championship. You've been aiming for that your whole life."

"My whole life was changed around the minute Lynda Dawn Austin walked into that first aid tent behind the chutes at the Dixie Stampede in St. George, Utah."

"Brady, I can't ask you to quit rodeo. That would be like . . . like you asking me to quit being an editor."

"Darlin', you didn't ask me to quit. This might come as a surprise, but my life dream is not a World Championship. That's for young men to fancy. What I want is a good home, a good ranch, and Lynda Dawn Austin. I didn't enter any June rodeos. Next week I'm going up to help them finish the house. I've got 200 cows and calves and 200 Black Angus heifers waitin' in Idaho, but I'm not truckin' them in until after the honeymoon. That is—providin' there is a honeymoon."

"Brady, I want to be real honest. Being with you in a log

house out in the wilds of Montana will be wonderful for a couple of weeks. But I really don't think I can live in a place like that. It scares me to death."

He glanced down at his brown cowboy boots and shook his head. "I reckon I got caught up in one too many dreams."

"You're serious about quitting rodeo?"

"Yep."

"I don't want you to quit, Brady. I've never wanted you to quit."

"Darlin', thirty-two is an old man in rodeo."

"But you haven't won the big one."

"Look, I don't know one ol' boy on the circuit who wouldn't trade every buckle and saddle he's won for what I've got. Darlin', for three weeks ever' month I'll be right there with you. On that fourth week, you'll be right here in your beloved New York City. I'll get you to the airport; I'll drive you home."

"Brady, how would you feel if we lived in my Manhattan condo?"

"Like a rattlesnake who woke up at the North Pole."

"So you know how I'm going to feel in Montana."

"There's a difference, Lynda Dawn Darlin'. Montana will make you readjust your schedule and some of your habits, but New York would break my spirit."

She slapped the silver server against the couch and shook her head.

"What's the matter?" he asked.

"How do you do this to me? You sweet-talk me into believing that I can do something totally impossible. Is it the dimples? The little-boy grin?"

"It's cowboy logic, I reckon."

"Okay, buckaroo, I'll try it—for a year."

"Three years. You've got to give it at least three years."

"One year. That's it."

"Two years. Try the ranch for two years. Lil' Brady will love it out there."

"Lil' Brady? You expect me to raise my children out there?" She could feel her throat tighten up again.

"Our children," he corrected.

Her shoulders sagged. "Please, Brady, just one year at a time."

"You're right, darlin'. No reason to get you to pledge more than that. I could be broke by next summer anyway." He reached his hand across to the middle cushion of the sofa.

Lynda laced her fingers in his. "Well, cowboy, shall we go cut the cake that's shaped like Wyoming?"

"Wyoming? I thought it looked like Colorado!"

Kelly Princeton stuck her head through the doorway. "Are you two ready to eat your cake?"

"Yes." Lynda smiled.

"Nope." Brady frowned.

"Okay, okay." Kelly backpedaled out of the doorway.

Brady's voice sounded stern. "I think we're only half through with this discussion."

"Look, I'm trusting you that I'll be able to survive in Montana. You've got to trust me that Cindy's manuscript's not publishable."

"No deal," he insisted.

"What?"

"A promise is a promise. You gave her a contract to publish her book. You didn't have to do that, but once you did, it became a promise. You've got to keep every promise. It's part of the code."

Lynda pulled her hand back to her lap. "Brady, don't lay that cowboy code on me. Our business practices are moral, legal, and ethical. The contract clearly states that if the author fails to produce a publishable manuscript, we may reject it, and the author returns the advance. I think we're going beyond our legal responsibility to offer her a kill fee. This is the way our business is done. The book just didn't meet our standards."

"Whose standards?"

"Atlantic-Hampton's."

"Who made the decision to axe Cindy?"

"We didn't 'axe' Cindy. I made the decision—by myself."

"Look, so it isn't a bestseller. Couldn't you bring it out anyway? You'll make enough off Joaquin's next western to offset a dozen Cindys."

"That might be true, but we are not going to lower our standards. We just can't do that."

"Standards? Almost half the books you publish are trash. You told me that!"

"But they're well-written trash."

"That makes a difference?"

"In our business it does."

"It can't be that bad."

"It is."

"But why did you get Cindy's hopes up?"

"Because the first sample chapters were alive and vital—fresh language and a freedom of expression and flow. After that, the book dies. It's like she got distracted."

"Have her rewrite the other chapters."

"She did."

"And?"

"It was worse. She decided to mention almost every dream she had while on pills and alcohol. Something happened, Brady. I tried to tell you about it over the phone. It's like she just didn't care after the second chapter. You want to look at the manuscript?" she offered.

"I guess so. But what if I like it?"

"You won't."

"But how can you . . . Cindy's a friend. She needs . . ."

"She needs a lot of things, Brady. But she doesn't need to be made a laughing stock over a botched story of her life."

"So you sent her a form letter and a check."

"It was not a form letter, Stoner. I tried to call her. Left word with L. G. in Nevada, Sheila in Idaho, and Heather in Utah. Heather said she thought Cindy was going to Santa Fe, but I couldn't reach her. I've left word for her to call me. I didn't know what else to do."

"You could go out and personally tell her."

"Brady, I don't even know where she is! For most of us, the West is a big place."

He pulled off his hat and cradled it in his hands. "Let's go find her."

"What?"

"Let's go find Cindy so you can talk to her face to face. That's the only way to handle this."

"Find her? Where?"

"If we found a lost manuscript and a final chapter, we can find a barrel racer."

"Brady, we don't even know where to start looking."

"Santa Fe."

"That's a big town."

"I've got some contacts."

She rolled her eyes to the ceiling. "Are you serious? You want me to dump my work and go searching for a gal who's obviously trying to hide?"

"What are you doin' next week?"

"Are you kidding? I've got a full schedule of appointments, manuscripts to read, and correspondence, and I've got to buy some clothes for life in Wyoming—I mean, Montana. Not to mention a wedding to prepare for. I can't believe we're moving to the Double Diamond."

"Bring your laptop; buy some things in Santa Fe. Give the rest to Nina and Kelly. You're always sayin' they need to be given more responsibility. We'll find her in two or three days. Then we can drive up to Montana and see how the house is coming along. You'll still have time to fly back here and pack up."

"Brady, I've got every day between now and the wedding completely planned. I can't run off to New Mexico—or wherever."

"Sure you can."

"This is crazy!"

"Lady, ever'thing we've done in the past year and a half has been crazy."

Lynda shook her head. "We'll be through by next Sunday night?"

"Trust me."

Lynda felt the tight wrinkles around her eyes relax. "If I go with you, are you going to try anything improper?"

The dimples hung like a parenthesis on the white-toothed grin. "Probably."

"Well, if you put it that way . . . I'll go."

"Darlin', I'm ashamed of the way I acted tonight with all those folks around. Maybe it's the jet lag or just being nervous about the weddin' like George said. It just caught me by surprise and I—I lost it. I wish I could promise you it will never happen again."

"Honey, it was me. I guess I'm a little edgy. No one at Atlantic-Hampton has ever seen me lose control like that before. If we're going to have a rip-roaring fight, why did it have to be with an audience of over 100?"

"Well, that's one advantage of livin' at the Double Diamond."

"You mean, we can argue without anyone knowing it?"

"You've got to shout awful loud for it to carry ten miles to the neighbors."

Lynda's eyebrows arched. "You said seven."

"Right. That's what I meant."

Lynda stood and brushed out her skirt. He eased up close beside her. "Brady Stoner, do we have any idea what we're getting into with this marriage?"

"Nope. I'm just countin' on the Lord havin' it figured out. Ain't it fun?"

"Not tonight. Brady, I really thought I was losing you. Even if it was only for a wild minute there, I actually contemplated calling the whole thing off. It was the most depressing, disheartening, spirit-crushing moment in my whole life. I don't want to ever, ever think like that again."

"There's no backin' out of it, darlin'. We're in it for the long haul."

"Well, in that case, shall we go cut the Wyoming . . . Montana cake now?"

"Nope."

"What now?"

"The best part of an argument." He grinned and then swung his arms around her waist and pulled her so close their big silver belt buckles clanked. "I really do love ya, Lynda Dawn."

"Well, cowboy darlin', I love you, too."

The applause broke out at the moment their lips met. She was vaguely aware of 120 pairs of eyes. For the first time in her life, Lynda Dawn Austin longed for the remoteness of the Double Diamond Ranch.

TWO

"Well, darlin', where do you want to begin?" His voice was like a waltz, never in a hurry to get to the end, concerned only with the next step.

Lynda Austin buckled the seat belt and patted the black and white one-eyed dog that sat between them. "Me? Where do I want to go? Brady, I flew to New Mexico because you said you had friends here, and we could find Cindy LaCoste. You're the one who knows where to look. I'm just along for the ride." She stretched out in the cab of the silver Dodge pickup and tugged the jeans leg of her black Lady Wranglers over the top of her gray cowboy boots. The cab smelled a little like straw, dirt, and dog. She hoped it would soon be filled with the aroma of Midnight Opportunity.

Brady gunned the rig out of the asphalt outdoor parking area at the Santa Fe County Municipal Airport. "So that's why you came out? Just for a ride?"

She grabbed the armrest to steady herself when the truck caught the edge of the curb as they entered the street. "That and the fact that I missed Capt. Patch."

Hearing his name, the reclining cow dog let out one staccato bark.

"Yeah, I should have known the Captain had somethin' to do with it."

"Come on, cowboy, you were with me last weekend. Surely you didn't miss me in three days." Lynda fought off the urge to pull down the sun visor and check her makeup in the mirror.

His brown eyes sparkled. Out of the corner of her eye she thought she could see the trademark dimples in his grin. "What I missed was that sweet-smellin' perfume. What's that one called, darlin'?"

Lynda glanced down at her bare arms and the silver and turquoise bracelet. *My arms are too thin and too pale. Maybe this sunshine will give me a little tan before the wedding.* "Brady, let's get something straight before we ever get married. The name of my perfume has nothing to do with how I'm feeling at the moment. I buy perfume because of its aroma—that's all. So you don't need to keep asking for the name. I don't intend on spending the next fifty years having to report the titles of my perfumes."

"Whoa, did you hear that, Capt. Patch? She's really touchy. Must be a mighty embarrassing name."

"Forget it, Stoner. I'm not telling you the name because it's not important. Just pretend that it's #12 or #25 or something. I don't even know why perfumes have to have names."

"I reckon because numbers don't sell well."

"Chanel No. 5 has done all right."

"Okay, you win!" He reached over and tousled the back of her hair.

She thought he started to turn toward her and then turned back. "What?" she demanded.

"I didn't say anything."

"I could see it in your face. You were about to say something."

"No, I wasn't."

"Of course you were. What is it?"

"Oh, I was thinking about calling that perfume LD #10."

"Lynda Dawn?" she mused. "But why #10?"

"'Cause whenever I smell it, I'd better count to ten before grabbin' and kissin' you."

"Look, cowboy, there's something you need to learn. Just because a woman wears nice-smelling perfume doesn't mean she wants you to grab and kiss her."

"It doesn't?"

"Of course not." Her face was turned away from him, as she gazed out the window at the northern New Mexico landscape.

"What?" he demanded.

"I didn't say anything."

"You were thinkin' it."

"Brady Stoner, how do you know what I'm thinking?"

"You're as easy to read as a Joaquin Estaban novel."

"I am not!"

"Are you telling me when you baptized yourself in L.D. #10, you had no thought of some cowboy smellin' that and wantin' to kiss you?"

"I do not baptize myself."

"That depends on what church you go to. Believe me, I've been to some where they didn't use that much liquid to baptize."

"Now I'll admit that lately I've had many thoughts of being kissed by one certain cowboy, but I certainly don't have to manipulate him with perfume."

"That's true."

"Of course . . ."

"Of course, what?"

"Everyone knows Brady Stoner is a pushover for sweet-smelling perfume!"

"Ah, hah! I was right! Didn't I tell you, Capt. Patch?"

The dog jumped straight up and stared out the front window.

"Speaking of churches, where in the world will we go to church in Montana?"

"The Little Belt Bible Church."

"Where's that?"

"About thirty-five, forty minutes from the ranch. Good folks there. I stopped by several weeks ago. I got us signed up for a Sunday school class."

"That's nice. What class will we be in?"

"In? Actually I, eh, signed us up to teach a class."

"Teach a class? You and me?"

"Yeah, it can't be too hard. It's not a very big church."

"What class will we be teaching?"

"Junior high and high school. Don't that sound fun, darlin'?"

That's his idea of fun?

Brady slowed down at a stop sign and signaled to turn right. "Downtown Santa Fe's up there. We'll check it out later. We are on our way to talk to none other than Mr. Rodney Hopewell III."

"Why is it I have some apprehension in asking this? But just who is Rodney Hopewell III?" *Brady needs a haircut. He always needs a haircut. Or maybe just a comb.*

"Big Rod Hopewell is an institution—that's what he is."

"And he lives in Santa Fe?"

"Almost. He lives right here on Rodeo Road. I don't think it's actually in the city limits."

"And what makes him so legendary?"

"He's a saddlemaker. He happens to make the best bronc saddles and bareback riggin' in the country. But he's a little . . . eh, eccentric."

"Coming from you, Stoner, that's ominous. Every friend of yours I've met is unconventional. Just what does this guy Rodney do that gives him that quality?"

"To start with, he lives in an airplane hangar."

Lynda lifted up the back of her hair to cool her neck. "He lives where?"

"He moved one of those huge, round-roofed sheet-metal hangers out to some acreage across from the rodeo grounds."

Lynda watched irrigated horse pasture and bleak, dry desert pass by her window. "And he made it into a house?"

"Not really. It's still just a huge old building. He sleeps on one side and does his work on the other. It's sort of a combination garage, home, shop, and bunkhouse all rolled into one gigantic room."

"A bunkhouse?" Lynda glanced up at the clear sky painted a southwest watercolor blue.

"That's the reason we're headed there. Anyone who's rodeoin' can stop there anytime and spend the night. Durin' the Santa Fe rodeo there must be dozens of people there ever' evenin'—sort of like a party. But even in the off season whenever I've stopped at Rodney's, there's at least two or three guys or gals hanging out."

"And you think Cindy might be there?"

"Not necessarily. But L. J. Minor said Cindy left in her old Cadillac pullin' a stock trailer she borrowed and carrying a horse named Early to Bed. Cindy's been training Early to run the barrels, so . . ."

"So you figure Cindy headed here to barrel race?"

"The thing is, this isn't rodeo time. I don't know why she came, unless there are some jackpot barrel races that I don't know about. But I know one thing, if she came to Santa Fe low on cash, she stayed at Rodney's."

"Did you call and ask him?"

"Nope. Rodney doesn't have a phone."

"He's in the saddle-making business, and he doesn't have a phone?"

"I told you, he's eccentric."

"How does he stay in business?"

"Guys just stop by and order or buy what they want. Usually it takes a year to get your saddle made. So you tell him one year and pick it up the next."

"He doesn't sound all that weird." Austin's voice was as flat as a public service announcer.

"He's a real big-hearted guy. You can stay at Rod's for free, but you might not get anything to eat besides chips and Mountain Dew. He's had some bad breaks."

"What kind of bad breaks?"

"Eh . . . Rodney's about six feet, six inches and works out bench-pressin' truck axles. I've never seen a man stronger. He tried wrestlin' steers years ago, but he kept breakin' their necks. They banned him from competition. So he just set up shop across the street. Then he got married years ago, but the gal stole his savings account and took off. If you get on Rodney's good side, he's a friend for life. 'Course, if you cross him . . . well, it's best to stay out of town."

"I trust you and Rodney are good friends?"

"Oh, yeah. I send him a NFR cap every Christmas, and he sends me a pint of cactus jelly."

"Cactus jelly?"

"Yep, it's almost as good as jalapeno jelly."

"Are you teasin' me, cowboy?"

"Why would I do that, darlin'? Anyway, I brought a 100-pound bag of Idaho potatoes one time, and he's called me Spud ever since."

Spud? Spud Stoner? No, please. "Someone actually calls you Spud?"

"Only if they're six feet, six inches, 300 pounds, and can bench-press a Volkswagen."

She glanced at her black duffel bag in the space behind the seat in the extended cab pickup. "We aren't planning on spending the night at the hanger, are we?"

"Nope. I called Doc Cartier at Los Alamos and arranged us a couple of guest rooms."

"Los Alamos?" Lynda peered at him over the rims of her sunglasses. "You mean, like where they developed the atom bomb?"

"Yeah. It's less than an hour up the road. I knew you'd want a little more privacy than Rodney's."

"Who's Dr. Cartier? I've never heard you mention him before. Does he work on nuclear bombs?"

"I suppose so, but she can't talk about what she's workin' on. Top secret, I surmise. I never ask."

"Does her husband work at Los Alamos also?"

"Here's the answer to your real question. Doc isn't married. She's about forty, has a doctorate in nuclear physics from Cal Tech, keeps rodeo stats in her computer at work, and can break and ride rank horses with the best of 'em. I met her one night at Rodney's. She wanted me to come out and look at some broncs."

Lynda threw up her hands in feigned disgust. "'Come up to my place and look at some horses.' Is that the Western version of 'come up to my apartment and look at some paintings'? I can't believe you fell for that."

"But, Lynda Dawn, all we did was look at horses and sit around talkin' rodeo all night long. You sure are a suspicious lady. I guess you Easterners just can't help yourselves."

It dawned on her that he had on the same blue shirt he had worn when they first met a year and a half earlier. "Stoner, you're either the most cunning or most naive man I've ever met." *Does he really only have three shirts?*

"You'll like Doc Cartier. She's a real sweetheart. You two can sit around discussing erudite topics like the impact French impressionistic painting had on historical novels of the early twentieth century and the appalling lack of moral imperatives in contemporary European fiction."

Lynda pulled off her sunglasses and stared at Brady. He faked a grin.

"You've been practicing that line for a month, cowboy."

"Three months. I was hoping to have a chance to use it at Gossman's party, but I couldn't find a time. Ever'one seemed to be bent on talkin' about rodeo, horses, and the West. What do you think? Did I pull it off?"

"To paraphrase Mark Twain: 'You got all the words right, but you didn't know the tune.' No matter what words come out of your mouth, you'll always sound like a cowboy."

"Is that all right, Miss Lynda Dawn?"

"That's why I'm marrying a bronc buster. I like all those 'darlin's' and the Western twang."

"Well, I say you're goin' to like Doc Cartier."

"What I'm going like is having you stay home on that Montana ranch and not roam a West that seems to be crowded with Stoner's sweethearts."

"All right! I knew you'd find some reason to like the place. Anyway, here's Rodney's."

"But there's nothing here but desert—and a big tin building." The tall, round-roofed building gave the feeling of an abandoned army base.

"Yeah, well, during rodeo week there will be fifty, sixty rigs parked all around here. Looks like Rodney's home."

"You mean, because the hanger door is open?"

"Nah, he leaves that open until winter."

"Even when he's gone?"

"Yeah, but there's usually always someone here. There's his rig."

"Which one is his?"

"The yellow one."

"What is it?"

"The Armageddon Express. It was a school bus, but he cut the top off and made it a convertible. We had over 100 in it one year. You should have seen their faces at the Burger Korral drive-through!"

Brady parked the silver and black Dodge next to two other pickups. One had the hood raised. Capt. Patch disappeared out the door the moment it opened. Lynda stretched her legs and then crunched across the dry dirt parking lot with Brady.

"T-Bob! How's it goin'?" Brady called out to the man with tan sleeves rolled up to his elbows and grease covering his hands.

"Wild Man!" the sandy blond mechanic grinned. "I thought you'd be out there rakin' in the sweets at all of them rich California rodeos."

"Me? What are you doin' at Rodney's?"

"Tryin' to get this old heap of a Chevy repaired so I can get on down the road. I'm about to get her whipped though." T-Bob nodded toward Lynda.

"T-Bob, this is my fiancée, Miss Lynda Dawn Austin."

"Howdy, ma'am. I heard he was gettin' married, but I figured it was jist a rumor. Facts can get pretty mixed up when you're goin' down the road. None of us was sure who Lynda Dawn Darlin' really was. Not that there weren't plenty of volunteers." T-Bob blushed as he stared down at his worn-out brown boots. "You sure are as purdy as a barrel racer but a tad pale to qualify as an outdoor girl."

"Nice to meet you, T-Bob." She started to reach out to shake hands, but the grease caused her to pull back. "Actually I'm a book editor from New York City."

"New York City?" He shook his head and pushed his tattered black felt hat to the back of his head, revealing the customary tan line across the forehead. "What in the world did you ever see in the Wild Man?"

"Why do you call him that?"

"You should see him whip up a crowd with that wild dismount."

"T-Bob exaggerates a tad," Brady explained. "It comes from all those nights of sleepin' in his truck."

"No, ma'am, this buckaroo once rode a bronc in Las Cruces, and after eight seconds he whips around in the saddle and rides the horse backwards for another eight seconds. The crowd came right out of the stands and tried to make him governor!"

She tried to smile. "Oh?"

"Ol' T-Bob's had too many kicks in the head. Can't tell fact from fiction anymore. They didn't say one word about makin' me governor. Mayor, yeah, but not governor."

"The truth is, Miss Lynda Dawn, ol' Brady is the most unpredictable cuss on the circuit. Did he ever tell you about the time he spent his whole paycheck renting an entire motel?"

Lynda smiled easily this time. "I don't believe I've heard this story."

"See, about thirty of us boys was trying catch some sleep at a rest stop east of Fort Collins, Colorado, but it was rainin' and startin' to snow and sleet. Well, it was too cold to sleep in the rig and too slick to drive tired. Brady had pulled first money that night, but the rest of us were nearly broke, as always. So the Wild Man drives down the road, bangs on the motel door, and rousts out the owner. Then Brady trades his check for the whole blame motel and breakfast for ever'one the next morning. We all had a warm room and a shower that night and steak, biscuits, and gravy the next mornin'. Yes, ma'am, you ask anyone goin' down the road—he's the Wild Man, all right, in the best sense of the term."

Brady took Lynda's arm. "Come on, darlin', before T-Bob gets really wound up. He'll be nominatin' me for sainthood or askin' me for a loan if we hang around much longer."

"Or both." T-Bob grinned.

"Is Rodney in a good mood?" Brady quizzed.

"He's been whistlin' for three days."

"That's good. Who else is here?"

"DeWitt and Morgan Stites have been hangin' around, but I think they caught a ride to town."

"Where are you up next?"

"Winslow—if I can get there," T-Bob reported.

Brady released Lynda's arm and stepped over to the grease-covered cowboy. She could see him pull something out of his wallet. Then the two men talked in hushed tones. Finally he returned, and they headed toward the hangar.

"Did you give him money?"

"Oh, just enough to get back on the road. He'll pay me back. T-Bob's a good man. If he doesn't do well this summer, I told him he could come up to the ranch this fall and work it off."

There is a bunkhouse at that ranch, isn't there? He doesn't expect them to stay in our house . . . surely. It's okay, Lord. He can't help himself. He's just everybody's friend.

Large, bright, bare lightbulbs hung straight down from the extremely high ceiling of the building. The door opening was twenty feet high and forty feet wide. Inside it looked more like a junkyard than a saddle-building shop. Truck chassis, horse trailers, industrial sewing machines, and partially repaired saddles were scattered among sleeping bags, boxes of auto parts, and cases of potato chips. The room was so vast Lynda could not see what was at the other end. Somewhere a stereo speaker amplified LeAnn Rimes belting out "Good Lookin' Man."

She and Brady walked straight toward a big man hunched over a workbench. Even though his back was toward them, she could see his massive hands clutching a wooden mallet and something that looked like a leather punch.

"Hey, partner," Brady called out, "haven't you got that saddle done yet?"

Rodney Hopewell III whipped around on his stool. A full smile suddenly appeared in the midst of a full reddish gray beard. "Spud! What are you doin' here?"

"I just stopped by for a friendly visit."

Hopewell didn't even glance at Lynda. "You're goin' to stay a few days, aren't you?"

"Afraid I need to push on this time."

"Hey, I heard the good news," Hopewell thundered. "Congratulations! The boys said it was all a lie, that no woman would ever hogtie the Wild Man. But when Cindy came through and told us all firsthand—"

"Cindy's been here?"

"Shoot, yeah! That's how I knew for sure you was gettin' married." A puzzled look in his deep blue eyes, he finally studied Lynda.

"Hi, Rodney, I'm Lynda Austin, Brady's fiancée."

The big man's smile dropped off his face like a leaf blown off a tree in fall. "You're his what?" he boomed.

"Rod, this is the gal I'm goin' to marry."

His face flushed red as Rodney growled, "You two-timin' romeo, you . . ."

The wooden mallet crashed into Brady's head.

Lynda screamed.

Rodney puffed.

Brady crumpled to the dirty concrete floor.

"Why did you do that?" she screamed as she dropped to her knees.

"Get that two-timer out of here before I hit him again!"

Lynda gently raised Brady's head. "Brady! Brady!" she sobbed.

She could hear cowboy boots run across the concrete, but she didn't take her eyes off Brady's unconscious face.

"Get him out of here, T-Bob, 'fore I get really mad!" Rodney growled. "There ain't nobody goin' to treat my Cindy-girl that way!"

"Back off, Rod!" T-Bob hollered. "Just back off and cool down. We'll get him out right now."

"If you know what's good fer you," Rodney pointed at Lynda, "you'll go back to New York. You got no business comin' out here and ruinin' folks' lives!"

Lynda's chest throbbed with rage. "How dare you," she sputtered.

"Come on, Miss Lynda Dawn from New York," T-Bob urged. "Let's get him out of here."

He grabbed Brady's shoulders and motioned for her to pick up his legs. They struggled out the door, Capt. Patch leading the way.

"Why did he do that?" she cried. "I can't believe this! I'm callin' the police! Where's the nearest phone? Where's a hospital? Oh, man . . ."

"And you tell that no-good bronc buster that he better never show his face around here again! He ain't welcome no more—ever!" Rodney hollered with a mallet in his hand from the doorway.

"Lay him across the seat," T-Bob ordered. "You have any water? A little water will bring him around."

"He could have a concussion!"

"Maybe, but a man don't ride broncs for a dozen years with a soft skull. He'll have a big lump, but I've seen ol' Brady take it worse than that!"

"Well, I haven't," she sobbed.

T-Bob splashed water from a leather-wrapped canteen on Brady's face and slapped his cheeks. "Come on, partner! You just got bucked off! Come on, open those big brown eyes! The buzzer already rang."

The voice was weak and tentative, like trying to start an old truck on a cold winter day. "Did . . . I . . . get a . . . mark?"

T-Bob brushed Brady's hair off the big knot forming on his forehead. "You got an 89, partner!"

"Did I win?"

"Nope, but you got third money."

Brady's eyes shot open. "Third money for an 89!" Then he raised his head up, stared at Lynda, and dropped back to the truck seat.

"Well, darlin', I didn't think you could get more beautiful, but you did."

"How did I manage to do that?"

"There's two of you now. . . . What a sight! 'Course there's a down side. There's two T-Bobs, too."

"Keep your eyes closed, partner. You've got to let your head clear," T-Bob insisted.

"Did Rodney coldcock me with that mallet?"

"Yep. He also banished you for life."

Lynda climbed up into the truck and cradled Brady's head in her lap. "Brady, we've got to get you to a doctor."

"I'll be all right. It could have been worse."

"Yeah," T-Bob added. "Rod could have been holding a sledge hammer."

"Why did your being engaged to me tick him off?"

T-Bob whistled. "So that's the reason."

"What's the reason?" Lynda demanded.

"Cindy LaCoste came by a couple days ago. None of us had seen her in what . . . four or five years? Anyway, she's lookin' tired but wanted to go to a motorcycle rally over at the rodeo grounds. Rodney volunteered to go with her. He's always been sweet on Cindy—joked and claimed he was next in line after Brady."

"A motorcycle rally?" Brady opened his eyes, glanced up at Lynda, and then closed them quickly.

"Yeah . . . well, when they get back, Rodney kind of hints that Cindy should just move in with him. But she up and says that she's getting married on June 12 to Brady."

"She said what?" Lynda gulped.

"None of us believed her but Rodney. We all knew about you. But Rodney gave her some space after that. The next day she loads up her pony and heads to Durango."

"Durango?" Brady repeated.

"Yeah, something about another motorcycle rally. I couldn't figure why she's haulin' a barrel horse to motorcycle rallies, but I was never one to figure out the ladies."

"But why did he hit Brady?" Lynda's eyes blazed.

"I guess he figured Brady was standin' up Cindy to marry you. He took it personal."

"Personal? The man's a psycho! I'm reporting this to the police!"

"No, darlin'!" Brady insisted. "That's the way Rodney is."

"Brady Stoner, he almost killed you!" she fumed.

He reached up and put his callused finger on her lips. "Rodney hasn't exactly had an easy life. I'm not goin' to make things worse. It's just a misunderstandin'."

"It's a concussion, that's what it is!" she protested.

He gingerly rubbed the knot on his head. "What's it look like, T-Bob? Like I been kicked by an unshod horse . . . or yanked into the back of a bull's head?"

"Kicked by a horse."

"Good. Probably only a mild concussion. I didn't vomit, did I?"

"Not yet, partner."

"Then there's no reason to go to a doc. Right, T-Bob?"

"He's right, ma'am. If you don't vomit, it probably ain't all that serious."

"You two are crazy! Brady's got his head cracked open, and you don't want me to report the assailant or take Brady to the doctor. I don't understand the West! Last year they shot at us, but we didn't go to the police. Why do you even have law enforcement out here?"

"For serious crimes, I reckon," Brady offered.

"Rodney means well, ma'am," T-Bob counseled. "He just sort of gets one thing on his mind at a time. And Cindy seems

to be on his mind. He thought he was protectin' her reputa-
tion."

Brady struggled to pull himself up.

Lynda put her hand on his shoulder. "What do you think
you're doing?"

"We better get on the road."

"You're in no condition to drive!"

"Then you drive. Cindy headed for Durango a few days
ago. She could be anywhere by now."

"What can I do to help?" T-Bob asked, wiping his hands
on his worn jeans.

"Tell Lynda how to get to Los Alamos. Then try to explain
to Rodney that I never was engaged to Cindy. She just made
that up."

Lynda felt herself tighten up all over. "Brady, you have to
go see a doctor."

"Darlin', me and T-Bob deal with this kind of thing all the
time. I'll be okay. If my vision doesn't straighten up by mornin',
then I'll go see a doctor."

T-Bob traced the route to Los Alamos in the dirt of the
parking lot and then stepped around to Brady's side of the
pickup. "If you don't hear from me sooner, I'll see you in the
fall. It's the Double Diamond in the Judith Basin, right?"

"You got it, partner." Brady shook his head to try to clear
his vision. "Both of you are invited."

T-Bob shot a glance at Lynda. "Take good care of him . . .
Lynda Dawn Darlin'."

Capt. Patch settled in the middle of the pickup seat as
Lynda shifted into low. She let out the clutch with a lunge,
spraying dirt in the air.

"You did it, Stoner. You got me to drive again. This wasn't
a secret plan of yours, was it?"

He softly kneaded the skin around his wound. "It was a
mighty dumb plan if it was."

"Is it any better?"

"The throbbin' in my head is keepin' time with a George Strait waltz, if you know what I mean. I'm glad the wedding isn't tomorrow. I'd sure look frightful. Lucky my hat took some of the blow."

"Your hat is completely crunched."

"Yeah . . . well, I didn't like that crown too much anyway. 'Course, with this knot I won't be wearin' a hat for a while."

Lynda pulled into a minimart and parked next to a pay phone.

"That's a good idea, darlin'. Buy me a bag of crushed ice and a Coke, would ya?"

"I'm going to find a hospital emergency room—that's what I'm going to do."

"Lynda Dawn, I aim to live a long, long time. And I promise you, I'll take care of myself. But I'm tellin' you, I don't need to go to the hospital. Take me up to Los Alamos, and let's see how it is in the mornin'."

"Brady, you are the most stubborn, hardheaded . . . well, maybe hardheaded isn't the right word." She couldn't help it. She cracked a wide smile and shook her head.

"Welcome back to the West, Miss Lynda Dawn!"

"The plane touched down almost two hours ago. This is good, Stoner. It took four hours to bust your knee in St. George. But then last fall you got shot on the streets of Jackson in less than an hour."

"That was just pretend."

"But the air let out of your tires was real."

"Okay, so things just seem to happen when I'm around you."

"When you're around me? You're blaming this on me? This is the way you live, Stoner. For you, this is just another day. Is this going to be our lives every day on the Double Diamond?"

"Lynda Dawn Darlin', it will be so peaceful up there you'll have to fly to New York to keep from being bored."

"Hah! Before I ever move to that ranch, I want the phone numbers of the nearest hospital, law officer, doctor, ambulance, and EMT."

"And vet. You got to know the vet's number."

She slid out of the truck. "*You* have to know the vet's number—not me, cowboy. I don't do animals."

◆ ◆ ◆

Lynda returned with a large bag of ice and a sack of apples, cheese, and crackers.

"There're some lunch bags in that yellow box. I thought you could make an ice pack out of them."

"Think I'll just put this whole bag on my head."

"That looks ludicrous, Stoner."

"Thank you, ma'am, but I bet you say that to all the battered cowboys."

Austin turned north on US 84 and drove toward downtown Santa Fe. "Why do you think Cindy went to a bikers' rally? After that attack by bikers, I'd think that's the last place she'd ever want to go." Lynda waved a hand toward the mini-mart sack. "Hand me one of those green apples, would you?"

Stoner dug into the white plastic sack. "I guess Cindy is lookin' for someone. Whoa, a dozen. I hope you're goin' to eat all of them 'cause me and the Captain would rather chew hay."

"You think she's trying to find the guys who jumped her?" Lynda took a large bite from the apple, leaving a trace of Autumn Rose Blush around the teeth marks.

"You saw how much of a bulldog she is once she sets her mind to somethin'. Vengeance is a mighty strong motive."

"But that was five years ago. Why didn't she go after them sooner?"

"Maybe this is the first time she's felt strong enough to do something about it. A lot of the past few years have been spent with a strong dose of painkillers and alcohol. Maybe she just got a lead—"

"After all our good spiritual discussions? I really thought she committed herself to the Lord."

"Maybe she did. That note you got in your Christmas letter from her surely sounded like a gal who knew the Lord. But we don't all act like saints immediately after belief."

"Brady, what will she do if she finds them?"

"Maybe she wants to tell them she forgives them."

"I wish I could believe that."

"Yeah . . . I wish I could believe it, too."

"They may attack her again. She could be worse off than before. Brady, we have to find her and stop her!"

"That could take awhile—especially if I keep runnin' into wooden mallets with my forehead."

She glanced at the five-pound sack of ice balanced on his head. "Is it feeling any better?"

Brady's eyes stayed shut. "I think the Advil's kicked in. Now it only feels like I caught a line drive right between the eyes."

"Well, truthfully, Brady, I can't stay out here any longer than Sunday. I've got a ton of things to do before the wedding."

"Let's give it a good chase for a few days and see what happens." The sound of an empty aluminum can crunching in his hand caused Lynda to jump. "Maybe we'll catch up with her. We do know she's drivin' that old green Cadillac and pullin' a horse trailer. And there's a chance she stayed in Durango for a few days."

"Why do you say that?"

"They have a nightly rodeo. She might need to make a few bucks before she pushes on. Why else would she trailer a horse if she didn't plan on ridin' him?"

Lynda looked at the eastern skyline as she wove through the afternoon traffic. "Is that downtown Santa Fe?"

"That's it. Sure is pretty, too." Brady sat up a little, peeked out the window, and then slumped back down and replaced the sack of ice. "One of the most historic towns in America. Founded in 1610 by an elegant hidalgo named Don Pedro de Peralta."

"1610?"

"Yeah, that was only four months after Henry Hudson sailed up a river he named for himself. Europeans were living right over there in those trees four years before that Dutch skipper and his crew camped on Manhattan Island."

"Where?"

"See all of those trees? That's the Plaza de Armas."

"I can't see anything! This reminds me of a now-famous trip through Yellowstone at night."

"We'll come back, darlin', I promise you. Santa Fe has attracted all sorts of strange folks lately, but she's still La Reina Vieja del Oeste—the old Queen of the West. I'm not sure she's ever lived up to the name Santa Fe."

"What does it mean?"

"The original name was Villa Real de la Santa Fe de San Francisco de Asis—the Royal City of the Holy Faith of St. Francis of Assisi. Doesn't that have a better ring than, say, New York?"

"Yes, it does. But it also sounds better than Buffalo, Montana. Is our mailing address actually going to be Buffalo?"

"That's the zip. The mail comes out of Judith Gap."

Lynda grinned. "What a relief. Well, what other tidbits of history do I need to know?"

"Santa Fe is over 6,996 feet in elevation, the highest of any state capitols. Those are the Sangre de Cristo Mountains."

"Sangre de Cristo?"

"The Blood of Christ. This is the upper end of the famous Rio Grande. But, most importantly, Santa Fe happens to be where I won my first silver buckle as a professional rodeo cowboy. I was just nineteen. Boy, I thought that was the greatest thing I ever did in my life."

"Where's the buckle now?"

"Up at my folks', I suppose. I've got a couple of apple crates full of buckles in my closet. Didn't I show you those things when you came out at Christmas?"

"The only thing I remember about your room was the one-eyed moose head over the bed."

"Delbert."

"And you promised me you wouldn't move him to our place, right?"

"I promised you he wouldn't be in the house. He can be in the barn." Brady peeked one eye out from under the melting ice.

She sighed.

"What's the matter, darlin'?"

"Mr. Stoner, I don't have any idea what I'm getting into marrying a cowboy and moving to the edge of the earth, do I?"

"No, ma'am, I don't reckon you do."

"I'm going to keep a journal from the very first day of our marriage."

"On the honeymoon?"

"Okay, maybe not the honeymoon. But at least from the first day we get to the ranch."

Brady sat up and placed the dripping sack of ice on the floorboard. They were past the city limits now.

"Your forehead's turning purple."

"I'll probably end up with two black eyes."

"He didn't hit you in the eyes, did he?"

"Close enough to make them black."

"Are you still seeing double?"

"Nope, but it's as fuzzy as tryin' to chase steers on a foggy day. Turn west at that Pueblo Indian village."

"West?"

"To your left."

"What's the name of that town over there?"

"I don't know, but it's off limits to all but residents."

"Do they all live in adobe homes?"

"Most all. Looks like a few of the younger ones have mobile homes."

"What are those huge mud beehive-looking things?"

"Ovens. That's where they cook their bread."

"Outdoor ovens? You mean, they still do that sort of thing?"

"Why not? It's done the job for almost 400 years."

Lynda focused on a green road sign. "What's LANL?"

"Los Alamos National Laboratory. It's over in the chaparral on that distant mountain."

"And Dr. Cartier—she knows we're coming?"

"Sure does. You're really going to like her."

She'll probably whop me in the head. Lord, I hope after we get married, my stomach won't tie up in knots every time I meet one of Brady's lady friends. "How long until we reach her place?"

"About twenty minutes. If she's not home, she said to go on in and make ourselves comfy."

"Oh, sure, that's what you said up in Montana last fall when the Mendoza woman was living at the Double Diamond, and she almost killed us. I am not entering a house where the owner is not present."

"That was totally different. I know Doc Cartier."

"I don't."

◆ ◆ ◆

The one-story, flat-roofed, thick-walled adobe ranch house looked old as the scrub cedars and piñon pines that surrounded it. In contrast, the huge metal barn looked new and modern. Stretched out behind it were several acres of sprinkler-irrigated horse pasture—each narrow, fenced five-acre parcel sloping up to the barn.

A four-foot adobe wall encircled the front red-tile patio. Outside the wall, among the scattered pine and cedars, drooping cholla cacti and a layer of white pebbles delineated the parking area.

"I don't see Doc's van. She must still be at the lab."

Lynda braked the truck in front of a black iron gate. "This house looks like something out of one of Georgia O'Keeffe's paintings."

"Or at least one of Stieglitz's photographs of her."

Austin pushed her dark glasses up on her head. "I'm impressed, cowboy."

"Santa Fe had a great retrospective exhibition of O'Keeffe works a few years back. There was a museum intern named April who showed me everything I wanted to know."

"Wanted to know about what?"

"About O'Keeffe and Stieglitz." It was a teasing response. "I like New Mexico. 'Course, it's totally different than Arizona. It looks great, doesn't it?"

"It looks a lot better than you do, cowboy." Lynda scooted out of the truck toward Brady. Capt. Patch was already exploring the barn.

"What color am I now?"

"Kind of reddish orange and blue, and your right eye is turning black. How's it feel?"

"Like my head's been inflated to the size of a basketball and a buffalo's sitting on it. Come on, we'll see if the Doc has something cold to drink in her fridge."

"Brady, I am not entering an unoccupied house again."

"Are you serious?"

"Try me."

Brady turned toward the barn. "Okay . . . let's go look at the horses."

◆ ◆ ◆

By the time the green GMC van finally rolled up the unpaved driveway, Lynda lounged on the open tailgate of the black and silver Dodge. Brady, eyes closed, sprawled across the bed of the pickup.

The van swung next to them. When the electric window descended, Lynda assessed the attractive middle-aged woman with auburn and gray-streaked hair, deeply tanned face, slight crow's feet at the corners of her sparkling green eyes, and four-inch dangling earrings.

Dr. Cartier smiled at them both. "Brady, you look awful as usual. Did you run into a horse hoof?" Her voice was deep and melodious, with a been-there, done-that tone.

"Worse than that. I smacked up against Rodney Hopewell's mallet."

Her smile turned to concern. "Sounds like a story I need to hear." She turned toward Lynda. "Hi, I'm Debra Cartier. You must be Brady's Lynda Dawn Darlin'."

Lynda stretched out her hand. "I didn't know that's how I was being talked about."

"Oh, honey, I meant it as a compliment, I assure you. You've got a cowboy who thinks his New York City fiancée outshines the stars in the heavens. And around these parts, the opinion of Brady Stoner is as good as gold. Why didn't you make yourself comfortable in the house?"

"Well . . . I—," Lynda stammered.

"We've been over looking at the horses, Doc. We were just headed that way."

Dr. Debra Jean Cartier winked at Lynda. "He can't lie worth beans, can he?"

Austin laughed an easy, comfortable laugh. "I was hesitant to go in. I just haven't gotten the hang of this Western hospitality yet."

"You'll soon learn. Just a minute and I'll join you."

Dr. Cartier flipped a couple of switches. Her entire van seat rolled backwards. The side door swung open, revealing the woman seated in an electronic wheelchair. With the flip of a couple more switches, a motorized ramp lowered her, wheelchair and all, to the ground beside them.

Brady closed the van door.

Lynda's face felt hot, her throat dry.

Dr. Cartier studied her. "I assume Brady forgot to tell you about my disability?"

"Disability?" Brady gasped. Then he looked at Lynda. "This lady is about as disabled as a mama grizzly protectin' her cubs. There is nothin' Doc can't do."

"I still can't dance the two-step, Brady Stoner."

"Shucks, Doc, neither can I."

Debra Cartier reached out to take Lynda's hand. "You grabbed the best one—you know that, don't you? Now come on, let's get some lemonade before we go ride those ponies." She glanced up at Lynda. "You ride?"

"Eh, I'm just learning."

"How about you, Stoner? You're not too bunged up to trot up into the hills, are you?"

Brady held out his wrist to her like a schoolboy about to be disciplined with a ruler. "Here . . . test for yourself."

With red-polished nails, Dr. Cartier pressed her fingers against the inside of his wrist. "Okay, cowboy, you've got a pulse. Let's go."

Lynda and Brady trailed behind Cartier's motorized wheelchair. "Now when is Atlantic-Hampton coming out with Martin Taylor Harrison's journal? I read about it last summer and am getting a little impatient . . ."

◆ ◆ ◆

The moonless northern New Mexico sky was ablaze with stars. The air, while still warm, held a hint of coolness. A soft glow of light radiated out from the open front doorway. Lynda, Brady, and Debra lounged around a patio table covered with the remains of three Navajo tacos and a spent pitcher of lemonade.

"Did you ever see anyone ride a pony like Doc?" Brady quizzed.

Lynda scrunched in her chair trying to find a position that wasn't painful. "I'm beginning to think Brady's right. You can do everything."

"Lynda, I was eight years old when I got bucked off into those rocks. I spent ten years hating horses, God, and mainly myself."

"What happened?"

"I decided to kill myself. I got mad and said if horses were going to cripple me, they could just finish off the job. So one night I went out to my father's barn and saddled up the rankest horse he owned. It took me three hours to get him saddled. I used the hay hoist to get myself up on top.

"I slapped him with the tail of my reins, and we went bucking off into the dark of night. I grabbed the fork of the saddle with my hands and held the reins in my teeth, and I made that pony keep running for two hours."

"You didn't get hurt or fall off or anything?" Lynda asked.

"Not a scratch. It was one of the Lord's many miracles in my life. We jumped logs, boulders, fences—it was an incredible ride. Finally, the big stallion was worn out and trotted back to the barn about daylight. I was in tears. A total failure. I couldn't even fall off a horse. I remember screaming at God, 'It's all Your fault that I'm a cripple.'"

"Did He answer you?"

"Yes, He did. He just seemed to say, 'Crippled? I didn't know you were crippled.'"

"Really?"

"At least that was my interpretation of the message. I figured if it didn't make one bit of difference to Him, it shouldn't stop me. So I packed up and went to Cal Tech in Pasadena. Ten years later, I moved back to New Mexico with a doctorate, a good job at Los Alamos, and a passion to ride fast horses. That was twelve years ago."

"Sounds like you have an exciting life."

"I like it. I like the breakthrough research. I like the rush of wind in my face and the power of a 1,000-pound horse beneath me. I like the New Mexico night sky . . . and a house with good friends—some old and some new." She peered across at Lynda's eyes as she finished the sentence.

"Did you ever think of writing a book about your life?" Lynda asked.

"Oh, if I ever do anything worth remembering, maybe I'll write. There's really nothing special to say—no 'slant.' Isn't that the correct term?"

"I suppose. But Brady mentioned all the awards and honors you received."

"Let me tell you about the greatest compliment I've had in the past ten years."

"You aren't goin' to embarrass me, are you?" Brady asked.

"Probably." There was a hint of deep laughter in her words.

"Eh, I think I'll go check the horses."

Lynda watched him and Capt. Patch slip out of the patio and head toward the barn.

"The first time I met Brady was after the rodeo in Santa Fe. I went out to Rodney's on a Friday night. Must have been 100 people out there. I wheeled myself in, trying to find a gal who had a barrel racing horse for sale. Well, Mr. Stoner pulled a crate up beside my wheelchair, and we must have talked for two hours about good horses and bad. Some of the others were dancing at one end of the hangar. When they finally played a slow number, he looked straight at me with those big brown eyes and said, 'Would you do me the honor of this dance, ma'am?'"

Debra Jean Cartier wiped the corners of her eyes. They heard the crunch of boot heels on the sand and gravel yard outside the patio. Through the shadows Lynda followed a familiar but hatless silhouette.

"That's when I first realized that in Brady's mind I wasn't crippled at all. It felt good, Lynda. Real good."

Dr. Debra Jean Cartier rolled her wheelchair closer to the table. "Lynda . . . I suppose you've figured this out by now, but Brady's a friend of most every woman between six and sixty in the eleven Western states. He's a straight shooter, girl. He makes you feel good about yourself. He makes you feel good about being a woman. That's why we all like being around him. He belongs to you. We know that. But you take good care of him. We'll be watching you." She leaned against the back of her wheelchair. "Now I'm beginning to sound like a mother."

"It's all right. I think I'm getting used to Brady's friendships."

Brady's voice rolled across the darkened patio. "You done talkin' about me?"

"Maybe, maybe not," Lynda teased.

"Let me finish the dance story." Debra Jean Cartier's voice was soft, yet steady, like a spring wind in the cottonwoods. "Ever since then, about once a year, usually in the middle of the night, I'll get a phone call from some cafe or truck stop and hear Brady's voice. He doesn't even say hello. He just says, 'Darlin', there's a big dance in Fort Worth on Saturday night. How about you and me going down there and showin' them some fancy stuff?'"

Brady plopped down in the chair next to Lynda. "Yeah, but do you know what this lady always tells me?"

"No, what?"

"Ever' time it's the same lame excuse. 'Oh, I'd like to, cowboy, but I need to stay home and wash my hair.' Don't that beat all?"

"I suppose I won't be getting those midnight calls anymore."

"Reckon I won't ask you to the dance, but I'll probably call you and ask if you can come up to the ranch and break a couple of wild horses for me."

"Now you ask me that, and you're likely to get a yes."

"No foolin'?"

Dr. Cartier glanced over at Austin. "Well, only if your Lynda Dawn Darlin' invites me. I'm kind of particular about that."

How big a house did Brady say he was building us? Why do I have visions of flying back from New York and finding twenty people living in my house, eh, our house?

"A visit from anyone would be delightful. Brady didn't happen to mention that the nearest ranch is ten miles away, and it takes an hour and a half to drive to the market for a loaf of bread?"

Debra Jean chuckled. "He did tell me it was a wonderful place to raise kids!"

"Yes, and it sounds like we won't have to worry about contagious diseases," Lynda added. "Or the neighbor kids stopping by after school. Or door-to-door salesmen."

"See, darlin', you're warmin' up to ranch life. Why, one of these days you'll actually want to move in."

"Oh?" Debra Jean quizzed, "Do I detect a slight disagreement?"

"Actually I wouldn't call it a *slight* disagreement," Brady mumbled.

"Brady! We said we would not bring up the subject until

after I've had a chance to see the ranch again," Lynda reminded him.

"My fault, guys," Cartier asserted. "Sorry to stir things up. But I'm glad to hear you challenge this grinning cowboy. You've probably learned it takes a firm hand and spurs to keep most buckaroos in line."

"Now this conversation is degenerating," Brady complained. "If you start sharin' manhandlin' secrets, I don't have a chance. Dr. Debra Jean, are you ridin' early in the mornin'?"

"I'll tell you what. When you called the other day and said you'd stop by, I scheduled a few days off in case you could stick around. But since you need to get to Durango, I thought I might just caravan up with you."

"No foolin'? That would be great!" Brady exclaimed.

"I want to test out that blue roan gelding on the barrels, and the Durango night rodeo might just be the place. I'll come as far as Durango."

"We can have supper at Casa de Oro." Brady turned to Lynda. "That's the Mexican place I've been tellin' you about."

The one with private booths where we could sit all evening long, holding hands and listening to live mariachi music?

"Oh, I don't want to crash in on—"

"Are you kiddin'?" Brady insisted. "We've got to spend at least a night up there. You and Lynda Dawn can bunk together."

"Oh, no, I didn't mean to—"

"It's a done deal. Me and the Captain will take one room, and you two can have the other."

◆ ◆ ◆

At Brady's insistence, Lynda left her window open overnight. She woke up to a soft, faintly cool breeze drifting into the room with its red-tile floor and adobe walls. The air was hacienda fresh, alive with historic anticipation. It was the most relaxed and comfortable she had felt since staying at her grandmother's in Key Largo as a child.

Brady, why didn't you buy us a ranch in New Mexico? I could get used to this.

A yell and a shotgun blast brought her straight out of bed. Lynda clutched at the oversized black National Finals Rodeo T-shirt that served as her pajamas. Every throb and pang pulsed from the previous evening's horse ride.

"Pull!" a woman shouted.

Then a blast.

Lynda shuffled by a huge rough oak dresser and peeked out into the front patio. *Someone's shooting trap?*

"Darlin'!" Brady shouted, waving a clay pigeon in one hand and a hand-held launch in the other. "Come on out and shoot. I think Doc can give you a match. I told her about how you blasted that manuscript down in the canyon."

A whiff of columbine, salsa, and gunpowder drifted with the wind.

"I need to clean up first!" she called.

"Me and the doc are packed up. She's got her horse already trailered. There's some *ranchos huevos* on the table in the patio. We'll just shoot a little while we're waitin'."

What time does he get up? Even when I'm with him, I never know what he's doing.

◆ ◆ ◆

It was an hour and several dozen shotgun blasts later when Lynda emerged from the house wearing jeans, boots, a scoop-necked flower-printed pink blouse, and a fragrance called Ultimate Fantasy IV.

Dr. Cartier buzzed into the patio in her wheelchair, a shot-gun lying across her lap.

"Doc's doin' real good, darlin'. She's only been shootin' for a year or two now."

"You shoot, too, Brady mentioned."

"Years ago. I don't have many chances any more."

"You know what I like about it, Lynda? I like having all that power right there in my fingers. I know that sounds weird, but when you're almost powerless from the hips down, having power and control is a treat."

Lynda joined Brady in making an egg and salsa burrito out of the huge tortillas.

"These are the best tortillas you'll ever eat," Brady bragged. "A gal from Monterrey, Mexico, lives just down the road and sells them out of her kitchen. It's a well-known fact that Monterrey señoras make the best tortillas in the world."

"I suppose they'll be hard to get in Montana," Lynda mused as she inspected the salsa.

"I bet you could learn to make 'em!"

"Stoner, I've told you that I don't—"

"That was a joke, Lynda Dawn. No problem. They have tortillas in the supermarkets in Montana. 'Course, they're frozen and taste worse than a cardboard plate."

"I told you you're getting macaroni and cheese every night."

"Yes, ma'am."

The ringing of the phone sent Dr. Cartier rolling toward the kitchen. She returned carrying a cordless telephone. "It's for you, Brady. It's Heather."

Heather Martin? Why's she calling Brady?

He grabbed the phone and wandered to the other side of the patio.

"Hi, Heather-girl. How's Utah in June?"

Lynda settled down in a patio chair, nibbled on a burrito, and tried to hear the conversation.

"Yeah, she's here. You want to talk to her? I'll tell her. You think so? That would be great. You might as well come on up and see the ranch. It's no bother really."

Stoner, we have to have a serious talk about Western hospitality!

"No foolin'? Cortez? That's a shame. Of course we will. No problem. I'll call you and let you know where we'll be. Tell 'em I'll be there by noon. Don't worry about it, Mama. I'll look after 'em."

Look after whom?

Finally Brady turned off the phone and laid it on the patio table. Dr. Cartier cleared the dishes as he came over and plopped down next to Lynda.

"Heather said to give you her greetings."

"That's nice. How did she know you were here?"

"Are you kidding?" Debra Jean interjected. "It's the Stoner network. All you have to do is call the next gal in line, and she'll know where Brady is." She wheeled a load of dishes to the kitchen.

"Anyway, here's the deal. Remember Heather's teenage girls? Well, Heidi and Wendy went on a trip with a friend of theirs and family to Mesa Verde. And this family just got word that the grandfather was killed in a car wreck in Salt Lake. So they had to cut the vacation short and drive right up there. They offered to take the girls with them or put them on the bus home, but Heather didn't like either option. Trouble is, she can't get off work to come get the girls until Saturday. She was wonderin' if I—if we could swing by Cortez, pick up the girls, and let them stay with us until Saturday."

"Stay with us? You mean . . . on the road?"

"Yeah. I told her it wouldn't be any problem at all. It's not more than an hour or two out of the way."

"And they're traveling in the truck with us?"

"Yeah. I knew you wouldn't mind, darlin'. You don't, do you?"

THREE

"Now let me get this straight." Kelly's voice rattled along like an elevated train on a cold winter day. "You're in Durango, Colorado, looking for one of Brady's old flames. Traveling with you is another of his former girlfriends, her horse, plus two attractive teenage daughters of some other gal who's sweet on Brady? Girl, that isn't a caravan—it's a harem."

"Not every woman he knows is an ex-girlfriend," Lynda protested.

"Hah! You forget, I've met Brady. And I've seen the troops march into your office when you're gone and gaze at your bronc buster photo display."

"Who? Who came into my office and looked at Brady's pictures?"

"Never mind. Listen, do you want to do that radio interview in Colorado Springs or not?"

"Give me the time and place again."

"Thursday at 4:00 P.M., KRMH. They want the whole story about finding the Harrison manuscript and a preview of what readers will find in Harrison's journal."

"Kelly, I'll have to call you back later. We might be in that area, but I won't know until after the rodeo tonight."

"He's all black and blue, huh?"

"He looks horrible."

"He is too sore to . . ."

"To what?"

"You know, to kiss and hug and stuff?"

"Of course not."

"You think you can keep him healthy until the wedding?"

"Probably not. Things just happen to Brady out of the clear blue sky."

"Well, it's not as boring as being an associate editor in Manhattan. I need a vacation. I'll be glad when your wedding finally gets here. Nina's got a cousin upstate who's going to let us borrow his van."

"You really are going to bring out all the presents?"

"Only if we get first dibs on Brady's cowboy friends."

"You can have T-Bob."

"Is he cute?"

"I wouldn't know. He was covered mostly with grease."

"Oh, great. Look, I've got to go. Call the radio station and try to get hold of Joaquin."

"He didn't say what it was about?"

"He doesn't speak to anyone but LDA."

"Is he at home?"

"He said to leave a note on his machine. He'll get back to you."

"Yeah, well, I'm on the road. It's sort of hard to make connections."

"I'll tell him to look for a caravan of Stoner's sweethearts."

"Yeah, right. Good-bye, Kelly."

◆ ◆ ◆

When Lynda got back to the table of the booth at Casa de Oro, Heidi had slipped into her seat next to Brady. Wendy sat across the table, and Dr. Cartier was in her wheelchair at the end.

Austin waited for the blonde seventeen-year-old to move back to her place.

She didn't.

"You get to sit next to Uncle Brady for the next fifty years!" she explained in a voice that buzzed like an annoying alarm clock in an unfamiliar dark room.

"And she gets to sit by me now. Go on, sweet Heidi, get over there by lil' sis." Brady tickled the pouting teen in the ribs.

"I'm not a little girl!" Wendy insisted.

"Nope. You sure aren't. You two are almost as purdy as your mama, that's for sure. But you will always be lil' sis, Wendy. That's what your daddy called you—that's what I'm callin' you."

"Are you goin' to introduce us to some of your cowboy friends tonight at the rodeo, Uncle Brady?" Heidi quizzed.

"Only the old, married ones."

"Brady, how about you and Lynda Dawn sitting in the stands," proposed Cartier, "and let the girls help me with Pedregoso?"

Heidi folded her hands in front of her and tilted her head. "You mean, we'd get to go behind the chutes?"

"No, you don't!" Brady insisted. "You have to stay down at the far end of the arena with the barrel racers."

"And ropers," Cartier added.

"You ain't helpin' this any, Doc," Brady protested.

"Well, if you'd rather have the girls sit with Lynda and you, I'd certainly understand."

Austin's elbow jabbed him in the ribs.

"Okay, okay, I'm outnumbered four to one. You girls help the Doc. But I'll be keepin' an eye on you."

"Yes, daddy dear," Heidi droned.

◆ ◆ ◆

The Tuesday night crowd at Durango was small and mostly rodeo illiterate. Nearly all the entries were local cowboys rather than circuit professionals. But the performance moved right along without the customary small rodeo headaches of broken gates and balky barrier strings. At least a dozen competitors spotted Brady in the crowd and lounged around him in the stands before and after their rides.

Lynda tried to keep up with the action in the arena and the conversation buzzing around her. "It's nice to have you surrounded by men instead of women. But I feel like a spring filly that everyone wants to stop by and have a look at," she managed to squeeze in as a clown with a miniature fire truck entertained the audience.

"Did you hear what Boots said about Cindy?"

"Boots? Which one is he?"

"Two rows down with neck brace . . . see him? Anyway, he said Cindy camped out in the parking lot and ran Early to Bed over the weekend. She won all three nights."

"What does that mean?"

"It means she's only a few days ahead of us, and she has several dollars in her pocket."

"Did he know which direction she was going?"

"Nope, but he did hear about some kind of wreck involving a biker north of town."

"Was Cindy involved?"

"He didn't know. But they do run a nightly up at Steamboat Springs. Could be she headed that way."

"But if she's trying to find a biker, why would she go to a rodeo?"

"That's what I'm thinkin'. Phil and Andy said they saw a biker rally camped out at Manitou Springs."

"Where's that?"

"Near Colorado Springs."

"Let's go there. Kelly set me up with a radio interview in

Colorado Springs tomorrow. Maybe it will work out for me to do it."

"I think Boots Young is going up to Steamboat. I'll have him look for Cindy. If he spots her, he could tell her we're looking for her."

"Will that be good or bad? Will she want to talk to us?"

"I was just wonderin' the same thing. She's liable to be pretty crushed, you going back on that book deal and all."

"I did not 'go back' on any book deal. Besides, she didn't receive the letter or the check for the kill fee. I've got it in my duffel bag."

Brady shrugged.

"But what?" she demanded.

"I didn't say anything."

"You were thinking it."

"Thinking what?" Brady carefully brushed the hair off his bruised forehead.

"You were sitting there thinking that it's somehow my fault that Cindy's on the run. If I published that book, she'd live happily ever after. Am I right?"

"That's not what I was thinkin'. I'm not blamin' you for anythin', darlin'."

"Don't jerk me around, Stoner. You're still extremely ticked at me."

"I'm grieved at the way the publishing business is run. All that's important is the bottom line."

"You just said it was a business, and you're right. You have to make a profit, or the company folds. The same is true in ranching, isn't it? You buy low and try to sell high. You don't sit around worrying about some family in Brooklyn paying more for a pound of hamburger, do you? Business is business."

Brady's eyes followed a long-legged sorrel stallion who defied those herding him out of the arena.

"Well?" she insisted. "Aren't you going to answer me?"

"Lynda Dawn, ever' answer I could think up would get me into more hot water."

"So you're not going to say anything?"

"I'll respond whenever my brain catches up with my heart and I can figure out how to answer in an intelligent way that still shows I'm crazy about you."

The Durango night air suddenly cooled. She stared at his bruised and battered face, carved-in-stone expression, dimple-less cheeks, and intense brown eyes. The scream of the crowd and an 81-point ride snapped her mind back to the rodeo arena.

Within seconds Brady was engaged in a debate over the score with a cowboy called Elkins.

I hate it when he does that, Lord. He just shuts up, and I blab on like a fool. Maybe I do feel a little guilty about Cindy's book. But we couldn't publish it. As much as I wanted to, it just didn't go anywhere.

She reached down into her purse and pulled out a small green bottle of Peek-a-Boo Fun and dabbed it behind her ears.

Maybe I'm in the wrong business. I do care about people more than I care about money. Maybe I should rewrite the letter to Cindy. Maybe it's a good thing it didn't get to her yet.

"They're settin' up the barrels, darlin'. I think Doc is first up." He slipped his arm in hers. "Sorry about barkin' at you like that."

"Maybe I needed to hear it," she murmured.

"Come on, Doc!" Brady shouted. "What did you say?"

"Eh, nothing. How does she keep her feet in the stirrups like that?"

"Velcro."

"Really?"

"Those jeans have the suede chaps sewn right in them. She puts Velcro on her cuffs and on the stirrup leathers. She's got some movement in her upper legs, a strong left-hand grip on the horn, and the best natural balance of anyone I've ever seen."

"Did you ever wonder how good she would have been without that accident?" Lynda asked.

His big brown eyes locked onto hers. "Nope. Guess I never did. I can't imagine her being different."

Dr. Debra Jean Cartier turned the blue roan horse away from the barrels as she entered the arena. She patted him on the neck and then took a deep breath. She slowly pulled his head around toward the barrel on the right. Unable to spur him, she slapped the gelding in the rump, and he galloped off.

He circled the first barrel tightly and sprinted toward the one on the left. With Cartier leaning toward the center of the turn, he slid a little past the second barrel, regained his footing quickly, and then dashed for the far end and the last barrel. Circling it snugly, Cartier slapped the pony's rump, and he sprinted with abandon back to the finish line. Her white straw cowboy hat blew off, and her auburn hair soared in the breeze.

Lynda was afraid she would crash into the wooden roping boxes at the south end of the arena, but she pulled up quickly to turn the horse just in time. One of the rodeo officials trotted over and handed her back her hat. The loudspeaker boomed her score.

"16.24—is that good?" Lynda asked.

"Sounds mighty good to me. 'Course, sometimes those barrels are closer than at other places. It all depends on the other gals. But she got to make her run on top the dirt. That always helps."

"On top the dirt?"

"Before the girls wear a rut in it. It's always best to draw toward the first of the pack."

About 400 men, women, and children lounged in stands that could hold over 1,000. Most were dressed in shorts, tennis shoes, and tank tops. A few sported brightly colored cowboy hats and big feather hatbands. But those wearing worn

Wranglers, taped-up Justin boots, and scars seemed to hover within shouting distance of Brady Stoner.

While Brady's eyes were fixed on every step of every barrel race, Lynda's attention waned to examining the crowd.

"Brady, do you know that cowboy sitting on the rail down there by the flagpole?"

"I can't tell. Hey, Elkins, who's the steer wrestler with the torn shirt?" Brady pointed to the distant end of the rodeo arena.

A thin, tough cowboy four rows in front of them grinned, revealing a couple of missing teeth. "It's that kid just out of high school from Grand Junction. State champ this year. But he needs a little more bulk to be a pro bull-dogger, don't you think? Believe his name is Tater or Tatum or Tippy or Tupulo. Somethin' like that."

Brady looked back at Lynda. "There you have it. I don't know him. Why did you ask?"

"Oh . . . nothing." She slid her hand over and locked her fingers into his.

Brady raised her hand to his chapped lips and gently kissed her fingers. "What do you mean, nothing? What about him?"

"Well, he's been following Heidi and Wendy around like a dog just let out of the pound."

Lynda's hand was abruptly dropped. "He's what?"

"From up here it looks like he's making a move on the girls."

Brady sat up straight and stared through the twilight at the south end of the arena. "How could you tell that from the stands?"

"Men on the prowl look the same at any age, at any distance."

Brady jumped up and yanked her to her feet. "Come on! I want to check out—eh, Doc's horse."

Lynda grabbed her brown leather purse. "Doc's horse?"

Brady tugged her down the steps. "I think I spotted a problem."

"And I think it might be best if we only have boys," Lynda stated as she tried to keep her teal boots from tripping on the bleachers. When they reached the dirt runway, she tugged at his arm. "You promise you won't horsewhip that young man?"

"I don't promise nothin'!" he growled.

◆ ◆ ◆

Eighteen-year-old Tyler Adams had a day job at a dude ranch at Hermosa Creek. He was six feet tall with brown shaggy hair, a mustache so faint it looked like it could be washed off, and dreamy blue eyes. Lynda learned all of this within thirty seconds of finding Heidi Martin.

"He thought we were barrel racers! Is that cool or what?" she giggled.

Lynda watched as Heidi and Wendy pulled the tack and rubbed down Pedregoso. Debra Cartier sat in her wheelchair at the rail to watch the other barrel racers compete. She visited with a blonde in a red, white, and blue sequined jacket who straddled a long-legged bay mare. Brady had moseyed up to the young man with the torn shirt and ushered him over to the peeling white wooden fence next to the roping boxes.

"Do you know what his name means?" Wendy asked her.

"Tyler's?"

"No, the horse," she sighed. "Tyler's not my type."

"He's my type," Heidi interjected.

"What *is* your type?" Lynda asked the younger sister.

"He's got to have brown eyes and be a bareback rider."

"You just want someone like Uncle Brady!" Heidi teased.

"I set my sights high."

"Oh? Are you saying that I'm aiming too low?" Heidi's long

blonde ponytail bounced in tune with the flash in her eyes and the crackle in her voice.

"I didn't say that . . . but if the boot fits . . ."

"Oh, yeah, sure. How about you? You went to the homecoming dance with the school dork!"

Wendy Martin's face tightened. "Jeremy Hacken is not the school dork!"

"Well, he's almost the school dork."

"Almost a dork is not the same as a dork."

Heidi scooted up closer to Lynda. They were exactly the same height. "Isn't Tyler a hunk?" she whispered.

Lynda inspected the pimply-faced, gangling, rawboned teenage boy. *Oh, to be seventeen and see the hunk in every boy!* "He does look like, eh, like he's all muscle and bone."

"You should see his smile! I thought my contacts were going to melt! What do you think Uncle Brady's talking to him about?"

Lynda shifted her weight from one foot to the other. "Rodeo, I suppose."

"Do you want to know what Pedregoso means or not?" Wendy interrupted. She held a palm full of rolled oats to the horse's slobbering mouth. "It means stony. Dr. Cartier named him after Uncle Brady."

A whoop and a holler from Brady caused all three to whirl toward the arena.

"She did it, darlin'!" Brady yelled back to her. "Doc won the first money!"

Cartier rolled toward the horse trailer.

"Congratulations!" Lynda offered.

"He could have done even better."

"You mean, cutting around that second barrel?"

Cartier stared up at Austin. "You are learning."

"I've got a good teacher."

"Doc?" Heidi was holding a curry comb in one hand and a

brush in the other. "What are Uncle Brady and Tyler talking about?"

Cartier glanced at the railing where both men stood.

"I think it's about steer wrestling. Brady was saying something about a sure way to get your face busted up."

With long, dark brown braids down her back, Wendy scampered over to them. "Doc, would you teach me to be a barrel racer?"

"I don't know. It takes a commitment. It's not something you learn in a few hours."

"I'm serious about it."

Cartier turned to Heidi. "How about you, big sis?"

"Me? Oh, I'm serious, too. Serious about Tyler!"

Cartier looked Wendy right in the eyes. "If you want to learn barrel racing from me, here's what it will take. Spend the rest of the summer living with me. You muck the stalls every morning, feed and exercise all the horses, and ride about four to six hours a day."

Wendy bounced up and down in her lace-up roper boots. "Really?"

"And here's what I'll do. I'll put you up, feed you, and at the end of the summer, I'll give you Pedregoso."

"You're kidding me!" Wendy squealed. "You're not serious."

"I'm serious, girl. Are you?"

"I can't believe this. I can't believe you said that!" Wendy twirled like a dust devil.

"I said it."

"Uncle Brady!" Wendy hollered. "Uncle Brady, I'm going to be a barrel racer!" She sprinted to the rodeo arena. Heidi handed Lynda the brush and comb and then trailed behind her younger sister.

"That's quite an offer you just made."

"I presume Brady's told you about how their daddy died?"

Lynda pulled at the short gray horsehair matted in the

brush. "Heather told me most of the details. Did you know him?"

"No, but it seems like the right thing to do."

"You're extremely generous."

"Lynda Dawn." Doc Cartier let out a deep breath. "Look at me. I'm forty-one years old. I enjoy my life. But only because I've come to terms with the fact I will never bear or raise children of my own. And it looks like I'm not going to have a husband either."

"Hey, don't give up yet—"

"Don't humor me. Men need a whole lot more than I can physically give. And don't feel sorry. The Lord and I have come to terms on that. But I will have neither a mate nor children to take care of me in my old age. The best time in my life is right now. Today. Tonight. I've learned to enjoy every moment. Who knows? Winning the Durango Nightly Rodeo might be the highlight of my career.

"So if I get a chance to have a teenage daughter, even for a few weeks, I guarantee I'll enjoy every day of it. And if I can teach a young lady self-confidence, responsibility, respect for people and animals, how to trust the Lord in everything, and maybe a thing or two about nuclear physics, my year, my decade, has been a success. That pony cost me $800 last fall at the auction. Can you think of anything better I could do with my money?"

"No. Sounds like you have it all thought through."

"Of course, I'm not sure Heather will want to give up a child for ten weeks."

"It will give Wendy something fun to think about anyway." She handed the horse brush and comb to Cartier. "Think I'll go check on that gang." She motioned toward Brady, Tyler, and the girls.

Lord, why do You do this to me? Why do You keep bringing peo-ple into my life who make me feel shallow? I spend a whole after-

noon worrying about perfume, while Debra is concerned with
strengthening a young girl's life. I resented having to have them
with us for even a day. Cartier wants one with her for the summer.
Doesn't Brady have any friends that are despicable?

◆ ◆ ◆

Pedregoso, with light gray blanket and empty oat pail, slept
standing, secure in a stall behind the rodeo grounds. Inside
Room 122 at the San Juan Motel, Heidi and Wendy in their
oversized T-shirts, both wearing two sets of pierced earrings,
giggled as the television blared. Dr. Debra Jean Cartier, single-
braided auburn hair almost reaching her belt, listened to a tape
of classical Spanish guitar music on her headset as she sat in
Room 121 punching numbers into her laptop computer. Tyler
Adams, still in dirty Wranglers and torn shirt, had visions of
blondes as he tried to find a comfortable position to sleep in the
cab of his 1972 Chevy pickup at Spring Creek Park.

Lynda Austin, freshly painted with an aromatic liquid
called Concealed Enticement, stepped out on the patio by the
swimming pool and plopped down in a white woven chaise
lounge next to a hatless cowboy with a black eye and bruised
head. A one-eyed dog lay next to him.

"I'm proud of you, Stoner. You didn't inflict any additional
injury on yourself—or others."

"Thank you, ma'am. It was a pretty borin' day."

The night felt a little cool. Lynda rubbed her bare arms but
decided against a jacket. "Boring? It's like being in a circus
troupe. I can't believe you invited young Tyler to go with us to
Colorado Springs. I thought you were going to chase him off."

"Well, darlin', turns out I once rodeoed with his Uncle
Wes. The kid's tryin' to work and learn a little rodeo. He
wanted to compete up at Castle Rock, but didn't think his old
truck would get him that far. Now when Doc said she wanted

to go up there and barrel race, I figured we might all just as well go. If Cindy went to Manitou Springs, we've got lots of reasons to head that direction."

"Have you thought through the logistics of this? Just where is Tyler going to ride? In the back of our—your pickup?"

"The girls can get along fine in the jump seat of my rig. Tyler can ride with the Doc and help her with Pedregoso. That'll work, won't it?"

"Oh, sure, providing you don't mind having a pouting, whining, sulking seventeen-year-old in the cab behind you."

"I'll have Heidi sit behind you."

"Thanks. Did you get hold of Heather?"

"Yep, me and the girls just finished talkin' to her."

"What did she say about Wendy spending the summer with Dr. Cartier?"

"She's got to think about it some. She's not feelin' too well. Thinks she's gettin' the flu or something. I guess the way things stand is, after the rodeo at Castle Rock, Doc will take the girls with her back to Los Alamos. Heather will meet them there and then decide what to do about the rest of the summer."

"You mean, after tomorrow it will be back to just you and me?" She reached over and rubbed the sleeve of his shirt.

"Looks like it. You won't be too lonesome, will you?"

"You'll just have to be extra friendly," she purred.

"I reckon I could do that. Sure hope we catch Cindy soon."

"Brady, we aren't even coming close to finding a trace of her."

"Not yet. Maybe she's just off rodeoin'. Maybe there's no big crisis at all. Maybe all this biker stuff was just a coincidence. Maybe we should just drive off and let her live her life."

"It's sort of tempting, isn't it? When will we have time to go up and see the ranch?"

"I've been ponderin' that myself. If we don't get up there by Saturday, maybe you ought to just stay out here next week, too."

"I'd love to, cowboy, but I'm getting married a week from Saturday. Did I tell you that? There are a few details to attend to."

"Married? You? No foolin'? Say, is it anyone I know?"

"Ever hear of the Wild Man, Spud Pedregoso?"

"Don't believe so. What kind of fella is he?"

"Well, if it gives you any indication—we're getting married on the back of a bucking bronc."

"Whoa, a short wedding, huh?"

"Eight seconds max."

Lynda took his rough, callused hand in hers.

"It feels good, doesn't it, darlin'?"

"Your hand in mine?"

"Yep. And the cool night air . . . the bright stars . . . and the thought that in a few days we'll be married. It just seems . . . right."

"You know what, Brady? I think I'm actually beginning to look forward to the peace and quiet of the ranch. Being married means I can chase all your friends off and have you all to myself."

"Ah, hah! The plan's workin', Capt. Patch! She's goin' to love the Double Diamond."

The black and white dog got up and trotted off into the night.

"You planned on having Rodney bust your skull? Come on, Stoner, everyone knows your life is just a series of unexpected crises."

"Darlin', my life is so routine when you're not around."

"Don't give me that baloney. You think I'm some tender-foot who just fell off the back of a Yellow Cab?"

"Can we get serious for a minute?" he asked.

"Are you planning to make a move on me?"

"Yes, ma'am, I reckon I am."

"Well, it's about time," she murmured.

"Darlin', I really do love you."

"Prove it!"

Brady pulled up from the chair and scooted into the chaise lounge with her.

Toe to toe, nose to nose, buckle to buckle—maybe we ought to get married tomorrow! Or tonight—

The door to Room 122 swung open with a bang and a shout. "Uncle Brady, Heidi's watching a show that Mother said we couldn't watch!"

A second voice blared from the room, "I am not! I'm just flipping through the channels, that's all."

"You were too! You had it on while I was brushing my teeth."

"Wendy, grow up."

"Me? You're the one acting immature."

"Girls, pipe down before the manager comes out. I'll be right there."

He pulled himself out of the chaise and shuffled across the concrete. "You want to come help me with this?" he asked her.

"No, I think this is strictly a job for Uncle Brady."

"Will you wait right there until I get back?"

"I'll wait for a few minutes, cowboy. But just remember, 'the time to dance is when the music's playing.'"

"Hold that thought, darlin'. I'll be right back."

◆ ◆ ◆

There was considerable discussion concerning who would ride where the next morning as they gathered around a brown formica table that housed eggs over easy, biscuits and gravy, oatmeal, and peach waffles. Wendy wanted to ride with Dr. Cartier and discuss the summer plans. Heidi and Tyler offered to ride in the back of the van and give Brady and Lynda some privacy.

Brady had a different plan. When the caravan finally pulled out from behind the rodeo grounds, a sheepish Tyler Adams rode in the truck jump seat. Wendy and a pouting Heidi Martin rode with Dr. Debra Jean Cartier.

The trip from Durango to Walensburg was filled mainly with rodeo talk. At least, that was the topic of conversation in the silver and black Dodge pickup.

Lynda and Capt. Patch dozed most of the way.

The caravan turned north off Interstate 25 and stopped in Pueblo about noon. When they finally left Fred's Front Range Bar-b-que Cafe and Bait Shop, Capt. Patch and Wendy rode with Dr. Cartier, and Tyler and Heidi were crammed into the narrow jump seat behind Brady and Lynda.

With serious conversation impossible, Lynda dug out a calendar and reviewed the next two weeks.

1. proof the finals on *Two Bullets and a Prayer*
2. meet with T. H., George, Julie, and Nicole on cover of *Death of the Steel Drum Band*
3. pick up dry cleaning at Les Boutique (Tues. after 3:00)
4. call Megan and see if she knows if William's coming to the wedding
5. check with Mr. Sylvanni about condo
6. lunch with Kelly and Nina on Monday (Pierre's???)
7. scan all the manuscripts in "In Your Dreams" file
8. take one whole day and do correspondence
9. manicure, pedicure, hair, (tanning booth?)
10. finish thank-yous for Gossman party

Ignoring the muted giggles in the backseat and the Sons of the San Joaquin harmonizing on the stereo, she glanced over at Brady, still hatless and bruised. He tapped his hand on the dashboard as he drove.

Lynda cleared her throat. "Brady?"

"Is this tape good or what?"

"Eh, yes, it is. Listen, I need to—"

"When those Hannah boys sing Charlie Daniel's 'Wyomin' on My Mind,' it's just a little touch of heaven."

"I guess I never thought of it that way. Honey, I've got to—"

"And 'Prairie Girl' and 'Is It Because?' Hey, you know what would be the greatest thing on earth?"

"You and me having dinner totally by ourselves at the lodge north of Jackson after our wedding and watching the sun slip behind the Tetons?"

He flashed a dimpled smile. "Besides that!"

"What other thing would be great?"

"Wouldn't it be a kick to have the Sons of the San Joaquin sing at our wedding? I met them once at the cowboy poetry gatherin' in Elko, Nevada. Did I ever tell you about that?"

"Brady, I have an extremely important question to ask you!" she huffed.

He punched off the tape player. "Go ahead—shoot."

"I won't need to if you'll sit still and listen."

Brady slapped the pickup seat and shouted, "Yes!" Then he glanced back at Tyler and Heidi. "When I met this lady, she was so citified she was afraid to relax and tell a joke. Now she deadpans with a Western metaphor."

"Stoner, I wasn't using a metaphor. Heidi, hand me the 30-30 under that seat."

"Whoa! Okay, what's your question, darlin'?"

"Do we have an address?"

"I thought I told you that when we were in New York. It's Rural Route 2, Box 34, Buffalo, Montana, 59418."

"No, I mean a street address."

"Darlin', we don't even have a street."

"Well, there's some kind of road. What do I tell UPS and Fed. Ex.? I'll need a street address. Where's our mailbox anyway? I don't remember a mailbox at the house."

"It's on the highway."

"The paved highway? That's five miles from the ranch."

"Seven."

"Seven miles! I can see it now: 'Honey, I'm going to get the mail. If the weather's good, I should be home by noon.'"

"I will personally deliver the mail into your sweet hands ever' day, darlin'."

All the tension in her neck seemed to release at once. "I like that, but I still have to have a street address."

"Okay, how about this? Double Diamond Ranch, Sager Canyon Road, Buffalo, Montana, 59418?"

"You think that will reach us?"

"That and a telephone number should do it."

"When do we get our telephone number?"

"Monday . . . I think."

"What do you mean, you think?"

"They weren't sure when the Judith Basin Auto Salvage and Saloon was closing. Either this weekend or next. Anyway, we get those two lines as soon as they're available."

"Does this mean we're going to get phone calls at 2:00 A.M. from wives wanting to know if their husbands are at the bar?"

"Oh, no, they change the numbers . . . I think."

"Okay, I now have a street address but no phone number. Is that right?"

"Exciting, huh?"

"On the edge of terrifying. Sometimes I feel like I'm jumping out of an airplane at night."

"Well, at least we get to hold hands doin' it," he smirked.

She shook her head and ran her hand through the curls of her wavy shoulder-length hair. "Okay, cowboy, you win again. But you tell them your fiancée is from New York City, and she wants a phone number by Monday or else."

"Or else what?" Heidi piped up from the backseat.

"When Lynda Dawn gets riled?" Brady laughed. "I don't even want to think about it. Just make sure you aren't in the same pasture."

"No kiddin'?" Tyler burst out. "Wow, that reminds me of a heifer I raised once."

"Enough of the Western analogies. Stoner, why are we pulling off the Interstate here?"

"Because that's the Pro-Rodeo Hall of Fame." He pointed at a large sprawling complex of buildings.

"Are we doing a tourist thing?"

"We're going to Castle Rock, but we had one report that Cindy might have headed toward a biker rally at Manitou Springs, and you have a radio interview at 4:00. So I thought Doc, the girls, and Tyler could check out the Hall of Fame. I've a card that will get two of you in the door. Tyler, you have a PRCA permit, don't you?"

"Yeah, but I haven't filed it yet."

"It will still get you and a friend in the door. You think you can find someone to go with you to the museum?"

"Uncle Brady, really!" Heidi griped.

"Lynda Dawn Darlin' and I will drive up to Manitou and see if there's any sign of Cindy. Then we'll meet back here and all traipse over to the radio station for the interview. We should still get to Castle Rock an hour or two before show time. Tyler, you look after the ladies."

He grinned at Heidi. "Oh, sure."

"All three of the ladies!"

Adams jumped to attention. "Yes, sir! All three ladies."

◆ ◆ ◆

Brady, Lynda, and Capt. Patch drove back through Colorado Springs and out Highway 24 toward the mountains.

"Were you like Tyler when you were eighteen?" Lynda asked.

"Nah. I was a self-controlled, mature, career-focused young man," Brady assured her.

"Whatever happened to you?" she teased.

"Guess I fell on my head too many times," he laughed. "How about you, Lynda Dawn? What were you like when you were eighteen?"

"Reasonable, clear-thinking, cautious, and eleemosynary."

"You were what?"

"Altruistic."

"Sometimes I wonder," Brady drawled, "if I know what I'm gettin' into, marryin' a book editor."

"Actually I was a lot like Heidi, only a little more shy. Especially around boys."

"Yeah . . . well, to tell you the truth, I was a jerk at eighteen. I knew everything there was to know about cowboyin', rodeo, trucks, girls, and especially bareback ridin'. It's a good thing you didn't know me then."

"You think maybe the Lord brought us together at the right time?"

"Yep."

When they pulled up in the campground at Manitou Springs, no more than a dozen motorcycles were scattered around the parking lot. Most of the black-leather-clad owners combed the grounds, picking up trash and cans.

"I'm not real comfortable in this environment," Lynda cautioned.

"Stick with me, darlin'."

"Like pine tar to your fingers, cowboy!"

Brady approached a big sandy-haired man with sideburns that attached to his mustache.

"Hey, dude," the big man called out, "what happened to you? Looks like someone dropped a meteorite on your head."

Brady leaned close to the man. "You didn't hear about that brawl down in Santa Fe across from the rodeo grounds?"

"No foolin'? I'm sorry I missed it."

"Looks like I'm the one that missed it." Brady pointed at the near empty campgrounds. "When did ever'one leave?"

"This mornin'. Just the cleanup detail left."

"I was lookin' for a gal drivin' a big green Cadillac and pullin' a horse trailer. Did she happen to swing by here?"

"Crazy Cindy? She ain't the one that did that to you, is she?" He pointed to Brady's black eye.

"Eh, no. Cindy was here?"

"Oh, she was here, all right." The big man dropped his black plastic trash sack and waved his hands. "She drove right into this lot on Friday night about sundown, jumped out of that Caddy toting a lever-action carbine, and screamed, 'I'm Cindy LaCoste. Which one of you is Lamont McGhee?' Mister, there were over 200 bikers here, and she's in the middle callin' Lamont out."

Lynda scooted closer to Brady. "What happened?"

"Well, doll, I'll tell ya. A couple dudes headed off to the pay phone to call the cops. Some of the others tried to get position on her. Most just scattered back behind a tree somewhere. She starts yellin' and screamin' and threatenin' to shoot us one at a time until Lamont shows himself. Well, I guess he was feelin' ashamed to let a cowgirl call him out like that, so old Lamont steps up and says he's never seen her before in his life.

"She dangles that 30-30 at her side, walks right over to him, and shouts, 'Oh, you've seen me before. You've seen all of me!' Then she bursts out cryin', and old Lamont reaches for the rifle. Well, before any of us could jump her, she cracks the barrel against Lamont's head, and he's crumpled on the parking lot. Her finger's on the trigger of that carbine jammed into his throat. She was cryin' and yellin' at the same time."

"What was she yelling?" Lynda asked.

"She just kept sayin', 'May God have mercy on your soul,' over and over and over. I thought she'd kill him for sure. But she didn't pull the trigger. I ain't never seen anyone snuffed, but

I figured it was goin' to happen then. McGhee is not the type worth losin' your life over."

"What happened then?"

"A deputy sheriff sirened in. When she heard him, she ran back to the car, tossed the gun into the backseat, and sat behind the wheel. Well, Lamont told us to not say anything. He didn't want the cops involved. Said he'd handle Crazy Cindy himself."

"And the deputy went along with that?"

"I think he was happy just to drive out of here. She pulled out ahead of him, and within an hour Lamont and that bunch left. We had a mighty nice rally after they were gone. Sort of wish she'd showed up and run him off earlier. They aren't exactly crowd pleasers, if you sniff my fumes."

"Do you have any idea where this Lamont was headed?"

"Nope. And don't care to. Oh, I'll see him up at Sturgis during Rally Week, but I won't miss him if I miss him. Maybe she was some old girlfriend, I don't know. Shoot, I'm gettin' too old for that kind of ruckus. I can still give and take a punch, but I don't have any intention of gettin' stung by a lead bee."

"You haven't seen Cindy or Lamont McGhee since last Friday?"

"Nope."

"Well, thanks, partner."

The big man with deep-set blue eyes ogled Lynda. "Have we met before?"

"No. I'm his fiancée—from back east." She held Brady's arm tight.

"You wouldn't happen to be an Amway salesperson, would you?"

"A what? Eh—no," Lynda blustered.

"I must have you mixed up with another gal. I need some of that extra-strength hand cleaner."

"Oh . . . well, I—"

"We got to get goin'." Brady pulled her toward the pickup. "Maybe we'll see you on down the road."

"You two take it easy—just one day at a time!"

Lynda's face was flushed and her breathing rapid when she got back into the pickup. She pulled down the visor and looked at herself in the mirror as Brady drove back to Colorado Springs.

"I take it you were a tad nervous," Brady commented.

"I can't believe you barged right in on the likes of them."

She could sense Brady's piercing glare. "Other than wearing black leather and ridin' motorcycles, they're no different than anyone else. Did you hear him say, 'Take it easy—just one day at a time'?"

"Yes. So what?"

"Those are buzz words for A.A. He's workin' on his alcohol problem."

"How do you know about things like that?"

"I've got a lot of friends in the same fix. Yeah, a few of the bikers can get pretty rough, and every once in a while there's a pack of crazies, but the same is true of cowboys, truck drivers, and tax accountants."

"I know," she sighed. "It's just not my element. I can go to Chinatown or Harlem or Little Italy or the lower east side and know my way around. Sometimes you forget I'm a tourist out here."

"Not for long, darlin'."

She shoved the visor back up. "Do I really look like an Amway salesperson?"

"I don't know, Lynda Dawn. I don't even know if that was a compliment or an insult."

"Brady, I'm frightened for Cindy."

"Me, too, darlin'. I don't know what got into her head. It sounds like she's wrestling something in her mind."

"You mean, like her mind is saying to find them and kill them all, and her spirit is tugging a different direction?"

"I hope it was that and not just the sound of sirens. One thing for sure, she's in deep water now."

"With that gang following her?"

"Yeah. Sounds like Lamont won't forget being put down like that. And it's a cinch it will be easy to follow an old Cadillac pulling a horse trailer."

"We've got to find her, Brady. We've got to talk to her before . . ." Lynda dug into the glove compartment, pulled out a brown paper napkin, and blew her nose.

"You okay, darlin'?"

"Brady, if they rape her again, she'll kill herself."

"I know, babe, I know. That's why we've got to keep lookin'."

The pickup followed the road as it curved through the mountains and led into the suburbs of Colorado Springs.

"What will we do now?" she asked.

"We'll drive up to the rodeo at Castle Rock. After the show Doc can take the girls back to New Mexico with her, and we'll keep searchin' for Cindy."

"I've been thinking. I don't need to go up to the ranch. I really want to, but I think Cindy needs us more."

"I reckon you're right. It's a fine-looking home, darlin'. You saw the pictures. 'Course, it will be unfurnished when we move in—except for the bed. I told you about the bed, didn't I?"

"No, buckaroo, you seemed to have forgotten about that."

"Tip and Ralph Lee—the guys building the house—are makin' us a custom bed. It's their weddin' present. A rough, massive pine four-poster."

"It's a king-size bed?"

"Nope. Just the bedposts are big."

"Queen-size?"

"No way." Brady glanced over at her and winked. "Didn't

you know those big beds are the cause of nine-tenths of all marital problems in America?"

"No," she snickered, "I'll have to admit I've never read that statistic."

"That's because statistics are gathered by people who sleep in oversized beds. They're ashamed to let the truth out."

"Well, Mr. Stoner, just what are the advantages of a regular size bed?"

"First, it's too small to have all the kids come runnin' and jump in bed with you. They have to stay in their own room."

"I see."

"Second, they're easier to make up in the morning and cheaper to buy coverin's for."

"That's true. But why is it I think you're holding back on the real reason?"

"Well, third, you can sleep back-to-back or belly-to-belly, but you can't run and hide."

Lynda fidgeted with her hands trying to keep them from crawling into her purse and pulling out a bottle of perfume. "Well, Mr. Stoner . . . do you have any other philosophical comments about the relationship of furniture and marital success?"

"Did I ever tell you about my philosophy of bathtubs versus showers?"

"Eh, no. Is this going to embarrass me?"

"Probably."

"Then how about waiting a week or two to tell me. I've got a feeling I have plenty of color in my face already."

"Blush pink is mighty purdy on you, Miss Lynda Dawn."

"We ought to get married, Stoner."

"Yes, ma'am, I do believe you're right. How about June 12 in Jackson, Wyoming?"

"I'll have to check my calendar." She pretended to scan an appointment book. "Can we do it in the afternoon? My morning's fairly tied up."

"Only if we could be done by four. I drawed good in Dubois that night, and first money pays $263."

"Well, we certainly wouldn't want it to interrupt your rodeo schedule."

"Thank you, ma'am, I knew you'd see it my way."

"Then it's settled. Say, where did you have in mind for our wedding night?"

"Oh, there's the purdiest little rest stop right outside of Rock Springs. The VFW has free coffee and cookies on the weekends."

"You tryin' to spoil me, cowboy?"

"Yes, ma'am. Nothin' but the best for my darlin'."

◆ ◆ ◆

The parking lot of radio station KRMH—Rocky Mountain High, 101.6—was large enough for about ten cars. By the time Brady's truck and Cartier's van and horse trailer pulled in, there was barely enough room for the black Lexus to sneak into a reserved spot. A tall, thin man wearing a short-sleeved black turtleneck shirt and black slacks walked over to the van.

Debra Cartier rolled down her window as Lynda also approached the van.

"Hi, I'm Gary Spruce. Are you my 4:00 P.M. interview?"

"I'm just a friend. Lynda's the one you want." She pointed toward Austin.

"Oh . . ." He gave a quick glance at her, from boots to silver dangling cowboy-hat earrings. "You're Lynda Austin?"

"Yep." Lynda grinned. "What's the matter, buckaroo? You expectin' some hard-driven New York City type dressed in a tailored suit and wearin' some slick Italian heels?"

"Yes, I guess I was," he admitted.

"Well, I'm slumming it. Hi, I'm the editor from Atlantic-Hampton."

"You compiled the Harrison journal?"

"Yes."

"Are you the one who journeyed down into that Arizona canyon and dug out the Harrison manuscript?"

Brady strolled up just then.

"Mr. Stoner here and I brought it out."

"Stoner? The cowboy? Great interview material. Can I get you both on the air today?"

Lynda glanced at Brady.

"Be happy to sit in the studio, but I don't imagine I'll have much to say," Brady offered.

"Are all of you headed to a horse show or something?"

"We're going to the rodeo at Castle Rock," Lynda offered. "Tyler's a steer wrestler; Doc Cartier's a barrel racer, when she isn't busy being a nuclear physicist at Los Alamos. And, of course, my fiancé is just about the best bareback rider in the world. Heidi and Wendy are good friends from St. George, Utah."

"The dog's name is Capt. Patch, and the horse is Pedregoso," Wendy piped up.

"This is great! I want all of you in the studio. We'll interview everyone."

"Really? Even us?" Heidi shrieked.

"Except for the dog and the horse." Spruce motioned for them to follow him into the single-story white stucco building. Then he turned around. "Come to think of it—bring the dog with the eye patch, too."

◆ ◆ ◆

Brady led Pedregoso out of the trailer in the big field next to the rodeo grounds at Castle Rock, Colorado. Doc Cartier showed Tyler, Heidi, and Wendy the way to the rodeo secretary's office near the concession booth under the stands. Tying the horse to the side of the trailer, Brady tossed a couple of scoops of alfalfa pellets into a plastic bucket hanging by the horse's nose.

"That was quite a radio interview, Lynda Dawn."

"It was supposed to be just twenty minutes."

"Well, twenty minutes for you, twenty for me, twenty for Doc—"

"Twenty for Heidi, twenty for Wendy, and even twenty for good old Tyler, whom none of us had met before this time yesterday. We were in that station for two hours. I thought he was about ready to interview Capt. Patch."

"Spruce said they had more call-in responses than they usually get in a month."

Lynda rubbed the blue roan's neck. "Yes, but I'm still not sure about him calling us the 'invasion of the Cowboy Gypsies.'"

"At least he didn't mention your being a CLS." Brady's brown eyes were sparkling.

"CLS?"

"Cowboy's Love Slave."

"That could have shortened his career considerably."

Brady nodded toward the horse. "Check out his hooves."

"They look fine to me."

"Ask him to give you a foot. See if he's picked up any rocks."

"Ask him?"

"Go on," Brady urged.

Lynda cleared her throat and tried not to giggle. "Excuse me, Mr. Pedregoso—a gelding is still a mister, isn't he—would you please give me a foot? Brady, I don't think he's listening."

"That's not what I meant, and you know it."

"Brady, I don't know how to get him to raise his hoof."

"Slide your hand down the front of his leg. When you get to the fetlock, tug on him a little bit and ask him again."

Lynda slid her hand down Pedregoso's left front leg. "About here?"

"Yep."

"Okay, Mr. Horse, lift it up . . . come on."

His leg lifted straight up. "Hey, he did it! Look at that. I got him to give me a foot!"

"What a gal!"

"What do I look for?"

"Any rocks jammed in down there?"

"Eh . . . I don't see any. What's all that?" She pointed to a mass between the bars of the hoof.

"The frog."

"The what?" She quickly dropped the foot.

"It's the soft part of his hoof. It's called a frog."

"You set me up for that, Stoner."

"I had to get even for that eleemosynary comment you made this afternoon. Is that really a word?"

"Trust me."

"Uncle Brady! Guess what." Wendy sprinted between the horse trailers and campers. "You're entered in the bareback riding!"

"I'm what?"

"Tyler entered you in the bareback riding, and Doc Cartier paid your entry fees."

"How can he do that without my PRCA number?"

"You mean this?" Wendy held up the card he had given her at the museum parking lot.

"You can't ride, Brady. You're all beat up and bruised," Lynda protested.

"Please, Uncle Brady, please! They complained that they didn't have many bareback riders entered. If you really do retire, this could be the last time Heidi and me get to see you ride."

"Brady, if you land on that head, you'll be in the hospital for sure!" Lynda insisted.

"Oh, well . . . the stock can't be all that rough at these little rodeos. Maybe I could just—"

"Stoner, I want you alive and well at the wedding!"

"Yes, ma'am. Eh, how about I go take a look at what kind of horses they're buckin'? Come on, lil' sis, which one did I draw?"

"One called Cowboy's Delight."

"No foolin'? That sounds like one of Lynda Dawn's perfumes."

"Really?"

Their voices faded into the crowd, and Lynda found herself alone except for the horse.

"Well, Mr. Pedregoso, he's going to ride in this rodeo no matter what I say, isn't he? In fact, for the rest of my life we'll pull into some little dinkwater town for supper, and before I get to the bread pudding, he'll be out trying to break his neck on some pony. It's an addiction. He's beyond cure. Maalox. I've got to get a year's supply and carry some with me at all times. Do you have any Maalox in that trailer of yours? No? Maybe I could just learn to chew rolled oats."

◆ ◆ ◆

Brady's black felt hat was pushed way back on his head past the bruises when the gate opened, and Cowboy's Delight leaped out of the chute. His spurs raked the horse's neck, his back slapped the flank strap, and his hat flew to the dirt.

By the time the buzzer sounded, Lynda could tell he thought he was in the money. Sliding off behind a pick-up man wearing red and white chaps, he hit the ground with a wide smile and both hands raised above his head. After retrieving his hat, he sailed it across the arena at Heidi and Wendy, who stood next to the rails by the roping boxes.

By the time he reached them, Wendy wore the black hat down to her ears, and the announcer reported his score: 79.

"Is that all? You were robbed," Tyler Adams complained.

"That will take home some sweets at a rodeo this size," Brady reported. "Cowboy's Delight flattened out at the end. I tried to scratch a little more out of him, but I think he was tired."

Tyler Adams threw his steer in a very quick 4.8 seconds, but he broke the barrier. With the ten-second penalty, he placed out of the money. Heidi Martin grabbed him by the arm and consoled him when he slumped back over to where the others were standing.

At least, Lynda thought that what she was doing.

Pedregoso made two wide turns but sprinted dramatically across the finish line. Doc Cartier was in third place with four more entries yet to ride. Brady and Lynda were helping her off the tall roan gelding when they heard the P.A. system over the din of the crowd: "Our next barrel racer is a Nevada cowgirl. Give a Colorado welcome to Miss Cindy LaCoste!"

FOUR

A sharp pain shot up from the heels of Lynda's denim-colored cowboy boots as they crashed into the concrete-hard dirt between Cartier's horse trailer and the rough wood fence. Her black jeans chafed her legs as she climbed the fence next to Brady. She hardly noticed the splintery boards probe the palms of her computer-keyboard-soft hands.

"Where is she?"

A hatless Brady Stoner stared off across the dimly lit arena. "No one's come out of the runway yet."

Lynda balanced on the top rail by locking her boot heels into the second rail as she clutched Brady's arm. Staring at the open gate at the dirt alley on the bleacher side of the roping boxes, she watched and listened.

"Looks like LaCoste is unable to make a run," the gravel-voiced announcer reported. "We'll move down to our next cowgirl. How about a big welcome for thirteen-year-old Missy Stonecreek from Pine Ridge, South Dakota!"

A dark-skinned girl with an eagle feather in her cowboy hat galloped a black and white Appaloosa out of the runway and began to circle the barrels.

"Brady, what does that mean, 'Cindy's unable'? Is she here? Where would she be?"

"It just means she didn't show. Must have signed up and paid her entry fees, but changed her mind."

"You mean she's been here tonight, and we didn't know it?"

"She could have entered any time today, even last night. I'll go check with the rodeo secretary. Maybe she knows." Brady jumped from the rail and then offered his hand to Lynda. "You and the girls comb both parking lots for that green Cadillac. I'll meet you back at Doc's outfit."

◆ ◆ ◆

The entire gang was huddled at the van when Brady finally returned. The narrowing of his brown eyes told Lynda there was little success.

"What did you find out?"

"Cindy ran last night and entered for tonight. She was around the grounds most of the morning, but no one's seen her since. They didn't remember her leaving. Did you find any trace of the Cadillac?"

"Nothing."

Brady stared out across the fairly crowded parking lot. "We're only a few hours behind her."

"But we don't have any idea what direction she's traveling." Lynda jammed her hands in her back pockets and drew the toe of her boot across the dirt.

Dr. Cartier, the girls, and Tyler Adams gathered around them.

"It's like a big game of hide and seek," Wendy offered.

"Yeah, with eleven Western states as the playground," Heidi countered. "What will we do now, Uncle Brady?"

"Someone must have seen her. Tyler, you and the girls help

the doc get loaded up. Lynda Dawn and me will keep asking around."

"I thought you already asked everyone," Lynda observed.

"I didn't ask the cowboys."

Brady dragged her by the hand through the contestant parking lot toward a fog of fine, buckskin-colored dust that swirled above horse hooves behind the arena. About a dozen cowboys on horseback waited for a pair of trick riders in red sequined blouses to finish their routines so they could begin the calf-roping competition.

The cowboys turned to face them as Brady tugged Lynda into the middle of the ropers. She felt like a steer about to be prodded through the squeeze chute.

"Stoner, what are you doin', slummin' this two-bit nightly jackpot rodeo?" The voice came from a denim-shirted man with wide shoulders and almost no neck.

"Boys, listen up," he called out. "I'm lookin' for a gal—"

"What's the matter with the one you got, Stoner?" A thin, tall, red-haired man laughed. He turned to Lynda, pulled off his black beaver felt cowboy hat and held it over his heart, revealing a tan line straight across his forehead. "Ma'am, if you ever want to dump that rough stock rider for a real man, I'd be happy to hep ya."

"Thanks for the offer," Lynda replied, tilting her head to the right and then gazing around at the others. "I presume you know some real men to introduce me to."

The cowboys hooted and hollered.

"You lose, Red!" one shouted.

"I reckon I did." He replaced his hat, tipped it at Lynda, and grinned.

Brady slipped his arm around Lynda's shoulder. "Boys, this is my fiancée, Lynda Dawn Austin."

"Who you lookin' for, Stoner?" asked a man holding a blue rope and missing his left thumb.

"Cindy LaCoste. She's a friend of me and Lynda Dawn's. She must have drawed out of the barrel race tonight. Have any of you seen her?"

"What's she look like?" One Thumb pressed.

"She's blonde, sandy blonde, about Lynda Dawn's height. She's pretty but has had a hard life, and she's, eh, well, eh, well framed and . . ." Brady stammered, "with a turned-up nose and blue eyes."

Lynda blushed and fought back the urge to glance down at her blouse. *Well framed? Well framed! Is that what you call her, Brady Stoner? And what do you call me? Weak framed?*

"Cindy's about my age," Brady continued.

"Hey, a senior citizen! She don't play bingo on Wednesday night at the Grange, does she?" Red jibed.

"Is it true that you and Casey Tibbs hung around together when you was young, Stoner?" another called out.

"Disrespectful kids!" Brady scowled. "They have no respect for experience and maturity. It ain't their fault, darlin'. It's a well-known fact ropers never go beyond the fourth grade."

"Say, Lynda Dawn," Red called out, "did anyone ever tell you why rough stock riders only have to stay on a horse for eight seconds?"

"I don't think so."

"'Cause that's as high as they can count!"

A muscular man with a solid black long-sleeved shirt and drooping brown mustache rode up next to them. "What kind of outfit did this Cindy have? I can remember a rig better than a purdy face."

"She drives a big old boat of a dark green Cadillac. It's a Fleetwood—early seventies."

"She pull an open-rack silver stock trailer with Nevada plates?"

"Probably. Did you see her?"

The man scratched the stubble of his two-day beard. "Yep.

Just south of Greeley about lunch time. There's a little mini-mart/gas station on this side of the South Platte, surrounded by a big irrigated alfalfa field. This sandy-haired gal with a pig-tail as purdy as a bronc rein . . ."

Lynda brushed her hand through her curling shoulder-length hair. *Is that the only way cowboys define hair: 'Purdy as a bronc rein'?*

" . . . driving a Caddy, pullin' a horse trailer, and wearin' a camouflage-colored tank top was fuelin' up and chewin' on a microwave burrito. Kind of a tough-lookin' purdy. You know the type. If a fight breaks out at the dance, you're hopin' she's on your side?"

Brady nodded. "That sounds like our Cindy."

"Well, I sidles up to her and asks if she needs any company goin' down the road. Being naturally generous and good-hearted, I offer to share expenses and save us both a few dol-lars and maybe have, you know, a laugh or two."

Lynda rolled her eyes toward the starry Colorado night.

"What did she say to your kind offer?" Brady asked.

The cowboy shifted in his worn tooled-leather saddle and fidgeted with the rope coiled in his hand. Then he glanced around at the other mounted cowboys. "She said she thought she'd pass. Said she already had bird droppings on the wind-shield and horse poop in the trailer, so she didn't reckon there was much I could add to her life."

Brady waited for the laughter to die down. "That was Cindy, all right. You didn't happen to see which direction she was travelin', did you?"

"Nope. I just assumed she was headed to Castle Rock. I went into the store. By the time I came out, she was gone. They've got two of them microwave burritos for a dollar. I cooked myself up a batch of 'em."

"Get 'em ready, boys!" came a shout from the chute boss.

Brady stepped over by the cowboy with the drooping mustache. "Were there any bikers hangin' around?"

"The Harley crowd?"

"Yeah, black leather jackets—all that?"

"None at the minimart. In fact, I don't remember any on Highway 85 all the way to Denver. Ain't much on that road today but hay trucks, swathers, and pickups."

"Thanks, partner. We'll probably head on up that way. If any of you run into Cindy, tell her Brady Stoner and Lynda Dawn Austin are lookin' for her." He gazed around. "Who drew the best calf tonight?"

"Ol' Red's got #236. That's the best draw. 'Course, Red cain't loop a fence post at four feet," One Thumb prodded.

"If I cain't beat you, I'll buy ya supper!" Red challenged and then turned back to Stoner and Austin. "Lynda Dawn, if that bronc rider gives you any more trouble, bust him in the other eye, ya' hear? I'm glad to see you ain't afraid to show him who's boss. Did any of you boys ever see a stock rider who didn't look like a cattle truck ran over him? I suppose they're jist born that way."

"Be seein' you boys on down the road." Brady carefully tipped his black hat that perched on the back of his head.

When Brady and Lynda made it back to the pickup, everything was loaded up, and Wendy handed him a check. "You won first-place money, Uncle Brady."

"Well, look at that, darlin'—we can retire!"

Lynda scowled. "It's $167 for first place? Is that all?"

"Yep. Now we can have that big weddin' you been dreamin' of."

"That won't even pay for the mints!" Lynda chided.

"We might have to cut back a little."

Debra Jean Cartier rolled over to them. "What did you find out?"

"One of the ropers saw Cindy up near Greeley around noon. We're goin' to head out that way."

"In the morning, I assume," Lynda added.

"Let's leave right now, darlin'. Maybe we can catch up with her tonight."

"More likely we'll drive right past her and go all the way to Canada without finding her."

Brady pulled a quarter out of his pocket. "Let's flip a coin. Heads, we leave tonight; tails, we wait until morning."

"Brady Stoner, I have never in my life made a decision based on the flip of a coin. I'm not about to start now."

"Really?" Wendy questioned.

Lynda brushed the hair out of her eyes. "Really."

"Wow, Heidi and I do that all the time. Like who gets the bed by the air conditioning at the motel, who gets the shower first, whose turn it is to answer the phone—"

"This might be a little more important than that," Lynda maintained.

"I've been wondering," Heidi inserted, "what you're going to do when you find this Cindy?"

Brady rocked back on the heels of his boots. "Well, we're going to find out what's this deal with the bikers and try to make sure she doesn't get herself in a jam."

"And I'll talk about the book . . . sort of," Lynda mumbled. Then she turned to Brady. "What are we going to do when we find her?"

"Well, you know . . ."

"She's a grown woman, and she can barrel race, follow bikers, or just drive down the road anytime she wants," Lynda admitted.

"We're going to try to talk some sense into her and get her to stay away from this guy, Lamont McGhee."

"What if she tells you both to get lost?" Heidi pressed.

"She'll listen to me," Brady huffed.

"Yes, and I'll give her the check for the kill fee. It's a generous amount. It's bound to come in useful. Then I'll tell her why we can't publish her book."

This time it was Wendy who, with wide eyes, quizzed them. "And what if she tells you to take your money and go back to New York?"

Doc Cartier used both hands to lift her legs up onto the foot rest of the electric wheelchair. "I think maybe you ought to wait and try to find Cindy tomorrow. Maybe you'll figure out what to say to her by then."

"All right, you all win. Let's get to the motel." Brady motioned to the rigs. "The girls ride with Doc, Tyler and Capt. Patch with us."

"How about her?" Wendy pointed to a black and gray dog with brown face and wagging tail that traipsed alongside Capt. Patch.

"Oh, no, you're not bringing any girlfriends along," Brady lectured the dog. He opened the pickup door. "Come on, Captain. You've got to kiss the girl good-bye."

Immediately, both dogs leaped into the truck.

"Hey, get out of there!" he hollered at the new dog. "Go on . . . get! Not you, Captain." Both dogs bounded out Lynda's side of the pickup. "Tyler, grab the Captain!"

Adams reached down and was greeted with a teeth-bared, curled-lipped growl. "You better grab him yourself, Mr. Stoner. I don't aim to get myself bit."

"Captain! Get in the truck!"

Again both dogs hurdled into the front seat.

"Hey, go on . . . git!" Brady shouted at the dogs, who quickly exited from Lynda's side. "Darlin', get in and close your door. Tyler, wait right there." Brady got in behind the steering wheel and closed his door. Then he started the engine and opened the sliding window at the back of the cab. "Come on, boy, come on, Captain. Time to hit the road!"

The black and white dog hurdled into the back of the truck, followed by the brown-faced dog. Then he jumped through the open window into the narrow backseat. Brady immediately slid the window shut. The other dog slammed into the glass. Capt. Patch stood on his back feet, stared into the bed of the pickup, and began barking furiously.

"You're a mean man, Stoner," Lynda shouted.

"What?" he hollered.

"The Captain is not very happy!"

"That's too bad!" Brady screamed. Each dog seemed to be trying to outbark the other. He rolled his window down an inch. "Tyler, chase that brown dog out of the truck, and you ride with the Doc!"

The young man with the torn shirt scooted closer to the window. "What?"

"Kick the dog out and ride with the girls!"

The brown-faced dog leaped from the truck the moment Tyler climbed on the back bumper. As soon as he trotted over to the van, Brady stepped on the gas and roared out of the parking lot. Capt. Patch continued his frantic barking from the backseat.

Lynda leaned forward and peered out at the sideview mirror. "I think she's following us!"

"What?" Brady hollered.

"The other dog is back there!"

"It looks fine the way it is!" Brady shouted.

"What looks fine?"

"Your hair!" he hollered, just as Capt. Patch stopped barking and flopped on the seat.

"Eh, sorry for yelling," Brady whispered.

"What about my hair?" Lynda asked.

"Don't change the color."

"I have no intention of changing the color."

"I thought you said something about your hair."

"I said that other dog was still back there."

"Oh, is she now?"

Lynda peered into the mirror. "I don't think so."

"Good."

"I've never seen the Captain go berserk like that."

"You've never seen him around a good-lookin' lady dog before."

"Good looking? She didn't seem all that different from any other."

"Didn't you see her eyes?"

"No, what did they look like?"

"Willing."

"Oh." Lynda glanced into the backseat. "At least he finally settled down."

"He's pouting. He'll be mad at me for two weeks now."

"Come on, cowboy, he's just a dog." Lynda reached into the backseat and scratched the dog's head. "What's the matter, boy. Did you lose your girl?" The Captain sad-eyed Lynda and licked her hand. "He might be a little depressed, but he's not mad," she reported.

"Yeah? Watch this." Brady slowly reached his hand back toward the black and white dog. Immediately, there was a snap of the teeth and a growl.

"Wow, he really is mad!"

"Yeah, I hope he doesn't start chewin' on the upholstery this time."

"What will you do with him tonight?"

"He has to stay in the cab."

"How will you and I get out without being trampled or bitten?"

"I'll give him Pee Wee."

"Who?"

"In the glove compartment—see that yellow rubber duck? Don't get it out."

"That's Pee Wee?"

"Yeah. It's sort of like a pacifier for him."

"I don't remember your having a rubber duck in the rig last fall."

"No, he drug that in at a rodeo down in Texas this spring . . . after I wouldn't let him bring a big Irish setter with us."

"He goes through this often?"

"Only since last fall. You're the cause of it, Lynda Dawn. It used to just be me and the Captain. But ever since you and me got engaged, he's started to—"

"Stoner, are you telling me your dog knows you're getting married?"

"Sure, he does, darlin'. You're the center of most conversations in the cab of this truck."

"What do you mean?"

"Well, I'll be drivin' down some dark highway and say, 'Captain, what do you think our Lynda Dawn's doin' right now?'"

"And what does he say?"

"Bark."

Lynda slumped down in the seat and leaned her head back against the cushion. "I've never owned a dog before."

"You're kiddin' me. You never had a dog when you were a kid?"

"No. I had a parakeet for a while. And a goldfish named Winston, who only lasted about six weeks. That was it."

"Well . . . a dog like the Captain purtneer takes care of himself. Oh, you might have to give him a bath now and then, spray him for fleas, give him a shot for tetanus . . ."

"I'm not going to—"

"Ever' once in a while pull the ticks out of his ears or a porcupine quill out of his lip, lance a boil and let the—"

"Stoner! Do you want me to barf all over this truck?"

"No, ma'am."

"Then keep your animal husbandry to yourself. I am not going to doctor sick animals, is that clear? You take care of the critters, and I'll take care of the children. Is that understood?"

"Yes, ma'am."

Dimples in the cheeks.

Sparkle in the eyes.

And a smile like a little boy with a double-decker chocolate ice cream cone.

What did I say? I'm taking care of the kids! By myself? He did that to me on purpose!

"What did you say, Lynda Dawn?" he chided.

"I didn't say anything."

"But you were thinking it."

"You think you can read my mind?"

"Yes, I do."

Brady looped his arms over the steering wheel. "Can you imagine what it will be like ten, twenty, thirty years from now?"

"Not really. But it sure is fun to think about. I love you, Brady Stoner."

"And I love you, darlin'."

Capt. Patch let out one lone bark.

Lynda leaned toward the dog. "I love you too, Captain. And so does Brady."

The dog glanced at Stoner, bared his teeth, and growled.

◆ ◆ ◆

Lynda sat on the dark green flowered bedspread and stared at six small opaque bottles lined up on the simulated wood formica top of the nightstand that separated the two beds in room 137 of the Fourteener Motel and Country Inn. Her wet dark brown hair lay limp against her head. Water dripped onto the white motel towel that caped her slightly sagging shoulders.

Her short-sleeved hunter green "Cowboy Up" sweatshirt

hung past the silver belt buckle on her black jeans. She wiggled her bare toes in the brown carpet.

I wore Designed Bliss all day, and he didn't say one word. Maybe I should try Provocative Proposal. But I was waiting to use that when I know we're going to be alone. Shy Anne's Radiance always brings a comment, but he's probably tired of that.

She picked up a small black bottle and unscrewed the tiny lid. Holding it to her nose, she sniffed lightly, then coughed.

Whoa! This stuff Kelly and Nina bought me is strong enough to lure a cowboy from across the arena, maybe across town. But I just can't wear something called Sinner of Attraction. Brady would ask me it's name for sure.

With a moderately long, unpainted fingernail, she picked at the gold foil label on the bottle until it was completely removed.

When I get back to the office, I'll print up a little label and call this L.D. #11. Maybe I should just mix a little Rosey Rose with Montana Mist.

The white-painted motel door opened, rattling the unused brass chain safety lock. With a backdrop of a star-filled Rocky Mountain night, Dr. Debra Jean Cartier wheeled into the room she was sharing with Lynda.

Cartier stopped at the far side of the full-size bed. "Are you still using the phone?" she asked.

"I'm waiting for Kelly to call back." Lynda returned the perfume bottle to the table and stood between the beds. "She was on another line when I called. Go ahead—you can use it. I'll get out of the way."

"No, no, stay right there, Lynda." Cartier's square-framed half-glasses perched low on her tanned nose. "I'll just use my cellular. I need to collect some messages at work and at home. Got to check on my babies, you know."

Lynda plopped back down on the bed and began drying her hair with the towel. "Your horses?"

"Yes." Cartier rolled over to her wide brown leather brief-case. "They miss their mama. At least, I hope they do."

Lynda turned each of the bottles of perfume so that their labels could not be seen by Cartier. "Who takes care of them when you're gone?"

"Pablo Hernandez de Peralta."

Lynda rubbed the towel on her head. "Peralta? Is that the family who founded Santa Fe?"

"Yes, I believe Pablo was there when it happened," Cartier teased. "He must be ninety, but he knows horses like no one I've ever met. Actually I don't think there's any family connection. Peralta's a common name in northern New Mexico." She glanced around the room and then pointed at the nightstand. "Could you hand me that green pen?"

Debra used the fountain pen like a pointer. "Are you trying to find the right fragrance?"

Lynda could feel her face redden. "Yeah. Kind of weird, isn't it? All these perfumes. I don't suppose you've ever heard of anyone so hung up with scents?"

"Nope." Using her arms, Cartier scooted herself back in the wheelchair and stretched her neck to the right and left. "But I like it."

"You do?" Lynda draped the towel back across her shoulders.

"Yes, I do. Oh, it's not for me. The only thing I dab behind my ears is a little Off when the mosquitoes and horseflies get too thick."

Lynda swept her left hand toward the nightstand. "You may borrow any of my perfumes if you'd like."

"Oh, no. It's your obsession. Mine happens to be horses. It's part of what makes us human, Lynda Dawn."

"Oh, I'm quite human."

"Brady has a pretty exalted view of your virtues."

"I don't know why. He's seen how horrible I can act at times."

Cartier pulled a cellular phone in a black simulated leather pouch out of her briefcase and laid it on her lap. "Brady has a marvelous ability to remember every woman's virtues and completely forget her vices. It think it's his God-given gift. I don't know if I've ever met anyone who could pull it off so sincerely."

"I know what you mean. He's one of a kind."

Cartier pulled a small address book out of her briefcase and tossed it on her lap with the phone. "Did you know that you're an answer to lots of prayers, Lynda Dawn?"

"I'm an answer to prayers?"

"Since the day I met him, I've known Brady and I would be no more than good friends. But I've prayed that the Lord would send just the right woman into his life. I have a feeling I'm not the only lady friend of his that's prayed that way."

"Being the answer to someone's prayers is a lot to live up to." Lynda flopped on her back across the bed.

"Not really, because all you have to do is be yourself."

"Debra Jean, be honest with me. Do you think I'm the right one for Brady?"

"Brady Stoner is convinced beyond a shadow of a doubt that you're the one."

"That's not what I asked."

"Lynda Dawn Darlin', you're the one, all right. I'm hoping you'll allow him to keep all his friends and allow him to roam around the West now and then. We need him, too, girl. People like Heather Martin and those two teenage girls and young Tyler and Cindy LaCoste and me—we need a Brady Stoner in our life, if just for a day or an hour or a ten-minute phone call."

"I know. I'm really trying not to be possessive."

Cartier leaned forward in the wheelchair and pulled her long auburn hair together in the back, wrapping it with a wide rubber band. "Well, I do have to make those phone calls, but listen—I've changed my mind."

"Oh?"

"Maybe I will use one of your perfumes."

Lynda jumped up. "Which one do you want?"

Cartier studied the little bottles lined up by the telephone. "Oh, I don't care. How about the one in the black bottle?"

She would select—

The telephone rang.

"Just toss it to me," Debra called out.

Leaving the motel door open, Cartier exited the room carrying a notebook, cellular phone, and a small black unlabeled bottle of Sinner of Attraction.

"Hello."

"Hi, girl. Nina's on the other line."

"What's going on, Kelly?"

"Most of the talk around the office is about the award-winning editor who's run off to Wyoming to marry the cowboy."

"Well, what's the verdict?"

"Oh, it ranges from 'she has no idea what she's getting into' all the way to 'I wish it were me.'"

"Who's saying stuff like that?"

"Mainly me and Nina. Have you called Joaquin yet?"

"No! I forgot all about it."

"He's called here several times. He says it has something to do with a wedding present. Wants you to call back right away."

"I'll call him tonight. What else is happening?"

"Did you know the Gossmans and the Hamptons are flying out to the wedding?"

"I thought Junior said they had to be in Toronto at some book fair."

"No, it's the Pan-Pacific show in Vancouver. He and Spunky are going to fly straight to Jackson on Friday night. The Gossmans will meet them. They're talking about looking at some property around Wyoming or Montana or something."

"I'm glad they're coming. It's only a little chapel, but you and Nina and Brady's folks hardly make a crowd."

"Hey, call your sister."

"Megan?"

"She's the only one you have, right? She called to say the whole family's coming to the wedding."

"What whole family?"

"Her, her husband, and the kids, plus your brother William and his family."

"Really? William can come after all?"

"That's the report I got. You call them."

"I can't believe they're all able to come. This is going to be the—the nicest—"

"The nicest wedding you ever had? You better call them. They want to know how to find it."

"There's a map in the wedding file. It's in the—"

"Second drawer down on the left, in the mist blue file folder?"

"How did you—"

"Just a lucky guess."

Wendy Martin barged through the open motel door. "Hey, guess what! Guess what! Isn't Uncle Brady in here? Oh, are you on the phone?"

"Just a minute, Kell, I've got company." Lynda took in the barefoot blonde in jeans shorts and navy blue Pro-Rodeo T-shirt. "Brady's next door, I suppose. What is it, Wendy?"

"Oh, man, it's so cool. My mom's sick, see—"

"What's cool about that?"

"Actually she's feeling a little better, but since we're this far north, she said—listen to this—she said we'd just meet up at Rock Springs, Wyoming, and all go to the wedding together! We get to go to the wedding!"

"But we aren't going to Rock Springs, are we? I thought we're supposed to get back to Santa Fe so I can catch my flight to New York Sunday afternoon."

"Uncle Brady said you weren't going back to New York."

"Oh, he did, did he? I offered to stay out a couple more days, but I have to get back and get packed, pick up my dress, settle with the condo association—not to mention show up at the office."

Lynda could hear Kelly trying to say something on the phone, so she put it back to her ear.

"Just a minute, Wendy. Kell, did you say something?"

"Girl, if you want to stay out West, let us know. Nina and I will take care of things back here."

"Thanks, Kell, but that would be impossible. I need to do a million things."

"Hey," Wendy called across the room, "why don't you ride with Dr. Cartier back to New Mexico? You can catch your plane, and Heidi and me can stay with Uncle Brady to look for Cindy. Then we can meet Mom at Rock Springs on Wednesday."

"Eh, well—"

"Lynda Dawn!"

Austin lifted the phone back to her ear. "Kell?"

"Lynda, stay out there with Brady. Let us handle New York."

"There's no way I can . . ."

Heidi glided into the room. "Hey, guys, guess what? Dr. Cartier just talked to Mom, too. Doc's going to take a week off and just drive on up to the wedding. We can all caravan. Is that cool, or what?"

"I have to get back to New York!" Lynda insisted.

"What's going on?" Kelly asked.

"Just a minute, Kell. Heidi, have you seen Brady?"

"He and Tyler are out in the parking lot."

"What are they doing?"

"Practicing roping, I think."

"What's Brady doing?" Kelly asked.

"He's practicing roping in a dark motel parking lot."

"Why?" Kelly pressed.

Lynda looked up at Heidi. "Why are they doing that?"

"Uncle Brady is teaching Tyler how to throw a hoolihan."

"He's teaching Tyler to throw a hoolihan."

"Who's Tyler?" Kelly quizzed.

"A steer wrestler."

"Is he cute? How old is he? Is he available?"

"Yes. Eighteen. No. Kell, I'll call you back when it's not so hectic around here."

"Don't hang up, girl. I've got someone on call-waiting. I'll be right back."

Lynda dropped the phone to her shoulder and glanced at the open doorway, now filled by a dimpled, grinning cowboy.

"Is this girl-talk, or can I come in?"

Wendy grabbed his arm and pulled him into the room. "Uncle Brady, we're all going to the wedding. Mom's driving up and meeting us in Rock Springs next Wednesday!"

Brady glanced at Lynda. "Well, I was just on the phone back home. Brock, Lorraine, and the kids are going to drive over, too! They'll stay with Lorraine's folks at Driggs."

"My brother's coming, too!" Lynda reported.

"You mean your family is actually going to meet my family?"

"That ought to be quite an event. I can't imagine anything Brock and William would have to talk about."

"Just the darling bride and the battered groom."

Lynda wrinkled her nose and scowled. "You'll look better by then."

"I could put some makeup on it, Uncle Brady," Heidi proposed.

"I do not wear makeup or earrings or nose rings or gold chains around the neck! Hey, if we get up to Lusk, Brock wants me to look at a bull."

"If we get up to where?" Lynda choked.

"L-U-S-K. Lusk, Wyoming. It's north of Cheyenne. There's a Black Angus-'Brahmer' bull for sale."

Lynda heard a faint voice and put the phone to her ear again. "I'm back. Is Brady there?" Kelly asked.

"Yes, he's in the room."

"Oh. I'm hanging up! I want you two to have time alone."

"Alone? We aren't alone."

"Well, then, what did he say about lust? I heard that part."

"We're going to look at a bull."

"What?"

"I'll call you later, Kell."

"Tonight?"

"If I get a chance."

Brady stood aside as Dr. Cartier rolled back into the room. "Am I breaking up a party?"

"Hey, Doc, you've been hanging around my Lynda Dawn too long. That perfume would melt the conchos off a man's chaps."

"It's kind of strong, isn't it?"

"Strong? It makes a rose garden smell like an old barn! What's it called?"

"It didn't have a label."

"Oh, she's letting you dip into her private reserve?"

"Hey, I've got great news!" Tyler boomed as he crowded into the room.

"Kell, I've really got to go."

"What's the great news?" Kelly Princeton implored. "Is that the eighteen-year-old cowboy . . . Taylor?"

"Tyler," Lynda corrected her.

Tyler Adams waved his shirt-clad arms as he talked. "I called my boss in Durango, and he fired me."

"I thought you had a few days coming," Brady observed.

Tyler sheepishly glanced at Heidi. "I forgot I used them up already."

"So you can go with us to Uncle Brady's wedding?" she squealed.

"Yeah, is that cool, or what?"

Heidi was bouncing up and down on her bare toes. "It's almost like the Lord's leading, isn't it?"

Brady scooted in between Tyler and Heidi. "I don't think the Lord wants us to neglect our job and get fired."

"It's okay," Tyler explained. "I didn't like the work anyway."

"Kelly, I'm hanging up. There's a circus act in my room."

"I don't hear any trained animals."

Lynda dropped the phone when a brown-faced dog, tongue lolling out of its mouth, bounded into the room, putting its front paws on the bed.

"Get out of here!" Lynda shrieked.

"Who are you yelling at?" Kelly asked.

"Everyone!" Lynda moaned as she hung up the phone.

◆ ◆ ◆

The few clouds that pocked the light blue Colorado sky were high and moved quickly toward the granite peaks of the Front Range of the Rockies. Lynda had the pickup window rolled down about two inches, and the still slightly cool morning air circled her hair and lifted her spirits. She wore a generous portion of Provocative Proposal. The little black bottle of perfume formerly known as Sinner of Attraction reposed in the dumpster behind the motel.

"Brady, why did they call that . . ."

His words blanketed hers. "I can't believe you . . ." He glanced over at her. "Go ahead, darlin'."

"I was wondering why they called that motel the Fourteener."

"People in Colorado are mighty proud of all the mountains over 14,000 feet high. They call them their fourteeners."

"Now please explain what's with the dog?" Lynda pointed to the back of the pickup bed. "You just picked up a stray?"

"Not me. That was Capt. Patch's idea, remember?"

"But you don't just drive down the road picking up dogs."

"I called the rodeo secretary, and she said someone had dumped the dog at the arena two weeks ago. They were about ready to call the pound. The Double Diamond is a mighty big ranch—even for a cow dog. I figured the Captain would want some company, too."

"He does seem quite pleased."

"Margarita's the right type for Capt. Patch."

"Margarita? She has a name?"

"The girls and I decided."

"And just what did you mean, she's the right type?"

"You know—affectionate and submissive."

"Are we talking dogs or women, cowboy?"

"Just dogs, ma'am. And there's a side benefit to the whole thing." He patted the pickup seat between them. "There's not room for two dogs in the cab, so they have to stay in the back."

Lynda scooted over next to Brady. "That's a good point, cowboy."

Brady put his hand on her jeans-covered knee. "And I can't believe you talked Doc into hauling Wendy, Heidi, and Tyler so we could have a few minutes alone."

"Talk Doc into it? You were the one I had to convince. And listen, buckaroo, I don't exactly call driving down the highway as prime time alone."

"Yes, ma'am."

He slipped his right arm around her shoulder. She reached up and clutched his dangling callused fingers and stared at the frayed but clean cuffs of the faded tan long-sleeved shirt.

"You need new clothes, Mr. Stoner. Where do you like to shop for clothes?"

"In Cheyenne."

"Are we going through there?"

"Maybe."

"Good. Let's buy you some new things."

"You're right. It is about time for my annual shopping trip."

"Oh?"

"Ever' year when I come to Frontier Days, I buy myself a new shirt—whether I need one or not."

"I'm not complaining exactly, but all the shirts you've worn on this trip, I've seen before. Which new shirt did you buy last year?"

"A purdy black and gray with a small turquoise arrowhead above the pocket. But a couple weeks after I bought it, I got pitched into a fence at the Caldwell, Idaho, Night Rodeo and ripped that sucker from collar to tail. I think it ended up as a grease rag or something."

"I presume ranching will be a little less strenuous on your wardrobe."

"I hope so. At least, they won't be crammed in a duffel bag all the time."

Lynda leaned her head on Brady's shoulder. "What kind of closet space are we going to have in that log home? I don't remember what the closets are like."

"Closets? You mean a pantry?"

"No, I mean closets. Like in the bedroom, for hanging clothes."

"Closets? You need closets?" he gasped.

She sat up and pushed herself away from him. "You mean to tell me I'm moving into a house without any closets?"

"Darlin', this is ranch life. It's different out here. There're pegs on the wall to hang up your other dress, if that's what you mean."

"My other dress?"

The sparkling, still-bruised eyes and dimpled grin gave him away.

"Stoner! Don't mess with me!" She clenched her fist and halfheartedly slugged him in the arm. "Tell me about my bedroom closet, and tell me right now!"

"Yes, ma'am. It's a walk-in closet eight feet wide and ten feet long, clothes racks runnin' down both sides and shelves for linens across the back."

"Wow, really?"

"Would I lie to you?"

"If you thought you could get away with it."

"And there's a skylight."

"In the closet?"

"Yep. Why is it closets are always dark? That never made sense to me."

"Our house has skylights?"

"Three of them. If the builders remember to put 'em in."

"But in the winter won't they be covered with snow?"

"That won't be any trouble. Every day when you get the vacuumin', dustin', washin', scrubbin', ironin', and cookin' done, you can climb up on the roof and shovel the snow off."

Lynda folded her hands under her chin and cooed, "Yes, dear, and while I'm on the roof, you'll be changing the twins' dirty diapers, right?"

"Eh—I'll take the roof; you take the diapers. Besides, all the skylights are on the southwest side of the house. Shouldn't have much snow up there. You saw how most of the snow in the Judith Basin blows sideways."

"You're really having them build a big closet?"

"Yep. I told you I added a few extras."

She scooted back over to Brady, grabbed his right arm, leaned over, and kissed his cheek.

A honk from the van behind them caused her to sit up and whip around. Wendy Martin, riding in the front seat with Debra Cartier, shook her finger at them. Lynda stuck out her tongue, threw her arms around Brady's neck, and gave him a long kiss on the neck.

"Hey, I need to get Heidi to tease you more often," Brady laughed as Lynda finally pulled back.

"Wendy."

"Wendy's in the front seat? I said they could all ride in the van only if Heidi sat up front!" He began to apply the brakes.

"Keep driving, Stoner!" Austin ordered.

"What?"

"If you expect to get another one of those kisses, keep driving. I'm not about to let you mess this up and put a pouting teenager in the truck with us."

"But that means Heidi and Tyler are in the backseat of the van and—"

"Back seats. Doc has bucket seats back there, too, remember?"

"But still they could . . ."

Lynda rolled her eyes toward the cab roof. "Please, Lord, please let us only have boys."

"That bad, huh?"

"Wretched."

"I've got a lot to learn about being a daddy. I guess I'd better learn in a hurry."

"Why? Do you know something I don't?"

"We are going to have children right away, aren't we?"

"Are we?" she prodded.

"Of course we are. Remember we got that all solved the night I called you from San Angelo."

"Where?"

"San Angelo, Texas. Remember? I called about 2:00 A.M., and we talked until daylight."

"Is that the night I had worked over the O'Brian finals until midnight for two weeks and kept falling asleep during our conversation?"

"Yep. That's the night."

"And I agreed to what?"

"To having six kids. So we should start right away 'cause you're not gettin' any younger."

"Not even in your dreams, cowboy! I've got to have a year in Montana to see if I can survive before I try it pregnant."

"I suppose we can talk further about this after we get married."

"Yes, we certainly will!"

Brady flipped on the tape player and then immediately turned it off. "If we don't find any trace of Cindy at the mini-mart, we'll be at the end of our trail."

"Are you changing the subject, cowboy?"

"Yes, ma'am."

"Good idea. Are you saying, if we don't find any trace of Cindy up here, we'll call off the search?"

"I'll want to make some phone calls. Cindy and I have a few mutual friends in the area—the kind of folks you stay with if you're rodeoin' up this way. I'll see if they've heard from her."

"What about those bikers that were after her?"

"If they were really chasin' her, I think they'd have caught her by now. But that calf-roper said she was healthy and by herself yesterday. I reckon she's all right, whatever it is she's doin'."

"Then you'll drive me back down to New Mexico to catch my flight?"

"I thought you wanted to go up and see the house and the ranch."

"Of course I do, but we can't do that and still make the Sunday flight from Santa Fe, can we?"

"Why don't you see if you can get the ticket changed to Great Falls . . . or Billings."

"I don't think they do that."

"You're flyin' United, right?"

"Yes."

"Call the 800 number and ask for Jamie Sue. She always lets me change my flights when I've got to get to a rodeo in a hurry."

"A real sweetheart, no doubt."

"She surely is. One time a few years back I was riding at the Rosemont, near Chicago, and Jamie Sue drove all the way out there after work just to personally deliver my ticket."

"What a dear! I hope you thanked her by taking her to supper."

"Yep. I did."

Lynda raised her well-defined eyebrows. "Surprise, surprise. So you really think I might get the ticket changed?"

"It's worth tryin', isn't it? And on our way to the ranch we'll look at that bull for Brock."

"In Lust, Wyoming?"

"Lusk. I told you it was Lusk."

◆ ◆ ◆

Brown's Corner Minimart at one time had been a vegetable stand. Its humble origins were still evident in the room additions—semitrailers laced together by lattice-covered decks. Both rigs pulled in for gas. Brady got out to quiz the attendant.

Doc got Wendy to lead Pedregoso out of the trailer and walk him around the dirt parking lot. Capt. Patch and Margarita explored a creek that ran between the dumpsters and the alfalfa field. Heidi and Tyler sauntered toward the snack counter. Lynda shuffled toward a graffiti-decorated outdoor pay phone.

She punched in a phone number and waited for the prerecorded message to end. "Joaquin, this is Lynda Austin. Pick up your phone because I have no intention of talking to a machine."

The voice was deep, melodic, like a bass singer's in an

a cappella male quartet. "Ms. Austin! So you're still in the country. How nice to hear your charming voice."

"Do you have *Massacre at Deer Creek* finished for me? Is that why you called?"

"Work, work, work—you've got to relax, Lynda Dawn."

"You don't have it finished?"

"I had to go to New York to a Long Island party last weekend, don't you remember?"

"Yes, and I believe you told me one more edit, and you'd have the final chapter done."

"Did I say that?"

"Yes, you did."

"Was that redhead with the long legs standing next to me?"

"Terri? Yes, I think she was."

"Oh, well, then you can't hold me accountable. I was blurting out a lot of things that weren't true."

"Is this why you wanted me to call, Joaquin? So you could tell me about a redhead with long legs?"

"No, no, Lynda Dawn. Are you and Brady still in Colorado?"

"Yes, along the South Platte south of Greeley."

"Perfect! You're in Brady's Dodge pickup?"

"Yes, why?"

"This is great because I have a little wedding gift for you and the cowboy. It's in Cheyenne, and they couldn't deliver it for a month, so here's what I want you to do—just stop by and pick it up for me. It's at Cheyenne Design, Inc. on Del Range Boulevard out by the airport. Brady can find it. I'll tell them you'll be by."

"What is it?"

"A surprise, Miss Lynda. A great big surprise. Does Brady have an eight-foot bed on that truck?"

"A what?"

"Is the cargo space eight feet long?"

"I don't have any idea."

"It might hang out the back some, but that won't matter."

"Joaquin, what is it? Is it really that big?"

"I think you'll really be surprised, girl. Listen, I still remember that I'm the one that got you two together. I had to get you something special. Unique. One of a kind. Now don't worry about *Massacre*. I've got it on the screen right now. I'll have it done next week. In fact, I'll give it to you at the wedding."

"Señor Estaban, don't you dare show up at my wedding handing me a manuscript. Fed. Ex. it to the office as quickly as you can."

"You're not scheduling in a little editing on your honeymoon?"

"Good-bye, Joaquin."

◆ ◆ ◆

Lynda saw Wendy lead Pedregoso back into the trailer under Dr. Cartier's watchful eye. "How's your pupil doing?"

"She's a natural."

"Natural?"

"You know how dogs can sense how you feel about them instantly? Well, horses are herd animals. There's a pecking order. Wendy's someone horses seem to recognize from the beginning as being in charge. In two days he's decided she can do anything to him she wants. It's fun to watch."

They were all loaded up and waiting for Brady as he took a turn at the phone. Fifteen minutes later he made it back to the pickup. He stopped by to say something to the crew in the van, whistled for the dogs to jump in the back, and then pulled up into the cab of the truck.

"Guess what," Lynda bubbled. "Your friend Jamie Sue was able to get my flight changed. I'm leaving from Great Falls

Monday afternoon. I have to pay an extra sixty dollars, but it's worth it. I'll get home by midnight. Then that will give me Tuesday, Wednesday, and Thursday to tie things together before I fly to Jackson on Friday."

"That's great! Maybe it will actually work out to see the house."

"And that's not all," she continued. "Joaquin said he has a wedding present for us that couldn't get delivered in time. He wants us to stop by Cheyenne and pick it up."

Brady headed the caravan over the bridge, going north on Highway 85. "What is it?"

"He wouldn't say. But he said it was big—that it might hang out the back of the truck some."

"You're kiddin'."

"That's what he said. What could it be?"

"I don't know. . . . What store was it at?"

"Some place called Cheyenne Design, Inc. Have you ever heard of them?"

"Nope."

"Did you hear him mention anything last weekend at Gossmans' party?"

Brady shrugged. "I didn't talk to him much. He was tied into that long-legged redhead."

Do all men notice Terri's legs? "Are we going to Cheyenne now?"

"Might as well pick this thing up."

"Are you going to buy some new clothes?"

"Yeah, I need a new shirt for the wedding."

"Why don't we spring and buy you a couple of shirts?" she suggested.

"I know what it is!"

"The present from Joaquin? What is it?"

"It's Leatherboy!"

"Who?"

"A big stuffed horse!"

"Stuffed, like in plush animal?"

"Stuffed, like in real animal taxidermied."

"We're going to put a stuffed horse in the back of the truck?"

"We could put him in the trailer with Pedregoso."

"Why would Joaquin give us a stuffed horse?"

"Last July at Frontier Days I ran across Joaquin having his picture taken on this stuffed bucking horse. They have a photograph in the background of a crowd scene, and it looks like you're really riding a bronc. Anyway, this ol' boy who had the business said he wanted to sell out, and Joaquin was jokin' and said he ought to buy the horse to make a good photo op for publicity pix. I teased him and said I'd like to have it out in front of a ranch house. 'Course, back then I didn't know we'd be havin' a ranch house. I bet when Joaquin found out about our ranch last week at Gossmans', he came right home and bought that bucking horse."

"We're goin' to have a life-sized, stuffed bucking horse in our front yard?"

"Is that great, or what?"

"Brady, aren't we going to have grass and trees and flowers and—"

"You're kiddin' me, right?"

"Am I?"

"Man, oh man, I can't believe it. This is the greatest wedding present anyone could give us! I think I'm goin' to cry."

"I was considering the same thing myself."

"And we have to go right through Cheyenne to get to Chugwater. It won't be any problem to pick it up."

"Chugwater?"

"Hey, I was so excited about our present I forgot to tell you about my incredible phone call. I called a friend of mine in Chugwater. His name is Riley Marks. He's got this place east of town, and I asked if he's seen Cindy. Well, he says he was surprised to hear from me so soon."

"So soon?"

"Yeah. Cindy stayed at his place last night. This morning when he went out for chores, she'd already pulled out. Only thing is, she left the trailer and the horse."

"She just drove off and left them?"

"Yeah, and a note sayin' the trailer and Easy to Bed belong to E. G. Minor in Ely. And—are you ready for this?—that Brady Stoner would be by to pick up the horse and trailer and take them back to Nevada."

"She told him that?" Lynda gasped. "She knows we're following her!"

"I believe you're right, Lynda Dawn Darlin'. Is this gettin' weird, or what?"

FIVE

Well, what do you think?"

"Boring, totally boring, Uncle Brady."

"What about you, darlin'?"

Lynda glanced up from sorting through a circular rack of brightly colored, long-sleeved Western-cut shirts. "I agree. It's a dud."

"Doc, how about you? Tell me the truth. Doesn't this look like the kind of shirt I would wear?" Brady held the tan denim shirt up to his chin.

Cartier leaned back in her wheelchair and nodded. "Yes."

He spun back around to Austin. "See!"

"You always dress totally boring," Cartier added.

Lynda held up an aspen green long-sleeved shirt with black horses thundering across the chest. "What do you think, ladies?"

"Definitely!" Heidi squealed.

"It's you, Uncle Brady," Wendy echoed.

Debra Jean Cartier rolled forward and crushed the material between her fingers. "It should hold you for a few rides."

"But I'm goin' to retire from ridin' wild broncs," Brady protested.

"Does he expect any of us to believe that?" Debra Jean quizzed.

Lynda flopped the shirt over her left arm with several others. "It's unanimous, Stoner."

"But—but—it's not . . ." Brady's eyes wildly searched the room as if to discover a deliverer.

"Uncle Brady, there are other colors in the world besides blue and brown!" Wendy insisted.

"Yeah," Heidi added, "and styles besides solids or stripes!"

"But I don't wear those kinds of shirts!"

Wendy waved her sixteen-year-old index finger at him like a seasoned schoolteacher. "That's only because you've never had four very attractive and fashion-conscious women along to help you shop!"

"I knew this was a mistake," Brady groaned. "I should have brought Tyler!"

"I told you not to leave him with the rigs," Heidi triumphed.

"Well, I . . . someone had to look after the animals. You gals go on over there and explore the ladies section. I'll—"

"Forget it, Stoner," Lynda announced. "Girls, I think he should buy this green one, plus the white one with the black design for the wedding, and the black shirt with the rose pink desert scene."

"Absolutely not! I will not now nor will I ever wear anything rose pink!" Brady declared. "It's completely out of the question."

Debra Jean Cartier rolled closer to Lynda. She pulled the black and rose shirt from her hand and held it up to a protesting Brady Stoner. "Brady's right."

"See!"

"A married man should never wear a shirt like this."

The look of triumph melted from his face. "What?"

"Gals, let's be honest. If any of us saw a cowboy like Brady wear a knockout shirt like this, there would be a tingle in our throats, we'd be a little short of breath, and our hearts would just skip a beat—wouldn't they?"

Heidi's smooth-cheeked smile slid into a scowl. "Yeah, I know what you mean. It would be distracting and unfair, I suppose."

"They're right, Uncle Brady," Wendy affirmed. "It looks a little too good."

"Are you serious?" Brady quizzed. "I know what you are up to! You're not going to con me into buying this shirt."

Lynda pondered over the shirt again. "I can see your point, girls. But what if I make him wear it only on our honeymoon and around the house when there's no company?"

"I suppose that would work," Cartier assented. "But only if he wears it on days when you weren't planning on getting any work done anyway."

Lynda raised her full, dark brown eyebrows and pulled her sunglasses back onto her nose.

Brady paced in front of them. "I don't believe this! This is a conspiracy! No shirt looks that good. Well, it won't work. Besides, I can't afford to buy three shirts! I have a bride to support and a ranch to pay for."

"I'm buying you the white shirt," Lynda said. "It's the only way I can make sure of what you'll wear to the wedding."

"Heidi and me want to buy you the green one with our own money. It's a special wedding present. That way you'll have to wear it."

Dr. Cartier just shook her head. "Oh, no, girls, I'm not buying the rose pink shirt for him. It's not fair. If I don't get to enjoy it, I'm not buying it. Besides, I'm not going to be a part of the lairs of temptation."

"Let's buy these two and go on across town. I'm getting anxious to find out what Joaquin's wedding present is," Lynda instructed in her commanding Manhattan voice. "Wendy, stick that other shirt back on the rack and—"

"Wait a minute." Brady halted his pacing. "Maybe I'm not being very sensitive about this."

"Oh?" Lynda prodded.

"I realize it's not right for me to tell others what they can or cannot buy me for a present. I know I should let you all just buy what you want."

Four sets of eyebrows raised at once.

"Now I'm not saying I will wear it often, but, you know, if you wanted me to buy it . . . It's not like I have to wear it to the National Finals or anything."

"Oh, no, darlin'," Lynda drawled, "don't you buy it just for me. It's too expensive just to hang in the closet. Come on, girls."

Looking like a professor addressing struggling freshmen students, Dr. Cartier clarified, "Brady, now don't think you need to do this just for us. We like you as you are."

"No matter how boring you dress," Heidi added.

"Get the shirt, Wendy!" Brady growled.

"If you insist, Uncle Brady. If that's what you really want." She poked Lynda as she rushed by.

◆ ◆ ◆

Cheyenne Design, Inc. was located in a large warehouse north of the airport near the corner of Powderhouse Road and Del Range Boulevard.

"It's a sign company!" Lynda blurted out as they pulled in.

"I'm sure it's just a place where they store the horse. Somebody had some extra space," Brady replied, as he steered around potholes in the small dirt parking lot. "It's pretty large, you know. Not everyone can stick something like that in their garage."

"Nor in their yard," Lynda said.

"You'll like it. You'll see. It's just hard to describe."

"It's hard to believe," she mumbled.

Brady pulled on his hat and turned off the engine. Lynda glanced out the back window. Doc Cartier parked the van and horse trailer at the curb.

He reached over and took her hand. "This is goin' to be great, darlin'! Whenever your friends from back east come to see us, they can have their picture taken on the back of a buckin' bronc. We'll tote it out to the corral, and all of us can be standin' around the railin' watchin'. It will look completely real. L. George Gossman will love it. I'll bet he blows up the picture and mounts it in his office."

My friends? If Barbara Washburn or Jacob Metzer see it, they'll bring their animal rights group out and picket our house night and day! Brady, I really, really do not want a stuffed horse in my front yard! He's like a little boy, Lord. I'm marrying a ten-year-old in a man's body. It's just like that Tom Hanks movie!

Lynda stared around the shop yard at discarded wooden, plastic, and neon signs that made the whole yard look like a strip mall in south Florida after a hurricane. "Maybe Estaban is giving us a sign."

"What kind of sign?"

"How about one for the ranch that says, 'Caution: Earth Ends, 100 Feet.'"

"Nah, it's not a sign," Brady insisted. "A stuffed horse! Open up the tailgate, and I'll ask around."

"We're putting it in the truck? I thought you said we could use the horse trailer."

"That's before I remembered it's a bucking horse. It's too tall to slip in the trailer. It will look cool back here. Think of all the attention we'll attract drivin' down the road!"

Lord, I don't think I can do this. Maybe I should just fly back to

New York from Cheyenne. Everyone will think we're idiots! A full-size bucking horse in the back of the truck? Please!

Lynda watched her slightly bowlegged cowboy saunter into the huge shop building, his black hat pushed far back on his now black and yellow head. She pulled down the tailgate of the Dodge pickup. Capt. Patch and Margarita bounded through the parking yard chasing real or imaginary prey.

Lynda stared at a blue upside down sign that at one time said, "The Daddy of Them All!"

"And what did you get for your wedding, dear?" "Oh, you know, the usual—dishes, linens, sterling, Tupperware, a stuffed horse!"

Heidi and Tyler strolled over to her. "Did you find out what it is?" Heidi asked.

"Not yet. Your Uncle Brady went to ask around. He's quite certain it's a stuffed bucking horse."

"Cool!" Tyler blurted out. "Maybe there's some way to motorize it. You know, like the buckin' machines? Then it could be used for bareback ridin' practice."

Heidi's face reflected a classic seventeen-year-old girl's sneer. "I think it sounds absolutely dreadful! He can't be serious about having it in the yard, can he? It would make your house look like a museum—like one of those geeky tourist traps in Nevada. That would be totally embarrassing."

Lynda glanced over the top of her sunglasses at Heidi's piercing blue eyes. *You know, Lord, I think I like this girl. Heather Martin, you raised your daughters well.*

"We'll find out what it is soon enough," Tyler reported. "Here he comes."

The three sat on the tailgate of the pickup as Brady approached, walking as slowly as a lad who had just witnessed his dog run over.

"What's the verdict, cowboy?"

The brown eyes did not glisten.

There were no dimples in his smile.

There was no smile.

Brady leaned his elbows on the back of the pickup rails and sighed. "I can't believe it. I just can't believe it!"

"What is it, Uncle Brady? Did you see it? Is it really mangy looking?"

Tyler tried to look into the open shop. "Did you get that buckin' horse?"

Lynda folded her arms across her chest. "Okay, Stoner, what did the world-famous western author Joaquin Estaban actually give us?"

Brady swept his arm across the yard. "A sign."

"A what?" Tyler pushed his black felt cowboy hat to the back of his head.

Lynda jumped to her feet and scooted next to Brady. "Joaquin really gave us a sign?"

His big brown Bambi eyes stared right at her. "I wonder if that stuffed buckin' horse is still for sale?"

Lynda grabbed his arm and pulled him back to the shop. "Where's the sign? Show it to us."

"What does it say, Uncle Brady?" Heidi quizzed.

"Is it nicely done?" Lynda pressed.

"Oh, it's a handsome sign," Brady mumbled. "But he knew I wanted that stuffed horse. I just can't believe he'd do this to me!"

"Is the sign embarrassing, or what? It isn't some obscure Spanish proverb, is it?"

Brady led the trio into the tall tin building cluttered with signs in various stages of completion. "It's over here." Brady pointed toward the far wall. "They finished it last Friday. Give me a hand, Tyler. We'll carry it out to the truck."

"That's it? It's enormous!" Lynda exclaimed. "I thought we were talking about a little something to hang by the front door."

"It's three feet by sixteen feet."

"Turn it over—let me read it."

Brady and Tyler swung the sign around. Huge Western block letters spelled out DOUBLE DIAMOND RANCH. On the left side two connected four-sided diamonds were burnt into the wood. The right side of the sign displayed a bucking horse and a cowboy clutching bareback rigging with one hand and waving the other in the air. In the same style of print but smaller, the second line read: BRADY & LYNDA DAWN STONER, BUFFALO, MONTANA."

"It's beautiful!" Lynda blurted out. "We can put it out at the gravel road above the corral gate where our driveway begins, right? Near the gravity-fed stock tank! Then people will know that it's really our place."

Brady started to perk up a little. "You remember the layout of the ranch."

"Honey, it really is a nice sign. We should put a small one down on the highway. But this is big. Will we be able to fit it in the truck?"

"I'll think of somethin'. It's heavy, Tyler. You ready to tote it?"

"Yes, sir, lead the way."

It took nearly half an hour to figure out how to secure the sign to the pickup. Finally, Brady lashed it to the outside of the truck on the passenger side. It stretched almost from bumper to bumper.

"So the rest of the trip I have to enter the truck through the driver's door?" Lynda queried.

"That's the best I could do."

"Don't you think it would have been better to have the lettered side toward the truck?"

"I didn't want to take a chance on it bouncin' against the cab and scrapin' the paint," Brady replied.

Heidi tilted her blonde head completely sideways. "But why did you mount it upside down, Uncle Brady?"

"I didn't want it to attract too much attention."

"You think having it upside down makes it less conspicuous?" Lynda questioned.

"All I know is that it's hooked up there good, and we shouldn't pull it down until we get to the ranch. Let's load up. Heidi, tell the Doc we'll take I-25 north to Chugwater and then 313 east for a couple miles to Riley Mark's place. Do any of you want to ride with us?"

Lynda's right boot heel mashed Brady's toe.

"On second thought . . . everyone load up just like they were."

◆ ◆ ◆

The rolling grassland north of Cheyenne exhibited an early June pale green. Up above, an occasional white cloud drifted by like a melting marshmallow in a warm cup of summer blue. For miles Lynda could see no trees or buildings, let alone a town.

She glanced out the window over the top of the big wooden sign. "I really like it, Brady."

"It's a mighty fine sign, isn't it?"

"You know what I like best?"

"The part that says, 'Brady & Lynda Dawn Stoner'?" he asked.

"Yeah."

"It's my favorite part, too, darlin'."

"We really are going to get married, aren't we, cowboy?"

"I reckon we have to now. It's in writin' over the corral. That makes it official. I guess we're stuck with each other."

"I suppose we'll just have to make the best of it." Lynda scooted closer to Brady, slipped her arm in his, leaned over, and kissed his cheek.

A sudden honk from the van caused her to sit straight up.

◆ ◆ ◆

The faded sign over the dirt road past the corrals and next to the half-dead elm tree read: "Bar-M-Bench Ranch, Adrian Marks, Proprietor."

"Who's Adrian?"

"Riley's daddy."

"Is he still alive?"

"Nope. Mr. Marks passed on ten years ago. Mrs. Marks moved to Casper and lives with a sister."

"Then why hasn't Riley put his name up there on the sign?"

"Just been too busy, I reckon. I'm sure he'll get around to it one of these days."

The first building to come in sight was an extremely old log cabin twenty feet wide and thirty feet long. The blackened logs still showed signs of being carefully dovetailed at the corners, even though the back end had slipped off its boulder foundation and caused the building to lean dramatically to the north. Several large brown and white steers grazed in and out of the edifice.

Abandoned piles of rusting farm and ranch equipment lined the drive like a junk yard fence. Brush corrals circled the huge barn. A dead elm had fallen across one corner of the corral and lay rotting in place. The barn itself had lost enough of the bleached gray unpainted siding that Lynda could look through it and see the sky on the other side. The roof had been covered with corrugated tin, but some sections had blown off.

Several outbuildings were propped up by fifty-five gallon oil drums and assorted tractor parts. The roof of one shed had completely collapsed and sprawled directly on top of a vintage, pre-World War II delivery truck.

The house was two stories, with a large balcony above the big front porch. At one time it had been painted white. Most of the paint was cracked and peeling, except for the bottom half of the west side of the house, which showed signs of someone beginning to paint it a light green. That paint, too, was chipped and faded.

The roof of the house was mostly covered with heavy cedar shakes. But the part just beneath the brick chimney was sheathed in a blue plastic tarp that the wind and sun had reduced to shreds.

The front yard was mainly dirt and dead tumbleweeds. The dogs—Lynda spotted three—had shredded something on the front porch. It looked like a load of laundry washed with a box of tissues.

On the left side of the porch, an eight-foot-high chicken wire fence separated the yard from a six-foot by ten-foot neatly manicured bed of pansies that bloomed in a kaleidoscope of bright summer colors. On the right side of the house, another eight-foot fence protected the perfectly straight, weedless rows of a large vegetable garden. A hand-painted sign above the garden entrance read: "Keep This Gate Closed or Else!"

When they parked the truck near the side door, Lynda could see that a large addition to the house had been started at the rear, but halted in progress—just the framed walls and the trusses in place. The wood was faded gray with age.

"Looks like Riley got them all built!" Brady grinned as he shut off the engine.

"Got what built?"

"The privies. Look at 'em. Last time I was here, they weren't half finished. Aren't they beauts?"

Lynda looked far to the right and spotted brand-new twin outhouses alongside two dead elm trees. They were cedar, dovetailed like the old log cabin. Both had new brown tin roofs and opaque fiberglass skylights. The sturdy cedar doors were equipped with modern hardware. On one was written "Buckaroos," and on the other, "Buckarettes."

"When were you here?"

"A couple years ago."

Capt. Patch and Margarita carefully sized up the Bar-M-Bench dogs as Lynda crawled out the driver's side behind Brady. Dr. Cartier and gang pulled in with a cloud of dust.

The tattered screen door flew open, and a parade of children swarmed outside, each one with bright blonde hair and blue eyes. They all wore jeans, boots, and T-shirts of varying sizes and colors.

"Brady!" a young girl hollered. "You have to come see my steer. I'm going to win grand champion with him!"

A boy about five tugged at his arm. "Brady, Brady, watch me rope! I'm a lot better than when you were here last time!"

Lynda looked down at the eager eyes. *Last time? He couldn't have been three last time.*

"How come you painted that sign upside down?" A pint-sized blonde almost stood on her head trying to read the sign on the side of the truck. Her pink T-shirt drooped around her neck.

"That sign goes on our ranch up in Montana," Brady answered as he picked up the smallest boy.

"Is this your wife, Brady? Mama said you were getting married! Are you already married?" the tallest girl quizzed.

"Ever'body, just wait a minute. I'll check out all your projects in a minute. This is Miss Lynda Dawn Austin. She's a book editor from New York City. Me and her will be gettin' married in about a week."

"She and I will be getting married," the tallest girl corrected and then grinned at Lynda.

"That's what I said. Now—" Brady dragged his boot heel across the dirt. "You all line up according to age."

The six children scampered to get in a line. Brady started down the line. "Summer is the oldest, then Riley, Jr.—but we just call him R. J., then Spring, then Lander—"

"My middle name is Brady!" the boy bragged, revealing several teeth missing from his smile.

"Then April, and finally Slate."

"Mama's givin' the baby a bath," Summer reported.

"What's the baby's name?" Lynda asked.

"Precious," Spring reported. "Isn't that a beautiful name?"

"It certainly is."

A tall, thin woman with bright blonde ponytail, wearing jeans, boots, and a fringed yoke T-shirt, banged out the back door with a wide smile on her face. Leather-tough creases lined her eyes. She wore no makeup. A scrubbed-clean baby hugged her hip, wearing only a white cloth diaper and scuffed brown cowboy boots.

Are they born with those on?

"Brady!"

"Sissy! You're as beautiful as always!" Brady replied.

The woman walked straight up to Lynda, who began to offer her hand to shake, only to find the baby shoved into her arms. Then the blonde threw her arms around Brady's waist and hugged him tight, laying her head on his chest.

Brady hugged her back. Real tight.

"It's so good to see you!" Then she spun around, retrieved the wide-eyed baby, and held out her hand. "I'm Sissy Marks. I'm so glad to finally meet Brady's Lynda Dawn Darlin'."

"I'm glad to meet you." Lynda shook the woman's callused hand.

"I've been a little busy this morning with the garden, and I have a sick calf in the bathtub," Sissy apologized, "so while Brady and the kids look over the place and hook up Cindy's trailer, you come in and help me finish fixin' dinner. How many in that other rig?"

"Doc Cartier and three teenagers."

Heidi and Tyler trotted up, surrounded by five tail-wagging dogs. Wendy was helping Dr. Cartier out of the van.

"Have the girls help us peel potatoes. The rest of you stay out of the house for a while. Maybe I'll get something done."

"Where's Riley hidin' out?" Brady asked.

Sissy Marks switched the baby to the other hip. "Oh, Pete Morega drove in right after you called and wanted Riley to ride up to Lusk with him and look at a bull."

"It's not that Angus-'Brahmer' cross, is it?"

"I have no idea. Riley hopped in Pete's truck and hollered that he'd be home by dark. He said he'd talk to you tonight. You all are spending the night with us, aren't you?"

Lynda looked at Sissy's dark-tanned face and perfectly straight white teeth. *This woman is delirious. She's been out here so long she doesn't even know what she's saying. When you have seven children, you don't invite six guests to spend the night . . . do you?*

Brady took her free hand. "Sissy, we'll have to take a rain check on the overnight. We need to catch up with Cindy and then get ready for the big weddin'."

Brady introduced Debra Jean, Tyler, Heidi, and Wendy to all the Marks gang. Dr. Cartier insisted on holding the baby.

Mrs. Marks locked arms with Brady on her left and Lynda on her right. "This is so exciting to have you two stop by. The truck threw a valve, and Riley hasn't got it fixed yet. So it looks like we're ranch-locked for a while. I guess we'll miss your wedding. But this is even better. I get to have you all to myself."

Lynda pushed her sunglasses to the top of her head. *Seven kids and six house guests is having us all to yourself?*

"This is really an answer to prayer. I was sitting around this weekend moping because we couldn't get to church, and we were going to miss your wedding, and the Lord seemed to say, 'Cheer up, girl. I've got this all in control.' Then yesterday Cindy comes by for the first time in five years. And today you two! Thank you, Jesus!" Sissy bubbled.

"I can't imagine six people, two dogs, and a horse being an answer to prayer," Lynda replied.

Sissy Marks stared at Lynda for a long, awkward moment.

"Did—did I say something wrong?" Lynda stammered.

"Oh, no," Sissy laughed. "I was just trying to remember what it was like before I became a ranch wife. You know what? I couldn't remember."

"You didn't grow up on a ranch?"

"Not me. Daddy's a doctor in Cheyenne. He specializes in setting broken bones. After I graduated from the University of Wyoming, I worked in his office. We always had a line of rodeo cowboys coming through the door. That's how I met Riley— and Brady."

"I know I have a lot to learn about being a ranch wife," Lynda admitted. "This is like a foreign world compared to New York."

"Honey, all you need to know is that you have a man who is crazy about you. Everything will find its place. Look around at this yard—is this a mess, or what?"

"Well, I . . . it looks like you have active children."

"Active children? Atlanta looked better after Sherman marched through. Yeah, I've got an active bunch. And a husband that just can't quite finish a chore. And it doesn't bother me a bit. You know why? Because Riley Marks, bless his soul, is thoroughly convinced that I'm the most wonderful woman God ever created. Isn't that right, Brady?"

"Riley drawed good. He figures he's the luckiest man in Wyomin'," Brady agreed.

"Seven healthy kids, a husband who loves me, and a Lord who looks after me. I'm happy, Lynda Dawn. Figure I've got more than most gals."

"I think you're probably right."

Sissy flipped sprays of blonde hair out of her eyes. "I just got your wedding present finished last Friday. Haven't had a chance to wrap it yet. Been meanin' to get to town and buy some paper and a card. Just have to make do with what we have, I suppose."

"That's very thoughtful of you." Lynda searched for a better response.

"I hope it's some of your pottery," Stoner blurted out. "I'll be mighty disappointed if it isn't."

"Brady!" Austin cautioned.

"Sissy's got herself a potter's wheel and a charcoal kiln out there in the barn. She makes some of the purdiest pieces in the state of Wyomin'. They have some in those fancy galleries in Jackson."

"Really?" Lynda turned to Sissy Marks.

Sissy swatted a horsefly away from the baby. "They want more. That's why we were headed to the wedding. I need to deliver some more pieces. But now with the truck broke down, I guess I'll miss most of this year's tourist season."

"Can I take them there for you?" Debra Jean offered. "We're headed for the wedding ourselves."

"Seriously? Do you have room?"

"It's a big van."

"Oh, thank you, Jesus! That would be wonderful! I'll have to get everything packed up."

"Me and Tyler will keep the kids busy out here," Brady offered.

"I'll watch over little Precious," Cartier offered, as she stared into the infant's big blue eyes.

"And Lynda and the girls can finish cookin' dinner while you pack up your pottery," Brady offered.

"Actually, I have most of it started, except for the apple pies."

Lynda tried to get Brady to look at her so she could flash her "you're-dead-meat-Stoner" look. But he didn't even glance her way.

"I can make the pies," Heidi offered. "I love making pies!"

I really, really like this girl!

Sissy Marks steered Lynda, Heidi, Wendy, and the baby-toting Debra Cartier toward the kitchen. It was a huge room with a ten-foot polished redwood picnic table in the middle. A wood-burning cook stove radiated heat, and the faded gray linoleum floor was spotless, like the rest of the well-ordered room.

"I hope we aren't putting you out," Lynda began.

"Are you kidding? It's always a treat to have company. Especially adult women. I seem to spend most of my life talking to children."

Lynda looked at an entire wall covered with crayon-drawn pictures. "Do you home-school your children?"

Sissy Marks looked at Lynda, then over at Dr. Cartier, and back at Lynda. "You've got to be kidding!"

◆ ◆ ◆

Cindy's horse Early to Bed was loaded in the silver stock trailer and hitched behind Brady's pickup. Tyler had exercised Pedregoso and secured him in Cartier's trailer. Capt. Patch and Margarita, after a boisterous and fur-flying fight with the Markses' dogs, retreated to the back of the Dodge. All the guests had filled their bellies with fried beef, boiled potatoes, thick dark gravy, fresh squash, homemade rolls, and apple pie.

In the jump seat of the Dodge was a complete four-place table setting of handmade blue-trimmed pottery sporting a blue Double Diamond brand in the middle of each piece. Three large boxes of Jackson-bound pottery were stashed in the Cartier van.

Brady hugged each child and then Sissy Marks. Lynda hugged Sissy, too. The caravan began the long trek down the dirt drive toward the paved highway.

"She wears me out," Lynda admitted. "That is the hardest-working woman I've ever met in my life!"

"Sissy likes to keep busy."

"Busy? Brady, most of us would have to hire six people to get that much done in a day. If that's your idea of the kind of wife I need to be, I'm already a failure."

"Darlin', Sissy is Sissy. That's all she knows how to be. You just need to be Lynda Dawn. I didn't fall in love with a ranch wife. I fell in love with an award-winning New York City book editor. That's all you have to be."

"It's a good thing, buckaroo. I was beginning to feel like queen of the wimps. What's this guy Riley like?"

"He's the best cowman I ever met. There aren't ten men in the West who know as much about cattle as Riley. The oldest girl—"

"Summer?"

"Yes. She's twelve. Has a bank account of $9,000 and fourteen head that are her own. Daddy's taught her how to raise steers and enter them in the county fair. Grand Champion beef sells for a tidy sum. The only competition she's had the last couple of years has been from her brother and sister. Soon as they're about five, they get a job that brings in some income."

Lynda faced Brady. She leaned her arm on the cardboard box full of dishes in the narrow backseat. "She just about talked us to death. There's a gal who's been away from other women way too long."

"What was the topic of conversation?"

"Horses, cowboys, children, pottery, the world condition, Debra Jean's job at Los Alamos, book publishing, ranch life, the Lord's return, and—perfumes."

"Perfumes?" Brady laughed. "I didn't think Sissy wore perfume."

"She doesn't. I gave her my Prairie After Dark, but she said she didn't know if she'd use it." Lynda chuckled. "How about you? I presume your conversation with her in the garden was more than a discussion of zucchini squash. Did you find out much about Cindy?"

"Sissy said Cindy never mentioned that we were right behind her—only that she was sure I'd be by fairly soon."

Lynda sorted through her brown leather purse and pulled out a very small white bottle. "But Cindy knows we're getting married next week. Why did she think you'd be way out here?" Without looking at him, she splashed perfume behind her ears and rubbed some on her wrists.

"That's what I was wonderin'. Sissy said Cindy asked about the back roads up to Fort Laramie. What's that one?" He reached out for the perfume bottle.

"It's called Scents & Sensibility. Is Fort Laramie a town or a historical site?"

"Both." Brady gently pulled his hat forward and slowed the rig as the pavement ended. "The town is up on the highway. The ruins of the old fort are down on the Laramie River."

"This is getting to be like a scavenger hunt. We get one clue, rush to that place, then one more clue. Only I don't know what the goal is or why we're doing this."

"It reminds me of last fall when Cindy kidnapped you and hauled you up on that mountain. Remember how she made you scatter your belongin's to leave a trail? She surely does know how to manipulate things."

"Leading us along is one thing; her being in serious danger is another. I wish we knew if it were one or the other."

"Maybe it's both." Brady glanced in the rearview mirror.

"You looking at your wounds, cowboy?"

"Oh . . . not really. I was checkin' on that horse trailer we're pullin'. We're stirrin' up a lot of dust."

"I guess it doesn't hurt anything. There's nothing out here for miles."

"I know. Kind of reminds you of some parts of Montana. Nobody for miles. I love this kind of country!"

"You're weird, Stoner. Really weird."

"Thank ya, ma'am."

Lynda glanced out the back window at sleeping dogs and a dusty trail. "I suppose it's awfully dirty back in the van."

"Doc can keep the windows rolled up and the air conditioner on."

"This is scary. I'm almost getting used to unpaved roads."

"Good thing. Look back there. This is like a covered wagon train."

"It's like a circus train."

"Full of animals?"

Lynda scooted closer to Brady. "Animals, clowns, tightrope walkers, lion tamers. We've got them all. It's a traveling zoo." Suddenly she threw her head back and burst out laughing.

"What's funny, darlin'?"

"Stoner, this is crazy! Absolutely completely loony. Last week at this time I'm sitting in my twelfth floor office on Madison Avenue, wearing a tailored suit, editing a novel. Now I'm traveling down some unpaved Wyoming road in a pickup with a head-busted cowboy, two amorous dogs, an upside down sixteen-foot ranch sign, a van driven by a gal with a Ph.D. in nuclear physics, three teenagers, two horse trailers, and two horses. I'm afraid to tell anyone what I'm doing for fear of being committed. Even when I have garlic and jalapenos on my pizza I can't dream anything this wild!"

"Now, Lynda Dawn Darlin', are you braggin' or complainin'?"

"I'm just thinking that I would really, really, really like to be sitting in a comfortable home with full utilities in some isolated location with nobody around but my own private cowboy."

"How's my head look?"

"Like you have a bad case of jaundice or malaria or something. It's a sickly yellow."

"Good. It's getting better."

She leaned over. The first kiss landed on his cheek.

He turned his head toward her.

The second kiss was lip to lip.

For the first time, the van behind them didn't honk.

◆ ◆ ◆

The dusty caravan proceeded mostly north as they skirted ranches, farms, and rolling hills and aimed for the Laramie River. Lynda rolled her window down several inches and allowed the warm June breeze to blow her hair. Most of the prairie was covered with thin, spindly wild grasses that were still green, but showing signs of beginning to dry. Cottonwoods and elms clumped around houses, barns, old homestead sites, and along water courses. The gray/green sage was short and scattered. The Herefords, Charolais, and Angus cattle bunched in draws and gullies. Most now stood rechewing their lunch. Several times Lynda spotted pronghorn antelope grazing among the cattle, as if trying to blend in with their larger domesticated range partners.

A few miles upstream from where the Laramie River ran into the South Platte, they crested a hill and looked down on the scattered ruins preserved as a National Historic Site. At one time, Fort Laramie was the largest and most important post on the northern plains. One hundred and ten years past its prime, it remains a major tourist attraction in eastern Wyoming. In the distance was a restored long two-story enlisted men's barracks, plus the captain's quarters called Old Bedlam. Several other buildings in various stages of restoration stretched off to the south.

In the foreground near a sandstone bluff were the blue and white flashing lights of a Wyoming State Highway Patrol car and the red blinking ones of the Goshen County ambulance.

"Brady! Is it Cindy?"

"I don't see the Cadillac."

Driving slowly on the gravel and dirt road, Brady rolled down his window as they neared a uniformed officer.

"Keep the rig movin', buddy!"

Brady leaned his head out. "What happened, officer?"

"A driver lost control on the corner and slammed into the sandstone."

"I was worried this might be a friend of ours we hope to meet at the Fort."

"What's his name?"

"Her name is Cindy LaCoste. She's drivin' a big old green Cadillac."

"This was a man riding a Harley-Davidson motorcycle like he was racing stock cars at the state fair."

"His name didn't happen to be Lamont McGhee?"

The officer glanced down at a small clipboard he held in his hand. "Nope. Rocky Taggun from Las Vegas, Nevada."

"Is the injury serious?"

"A broken leg and a busted wrist. It could have been worse."

"Thanks, officer!"

"Keep it moving."

"Yes, sir."

The parking lot at Fort Laramie consisted of five acres of packed sand and gravel. With only a couple dozen cars in the front row and two tour busses to the right, Brady pulled the truck and horse trailer to the back of the lot.

"Brady, was that guy with Lamont McGhee?"

"I don't know. But he was from Las Vegas. We were told down at Manitou Springs that the bunch that followed Cindy was from Las Vegas."

Heidi, Wendy, and Tyler piled out of the van. Doc Cartier rolled down her dusty window. "What was all that back there?" she asked.

"A motorcyclist lost control."

"Is Cindy's rig here?"

Brady stretched his back and stared across the nearly empty parking area. "Nope."

"What do we do now?" Heidi quizzed.

"That's what we're trying to figure."

"Uncle Brady, can we go look at the Fort?" Wendy pleaded.

"Doc, do we need to stretch the horses yet?"

"They're fine."

Brady turned to the others. "You all go look around a little."

"What are we going to do?" Lynda shaded her eyes with her hand.

"Go for a hike."

"Where?"

He pointed to the west. "Up to that bluff."

"Why?"

"To ponder."

"To ponder?"

"Yeah." Brady pulled off his hat and ran his fingers through his shaggy brown hair. "For instance, was Cindy here? When? Did she run that guy off the road? Or did he take the corner too fast because he was pursuing her? Where is good old Lamont and the others? Could they have caught up with her by now? If they were all here in the parking lot a couple hours ago, they can't be too far now. But which direction would they head?"

Lynda tucked her mauve blouse more securely into the back of her black jeans. "We're going to find answers to all that up on the bluff?"

"Well, if we don't," he said grinning, "we'll just sit and neck."

Lynda's face warmed. "You mean we're going up there by ourselves?"

"Just you and me and the Captain and Margarita. No dogs

are allowed on the grounds of Fort Laramie unless they're leashed."

They hiked for the sandstone bluff, which turned out to be two hills instead of one. From the parking lot it had looked like a fairly steep climb to a mesa that overlooked the region for miles. But as they reached the top, they found that it dropped down into a little grassy swale before it climbed back to cliff dimensions overlooking the scene of the accident.

Capt. Patch and Margarita were out of sight and barking by the time Brady and Lynda panted their way, hand in hand, to the top of the first ridge. Parked in the coulee below them, completely out of sight of the parking lot and the entrance road, were five chopped-down Harley-Davidson bikes, four leather-clad riders, and two yapping dogs.

Lynda grasped Brady's arm. "The bikers!"

"There's only four of 'em. Someone's missing."

"The man who had the wreck?"

"Nope, his bike is down below."

"I think they've spotted us."

"Wait here," Brady instructed.

"What are you going to do?"

"Go get my dogs."

"Brady, it's dangerous!"

"That's why I want you to stay right here. If anything happens, or anyone starts up your way, head down the hill and report it to that patrolman."

"Brady, I don't want you going down there!"

"It's too late, darlin'. If I don't head that way, they'll come this way. They don't know me from Joe Tourist. I'll just grab the dogs and see if I can learn anything."

Lynda reluctantly released his hand. "What do you want me to do?"

"Just smile and look touristy."

She started to clasp her hands in front of her, then shoved

them into her jeans back pockets and tried to relax. *Joe Tourist? He could no more look like a tourist than I could look like a fashion model. Lord, this isn't good. I want to marry that cowboy, and I don't want him all beat up.*

Lynda strained to hear the voices below her in the coulee. "Hey! Capt. Patch, come on!" Brady yelled. "Come on, dogs. Sorry, guys, I didn't know anyone was over here."

A thin man with full, untrimmed beard and shoulder-length hair stepped toward him. "We was just lookin' for a place to have a picnic and take a siesta."

The Captain and Margarita circled the motorcycles barking and snapping at tires and boots.

"Can't you shut them up?" the man asked.

"Sorry, they're just a little excited. We traveled·quite a way to see the Fort."

"If they hike a leg on a bike, they're dead. You understand me?" the man threatened.

"I'll take them back to the parking lot. Hey, those are nice bikes."

"Are you leavin' or not?"

"I'm goin', I'm goin."

A pasty-complected man with bulging eyes pointed up toward Lynda. "Is she with you?"

"Oh, yeah. There's a whole group of us. Kind of like a tour," he explained. "Come on, dogs!"

Capt. Patch and Margarita scurried to his side, still releasing an occasional bark.

"What's with the patch on the dog?" one of the leather-clad men asked.

"Got in a fight over a lady dog and lost his eye. He likes wearing the patch."

"No foolin'? That's real jack. Lamont, we ought to have us a dog with a patch."

Lynda watched to see which one admitted to being

Lamont. It was the tall one with full brown beard and large bruise on the right side of his head. "We don't need no animals," he groused.

She noticed Brady trying to size him up. *For goodness sake, Brady, don't start a fight or something!*

"Say," Brady blurted out, "did you see the guy on the bike who wrecked down at the corner? He bent the fork of that bike in a ninety-degree angle. Cops said he'd be all right. He's got a couple broken bones, but it could have been worse. Was he ridin' with you?"

"Do we look like the type who would lose control and slam into a cliff?" the man gruffed. "Now beat it, dude, or we'll not have time for a siesta."

"Oh, sure. Come on, dogs!"

As Brady turned to climb back to Lynda, a man rose up out of the brush on top of the cliff overlooking the accident and hiked down toward the others. "Hey!" he shouted. "What's Stoner doin' here?"

Brady whipped around. The biker slid down the embankment by stabbing his heels into the soft dirt. He stumbled past the scattered boulders and sage.

"He's a friend of Crazy Cindy's!" the man hollered.

Lynda's mouth went dry. *He knows Brady?*

McGhee started up the hill after Stoner, but the growl of the dogs kept him back.

"Brady, honey," Lynda called, "the children are waiting!"

For a moment all the men in black leather froze and stopped to stare up at her. Brady kept climbing the hill. When he reached the top, he grabbed her hand, and they hurried in the direction of the parking lot. Capt. Patch and Margarita raced ahead of them.

They saw Heidi and Wendy waving their arms.

"Whoa, the children really are waiting."

"Uncle Brady!" Wendy shouted.

"I thought they went to look at the Fort."

"That was Lamont McGhee, wasn't it?" Lynda asked.

"Yeah."

"Some of them knew you?"

"Only one."

"Who was he, Brady? How did he know you?"

"I met him in a parking lot in Las Vegas, remember? He was one of the thugs Joe Trent sent to 'talk' to me."

"Trent? But aren't those the bikers who chased Trent off when they attacked Cindy years ago? He said they would have killed him if he stayed to help her."

"That was Trent's story."

"You mean, he might have been in on it all along?"

"I don't know. That was years ago. Since then Trent's made a lot of lousy friends. All I know is that the one on the hill used to work for Joe Trent, or still does."

Brady was now tugging on Lynda's arm so hard she had to jog to keep up. She could feel her toes cramp in the points of her cowboy boots.

"Uncle Brady," Heidi hollered as they approached. "Look!"

He dropped Lynda's hand. She turned around to see five motorcycles perched on the top of the hill pointed down the incline she and Brady had just descended.

"Are they the bikers from Manitou Springs?" Doc Cartier inquired.

"Yep," Brady replied. "I want everybody to load up right now! Heidi and Wendy, get in there with Doc. Pull that outfit up alongside mine."

"Circle the wagons?" Cartier questioned.

Brady directed traffic with his hands. "Yep. And lock the doors. Lynda Dawn, put the dogs in the truck with you and get behind the wheel. Tyler, grab me a couple ropes out of that bag in the back of the truck. Darlin', hand me the 30-30."

"Are you ser—serious?" she stammered.

"Just in case."

Brady grabbed the carbine, checked the lever, then released the hammer to the safety position, and put the gun on the seat of the pickup.

"What are we goin' to do?" Tyler asked as he handed Brady a rope.

"Wait—and see what they're up to."

Lynda kept the door of the truck open as she sat behind the wheel. Wendy rolled down a window in the van. "Uncle Brady, she's been here!"

"Who?" Brady shouted back, keeping his eye on the bikers still perched high on the distant bluff.

"Cindy LaCoste. It's right there in the registration book at the beginning of the self-guided trail. That's why we came right back."

"What did it say?"

Tyler coiled a loop and began to swing it above his head. "I saw it, too. It said, 'Cindy LaCoste, Beaver Creek, Nebraska.'"

"Is that the same Cindy, Uncle Brady?" Wendy called out.

"Where's Beaver Creek?" Lynda asked.

"I have no idea."

Tyler tossed his loop at an imaginary target in the parking lot and then began to coil his rope again. "Do you think they're comin' down here?"

"I suppose."

"Why are they waitin'?"

"For that!" Brady pointed to the state patrol car as it crested a distant hill and left the area.

With a roar of engines and a cloud of dust, the five motorcycles ripped down the bluff and into the mostly empty parking lot. Brady and Tyler sat on the side of the pickup bed, their feet dangling over the edge. Both had cowboy hats pushed back on their heads and fiddled with the coiled ropes in their hands.

Flinging dust and rocks, the chrome and black Harley-Davidsons circled the two outfits. Lynda slammed her door and locked it and then rolled the window down a few inches. Both horses pranced and kicked in their respective trailers. Capt. Patch and Margarita began a half-hearted duet of protest. In the sideview mirror she watched Brady's face.

No smile.

No dimples.

No relaxed, easy-going pose.

Just fire in the eyes.

Intensity in the expression.

Controlled power.

Like a cat ready to pounce.

Or a bareback rider about to nod for the gate to be opened.

Or a cowboy defending his loved ones.

Lord, that just might be the second favorite thing I like about that man.

With the timing and precision of a horse club drill team, the motorcyclists pulled up in front of Brady, each pointing his bike straight at him.

"I don't like you, Stoner!" the one biker growled.

"That doesn't exactly break my heart."

"What are you doin' here?"

"Sightseein'." Brady had an anytime, anyplace kind of smile of his face.

Don't let him get beat up, Lord, please!

"Is Crazy Cindy travelin' with you?"

"Nope. She's not with us. And she's definitely not crazy."

"That's her horse trailer."

"No, it belongs to L. G. Minor in Ely, Nevada. But Cindy was pulling it."

"What are you doin' with it?"

"Takin' it home."

Lamont McGhee shoved down the kickstand, still straddling the motorcycle. "I want to know where Cindy is."

"Why?"

"It's personal. Where is she?"

"Can't say. It's personal."

McGhee stepped off his bike and pulled a large survival knife from his boot. "Stoner, you're wastin' our time. Where is she?"

"You don't want to find her. Cindy's a little ticked at the moment. Push her one more click, and she'll put a thirty-caliber bullet in one of your heads. Your best bet is to get on the road and put some miles between you and her. If you keep on following Cindy, she'll end up shootin' one of you. And I can tell you from personal experience, she will pull the trigger."

"Following her? That stupid blonde witch has been doggin' us down every road for days! We've been tryin' to lose her. But that ain't workin'. So now it's time to try somethin' different."

"She's been stalkin' you?"

"What do you think we've been talkin' about, man? She put Nicky in jail in Durango, Kite's in a hospital in Denver, and now she ran Rocky into that bluff. She ran right at him with that green Cad not more than two hours ago."

"Nice of you to stop and help him out," Brady chided.

"We've got our reasons for not wanting to talk to the cops. Where is she? This time we'll go straight after her. We're going to get this settled right now."

One of the men left his bike standing and hiked over to Dr. Cartier's rig. He peered through the shaded windows. "Hey, the van is full of babes. Maybe it's pay-back time right now! You ladies like some company?" He reached his hand up and tried to open the locked van door.

The loop of Brady's rope circled the handlebars of the

man's abandoned motorcycle and instantly toppled the bike to the dirt.

With shouts and curses, the man charged Brady as the others dismounted. Tyler's coiled, hard nylon rope caught the attacker across the face like a whip. He staggered back and fell to the ground, clutching his bleeding nose.

The other four came at Tyler and Brady from different angles carrying chains and knives. One of them stopped his advance by Lynda's window. "When we put the cowboys down, I get this one!" He waved a switchblade knife toward her.

Lynda grabbed the carbine and shoved the barrel out the partially opened window and pulled the hammer back. The gun was no more than two feet from the biker.

"Careful, darlin', there's a cartridge in the chamber," Brady hollered, never taking his eyes off the other three advancing men.

"Should I aim at his head or his chest?" Lynda called out.

"Wait, darlin', don't pull the trigger. It ain't right."

"This man was threatening us with a knife. It's self-defense!"

"You're right . . . it's just, well, I don't think he meant it," Brady shouted. "Mister, put the knife in your boot and slowly move away from the truck!"

The others stopped their advance.

Capt. Patch and Margarita began barking vigorously from the backseat.

"She's as crazy as Cindy!"

"Why are all the women comin' after us with guns?"

"She ain't goin' to pull no trigger!"

"Darlin', if you have to shoot somethin', just shoot the tires off those bikes . . . or maybe the gas tanks."

"Will they blow up nice and purdy?" Lynda shouted.

"Wait!" McGhee shouted, backing up toward his bike.

"Don't shoot Lamont's bike. Shoot one of the others," Brady called out.

"No! Wait!" All five men scurried back to their bikes. The injured man tossed Brady's rope to the dirt and pulled his bike off the ground.

"Stoner," McGhee shouted, "you just made a big mistake you'll spend the rest of your life regrettin'! This ain't over! I ain't the kind that forgets!"

"Neither is Cindy LaCoste."

"You tell that blonde witch that next time we see her, she's goin' down!"

"'Goin' down'? Come on, McGhee, you can be more creative than that," Brady riled.

The roar of a tour bus pulling into the parking lot caused Lynda to glance to the right. She pulled the carbine down out of sight. The five bikers rode off across the empty parking lot.

Lynda pushed her door open. The dogs bounded out in mock pursuit of the Harleys. Lynda rushed to Brady's side as he re-coiled his rope.

"You done good, darlin'." He nodded.

"Good? Look at me—I'm shaking all over!"

"Me, too!" Tyler admitted.

Heidi and Wendy trotted over to them, and Dr. Cartier lowered herself from the van.

"Were you really going to shoot that man?" Wendy asked. "I've never seen anyone get shot in real life."

"I hope not. But I was so scared for Brady and Tyler I just about lost it."

"I know what you mean. I thought I was going to wet my pants!" Heidi confessed.

The door of the big silver bus swung open, and the parking lot began to fill with Japanese tourists. They filed out and stood in a line in front of the bus. Each one had a blue canvas hat with the words "Wild West Excursions" embroidered on the front. And each sported at least one camera around the neck. A woman with short black hair, a navy blue pants suit, and a bronze name tag reading, "Jeannine Katomo, Tour Guide," scampered over to Brady.

"Excuse me! Would it be all right for our people to pose with you and take a few photos? They're all very excited to meet some real cowboys and cowgirls!"

SIX

W"here are you now?"
"Lusk."

After a long pause, Kelly Princeton cleared her throat. "Yeah, right. And you're looking at a bull?"

"Brady's looking at the bull. I'm looking at a rack of postcards of 'Scenic Wyoming: Like nowhere else on earth!' at Marty's Eastside Minimart and Taxidermy Shop."

"Taxidermy? So it's not a real bull?"

"It's a real bull, all right. I left the others at a ranch a few miles from town and came in to call you."

"It's a good thing you did, girl. Nina and I were just leaving to go over to your place and load up all the wedding gifts."

"I can't believe you're really going to drive out here." Lynda shifted her weight to her left foot, trying to find a comfortable position as she huddled against the wall. *This pay phone's so low even Henri de Toulouse-Lautrec would have to bend down to use it.*

"Neither can we. Around the office we're being accused of pulling an 'Austin.'"

Lynda stood up, stretched her back, and then loosened the tension on the phone cord. "An 'Austin'?"

"You know, a totally irresponsible and reckless act of der-ring-do."

"I am not irresponsible and reckless. I like to think of it as occasionally adventuresome and out-of-character."

"You call pointing a gun at a vicious motorcycle gang and threatening to blow them to kingdom come a normal, every-day activity? That's pretty wild even if you're in the Bronx—let alone 'scenic Wyoming.'"

Lynda took a deep breath. She couldn't decide if the store smelled more like stale burritos or fresh-tanned leather. "It wasn't all that big a deal."

"Whatever. Do you want us to bring your wedding dress and more of your clothes?"

She tried flipping several errant strands of dark brown hair out of her eyes. "No, I really am flying home for a couple of days."

"Yeah, right," Kelly prodded. "What are you going to do now?"

"You mean, after we buy the bull?"

"So he's really buying it, huh?"

"He says it's a really great bull."

"What makes a great bull?"

"I have no idea in the world. Brady and his brother Brock are going to share the bull." The store clerk turned on a stereo, and the pounding music boomed off the bare linoleum floor.

"Say, what?"

"We'll put the bull in with our cows, and he will . . . you know, do his thing. Then we'll ship him over to Brock, and he'll do the same over there." *Linda Rondstat? I haven't heard one of her songs in fifteen years.*

"I don't need to know the parentage of my Big Mac. I'm not into this cow thing."

Lynda hooked the toe of her boot on a stack of Dr. Pepper 24-packs and tried sliding them toward her. "I thought you were coming out here to look for a cowboy. These are the kinds of things you'll have to learn about."

"Hey, I've watched *Dallas* reruns. I'll just marry a really rich cowboy."

"Get real."

"Okay, maybe I'll look for a doctor who wears a cowboy hat and likes to raise horses for a hobby. But you didn't answer me—what are you doing after you buy the bull?"

Lynda sat down on the Dr. Pepper cases and switched the receiver to the other ear. "We might be going out to Beaver Creek, Nebraska."

"Nebraska? Nina and I are going to be driving through Nebraska. Should we meet you somewhere?"

"No! We're not going to be there long. I'm flying home, remember?" *We absolutely do not need any more people to travel with us!*

"I'm bringing your wedding dress with me."

"No, you're not, Kelly! I want to come home."

"Come home? Your home is now on the range where the deer and the antelope play, remember? Do you have deer and antelope on your ranch?"

"I never thought about it that way, but Brady says there are plenty of both."

"Now that is cool. It's like you're moving into a fairy tale or something. Anyway, where are your shoes and other things?"

"You are not bringing my wedding dress. All the accessories are in those white boxes stacked under the window facing the street in my bedroom."

"Good. How much of your closet do you want us to bring? It's a big van."

"Kelly, I'll come home and—"

"It's Monday. You're getting married Saturday. You aren't coming back. Even if you do, you can't take all those clothes on a plane."

"But I need to be there to tell you which ones to bring."

"You want us to bring just the summer things?"

"Kelly, you're not listening to me."

"I most certainly am. Bring everything, right?"

"Right. Actually, I have all my clothes already packed up in the moving boxes."

"And the perfume cabinet?"

"Yeah, it's boxed, too. Do you have room for it?" Lynda sniffed her wrists. *I'm in a minimart for ten minutes, and I smell like cigarette smoke and fried chicken wings.*

"We'll make room, Lynda-girl."

A lanky, tanned man in a white straw cowboy hat and worn brown boots sauntered by where Lynda sat.

"Howdy, ma'am." He tipped his hat toward her.

"Howdy!"

"Who was that?" Kelly quizzed.

"Just a drifting cowpoke."

"Is he cute?"

"I can't tell. He's over at the beer rack."

"Maybe he's buying it for someone else."

"Relax, Kell, you'll be here soon enough."

"Yeah, but I still can't believe it."

For a moment both were silent.

Lynda's voice was very quiet. "I'm not going to get to come home, am I?"

"Nope."

"I don't even know why I make plans. From the day I met that cowboy behind the chutes at the Dixie Stampede in St. George, Utah, absolutely nothing has gone according to plans."

"You bragging or complaining, girl?"

"Now you're sounding like Brady."

"Look at it this way. It's best that you're with him this week. That way you can make sure that he's there for the wedding."

"That's the first good reason for going through all of this

I've heard." Lynda leaned against the green-and-dirt-colored wall and stretched her legs across the aisle toward the one gallon containers of antifreeze.

"If I don't get another call from you before six in the morning, we bring everything we can cram into the van. Maybe we'll rent one of those moving trailers."

"Kelly, did you ever have dreams when you were a teenager of how you wanted your wedding to be?"

"When I was a teen? You're kidding. I'm still dreaming, remember?"

"Well, when I used to think about my wedding, it never even faintly resembled what's going on now. Remember how I spent most of the spring planning each day before the wedding? I can't even find the list, let alone follow it! I feel like I'm caught in a swift river and can't make it to shore."

"It'll turn out fine. Where's your faith, kiddo?"

"That's the crazy thing. Even in all of this, it all has the feeling of being the Lord's will."

"Then enjoy it! We'll see you in Jackson, Wyoming. Wow! I've always wanted to say that."

"You won't get lost, will you?"

"Are you kidding? Nina's dad in Wisconsin faxed us a detailed map of the entire route, including where we should spend the night and how often to call him."

"Good for Mr. DeJong."

"I think we're going to stop by and see them on the way home—if I don't elope with a cowboy or something."

"I've got to get back to the bull, Kell."

"Yeah, me, too. I'll tell 'em you won't be in this week. Good thing you're three years behind on taking your vacations."

"Thanks, Kell. I couldn't do all this without you and Nina helping me."

"You owe us, girl. And we intend to collect."

"I'd better hang up. There's a cowboy wanting to use the phone."

"Yeah? What's he look like?"

"He's a looker, all right. Of course, he'd look even cuter if he had some front teeth. Here . . . you can talk to him."

Lynda could hear Kelly's phone click even as she handed the receiver to the seven-year-old impatiently waiting in line.

◆ ◆ ◆

Debra Jean Cartier was riding Pedregoso. Brady was mounted on Early to Bed. Tyler, Heidi, and Wendy sat on the rail of a corral welded out of oil field pipe. L. G. Minor's stock trailer was backed to the gate. With Capt. Patch and Margarita nipping at his hooves, a brindle-colored bull with a black R-43 painted on his hip was being slowly encouraged to enter the trailer.

Lynda climbed up on the rail next to Wendy. "So he bought the bull?"

"Uncle Brady called his brother. They talked it over and decided to go ahead."

"Called him? There's a phone out here?"

"The vet had a cel-phone. Guess what? Brady said Brock's buying the bull himself and giving you and Uncle Brady half interest in it for your wedding present."

Lynda stared across the pasture at the rolling green hills. *I get half a bull for a wedding gift? How do you write a thank you for that? Which half do we own anyway?*

She glanced back at the multicolored hornless bovine. "Isn't he kind of . . . big for a bull?"

"Not really," Tyler spoke up. "I suppose he'll come in at nearly 2,000 pounds."

A ton of bull? He weighs more than an entire motorcycle gang. "Can you put him in there with Cindy's horse?"

"We don't know if we can trailer him at all. But Uncle Brady said we'd put both horses in Doc's trailer," Heidi reported.

"Hey, how about a little help here," Brady called from inside the corral. "You four block off the middle, and Doc and I'll keep him moving away from the fences. Maybe the Captain can pester him enough to hop up in that trailer. Don't get too close, and if he breaks toward you, head for the fence."

Lynda followed Tyler and the girls into the middle of the corral as they fanned out to make a human barricade. "Are you sure this is safe?" she grilled.

"They say he's easy to handle on the ground, but he doesn't like trailers," Brady called out. "Just keep him headed this way."

Lynda turned to Tyler. "Just how do we do that?"

"Wave your arms and hat. Holler at him," Tyler instructed.

The big bull stopped his movement toward the trailer as soon as the four on the ground began to make noise. He turned his massive head back around and stared at each of them.

"What's he doing?" Lynda called out.

"Contemplating his next move," Brady replied. "Heyaaa! Let's go! Move it, bull!"

Lynda joined in the chorus of noise, waving her arms and advancing toward the bull. *What am I doing? I can't even get a two-pound cat to mind. This is not good. What if he charges right at me? I'm glad he doesn't have horns. I'll merely be trampled to death. "Yea, though I walk through the valley of the shadow of death, I will fear no evil" . . . except big bulls! Be cool, Austin. Show Brady you have what it takes to be a ranch wife. I wish Sissy were here. She'd know what to do. Or Summer or R. J. or any of the kids. Stoner, this is not a good idea!*

"He's not moving, Brady! Why don't you rope him?"

"He's too big. He'd rip this saddle up and might injure Early."

That's nice. I'm glad he's looking after the horse. How about those of us on the ground?

"Maybe I need to spank him a little," Brady called out. He widened the loop of his nylon rope and slapped it into the rump of the bull. R-43 broke into a run straight at Lynda, in the exact opposite direction of the trailer.

I'm dead! I won't live until my wedding day!

Lynda was unaware that Heidi, Wendy, and Tyler had scampered to the top rail of the corral. And she did not hear Brady holler at her. She heard only her own piercing and petrified scream. "Noooooooooo!" Lynda held her hands straight out in front of her and closed her eyes.

It didn't feel like a train ran over her.

Nor the entire defensive line of the Green Bay Packers.

There was no collision . . . no pain . . . no trampling . . . no bull.

When the crowd on the fence let out shouts and applause, she opened her eyes. Brady shoved the doors closed on the trailer.

"He went in the trailer?" she gasped.

"It was that scream of yours that did it," Wendy reported from the rail.

"He just turned around and ran right in there," Cartier added. "Nice job."

"You said he was tame, Brady Stoner!"

"He is. Soon as you showed him you were serious, he high-tailed it out of the corral."

"Serious? I thought I was going to die!"

"Now, darlin', you shouldn't make somethin' like this so dramatic."

"Stoner, the next time I'll ride the horse, and you work the ground."

"Did you all hear that? Lynda Dawn is plannin' on workin' cattle after all."

"That is," she hurried to correct, "if I ever decide to do this again."

"When we get to the ranch, you can ride Bullet," Brady offered.

"You mean X-it? That horse you bought along the road up at Holter Lake?"

"Yeah, he calmed right down for me this spring."

"I don't ride horses that buck, kick, bite, or have the faintest notion of running off."

◆ ◆ ◆

All five booths at the Texas Trail Cafe were taken, so they filled the counter, sitting on duct-tape repaired green Naugahyde stools that only partially swiveled. The order was simple—five chicken-fried steaks and one chef's salad with lite vinaigrette dressing.

"There was actually a trail up from Texas that came through here?" Lynda quizzed.

"The Texas Trail intercepted the Deadwood-Cheyenne stage road right here."

"Oh," she mumbled.

"Yep," Brady waxed on, "located on the beautiful Niobara River, Lusk, Wyoming—houses the historic Stagecoach Museum and is the site of one of Tap Andrews's early show-downs. 'Course, it was called Roaring Water back then."

"Who?"

Brady rolled up his sleeves and began to spear a mound of mashed potatoes and brown gravy. "Mr. Tapadera Andrews. He happens to be a distant relative of mine and one of Montana's pioneer ranchers, that's who. You know—Granville Stuart, Con Kohrs, and those boys? You do know a little Montana history, don't you?"

"Stoner, don't you give me that Montana history baloney.

Until about two weeks ago, I thought we'd be living in Wyoming, remember? I don't have to learn any history until we're actually moved in somewhere. I don't even know where we're going to spend the night, let alone where I'm going to live after we're married."

He spiked a bite of batter-fried beef about the size of a small frog and popped it into his mouth. "We'regonnaliveinmontana," he mumbled.

"I assume that was a nod to Montana. But how about tonight? Are we really headed toward Nebraska?"

"It's only thirty miles down the road."

"What then? Do we just keep following these clues? What if Cindy's doing this on purpose? What if she changed her mind and decided to get even with you after all? What if she's trying to ruin our wedding plans? Three days ago I was worried about her safety. Now it seems like she's the only one who knows what's going on."

"I know what's goin' on," Brady announced. "You told me you've decided not to go back to New York, right?"

"I decided? I've been trying to get to an airplane for a week. Now Kelly and Nina have packed up all my things and are leaving in the morning." Lynda threw up her hands, took a deep breath, and sighed. "I don't have anything to go home for."

A dark-skinned waitress leaned forward on the counter with a coffeepot. "Honey, I know what you mean. Ever since Vince ran off with that flop, Louisa, I've felt the same way."

Lynda gave the woman a startled look.

The waitress stood straight up. "Oh, excuse me. You want some more coffee?"

"Thanks, Monica," Brady hummed, "and while you're at it, why don't you just cut that banana creme pie into six pieces and put it right down here on the counter."

With the waitress gone, Lynda leaned toward Brady and whispered, "Do you know her?"

"Nope. But she seems like a real sweetheart. It says 'Monica' right there on her blouse."

"But that doesn't mean you're supposed to call her that."

"It doesn't? What does it mean?"

"Never mind, Stoner." She sat up and resumed a normal tone. "What's the plan now? We have the bull. Where do we go from here?"

"We're going out to Beaver Creek. No matter what we find there, we're headed up to Rapid City, and we'll spend tomorrow night in Sheridan, Wyoming. I've got a friend we can stay with there."

"Buckaroo, are we going to have any time to ourselves this week?"

Brady leaned so close to her she could smell the gravy on his breath. "We're by ourselves right now."

"By ourselves? We're in a crowed little cafe in some Wyoming cow town," she pouted. Then she reached down into her purse, pulled out a clear bottle of golden liquid, and proceeded to splash it on her neck. "Don't ask!"

"Well, I reckon it's better to be alone after the weddin' than before, if you get my drift." He grinned.

The waitress shoved a pie with a three-inch meringue crest and a stack of plates in front of them. She sniffed at the air. "Someone is wearing Remember That Night. It was Vince's favorite—the jerk!"

"Remember what night?" Brady teased.

"There have been a few memorable ones, cowboy. Like the night last fall when we were huddled by the campfire next to that lake in Montana."

"And we wrapped up in a sleeping bag to stay warm?"

"And there was no one around for fifty miles!" Lynda added.

"Oh . . . that night. There will be more of those, darlin'."

"When?"

"How about next week at this time? One week's a mighty short time."

"Not when I'm with you, Brady Stoner. Somehow a whole year is crammed into every week." She stabbed a piece of pressed turkey and tried to dip it in the dressing. "Where are we going after Sheridan?"

"On Wednesday we'll visit the ranch, see if the house is finished, leave off the horse and bull, and then travel down to Jackson on Thursday and lounge around until the wedding on Saturday."

"What do you mean, see if the house is done? I thought you said they guaranteed it."

"They did, they did. And their word's good, too."

"So what's the problem?"

"I want to find out if they use the word *completed* in the same way that I use it."

"You're not going to tell me we have to live in that horrid old house until ours is ready."

"Nope. I can guarantee you won't stay in the old house. They bulldozed it into a pile and burned it to the ground."

"That's the best news I've heard in a week. Now where are we going to spend the night tonight?"

"Somewhere over in Nebraska. There's bound to be a motel along the highway."

"What if there's not?"

"I've got a friend who has a big place in Smiley Canyon near Fort Rob."

"I thought you said you've never been in that country."

"I haven't."

It was 9:30 and new-moon dark when they pulled up to a single-wide trailer and an extremely faded sign that read: "Smiley

Canyon Land and Cattle." Brady was in the dimly lit house for twenty minutes before he came out carrying a Coleman lantern.

Lynda lounged beside the open window of Debra Cartier's rig. "What's with the lantern, cowboy?" she asked.

"Duane invited us to spend the night, but he's got four kids in a two-bedroom mobile home."

"I thought you said he had a big place."

"Oh, he does—6,200 deeded acres. But he hasn't got around to building the house yet. 'Course, they've only been married eight years."

"That certainly explains it," Lynda returned. "Does this mean we go down the road looking for a motel?"

"He said there was nothin' this side of Gordon, but we could use the barn."

"Good," Cartier replied. "I presume we can turn the livestock out?"

"Yeah, Duane said to put the horses in the cedar corral, and the bull we can keep in the round pen. There's roundup bedrolls in the tack room and plenty of room in the loft to camp out."

By the time Lynda, Heidi, and Wendy staked out the loft into "boys" room and "girls" room, Brady and Tyler had put up the horses. Debra Jean Cartier turned down Brady's offer to carry her up the loft ladder. She opted to spend the night in the van.

Lynda and the girls stood at the barn door watching as Brady and Tyler tried to get R-43 to leave the trailer for the expanse of a dark and ominous round pen. Brady beat on the side of the trailer. He reached through the metal slats to prod the bull with a stick.

"He ain't budgin'," Tyler reported.

"We need Lynda Dawn to yell. That's the only time he's moved quick all afternoon," Brady mumbled as he reached inside the trailer and tried to pop the bull on the nose with his rope. "C'mon! Get outa there! Yeeahh!"

Heidi nudged Lynda. "Why don't you go over there and scream?"

"That was a death scream. I just can't come up with one of those any time I want."

"Maybe you could," Wendy encouraged. "Mom's pretty good at knowing how to get our attention any time she wants."

"I don't know anything about animals," Lynda protested.

"Come on, let's hear your best shot," Wendy urged. Carrying the lantern, she led Heidi and Lynda over to the round pen.

With Brady and Tyler still poking, prodding, and yelling at R-43, Lynda marched near the trailer. She looked back at the girls. They nodded. She took a long, slow, deep breath, shook her finger, and screamed at the top of her voice, "Bull, get out of that trailer, and get out of there right now!"

Brady and Tyler turned and gave her a silent stare.

Capt. Patch and Margarita cowered down in the dirt.

Heidi and Wendy burst out in hysterics.

And R-43 meekly backed out of the trailer and trotted to the far side of the round pen.

Brady drove the truck and trailer forward. Tyler closed the gate. Lynda watched with her mouth open.

"She's got him buffaloed," Tyler hooted as they met back at the barn door. "He's decided that she's boss."

"I think he's got delicate eardrums," Brady teased. "Come on, gang, time to get some rest." He tugged Lynda back inside the barn as the others followed.

"Are you saying I have a piercing voice when I scream or yell?"

"Yep. And that's a mighty good quality when your nearest neighbor's going to be twelve miles away."

"You said ten."

"Whatever."

◆ ◆ ◆

Pancakes were served on paper plates at the back door. Lynda felt uncomfortable wearing the same clothes as the previous day. "We will have baths tonight, won't we?" she quizzed.

"Yep. They've got a big bunkhouse in Sheridan. Showers and everything. Think I'll wear one of those new shirts after we get scrubbed up."

"Which one?"

"The green one."

"Good. I'll wear a green blouse tomorrow."

"Why?"

"So we won't clash."

"Are we going to have to start coordinating all our clothing?"

"Certainly. But don't worry," she said smiling, "I'll have a clothing selection chart for each week."

Brady's mouth dropped open, and he scratched the back of his head. "You know, I don't have any idea what it's like to get married to a New York City book editor."

"Chill off, cowboy, I was just spinning your rowels."

"I hope you have lots of browns and blues."

"You're going to have one less blue shirt."

"Oh?"

"I'm burying that shirt. It's the third day in a row you've worn it."

"Fourth."

"I look forward to getting off the road and into our house where we can have some kind of normal routine."

"Normal?"

"Washing clothes, eating meals—things like that."

"I'm looking forward to turning west today. It's sort of like we're finally getting closer to Jackson with every mile."

"Did you find out about this Beaver Creek?"

"Yeah, Duane pointed me right to it. But it's mostly all private property and fenced in. He can't figure out why Cindy would be goin' there."

"Neither can we." Lynda tossed her empty paper plate into a large black plastic sack.

"That's what I told him."

"Did you ever consider that maybe Cindy's not going to Beaver Creek? Perhaps she's just trying to get us off her track."

Brady stooped and brushed straw off the legs of his Wranglers. "Yeah, I considered that."

"And?"

"Well, if she's there and needs help, we'll find her. If she's trying to dump us, then let's pray the Lord's protection on her and go get ready for a wedding. It's mighty hard to help someone who won't let you."

"Is Beaver Creek a town or something?"

"Nope. Just a crick. But Duane did tell me about one place where they hold a Mountain Man Rendezvous ever' year. It's near some Indian historic places."

"What do you mean, historic places?"

"Old camp sites, sun dance grounds—things like that."

"You think Cindy's gone there?"

"I've given up tryin' to figure her out. But she does know quite a lot about Indian history."

"None of this makes sense to me, Brady. She's chasing down bikers and knows we're on her trail, so she heads to Nebraska? What does that have to do with anything?"

"You're the one who edits fiction."

"This is getting too weird for fiction." Lynda scrunched down and glanced at herself in the sideview mirror on Cartier's van. "Does my hair look all right?"

"It looks great, darlin'. Straw gives you that hearty cowgirl look."

"Straw? Really?"

"Just a little. Darlin', did you ever try braiding your hair?"

"No, it's still too short for a decent braid." *And don't tell me it would look as "purdy as a bronc rein."*

"That's too bad," he said. "I bet it would look as purdy as a bronc rein on a good buckin' horse."

"Are we going to be leaving soon?"

"As soon as we get this circus train loaded up."

◆ ◆ ◆

Brady rolled down the window of the Dodge pickup and waved his arm out at the hillside. "Would you believe this country? This is Nebraska, the Cornhusker state. Where's the corn? Where's the irrigated farmland? Mountains. Evergreen trees. Look at those logs—those are Ponderosa pines. I don't believe this!"

"You mean to tell me there are some places in the West where Brady Stoner has never gone?"

"This is not the West! This is Nebraska! Sure, there are some cattle ranches along the North Platte, and everyone's heard of the Sand Hills. But this is like the Black Hills or something. It's beautiful."

Lynda scooted closer to Brady, and his right arm slipped around her. "So what exactly are we looking for?"

"A green Cadillac."

"Do we look in the trees or along the road or where? Brady, there aren't even any houses back here."

"But there's a road."

"A dirt road."

"Hey, we live on a dirt road, remember?"

"I live in a sixth floor condo in Manhattan, at least until Saturday. You think the Cadillac will be out here on the road?"

"Probably not. We'll drive a loop through these mountains. Duane drew me a map. If we don't see any trace of Cindy, we'll be on our way to the ranch. I started out tryin' to help her out of a jam, but now it's like she's stringin' us along. I'm really gettin' tired of this." Brady repeatedly rapped his fingers on the silver-colored steering wheel.

"Is Brady Stoner losing his cool?"

"I don't like being manipulated, especially by pushy women."

"Like me?"

"No, no, darlin', I like bein' manipulated by you."

"So I'm a pushy woman, am I?"

"Darlin', you can push, pull, poke, hug, kiss, snuggle, or do anything you want."

"Okay, you squirmed out of that one, cowboy."

"But I still don't know what to do about Cindy."

"Pray about it."

"What?"

"Let's pray about it."

"What's prayer got to do with it?"

"It just dawned on me that we don't like playing Cindy's game because we want to play our own game."

Brady pulled his arm away from her shoulder and reached down and shifted into a lower gear. "We have a game?"

"Not a game but our own agenda. What we want to know is the Lord's agenda. We want to be headed to Jackson; Cindy wants us traipsing out here, but what does the Lord want?"

Brady was silent for several moments as they continued to circle through the small green meadows along Beaver Creek and into the pine-covered hills. "Lord," he finally began, "Lynda Dawn is right. Help us do the right thing. Show us what You want us to do with the next four days. Maybe . . . maybe we need a sign or something."

"Brady, stop the rig!"

"I'm praying!"

"I know, but I think your prayer was answered."

"What do you mean?"

"You asked for a sign, right? Look over there!"

"The paper plate stapled to a fence post?"

"What's it say?"

"'BB & CLS —' What's that all about?"

"CLS . . . Cowboy's Love Slave?" Lynda suggested.

"BB—that's the rodeo code for bareback rider."

"It's a sign!" she reiterated.

"But when I prayed for a sign," Brady stammered, "I didn't mean a sign."

"There's no road up that mountain. What are we supposed to do now?" she asked.

Brady waved at a barren dirt turnout about 1,000 feet ahead on the right. "I'll park up there by the crick, and we'll hike back and check this out."

Cartier and Wendy volunteered to stay with the rigs and livestock. Brady and Lynda led Heidi, Tyler, Capt. Patch, and Margarita back up the dirt road to the paper plate.

"Where do we go from here, Uncle Brady?"

"Well, Heidi-girl, I'm not sure. Look at this little valley. It's beautiful. Plenty of green grass, fresh water in the crick, and pine-covered mountains. This can't be Nebraska. We must have taken a wrong turn at Lusk."

"Hah! That's what they all say," Lynda replied. "Do you suppose there's another paper plate marker up on that mountain?"

"Only one way to find out," Brady replied. "Tyler, I'll lead the way, but I want you at the end of the line. I don't want trouble sneakin' up on us from behind."

Tyler dropped back behind the ladies. "What kind of trouble you expectin'?"

"Who knows? Someone must be running cattle in here. I don't want some protective mama cow thinkin' we're sneakin' up on her baby."

"We could always have Miss Lynda Dawn scream," Tyler teased. "That would keep them cows at a distance."

"Am I going to have to live with that label the rest of my life?"

"It's a compliment, darlin'. Here's a city gal that can work cattle. It's a little unconventional, sure, but she tells them who's boss in no uncertain terms."

"She could always get a job for a rodeo contractor. She could just yell the arena clear," Tyler bantered.

Under a clear blue June sky they trooped across the slightly damp foot-tall grass. The slight drift of wind from the northwest hinted cool, and Lynda occasionally rubbed her bare arms. The soft ground turned rocky as they reached the timberline. Last season's pine needles wove themselves into a carpet of brown around granite outcroppings that looked like scattered chairs after a dance.

Brady halted near a pile of barren rock big enough to build a cabin with. "Do you guys see any more signs?"

"Nothing so far," Heidi replied.

"How far should we go in this direction?" Lynda asked.

"I've been wonderin' the same thing. If Cindy just wanted to get us off the trail, this would do it."

"She had to be here recently to put up that sign on the road," Lynda suggested.

"Or she could have put it up two weeks ago before this whole thing began."

"She knew we would follow? We didn't even know that."

"Maybe she has friends out this way and called ahead to set up a decoy," Brady offered.

"Or a trap," Tyler added dramatically. "Did you ever read *The Ambush of Waco McGraw*?"

"Is that one of Anthony Shadowbrook's River Breaks Series?"

"Yep. See, Waco is chasin' the Rupert brothers and can't

find the trail. But being a former army scout, he finally spots a tiny piece of cloth from a shirt that Burleigh Rupert was wearin', and he knows he's on the right trail."

"Is this going anywhere?" Heidi asked.

"Well, Waco was thankin' the Lord for this sign when he stumbles into Desperation Canyon and is ambushed by the Ruperts."

"You mean they purposely left that little clue?"

"Yep. But he got so excited with his ability to track that he walked right into their trap."

"What happened to him?"

"He took a slug in the left arm and another in the thigh, but he did manage to lead them down."

"Oh!"

"Shot 'em right between the eyes, he did."

"Are you sayin' this could be a trap?" Heidi asked.

Tyler shrugged. "Could be."

"Why would Cindy want to trap us?" Lynda asked.

"Maybe she *did* read your kill-fee letter and has decided to get even," Brady replied.

"The letter came back unopened. Undeliverable," Lynda insisted. "She has no idea about the book. This is something completely separate. Come on!"

They climbed another 200 feet higher before stopping again. Lynda put her hands on her hips and stretched her back. "There's nothing up here, Brady."

"Looks that way. Let's hike to the crest anyway."

"The last time we hiked to the crest there were bikers below," she reminded him.

"Too remote for bikers. They won't go anywhere they can't ride to."

"What do you expect to find up here, Mr. Stoner?"

"A good view, soon-to-be Mrs. Stoner, a very good view, if nothing else."

"I think that's the spot for a view." Tyler pointed to a granite spire on the crest of the mountain.

"Let's hike up there and take a look." Brady turned back and offered Lynda his hand. "You doin' all right, darlin'? Cowboy boots weren't made for hikin'."

"I'm doing okay. Just a little winded. The only time I have to hike like this is when the elevator breaks down at the office."

"What floor do you work on?" Heidi asked.

"The twelfth," Lynda panted.

"How many are there?"

"Twenty-four."

"Wow, I didn't know your publishing house was that big!" Heidi gasped.

"It isn't. All of our offices are on the twelfth and fourteenth floors."

"What's on the thirteenth floor?" Tyler asked.

"There isn't a thirteenth floor. It skips from twelfth to fourteenth. No one wants to rent office space on the thirteenth floor of a high rise."

"Hey," Brady called, "climb up here, you guys. Look at this view! If you look through that gate in the mountains, I bet you can see all the way to Wyomin'."

"It's beautiful!" Lynda sighed. "I think I like Nebraska."

"Wow, look down there!" Heidi yelped. "There's our rigs. I wonder if Wendy and Doc can see us?" She began to wave and then shaded her eyes. "I can't tell if they see us."

"You know, if I was a band of Sioux camped in that valley, I'd keep one scout up here to warn of anyone coming into the area. You'll have to tell Estaban or Shadowbrook to write a book about this place."

"No one tells those two what to write." Lynda inched her way a little closer to the edge of the bluff. "I'm glad we hiked up here, but we didn't find one thing that gives us a clue about Cindy."

"We could have misread that sign on the fence post. Maybe it stood for a wedding reception for Butch Benson and Claudia Louise Sandini."

"Who?" Tyler quizzed. He tried to move over next to Heidi, but Brady nonchalantly stepped between them.

"There wouldn't be a wedding reception up here, Uncle Brady!"

"We could keep marchin' north—the direction the sign pointed. But if we haven't found anything by now, then the whole thing is too obscure anyway."

"So what do we do now?" Lynda asked.

"I was just thinkin', ma'am, why don't we swing up to Montana and unload some of this baggage. Then how about you and me drivin' to Jackson Hole and gettin' married?"

"This weekend?"

"Yep."

"I'll have to check my calendar."

"Sure hope you can make it."

"I've been wanting to do something like this for several years, but I could never find anyone with the same goal."

"Looked around quite a bit, did you?"

"Oh, you know . . . whenever I had a chance."

"Come on, you two." Heidi grimaced. "You're starting to sound really weird. Let's head back down. Tyler and I will lead the way."

"Tyler can lead on his own. You walk behind him," Brady lectured.

"Uncle Brady!"

They had descended from the granite point but were still on the crest of the mountain when they heard the dogs barking.

"I hope they didn't find a skunk!" Lynda said.

Brady glanced back over his shoulder. "Or a porcupine. All we need is a couple of dogs with quill mustaches. Go on down. I'll get the dogs."

"I'm sticking with you, cowboy," Lynda insisted.

Heidi peered back up the mountain, bare arms folded across her chest. "You two aren't going to sneak up there and make out, are you?"

"The thought never crossed our minds!" Brady laughed.

Lynda lifted her right arm and sniffed at her wrist. *It crossed my mind, cowboy. It definitely crossed my mind! This would have been a good day for something a whole lot stronger than Paris Mist.*

Brady and Lynda trailed the sound of barking dogs to a tree-covered rocky bluff several hundred yards to the west. Sometime, years before, a huge slice of the granite bluff had flaked off, leaving a pile of boulders and rock the size of a small swimming pool. Trees surrounded the rock, and limbs from the evergreens drooped over the rocks and shaded them.

Capt. Patch and Margarita pranced beneath one of the trees that leaned over the rocks, barking at something in the tree.

Brady broke into a trot. "Did they tree a raccoon?"

Lynda kept a slower pace. By the time she caught up to Brady, he was staring at the trees around the rock pile at the base of the outcropping.

"What's all that stuff in the trees? Are those ribbons tied up there, or did they . . . Brady, look over here! It's a—a—"

"A homemade bow and arrow? Look at those little pouches tied to the limbs."

"What's in there?"

"Tobacco, I would imagine," Brady said.

"Tobacco?"

"I rodeoed with Lincoln Tallman who was a Sioux from the Standing Rock Reservation. When his grandfather died, he went home to tie a tobacco pouch on his grave and plant seeds."

"A sacrifice to pagan gods?"

"Not really. It's more like showing respect for the dead.

Symbolically, it gave the deceased something to put in his pipe as he headed for the next world—or something like that."

"You mean someone's buried beneath the rocks?"

"I reckon so. See the four colored ribbons over there?"

"Red, yellow, black, and white?"

"Yeah, those represent the four winds."

"How about the bells? That seems to be what the dogs are barking at."

"I don't know about those. But this guy must have been important. Look over there. That's a hand-carved walking stick."

"It looks new. You think someone was just buried here?"

"No, look at the moss on these rocks. They haven't been moved for a long time."

Lynda stepped toward the base of one of the trees. "They're littered with tiny ribbons and pouches."

Brady squatted down and patted the dogs silent. "A long time ago. Darlin', those are scrubby-looking cedar trees. I bet they're a hundred years old, and they were planted in a straight line."

"Planted? You mean they didn't just grow here?"

"We haven't seen one cedar on this whole mountain, and the ones we did see back down the road had straight trunks."

"What does that mean?"

"I told you Lincoln went to plant seeds at his grandfather's grave."

"Yes?"

"Cedar seeds. From some kind of tree that grows in the Black Hills."

"So you think someone was buried here a hundred years ago, and someone keeps leaving things as a memorial?"

"Yeah."

"Who?"

"I don't know. I didn't even know these mountains existed, let alone what happened here."

Lynda reached out to touch one of the pouches hanging on the tree limb and then pulled her hand back. "What does all this have to do with Cindy?"

"I don't know. I told you Cindy always knew a lot about Indians, but I just figured it was from her grandma who was half Cheyenne . . . or some plains tribe. I don't remember. Anyway, I have a feeling she knows what this is, but I don't."

Lynda stopped to gaze at the hand-carved walking stick propped in the rocks. "Didn't you tell me when we were at Fort Robinson Historical Site that Crazy Horse was killed there?"

"Yeah."

"Well, maybe this is where he was buried," Lynda announced.

"No one knows where he was buried. I read that on a plaque over at the Crazy Horse Memorial south of Mt. Rushmore. It said his parents hid his body so that no one could dig it up and get the reward money. The hunt for his burial place has gone on for over a hundred years."

"Maybe this is it."

"Now that, Ms. Lynda D. Austin, senior editor for Atlantic-Hampton, is a startling thought."

"Brady, I don't think we should be here. Whoever is buried is very important to some other culture than ours. It's a special place for them."

"I agree with you, darlin'. I don't know if this place is demonic or sacred, but it's surely not our place." He turned away from the rock pile. "Come on, dogs."

"Maybe some Christians come up here, too." Lynda pointed to a white cotton pouch tied to a tree limb. "Look at that one. It has 'Gal 6:7' marked on the outside."

Brady stepped toward the cedar and reached up for the little cloth sack, no bigger than his fist. "'Do not be deceived. God cannot be mocked. A man reaps what he sows.' Isn't that what Galatians 6:7 says?"

"Brady, don't touch that! It's not right to . . ."

He jerked it off the limb and stepped over to her.

"Why did you do that?"

"What's that symbol under 'Gal 6:7'?"

"A double diamond? That's us! You think this is what Cindy wanted us to find?"

Brady unwrapped the cloth pouch.

"What's in there?"

"A key."

"What kind of key?" Lynda pressed.

"An old worn General Motors key."

"To the Cadillac?"

"Maybe."

"What does the note say?"

"It's hard to follow—on the back of the cloth."

"Read it to me."

"CH is still waiting for justice."

"CH?"

"Crazy Horse, I suppose."

"Then this is his—"

Brady continued to read. "'But I won't wait that long. No vengeance, merely justice. HR 1-92.'"

"Vengeance? Justice? Brady, she's after the bikers, isn't she?"

"Yeah, but I don't have any idea why she wants us to follow her around."

"What does HR 1-92 mean?"

"Post office route #1 . . . and box #92."

"Where? She doesn't say where!"

"Along this road maybe. When we came through that pass, there were two mail boxes. The one I could read was #142."

"Brady, if Cindy's not in trouble and just wants to divert us from Jackson, then I want to go get married. I've got better things to do than be a witness to a woman's fanatic vengeance."

"I'm beginning to think you might be right. All of this is just so she'll have an audience."

"Then we're headed to the ranch?"

"Today's Tuesday, isn't it?"

"Yes."

"We can still get to the ranch by tomorrow and make Jackson by Thursday night. When are Kelly and Nina arriving?"

"By Friday noon."

"Great! We'll be able to relax in Jackson for a day or two before the wedding."

"I'd really, really like that."

Brady led Lynda and the dogs down the mountain. "What do you think that key means?"

"I have no idea. Cindy seems to be getting more and more cryptic. I keep expecting Hercule Poirot or Jessica Fletcher to step into the scene and solve this mess."

When they reached the others, they spent ten minutes explaining.

"So you think Crazy Horse was buried up there?" Cartier asked.

"I don't know, but I think there are some people who believe that."

"Are we really going to your ranch?" Wendy asked.

"Yep!"

"But Mom's supposed to meet us in Rock Springs!"

"Well . . ." Lynda slipped her hand into Brady's. "Let's send you four in the van to meet Heather in Rock Springs, and Uncle Brady and I will swing up to the ranch and then meet you all in Jackson—Fridayish or so."

"Darlin', that's a good plan, but it won't work."

Lynda dropped his hand. "Why?"

"We've got to take both R-43 and Early to Bed to the ranch, and they won't haul in the same trailer."

"So we do have to go up to Montana?" Heidi asked.

"If I can get ahold of your mother before she leaves St. George, maybe we could meet somewhere else."

"Maybe we could meet at our Aunt Jean's in Cody," Wendy suggested.

"When we get to a pay phone, I'll try to call her. . . . Let's load 'em up, gang. Doc, are you doing all right with that troupe of teenagers?"

"Hey, they're a great bunch."

"Doc's got three rules," Wendy announced.

"What's that?"

"Have fun, keep your seat belts on, and she gets to pick the music."

"Well, if you need to boot any of 'em out, Lynda and I can always haul a couple. Right, darlin'?"

No! We haven't had ten minutes of quality time together in a week except in that truck, and I'm not about to forfeit what few minutes we have to discuss things privately. Just me and you, cowboy, that's it! No more. Zero. None. Nada. Zilch.

Lynda mustered up her best making-the-peace voice. "Oh, sure, we've got room."

Please, no—please, no.

"I've learned more about teen culture in the last six days than I have in the last six years. This is a riot. And to think, I could be back at the lab editing grant proposals. For a stay-at-home person like myself, this is quite an adventure. This gang is definitely riding with me." Cartier winked at Lynda.

Yes! I like this woman! Lynda mouthed the words, "Thank you."

With a minimum of dust, the caravan reentered the dirt and gravel road heading east. The pine-tree-lined road began to swing around the mountains toward the north.

"There aren't any houses or ranches out here. Is this government property?"

"There are some houses in there. We just can't see them. See those mailboxes? There must be a house or two up on that mountain somewhere."

"What number was on that box?"

"120."

"If this is HR 1, then we might be getting close to Cindy's next clue. If it's not out of the way, let's check it out."

"Oh, sure. We're this close—we might as well. But here's the deal," Brady explained. "We're headed to the ranch. If Cindy has time for all these games, she's doin' all right."

"Brady, I'm really glad we're going to the ranch. I've been real nervous about it for the past two weeks."

"You're worried that it will look just as bad as it did last fall?"

"I guess." Lynda bit her bottom lip. "Sometimes, if I think about it a lot, I almost panic. It reminds me of Central Park at night."

"How in the world do you see any similarity?"

"Because you don't know what's out there, but you can pretty well count on getting hurt."

"But that's the point." Brady's voice rose with each word. "There's nothin' at the Double Diamond—only horses, cows, dogs—and you and me."

"And snakes, wolves, coyotes, drunken hunters, ding-a-ling loners, and para-military militia."

"Now, darlin'," Brady drawled with deliberate slowness, "don't you be talkin' about the neighbors before you've met them." The classic dimpled smile returned to his face.

Lynda stared at Brady. "Have you met the neighbors?"

"The ones that live fourteen miles away?"

"You told me seven miles!"

"Oh, those neighbors. Yep, I met them . . . and I like 'em.

Good cattle folks. Remember that twelve-year-old girl that shot the tires off my rig last year?"

Lynda raised her eyebrows. "They are our closest neighbors?"

"Yep. They think we're movin' up from Texas."

"Texas? Who told them we were from Texas?"

"Your buddy from the cafe in Lewistown, Emmit Earl, told them that his good friend, Miss Lynda Dawn from Austin, was marrying some Idaho yahoo and taking over the Double Diamond. I think ol' Emmit has sort of adopted you."

"Well, buckaroo, just remember, I do have friends in the area! So you'll need to watch your behavior."

"Yes, ma'am. Do I need to watch it right now?"

Perfume. I should have used Nueva Amor.

Brady patted the pickup seat between them, and Lynda scooted over. *Hopefully I don't still smell like that barn we slept in. On the other hand, maybe he likes the smell of a barn.*

"I bet you can't guess what I was thinkin'," he challenged.

"Is it rated G, PG, PG-13, R, or X?"

"Darlin', I hope you're not disappointed, but it was strictly a G-rated thought. I was just thinkin' about all these unexpected folks showin' up at the weddin'. Jackson's full of tourists in the summer. I hope they can all find a room for the night."

"We are not sharing our room, Brady Stoner!"

"That's something we fully agree on. Did I tell you that I reserved the room at the lodge with the Teton view and the hot tub on the balcony?"

"You did?" She slipped her arm into his and leaned her head on his shoulder.

"'Course, I could only afford it for thirty minutes. We get it between 3:30 and 4:00 in the morning."

Lynda sat straight up. "What!"

"Just teasin' you, darlin'."

She cozied back up to him and kissed the two-day stubble of beard on his cheek. "Are your thoughts still G-rated?"

"Eh . . . not exactly."

Lynda pushed his cowboy hat back and kissed his ear gently. "I really love you, Brady Stoner."

He threw his left foot on the clutch and his right on the brake and leaned back against the seat. "Darlin', we've got to stop!"

"Wh-why?" she sputtered. "We are getting married in three days."

He waved his hand toward a mailbox. "No—we've got to stop at this place. Look, it's box #92."

"Oh . . . yeah." Lynda let out a long, deep breath.

The faded hand-painted sign under the mailbox read: "Milton Kaylecki's Plumbing."

"A plumber lives back here? Where's his customer base? There isn't a town for fifty miles!"

"Twenty-five miles."

"But—a plumber?"

"And gemstones." Brady was looking in his sideview mirror. "Did Doc see us turn off?"

"Yep, they're right behind us."

Lynda tried to glance back in the sideview mirror.

"Hey," Brady exclaimed, "there's a sight you don't see ever' day. A commode-lined driveway."

Lynda spied the mostly white discarded toilets that lined both sides of the dirt lane. "This is incredible!"

"I guess ol' Milt really is a plumber."

"Why would anyone destroy the beauty of such a place?"

"Maybe he likes it. Ever'one of them represents money in the bank. Besides, they do make great planters. Pansies in the tank, petunias in the bowl—it's quite colorful."

"Brady, this is the tackiest thing I've ever seen in my life!"

"To each his own. It's a great country, isn't it? Ever' man can just be himself."

"And every wife can be humiliated."

"Chances are, she's the one who planted the flowers."

A white clapboard-sided house was almost out of sight behind trees, and a very cluttered metal-sided building served as garage, office, and warehouse for Milt's Plumbing and Gemstones.

"Look, Brady! That's Cindy's car! Maybe she's here."

"It's her car, all right." Brady parked the rig in the clearing and stepped out of the pickup, waiting for Lynda to scoot over and follow. Cartier's van pulled up and parked beside them.

Wendy rolled down the window. "Did you see that driveway, Uncle Brady?"

"Picturesque, isn't it?"

"Is that Cindy's car?" Cartier called out.

"Yep. We'll check it out."

"And we'll wait here," Wendy insisted.

With Capt. Patch and Margarita investigating the petunias, Brady and Lynda hiked to the open door of the garage/plumbing office. A middle-aged man wearing a faded University of Nebraska baseball cap and coveralls walked out to greet them.

"Howdy, folks, anything I can do for you? Need some plumbin'?"

"Eh, no," Brady began.

"Too bad. We're runnin' a special on pink low rises."

Lynda glanced around at the yard. *A special? Pink toilets? You don't have any customers out here. How can you have a special?*

"How about gemstones? I've got Bisbee turquoise 40 percent off for a limited time only."

Lynda absently rubbed her hands up and down her jeans. *This guy is delusional. There's no business out here.*

"We do need a little information," Brady responded. "That

green Cadillac belongs to a friend of ours, and we were wonderin' if she's still around?"

"Miss Cindy! You know Miss Cindy? Well, I'll be! Didn't reckon you'd be by so soon. Have you got the key?"

Brady reached into his pocket and pulled out the General Motors key wrapped in the white cloth. "Yep."

"There she is—you can drive her off."

"Cindy's not here?" Brady pressed.

"Oh, no, she left last night."

"How did she leave if her car's here?"

"She bought a pickup truck from me. Said some cowboy would come by with the key and drive off the green Cadillac. If that key works in the ignition, I reckon you're the cowboy."

"Where did she go?" Lynda questioned.

"She didn't say, but she did ask how long it would take to drive to Mt. Rushmore."

"Mt. Rushmore?" Lynda exploded. "You mean the monument?"

"Well, by golly, I do know where she headed. I reckon she's on her way to Rushmore." Milton's wide smile revealed his tobacco-yellowed teeth.

A woman around fifty with bleached blonde hair and wearing a knee-length house dress came out of the office and scurried toward them. She held a small blue scrap of paper in her hand.

"Lola, these folks came for the Caddy. They're friends of Miss Cindy's."

"Good," the woman barked in a voice meant to quiet ocean waves on a stormy day. "Maybe they can tell me if this is any good. That Cadillac stays in this yard until I find out if you've been swindled or not."

"Swindled?" Lynda asked.

Milton grabbed the paper and shook it. "I sold her my 1982

Ford pickup. She paid for it by signing over a check. We were going to the bank this afternoon to see if it was any good."

"She led this silly old man around by the nose and swindled him, that's what she did," Mrs. Kaylecki insisted.

"Now, Mother, that's not so. She was just a gal a little down on luck and needin' a helpin' hand."

"Can I see the check?" Brady asked.

He handed it to Brady. "You think it's good?"

Brady whistled. "My-oh-my, yes. I do believe it's good. In fact, Lynda Dawn is the one who issued the check."

"No foolin'?" Mrs. Kaylecki replied.

"See, Mama!" Milt triumphed.

"Well, I was mighty suspicious when I saw those words *kill fee* written on the corner of a New York check," Mrs. Kaylecki replied. "Sounded like Mafia money to me."

"What?" Lynda plucked the check out of Brady's hand. "That's our company check, but—but—but I've got the kill fee in the envelope in my purse!"

Brady narrowed his eyes. "Are you sure?"

Lynda pushed her dark glasses to the top of her head. "I certainly know what I stuffed into the envelope."

"When you got it back, did you open it to see if the check was still there?"

"Of course not. It said, 'Undeliverable. Moved. No forwarding address.' The enveloped was sealed. She couldn't—"

"She did. She knows about the reject. She had the check all this time."

"If she had the check, then what's in my envelope?" Lynda queried.

"That, Lynda Dawn Darlin', is a very good question."

SEVEN

R ead it to me again."
Lynda rolled down the window and let the Nebraska summer breeze blow her hair. "It just says, 'It won't have a boring ending now. Come and see. Pray for me. C. L.'"

"A boring ending? Did you tell Cindy that her life story had a boring ending?"

"Of course not. It's not a critique of her life anyway; it's an evaluation of a book about part of her life."

"But you insinuated the book was boring. A lady who has lived the past five years in daily trauma, fear, and flashbacks after a vicious attack is told that all of that is boring?"

"Brady, we talked about that in New York. The manuscript lacked purpose, focus, and punch. No matter how neat a person Cindy is, no matter how much she wants to tell her story, people would not read it. That's not a critique on Cindy's life. It's a commentary on what people read."

"How can you be so sure? I'd read it," Brady insisted.

"Yes, and so would I—and so would all of Cindy's friends. How many copies would that make?"

"Eh . . . maybe fifty?"

"Precisely. And we like a first printing to be at least 25,000."

Brady rubbed his hand across the stubble of his beard. "Then you shouldn't have encouraged her in the first place."

"Stoner, you're laying a guilt trip on me. You're setting me up to carry the entire blame if anything happens to Cindy while she's on this spree. Well, I won't carry that load, buckaroo. That's not fair. Sometimes life is like a rodeo. You draw a horse, and you take a chance. As far as I know, no one wins the buckle just because he got hurt the worst. Cindy drew a rank ride and got hurt bad. I have shed tears for her on more than one occasion, and I'll probably shed more in the future. But that doesn't mean her story will automatically translate into print. Maybe the Lord has some other use for her story." Lynda reached into her purse for a tissue and wiped her eyes.

"Darlin', don't get me wrong; it's just that I can't figure out why you couldn't have—"

"Brady," Lynda sucked in air to try to keep from crying, "I do my job the very best I know how. I work hard at it. I am not insensitive to the feelings of others. And I will not have you or any other person label me otherwise!"

"No, no, darlin' . . . what I meant was—"

"Look," Lynda sobbed, "I feel crummy about this. But it has to be done. I have to live with myself. I have spent my life pushing for excellence; it's the only way I know how to operate. Can't you understand that?"

"Wait a minute, darlin'—come over here." He patted the pickup seat near him.

"I don't want to come over there," she sniffled.

"Soon-to-be Mrs. Stoner, I really need you over here."

"Can I blow my nose first?"

"Wipe your eyes, blow your nose, put on more perfume, but please scoot on over here."

She flipped down the visor and stared into the vanity mirror, carefully wiping the tears out of the corners of her eyes. *Stoner, I have never given you a critique of your bareback riding. Don't tell me how I ought to operate as an editor.* She blew her nose and then pulled out a small green bottle and splashed Vanilla Dream on her neck. The aroma of the perfume seemed to relax the tension she felt. After shoving everything back into her purse, she flipped up the visor and scooted next to him.

"Lynda Dawn Darlin', I need to apologize. I know I sounded unjustly critical. I had no intention of makin' you cry."

"And I had no intention of crying."

"I think you're a wonderful editor. Darlin', I'm hurtin' so much for Cindy that I forgot about how I'm grievin' you. I'm really scared that Cindy's going to get herself in serious trouble—either with a biker or the law. I know you're right. I just don't know what to do. Do you have any idea what it's like to spend your life as a person who's always there to help his friends—and then have to just sit and watch?"

She slipped her fingers into his. "I really hurt for Cindy, too. Why else would I give up the week before the wedding to traipse all over the West?"

He raised her hand to his mouth, and she felt his slightly chapped lips kiss her hand. "Are we making things worse by givin' her an audience?"

"I was wondering the same thing."

Brady loosened his grip and banged his fist lightly on the steering wheel. "I wish we could just catch up with her, have a real good talk and—and—"

"Pray with her?" Lynda posed.

"Yeah, that too. Did you ever think, darlin', how much simpler life would be if a person was totally self-centered? Just do whatever was best for you and tell the rest to get lost."

"Yes. But you and I know that would make life meaningless and shallow."

"There is nothing more boring than being stuck with no one but yourself," he concurred.

"Well, cowboy, this past week hasn't been boring. I've spent the week laughing and crying and everything in between. Well, not exactly everything." *Relax. Smile. Don't blush, Austin. Maybe he didn't catch that.*

"I know what you mean. You want to hear somethin' wild I've been thinkin' lately? I surely would like to take you to a drive-in where they were playin' a couple of borin' movies."

"A drive-in movie? Get real, Stoner, there aren't any of those left in the world."

"There's one still open about fifty minutes north of my folks' ranch in Idaho."

"Oh? Do you go there often?" She poked him below the ribs with her finger. Nothing but muscle.

"Not anymore. Not much since I was a teenager."

How does he do that? Eyes sparkle. Smile dimples. Voice tickles. Relax, Lynda-girl. Four more days. "Speaking of teens, I was surprised you let Tyler drive Cindy's car. I thought for sure I'd get stuck with it."

"Darlin', there is no way I'm goin' to let you out of this truck."

She kissed his cheek. "Good."

"'Course, I thought Heidi would never stop pitchin' a fit when I said she couldn't ride with him."

"I think you made a good point. If those bikers are looking for a gal in an old green Cadillac, you don't want them coming upon Heidi."

"That, of course, was only the second reason for makin' her ride with the Doc."

"Yes, well, I think the girls know a whole lot more about Uncle Brady than they ever did before."

"I'm glad babies start out little. Maybe I'll learn how to be a better daddy by the time they get to their teens."

Lynda began to snicker.

"What's the matter? What'd I say?"

"Can you imagine either one of us being parents?"

Brady joined in the laughter—then stopped.

"Darlin', before I met you, I couldn't imagine being a daddy, that's for sure. But now, actually, I can imagine it real vivid."

Lynda laid her head on his shoulder. "Cowboy, you are the sweetest-talking man I've ever met in my life. Every time . . . whoa!"

Brady swerved the truck to the right shoulder to miss a shining object in the dirt road.

Lynda straightened back up and peeked in the sideview mirror but could only see the horse trailer behind them. "What was that?"

"It looked like the handlebars off a motorcycle and maybe a few—"

"A motorcycle?" Lynda gulped.

Brady immediately slowed down and pulled over near the brush-tangled barbed-wire fence that lined the road. The green Cadillac pulled in behind them, followed by Cartier's van and horse trailer.

"You think it has something to do with Cindy?" she asked.

Brady crawled out of the truck and waited for Lynda. "Maybe. She didn't leave any clue except Mt. Rushmore. But this road is the quickest way to get there. She must have figured we'd drive this way."

Lynda hopped out and tucked the back of her pink short-sleeved blouse into her jeans. "Are we getting jumpy, or what?"

"Could be. Tell Tyler and the ladies what we're doin'. I'll go toss that handlebar out of the road if nothin' else."

Heidi had already slipped out of the van and was visiting with Tyler by the time Lynda reached the Cadillac. *Oh, to be young, long-legged, and tan!* When Lynda reached Doc Cartier's van, the window was rolled down.

"Is Brady worried about those motorcycle parts?" Cartier asked.

"Yes. This whole trek seems to get more bizarre every hour. Are you sure you wouldn't get more accomplished at Los Alamos?"

Dr. Debra Jean Cartier patted Lynda's hand. "Are you kidding? Next to that all-night ride on my dad's pony that I told you about, this trip has turned into the highlight of my life. I think you and Brady ought to sell tickets. You could make a bundle just letting us ordinary people travel along and watch."

"Actually it's not like this—"

"Darlin'!" Brady hollered from somewhere down the road. "Come quick. You've got to see this! It's totally incredible!"

"You were saying?" Cartier prodded.

"Eh . . . I'd better go see what he's yelling about."

Cartier turned to Wendy, who sat in the other front bucket seat. "Come on, Miss Martin, let's go see what kind of mess your Uncle Brady's in now!"

Lynda jogged to the spot in the road where she had seen the motorcycle handlebars. Brady waved at her from a clump of small cottonwood trees growing along a creek about fifty yards from the roadway. "Over here, darlin'. Come see what I found."

Lynda made her way along a trail of rather burnt-looking motorcycle parts that littered the weeds and grass.

"What happened?" she called out.

"I'm not sure, but I figure he'll tell us."

Brady pointed to where a black-jacketed man sat on the ground, leaning against a tree. He was secured by an enormous amount of gray duct tape. His boots were also taped together, and a small piece covered his mouth.

She bent low and stared at the man's angry brown eyes. "He's one of the bikers from Fort Laramie."

"Yep."

Lynda stood up and jammed her hands into the front pockets of her jeans. "I think he wants us to cut him loose."

"I reckon."

Heidi and Tyler trotted up. Wendy pushed Cartier's wheelchair across the packed dirt toward them.

"I presume he's had a run-in with Cindy LaCoste," Cartier called out as she rolled closer.

"That would be my guess," Brady agreed. "Either that or a pack of talented and tape-totin' timber wolves."

Tyler picked up a six-inch chunk of tire. "What happened to the bike?"

With the toe of his dark brown cowboy boot, Brady kicked a jagged part of a gas tank. "I think it blew up."

"On purpose, no doubt," Lynda suggested.

Brady pushed his hat back and stepped toward the bound man. "Let's see what this hombre has to say for himself."

The others huddled around the man with the wild brown eyes and shoulder-length hair as Brady slowly tugged the tape off his mouth.

The man gasped for breath and then screamed, "She blew up my bike!" His face and neck turned red.

"Was it Cindy?" Lynda asked.

"The woman's nuts. She should be committed before she kills someone—or someone kills her! Cut me loose. I've lost all circulation in my hands and feet."

"First, we want to find out what happened here," Brady insisted.

"Cut me loose or else!" The man began a string of profanities.

Brady immediately slapped the tape back over his mouth. "Listen, hombre, and listen carefully. I want to find out what happened. There's a good chance I'll cut that tape off of you. But if I hear one more curse, just one word, I'll drive off and leave you here taped to a tree, do you understand that?"

The man vigorously nodded his head.

Brady yanked the tape off this time.

The man said nothing.

"Hey," Wendy hollered. "He really is one of those guys from Fort Laramie! I remember him. This is the one who stormed over to the van."

"I don't need a whole da—"The man bit his lip and looked up at Brady. "A whole army standing around staring at me."

"We can all leave," Brady offered.

"No . . . look, this thing is nuts. I'll tell you about it. Cut me loose."

"You talk—then I'll cut you loose."

Some of the flush drained out of his face. He slumped back against the tree. "We were on our way up to Rally Week at Sturgis."

"That's not until August," Brady remarked.

"We like to take our time getting there."

"How charming—an all-summer camp-out," Lynda chided. "Just how do you finance such an extended vacation?"

"Oh, we, eh, sort of live off the land, you know."

"Not really."

"I'm thirsty. Have you got a beer?" the man asked.

Brady shook his head. "Nope. Finish your story."

"Well, anyway this one they call Crazy Cindy just keeps doggin' us. Like she knows our route. Other than the first time in Manitou Springs, she stays out of sight until she can pick us off one at a time."

Brady cut him off. "We know all of that. What we don't know is what happened here."

"The others decided to head right up to Deadwood. We've

got a campsite there we use ever' summer. They figured to set a trap for her rather than let her surprise them along the way."

"So what are you doin' in this place?"

"We surmised you all must know where she went, so I volunteered to trail you and scout out the situation."

"You were following us?" Lynda prodded. "And we didn't know it?"

"You ain't hard to follow. It's like trailin' a covered wagon train across the prairie. Except I figured you'd stop before dark last night. I didn't see you turn off and couldn't spot any trail in the dark. So I camped out near a creek a few miles back."

"In Beaver Valley?"

"I don't know what it's called. I don't even know where I am now. Anyway, when I got up this morning, I didn't know if you were behind me or ahead of me. So I figured I'd cruise along slow and see if I could pick up your trail."

Lynda pointed at the motorcycle parts around the field. "This just happened this morning?"

"I'm coastin' down this road when I notice a Ford pickup over here near these trees. The hood's up, and some dark-haired babe with a long braid is wearin' short shorts and tryin' to get the rig goin'."

"Dark hair?"

"Yeah . . . about your color." He pointed to Lynda. "Anyway, it wasn't the Cadillac or a sandy blonde, so I . . ."

"Wanted to help a lady in distress?" Lynda tugged her dark glasses down until they rested on the end of her nose.

"Eh, yeah. Well, she didn't even turn and look at me when I drove up. So I strolled over to her. I . . . you know, slipped my arm around her waist—"

"How sweet of you."

"As you can see, she clobbered me alongside the head with something. I don't know what she had in her hand. When I came to, my head was throbbin', and she had me taped to this tree. Her truck was out on the road, and she had two sticks of dynamite strapped to my bike—right out there in the clearin'."

"This dark-haired lady was Cindy LaCoste?" Brady quizzed.

"Oh, yeah, it was Crazy Cindy, all right. She was wearin' a wig. She set the whole thing up. She knew I was coming, but I don't know how she knew."

"Probably she was up on the rocky point when you drove into Beaver Creek Valley. You can see everything from up there," Heidi chimed in.

"Anyway . . . I start yellin' and screamin' at her, and she threatens to light the fuse if I don't tell her where the rest of the guys are headed. I figured it was all a bluff."

"Why would you think that?" Cartier pressed. "The woman's clearly a person of action."

"I still can't believe she did it. She lit that sucker and ran for the road. The dynamite exploded the gas tank, and the whole bike blew up like a bomb. I could have been killed! I never felt so helpless in my life!"

"Cindy has. One night years ago in the Arizona desert." Lynda looked over at Cartier and then at the girls. "You're lucky. I probably would have stuck the dynamite in your ears."

"I'll get even with her!"

"Even with her? She's not *even with you* yet. Not until you're in prison serving ten to twenty," Brady insisted.

"She can't prove nothin'."

Wendy picked up part of a black leather motorcycle seat. A white skull and crossed bones were on the side. She tossed it in the man's lap. "She proved she can get the best of you."

"So your buddies are campin' in the woods between Deadwood and Lead?" Brady pressed.

"Yeah, we got . . ." The man's voice trailed off. "Eh, we got several places in the Black Hills to camp. I'm not sure which one they'll choose."

Brady waved his arm. "Okay, let's load up."

"Hey, you've got to cut me loose."

Brady ignored the man. "Doc, you and Tyler honk when you're in your outfits. Wendy, make sure the dogs get loaded up."

While the others returned to the road, Lynda waited with Brady.

"You can't leave. You've got to cut me loose!" the man screamed. "You promised!"

"Did I promise that?" Brady asked Lynda.

"I believe you did."

There were two honks from the road.

"Well, I'm a mighty generous man. I don't know if you deserve to be cut . . . loose." Brady pulled out his pocketknife and sliced through the gray duct tape on the tree. The man hurriedly ripped the tape off his chest.

"My feet—cut it off my feet!"

"You can pull that off yourself. We've got to get going."

"Wait, you can't leave me out here. I need a lift to town!" The man frantically pulled on the wide gray tape around his ankles.

"You've got to be joking!" Lynda replied.

"Your best bet is to hitch a ride back to Las Vegas and hang around with losers like Joe Trent."

"But Joe's supposed to meet us in the Black Hills!"

Lynda stared at Brady's troubled brown eyes.

"Trent? Come on, darlin', we've got to catch up with Cindy!"

They scurried toward the roadway as the man pulled the last of the tape off his boots.

"Wait!" he screamed.

Lynda turned back to see him take two steps toward them and fall on his face.

"My legs are asleep," he yelled. "I can't walk!"

"If I were you, I'd just sit there until I felt better."

"It ain't right."

"I can't imagine what the basis of your ethical statement could be," Lynda mused.

"Hedonistic neo-utilitarianism, I reckon," Brady proposed.

"Wait! I can't believe you're going to leave me out here."

Brady glanced back at the man. "From time to time we all need to reevaluate our beliefs."

◆ ◆ ◆

Dust drifted high into a slightly cloudy Nebraska sky as the caravan worked its way out of the trees into the rolling prairie near the South Dakota line. Lynda glanced over her shoulder at the horse trailer. "Do you think he'll try to follow us?"

"He's not too bright, but I don't think even he would do that."

"Why not?"

"He can't go to the police because Cindy can accuse him of the Nevada attack. He can't show up on foot and tell the others she got the best of him. I figure he'll try to hike back to Las Vegas."

"Speaking of Vegas, why would Joe Trent come to the Black Hills?"

"I don't know. It's crazy. What in the world does Trent have to do with this bunch? He's like a noxious weed in the garden. Ever' year you dig it out; yet next season it comes back."

Lynda scooted over closer to Brady and began to rub the back of his neck. "Cindy's narrowed the gang down to four. I don't suppose she'll stop until she catches up with them all."

"But we know more about where they are than she does. He said he didn't tell her anything."

"She knew enough to go to Rushmore. Is that on the way to our ranch?"

"Yep. We have to go up there on our way to Interstate 90. Chances are we'll catch up with Cindy today. She can't be more than a couple hours ahead of us now."

Lynda stopped rubbing his neck but left her arm on his wide shoulders. "What are we going to say to her: 'Stop this foolishness and go home'?"

"I don't know, darlin'. Maybe we could invite her to the wedding." He let his right hand rest on her leg.

"I sent her an invitation last spring."

"Maybe you can tell her she's in the wedding party or something."

"Wedding party?" Lynda pulled her arm back from his shoulder. "That's been planned for months. My sister Meg will stand with me—your brother Brock with you. My brother William will walk me down the aisle. We don't need anyone else, and you know it."

"Well, if we had something for her to do, we might get her off this crusade."

"Brady, I'm not changing my wedding plans just to find something for someone to do!" She picked up his hand from her leg and plopped it back on the steering wheel.

"We'll think of somethin'." Brady put his hand back on her leg. "How about hirin' her to stay at the ranch with the livestock while we go down to Jackson?"

"Brady, I think Cindy is ticked with me." She shoved his hand out to her knee. "I really don't think she'll want to do anything for us. Besides, why would she quit this revenge quest? It's been quite successful so far."

"It's not revenge—it's justice," Brady corrected.

"I don't think so. Justice means you go to the police and file charges. Vengeance happens when you decide to even the score yourself."

"Cindy reported all of this to the police over five years ago. They haven't been able to do a thing."

"But when did she know which group was responsible? And why didn't she take that information to the police?"

"I don't know. But I surely aim to ask her."

"How long will it take us to get to Mt. Rushmore?"

"Depending on where we are . . . two . . . two and a half hours."

"Will we get to Sheridan tonight?"

"I don't see why not. Might be a little late."

"Brady, I want a hot shower and a clean bed tonight. No barns or bunkhouses."

"We've got to find a place where we can turn the animals out."

"You can just leave me at a motel. You go turn the animals out, or whatever."

"Are you gettin' worn out?" Brady's hand slipped up a little higher on her leg.

"I'm getting extremely nervous about the wedding. We don't seem to be getting any closer to Jackson."

"You afraid you'll miss it?"

"As long as I'm with you, I won't miss it. But we could really mess it up."

"Did I ever tell you how I dreamt about being late for our wedding?" He lifted his hand and put it back on the steering wheel.

"Yes, you did, and I don't want to talk about it." She tugged his hand back down to her leg.

◆ ◆ ◆

Lynda shoved her dark glasses to the top of her head and pointed. "I can't believe it! It's just like the pictures!"

"Amazing, huh? Every time I see Mt. Rushmore, I marvel at how someone could even come up with the concept—let alone pull it off." Brady reached back and slid the back window open. "Captain, come on!"

"What are you doing?"

"Dogs have to be kept on a leash. We'll have to leave them in the cab."

The dogs both cocked their heads but didn't move. "I don't think the Captain trusts you," Lynda observed.

"We have to get them in the cab before we move up the line to the entry. You try it. Call Margarita."

"She doesn't know her name yet," Lynda protested.

"Give it a try."

"This is dumb, Stoner. I had a cat for over a year, and he never once minded me."

"These aren't cats."

Lynda leaned back and called, "Margarita, bring the Captain, and come here. We, eh, need to talk to you two!"

Brady shook his head and grinned. "That's the dumbest thing I ever—"

The brown-faced dog hurdled through the open back window, followed by the black and white one with the patch over one eye.

"They did it!" Lynda squealed.

Brady slapped his knee. "You and animals—why you're a regular Dr. Do-Gooder."

"Dr. Doolittle."

"Whatever. Open the window a couple inches. Then shove that brass pin through the lock."

Lynda gave the orders. "Listen, dogs, you have to ride up here for a little while, but don't dig in the boxes of dishes, and stay off my duffel bag."

The Captain let out two barks, and both dogs settled down.

"He usually only barks once at me," Lynda remarked.

"Maybe he was answering for Margarita, too," Brady teased.

"Roll down your window, darlin'. Looks like the ranger takes the money over there."

A blonde in her mid-twenties wearing a dark green park service uniform and no makeup strolled up. "Well, if it isn't Brady and Lynda Dawn Stoner from Buffalo, Montana. How's everything on the Double Diamond?"

I can't believe it. Every good-looking woman in the West knows his first name. But how did she . . .

"I read your sign." The gal grinned and pointed to Lynda's side of the pickup. "It's getting a little dusty."

Okay, Austin, you were wrong. Just relax.

"It'll be just a minute. We've got to let a few rigs out first. Hey, are you the Brady Stoner that used to ride bareback?"

"Used to? I still do—I mean, until quite recently." He looked at Lynda like a scolded puppy.

"Did you take a kick in the head?" the gal added.

Lynda leaned back as the woman stuck her head in the window to talk to Brady. *I need more perfume. I bet rangers aren't allowed to wear it. Probably just bug repellant.*

"Have we met?" Brady asked.

"Nope. My name's Lacy, but you dated my sister one time down in Pueblo. Remember Kristi Carter? She used to barrel race."

Lynda found herself rapping her fingers on her knees. *I was right! Why am I not surprised?*

"Boy, I surely do. Kristi had the purdiest black . . ." He glanced over at Lynda. " . . . eh, horse I ever saw."

"He was sorrel," Lacy corrected.

"Yeah, that's what I meant. How's your sis?"

"She's doin' her internship at Denver General."

"You aren't the lil' sis that hid up in the tree when Kristi and me were parked in the driveway, were you?"

I don't want to hear this, Stoner!

"No, that wasn't me."

Good.

"That was my sister Jamie. She told me all about it. Like the time your shirt got ripped off on the chute, and you had to . . ."

Lynda pointed to a large truck and a flashing blue and white light. "What happened up there? Was there an accident?"

Lacy yanked her head out of the cab and glanced over her shoulder. "Oh, no accident. But it was exciting for us. You see those three motorcycles they're impounding? The sheriff arrested three guys from Las Vegas trying to sell five pounds of marijuana."

"Five pounds? At Mount Rushmore?"

"They were meeting some locals out of Rapid City, and I guess they figured no one would be suspicious in this crowd. Anyway, they hauled the guys off, and now they're loading up the bikes and taking them in for evidence."

"Just three guys—not four?" Brady asked.

"Only three. Do you know them?"

"No, but we ran across some suspicious guys on bikes yesterday."

"And there were four of them?"

"Five, but we left one in Nebraska," Brady said. "How did the sheriff find out about them?"

"Rumor around here is that some woman, one of the tourists here at the monument, phoned the sheriff's office." The ranger stepped back to look at the line behind them. "You traveling with that van and horse trailer?"

"Yeah, we've got a bull, and there are a couple horses in the other trailer. And the Cadillac in between," Brady announced.

The uniformed ranger glanced back at the line again. "Those two in the Caddy are chummy, aren't they?"

"What?" Brady's door flew open.

Lynda tugged hard on his blue shirt sleeve. A pickup leaving the parking lot had caught her attention. Her eyes met the driver's. "Brady! It's Cindy!"

"What?" By the time he looked up, the two-tone blue Ford had turned north on the entrance road. "Are you sure? It looks like she has dark hair."

"It's Cindy in a wig! Remember?"

Brady slammed his door. "Let's go!"

Ranger Lacy Carter stepped back away from the truck. "Aren't you coming in to see Mr. Rushmore?"

"Nope. Can I swing a U-turn between here and that gate?"

"Take it real slow," the ranger cautioned.

"We'll make it. Bye, Lacy. Tell Kristi hello and that central Montana would be a great place to set up a medical practice."

Lynda feigned a smile. *No, it wouldn't. It would be absolutely lousy. She wouldn't like it. Trust me.*

As Brady cranked the steering wheel, they could both see Heidi sitting next to Tyler in the Cadillac.

"Get in the van, Heidi!" Brady shouted.

"But I was helping Tyler. He has a bug in his eye."

"And I've got fire in mine!"

Heidi hopped out of the car and scampered back to the van.

Within minutes all three rigs had made a U-turn and headed north on Alternate Highway 16.

"I know, I know. I blew it with Heidi again. Remind me to have a talk with her and apologize."

"When?"

"Tonight."

"How do you know Cindy turned north?"

"There's one more guy out here somewhere, and Deadwood is north."

"Surely, he's not going to some campground by himself."

"He will if he's supposed to meet Joe Trent."

"You think Trent's in on the drug deal?"

"That's the kind of guys he associates with. Maybe Joe's the mule who packs the drugs between Vegas and this road gang. Then they sell it on the street, so to speak."

"Or peddle it to Rapid City dealers?"

"Yeah. That seems kind of dumb, but maybe Cindy has pushed them out of their pattern a little."

"You think she knows Trent's in on this?" Lynda asked.

"I don't know. I don't know how she knows anything in the first place."

"Don't we need to hurry to catch up with her?"

"These rigs can't go any faster in the mountains. Besides, she saw us. She knows we will follow. She'll leave us some kind of sign." Brady pointed up at the mountain to the right. "Look up there, darlin'!"

Lynda leaned forward, staring up and out the window. "Washington, Jefferson, Roosevelt, and Lincoln—they're . . . they're . . . gone!"

"We'll come back."

"I just made up my mind, Mr. Stoner."

"About what, Mrs. Soon-to-be-Stoner?"

"About vacations after we're married. I get to plan all of them."

Brady looked over at her and winked. "Denver in January, Cheyenne in July, the N.F.R. in December—how many vacations do we need?"

"Afraid not, cowboy. It will be Key Largo in January, Banff in July, Rockefeller Plaza in December . . ."

Brady looked incredulous. "Surely you can't be serious!"

"You better believe it, buckaroo." Lynda grinned from dangling earring to dangling earring. "And don't call me Shirley."

When Brady reached the junction at Highway 16, he turned north toward Lead. Lynda opened the back window, and both dogs vaulted for the freedom of the pickup bed. She scooted across the Indian blanket upholstery. "What kind of sign do you think Cindy will leave this time?"

"I don't know, but I don't expect anything until we get past Lead."

"Looks like this might be the day we end the whole chase."

"That's what I'm thinkin', darlin'."

"I was supposed to be back at the office today. Look at me! I feel like I'm part of a traveling band of Gypsies."

"At least, you're the queen of the Gypsies."

"If I'm the queen, why is some other woman dictating every move? I've been thinking, Brady . . . what would Cindy do if we just drove off toward Montana?"

"You mean, if we let her know where we were headed?"

"Yes, what if we set the direction? Would she follow?"

"How would we let her know where we were going?"

"Do you have a mutual friend in the Black Hills that she might be headed toward? Maybe we could call ahead and leave a message."

"No mutual friends, but we do have a mutual enemy."

"There's another man besides Joe Trent who hates the amiable Brady Stoner?"

"Not man—woman."

"Oh, no! Another story from Stoner's sordid past."

"Now, Lynda Dawn Darlin', you're just too suspicious."

"Well, cowboy, give me the details." Lynda dug in her purse for the bottle of Vanilla Dreams and glanced out at the pine-covered mountains racing by her.

"You watching out for a Cindy sign?" Brady asked.

"Are you going to tell me about this mutual enemy who, no doubt, was a real sweetheart with long hair as purdy as a bronc rein?"

Brady slapped his knee and began to laugh. "Okay, okay. It happened when Cindy and me were running horses for that movie deal."

"What movie deal?"

"Remember, I told you about that made-for-TV movie they were making down near Four Corners? That's the one where Cindy and me were wranglin' horses and doin' some stunts."

"What are you talking about? Brady, you never told me about any movie."

"I didn't?"

"No, you didn't. That's something I would have remembered, even on the telephone at three in the morning," she huffed.

"I guess it slipped my mind."

"I can't believe this! You were in a movie, and you never told me about it. What are you trying to hide?"

"It wasn't a very good movie."

Lynda raised her dark brown eyebrows far above her sunglasses. "Stoner?"

"Here's the brief version."

She slumped against the door and stared straight ahead. *I want to hear the long version. I think.*

"An uncle of Cindy's has a ranch southwest of Cortez, Colorado. He contracted to supply horses for the movie and—"

"What was the name of the movie?"

"Eh . . . it wasn't much of a—"

"Stoner?"

"They changed the title a few times but ended up callin' it *Bad Girls with Good Guns.* It was supposed to be a female western—sort of. Anyway, I was laid up with a sprained wrist and couldn't rodeo for a couple weeks, and he offered me and Cindy a chance to earn $100 a day. All we had to do is herd the horses around in the desert, then bring them in and saddle them up for the stunt people."

"So you weren't actually in the movie?"

"Yes and no. It ended up that they needed extra riders for

several scenes, and Cindy and I got in on quite a few of the shoots. But our parts were all edited out."

Lynda flipped down the visor and glanced in the vanity mirror. *I wonder what I would look like with long hair?* "What does all this have to do with some woman in the Black Hills?"

"I was gettin' to that. One of the gals in the movie got mad at Cindy and had us both canned, so they edited us out of the film. Which was probably the Lord's blessing. It was a lousy film."

"Why was she angry at Cindy?"

Brady plucked a toothpick off the dash and shoved it into the corner of his mouth. "Cindy punched her in the nose and delayed shooting for two days."

"Cindy hit her?"

"Not until after she knocked Cindy off the bay mare."

"They had a fight?"

"Yeah, the whole crew was standing around rooting for Cindy. I guess none of them liked Joysee."

"Joysee? Like in Joysee Draper—Miss Universe, queen of magazine centerfolds and B movies?"

Brady pulled the toothpick out of his mouth and glanced at Lynda. "Yeah, you know her?"

"Of course not. What were they fighting over?"

"Eh, well . . . you know how those actresses are. They can be sort of possessive."

"No, I don't know. What was she trying to possess?"

"Eh . . . me," Brady mumbled. "Hey, look! Is that Cindy's rig up there?"

"Who gives a squat whose rig's up there? Finish the story, Stoner. You've left me with a barrel racer and a silicone-improved movie star fighting over you."

"No . . . that's not Cindy."

"Stoner?"

"Well, we were told not to come back. We were paid off, and that's the end of the story."

"And Joysee Draper lives in the Black Hills?"

"She owns the Deuces Casino and Hotel in Deadwood. Lives there part of the year when she's not making a movie."

"And how do you know that?" Lynda sighed. "Or do I want to know?"

"I read it on the cover of a tabloid while standing in line at a supermarket. But, like I said, I don't think Cindy would head for Joysee's."

"Brady, why didn't you tell me about this movie before?"

"Darlin', I'm so busy daydreamin' ever' wakin' minute about how incredible it's goin' to be married to you that I forget ever'thing in the past."

She looked over at him and shook her head. "Stoner, you could talk a mama bear out of her only cub."

"Thank you, ma'am." He tipped his hat in her direction.

Pine trees, weathered cedar fence posts, and yellow lines in the center of the blacktop road whizzed by before they spoke again.

"I was wondering, how does a woman who jiggles her way through lousy movies make enough money to own a whole casino?" Lynda questioned.

"Oh, I doubt if she owns it outright. I hear she has connections in Las Vegas."

"The tabloids again?"

"All-night talk radio. I have to listen to something to keep awake on the road."

"Joe Trent has Las Vegas connections, doesn't he?"

"Joe's just a two-bit player in a mega-buck town."

"But he'd like to move up into the majors, right?"

"I suppose."

"And Joysee Draper would like to move up in the business, too, right?"

"You're stretchin' it, babe," he cautioned. "We don't know any of that."

"But it makes a good story."

"You writing fiction or nonfiction?"

"If I were a writer instead of an editor, I'd hang on to that storyline. It has possibilities." She pulled off her dark glasses and looked at Brady. "For the first time in a week, I was actually thinking about work."

"You like being an editor, don't you, darlin'?"

"Yes. I love it."

"It's a good thing. With the price of cattle like they've been the past couple of years, we're goin' to need some way to pay for groceries."

"Are you worried about finances already?"

He reached over and drew his strong, callused fingers across her cheek. "I'm worried about providin' for you at the level to which you are accustomed."

She reached up and took his hand in hers. "I'm accustomed to eating dinner by myself with a manuscript in my lap and an old movie on TV. I'm accustomed to foul-smelling subways and cabs, crowds shoving me across crosswalks, sirens blaring, and people screaming anytime night or day. I'm accustomed to three locks on my front door and a canister of mace in my purse. I'm used to spending my days off standing in a long line in Times Square waiting for discount theater tickets and spending most of my evenings with nothing better to do than plan my perfume for the next day. If you provide me with that lifestyle, I'll scream. In case you can't tell it, cowboy, I'm due for a change."

"Three locks on the door?"

"A condo association rule states that each door must have a minimum of three locks and a peephole or surveillance camera on every unit. How many locks do we have on the front door of our new house?"

STEPHEN BLY

"I think there might be one," Brady admitted. "Locks come in handy to make sure the door doesn't blow open during a windstorm."

Lynda scooted over closer to him. "I wish we were there, don't you?"

"At the house?"

"Yes. I wish we were married . . . and everyone else gone . . . and we were sitting in the living room just waiting for the wind to blow open the front door. It sounds so peaceful."

He combed the back of her hair with his fingers. "It's like waitin' for Christmas."

She laced her fingers in his. "When I was little, we spent every Christmas in Key Largo at Grandma's. It was always warm. My grandmother gave me a typewriter when I was ten."

"And you've been editing ever since?"

"Not really. I remember being disappointed. I had wanted a pair of pink ballet slippers."

"I didn't know you knew how to, you know, ballet."

"Oh, I don't. I just wanted pink ballet slippers. How about you, cowboy? What was your favorite gift as a kid?"

"When I was seven, my dad had a friend of his make up a fancy pair of chaps with my name branded in them. I dug through the tack room about the first of December and came across them in a box."

"So you knew what you were getting."

"Yeah."

"Did that spoil Christmas for you? I hate knowing ahead of time what I'm getting."

"Nope. But it surely made it tough to wait. I knew they would be wonderful, but I couldn't try them on for four weeks. I couldn't stop thinkin' about them day and night."

"Were you disappointed when the day finally got there?"

"No way. I was the most thrilled and relieved kid in Idaho. I wore them twenty-four hours a day for a week."

"For a whole week, huh? Cowboy, are we talking about waiting for Christmas or waiting for your wedding day?"

"Both, I reckon. What do you think?"

Lynda lifted his right hand to her lips and kissed his fingers. "I reckon you're right, Mr. Stoner."

She stretched her legs back toward the glove compartment and rested her head on his shoulder. Brady's hand slipped out of hers and soon lay across her shoulder. He held her tight. Lynda let her eyelids droop, then close.

Lord, why is it I feel so great just being near this guy? It's like decades of worry over how I look, what others think about me, if I'm disappointing someone—all of it just fades away when I'm with Brady.

This has been the craziest week of my life.

Well, one of the craziest, but it's okay.

I know I'm where I ought to be.

Thanks, Lord.

"Looks like we're headin' into a storm, darlin'."

Thanks even for the storms.

Dark clouds covered the sky to the north when she once again opened her eyes. "Is that lightning?"

"Yep. Must be rumbling along up at Deadwood."

"Isn't Deadwood where Wild Bill Hickok got shot in the back of the head by Jack McCall while he was holding black aces and eights at the #10 Saloon, with his back to the door on Wednesday, August 2, 1876, at 4:15 P.M.?"

"Whoa!" Brady threw back his head. "You've been practicing that line for a month."

"That's not true. Two weeks, tops! I had Joaquin write it out for me when he was in New York for the party at Gossmans'. Are you impressed?"

"Impressed? I'm shocked. I had no idea Wild Bill was shot on a Wednesday afternoon at 4:15. You have any other lines to surprise me with?"

"I do."

"Oh, yeah? What else?"

"I do."

"You said that. What's the other line?"

"I do!" she snapped. "That's the line I've been practicing."

"Oh . . . yeah . . . like in wedding vows."

"What a bright fellow you are."

"Thank ya, ma'am!" He tipped his hat again. "It's starting to rain. See if you can coax the dogs in here." He reached back and slid the window open.

Lynda turned around and shouted in the wind, "Margarita!"

Both dogs scampered into the crowded backseat.

"These mountains are covered with green trees. Why do they call them the Black Hills?" she asked.

"Haven't you ever heard the story of Jedediah Black?" Brady turned on his windshield wipers.

"You're joking."

"Yep. They say comin' across the prairie in the summer, they look black on the distant horizon. Look at that! It's slamming down out of the sky like water over a dam in springtime."

Lynda watched the water pile up on the two-lane blacktop road. For the next several minutes the heavy rain fell in waves—downpours at the crest of the hills, lighter rain in the valleys. By the time they drove under the city limit archway at Lead, South Dakota, the rain had settled into a slow, constant drizzle.

"I never could understand why a person would want to ride a motorcycle through a rainstorm."

"I suppose they're hopin' for good weather like the rest of us."

"What's that over there? It looks like a canyon."

"It is. It's the open pit of the Homestake Mine."

"They dug that out of the mountains on purpose?"

"Yep. 'Course they're still runnin' the underground operation, too. They've been diggin' there for over 100 years. Underground, that is. Some shafts go down 7,000 feet, I hear."

Lynda stared at the giant hole in the ground. "This is weird."

"Why do you say that?"

"Gold mines were supposed to pass away at the turn of the century along with stagecoaches, Indian wars, and . . ."

"Cowboys?"

"You know what I mean."

"Come on, let's go take a look at a real gold mine." Brady pulled into the Homestake Mine parking lot and guided the pickup and stock trailer toward the long spaces reserved for recreational vehicles.

Brady slammed on the brakes. Capt. Patch tumbled off the box of pottery and bounced into the front seat. A loud crash and rocking of the stock trailer warned of R-43's displeasure at the sudden stop.

"Look!" Brady shouted.

"What is it?"

"A motorcycle and a two-tone blue Ford pickup."

"Nebraska, TYU 385. That's Cindy!"

Brady scanned the parking lot. "It's her outfit, but I don't see anyone around."

"Brady, how did she know we'd turn into the parking lot? Her pickup is parked over here behind the motor homes. There's no way we would have seen that from the road."

"It makes me think this isn't exactly in Cindy's plans."

"Where could she be?"

"There's a tour of the underground operation and an observation platform for looking at the open pit."

"And a gift shop over there in that old church building." Lynda pointed to the west end of the parking lot.

"You ready to get drenched?"

"How about the others?"

"I'll take Tyler with us in case a biker's lurking about."

"He's just a teenager."

"He's rodeo tough. That's all the help I need. You can wait here if you want."

"I'm coming, too. If Cindy's here, maybe I can help her."

Brady opened the door. "Stay in the cab until I tell the others. Then make a run for the information booth. Looks like there's covering over that deck."

When Lynda saw Brady and Tyler run for the covered observation deck, she jumped out of the truck, the two dogs following her. She sprinted across a half-full asphalt parking lot, dodging most of the large puddles of water. Capt. Patch and Margarita sprinted toward a display of mining equipment that roughly resembled fire-hydrant heaven.

"Doc said those horses were gettin' a little restless," Brady reported. "Remind me to find someplace to exercise them before dark."

"We aren't going to make it to Sheridan tonight, are we?"

"We'll make it, but it might be late."

"Where do we look for Cindy?"

"Darlin', why don't you—no, me and Tyler have the hats on. Tyler, how about you runnin' down to that gift shop?"

"What's Miss Cindy look like?"

"Like a tough thirty-year-old barrel racer with a long braid that's—"

Don't say it, Stoner!

"—as purdy as a bronc rein."

"If she's there, what do I do?"

"Tell her to come talk to us."

"And if she don't want to?"

"Come get us, but don't let her drive away."

"Yes, sir." Tyler cantered down the sidewalk through the rain to the gift shop.

"Darlin', I'll check the people out here. You want to ask

inside about the underground tour? She could be in there or on a tour or somethin'."

"It doesn't make sense. After two weeks of chasing bikers, why would she stop and take a mine tour?" Lynda mused.

"Or, for that matter, why would good old Lamont McGhee stop here?"

"You think he's the one who's left?"

"Yep. That's his bike out there."

"How do you know that's his bike? They all look the same."

"The same? That's about like sayin' all cows look the same."

Lynda pushed her way though the swinging double doors. *All cows* do *look the same—don't they?*

Lynda was settled on an empty wooden bench in the sparsely filled waiting room when Brady and Tyler burst through the door, rain still rolling down the brims of their cowboy hats and splashing on the bare, unpainted concrete floor. "You boys ain't been out there roundin' up them dogies again, have ya?" she drawled. "You two is wetter than a beaver in springtime."

"Don't you just love it when she talks that way?" Brady glanced at Tyler, then drawled back, "Actually, ma'am . . . we've been a whole lot wetter than this before."

Tyler tipped his black felt hat at her, and the water poured down the back of his long-sleeved shirt. "Miss Lynda Dawn, you could make a mighty fine cowgirl if you—"

"If I had a long braid as purdy as a bronc rein?"

His nineteen-year-old face lit up. "Yes, ma'am. I told Miss Heidi she'd be even more handsome if she let her hair grow out. You reckon that's possible?"

"For her hair to grow?"

"No, ma'am. That she could be even purdier than she is now?"

Maybe Brady's right. He should keep those two apart. "It's hard to improve on perfection."

"Yes, ma'am. I believe you're right about that."

Oh, brother.

"No sign of Cindy outside," Brady reported. "How about in here?"

"They don't keep records of people's names, but the last group should be back within fifteen minutes. I suppose we should wait."

Brady plopped down on the bench beside her. "I guess someone could park in the lot out there and walk uptown."

"In this rain? That doesn't make sense."

"Not much about this whole week makes sense."

"I'm glad you said that. I was beginning to think it was just me."

"Miss Heidi says that things like this always happen to her Uncle Brady," Tyler mentioned.

"Well, the handsome Miss Heidi is certainly right about that," Lynda assured him.

"I don't know why you always say that," Brady protested. "My life was as boring as mud before you came into it."

Lynda turned and stared at Tyler's wide brown eyes. "Do you believe that, cowboy?"

"No, ma'am. I surely don't."

"Neither do I."

Tyler shook the rain off his hat and jammed it back on his head. "You want me to wait outside just in case Miss Cindy shows herself?"

"That might be good. She doesn't know you and won't be suspicious. If you see anyone fitting her description, come get us," Brady instructed.

After Tyler left, Brady slipped his cool and very damp hand into Lynda's. "He reminds me a lot of myself at that age."

"Is that good or bad?"

"Some of both, I suppose. I'm goin' to be glad to deliver the girls back to their mother. Then it's Heather's worry."

"Once they're out of sight, you'll forget all about them?"

Brady shook his head. "Okay, I'm goin' to be worryin' about those girls the rest of my life. I suppose I'll never stop prayin' for them and their mama."

"Richard wouldn't want it any other way," Lynda agreed.

"I promised him out in that Kaibab blizzard that I'd look after them 'til my dyin' day."

"I like a man who keeps commitments. For instance, when one says, 'I'll take you to see the ranch before the weddin' on Saturday.'"

"Now, darlin', I'm goin' to get us there."

"I believe you."

They sat hand in hand for several moments. Then Lynda patted the top of his hand. "Do you like motor homes?"

"What?"

"Would you ever like to travel in a motor home?" she pressed.

"I'd hate it! I'd rather sleep under the stars in the back of my rig than in one of those."

"Even with your wife?"

"Ooooh! Yeah . . . well, what I'd really like is a first-class horse trailer with living quarters up front. That way we could take the horses with us."

"Why would we want to do that?"

"So we could ride, of course. What kind of vacation would it be if we didn't go horseback riding?"

The man's serious! It must have been that blow to his head. He can't even think straight.

Heidi burst into the room shouting, "Uncle Brady! Come quick!"

"Wha-what happened?"

Brady and Lynda jumped to their feet.

"I was waiting out front with Tyler when Capt. Patch and Margarita started barking at two men jogging toward that blue travel home over near the Ford pickup and the motorcycle. Then a man wearing black leather began to kick at the dogs. After that, he hopped on the motorcycle and took off."

Brady yanked Lynda along by the arm.

"There it goes! The motor home is leaving, too!" Tyler reported as he pointed across the parking lot. "The other man got into that motor home."

"Are we going to follow them, Uncle Brady?"

He looked across the parking lot. "Cindy's truck is still here."

"Maybe they kidnapped Cindy in that motor home," Lynda suggested.

"That's a horrible thought." Brady banged the palms of his hands together. "Listen, I'm going to follow that rig for a few miles and see where it's goin'. The rest of you wait here in case Cindy shows up for her truck. I'll be back no later than an hour."

Lynda latched onto his arm. "Cowboy, you aren't getting out of my sight!"

"Darlin', I promise to be right back."

"No way, Stoner. You aren't going without me."

He stopped, and his eyes met hers. "Eh, no, I guess I'm not."

She shook her head just as a loud siren blared from under the deck covering. A woman from inside the information office came running outside. "Clear the platform! All tours are closed! Please return to your vehicles!" she hollered.

"What happened?" Brady asked.

"There's been an accident."

Lynda clutched Brady's arm. "Where?"

"Down at the east observation deck! Over there!" the woman huffed, pointing across the parking lot.

"I don't see anyone," Lynda said.

"Come on, folks, clear out of here!"

"What happened?" Brady pressed.

"Some tourist must have climbed over the guardrail and fell into the pit."

Lynda stared down into the man-made grand canyon. "Down there?"

"She fell about 100 feet and is wedged on some rocks."

"She?" Lynda felt her stomach sink and her knees shake.

EIGHT

"Tyler, grab the ropes out of the back of the rig," Brady hollered as he jogged through the drizzle. The dark clouds hung low, speared by the pines and power poles.

Lynda tried to avoid the puddles as she sprinted next to him. "Brady, what are you going to do?"

"I'm going to get her. I'm afraid it's Cindy." He reached back and grabbed her hand, tugging her across the blacktop.

"But shouldn't you wait for the rescue team—the EMTs?" Her boot heels slammed hard into the asphalt at every step. Her chest heaved. *Search and rescue? That could be the title of a Brady Stoner autobiography.*

"If it's her down there, and she's still alive, she needs help right now!"

Brady reached the small, uncovered wooden observation deck a couple steps ahead of Lynda.

"How does anyone accidentally fall over an eight-foot fence?" she asked.

"Looks like the chain was busted on the safety gate."

"Brady, be careful!"

He stepped onto the bottom pipe of the chain-link fence

gate and swung himself out over the man-made crevice. Then he leaned out as far as his stretched arm would allow him.

"Brady, that scares me. Please don't. It's just like that narrow trail along the Grand Canyon!"

"There is some slope to this one, darlin'."

His voice seemed distant. Her vision narrowed. Lynda gulped in a huge breath of fresh air.

"But it's muddy and slick. Brady Stoner, get . . . get back in here! Brady!" Panic rose inside her.

Get a grip, girl. Breathe deeply. It's just a man-made hole. You're safe; he's not. He's going to fall off and die, isn't he, Lord?

"There she is! I can see her!"

Lynda scurried to the fence and laced her fingers through it. "Is she . . . okay?" She felt every muscle in her body lock tight as she gazed into the abyss.

"She's not movin'," Brady shouted. Then he swung himself back to the platform. He scooted over and put his arm on Lynda's shoulder. She shuddered but didn't turn loose of her white-knuckle grip on the chain-link fence. "Are you all right, darlin'?"

"I think I'm going to throw up."

"Move back away from the edge."

"No!" she shouted. "Get your hands off me!"

Brady slipped both arms around her waist and yanked her away from the fence. "No! Don't! I mean it!" she screamed in terror.

Lynda tried to kick him and slug him with her fists but couldn't land a blow. She kept screaming, "No!" He carried her to the back of the platform, twenty-five feet from the edge of the pit.

"Yes! Yes!" she groaned her way into a sob. "Thanks."

"It's okay now, darlin'."

Heidi and an umbrella-carrying Wendy hurried behind Tyler as he hustled to the platform.

"Here's some gloves and three ropes. That's all I could find," Tyler called out.

"You girls stay at the back of the platform, and keep Lynda Dawn with you," Brady called out.

Lynda stumbled under Wendy's umbrella. Her head was still spinning, her vision blurred. She was vaguely aware of dogs barking, a crowd gathering, and a siren blaring in the background.

For the next fifteen minutes Lynda stood frozen in place, getting progressively soaked as Brady and a rescue crew of three men and a woman pulleyed Cindy LaCoste up out of the pit. Thick red clay stuck to Brady's boots, which looked as if they were mud snowshoes. His shirt and jeans were drenched. His black felt cowboy hat drooped down, soggy, yet still funneling off a stream of water.

The throbbing in Lynda's head had begun to ease when she heard Brady shout, "It's Cindy! She's alive!" When he finally climbed out of the pit, Lynda's head cleared.

"Darlin', you look pale."

"I am pale," she murmured. "I'm from New York where everyone looks like they crawled out from under a rock, remember?"

"What I meant was, how's the stomach?"

"Better. Listen, cowboy, the next time you risk your life, do it when I'm not watching. I really can't handle this kind of thing. It's too intense."

He pulled off his gloves and ran his fingers through her damp hair and then kissed her gently on the right cheek.

How can his whole body be wet and cold and his lips still be so warm?

Brady pulled back. "Sorry, darlin', I didn't mean to make you fret."

"Fret? This wasn't a 'fret'! It was teetering on the verge of hysteria." She leaned forward and offered him her left cheek.

He kissed it. Twice.

"What do they think about Cindy?" Lynda asked. "Is she conscious? Did you find out what happened?"

Brady huddled under the umbrella with Heidi, Wendy, Tyler, and Lynda. "Listen, gang. Here's my thought. Homestake has a company hospital and emergency room here in town. That's where they're taking Cindy. The rescue guy named Gary has a few acres down there where we drove into town. Remember the corrals with the white board fence? He said we can turn the animals out there for tonight."

"We're going to stay here tonight?" Wendy asked.

"We've got to stay with Cindy. Right, darlin?" His soft brown eyes searched for confirmation.

No Sheridan. No ranch visit. He's right, Lord. But why does this have to happen to me?

"Right. We should stay here tonight," she repeated in a soft monotone.

Lord, help me to be more generous. I'm ashamed that I resent Cindy's accident.

Brady tried scraping some of the mud off his boots onto the edge of the platform. "Tyler and Doc can take the girls and go turn the animals out at Gary's. He said he'd call his wife and let her know we're coming over. Tyler, you drive my truck. Then swing on by a motel and have Doc rent us three rooms for tonight. There's some motels on the north side of town—on the back way to Deadwood. Lynda Dawn and me will go to the emergency room and see what we can do for Cindy."

"What will we drive?"

"Let's take both of Cindy's outfits."

"Did you get the keys to her pickup?"

"Yeah, I had to search her all over to find them."

All over? All over where, buckaroo?

"You need dry clothes. You're soaked to the bone," she cautioned.

"So's Cindy."

"Do you want us to come to the hospital after we check into the motel?" Heidi asked. Her thin shorts-clad legs were almost purple.

"Nope. Just call the hospital waiting room and let me know where you settled in. Warm up, put on some dry clothes, and have some supper. Let's get goin'."

As they started across the parking lot, he hollered, "Heidi, you and Tyler take the dogs with you in my pickup."

Lynda could see the gleam in the seventeen-year-old's eyes even in the drizzling rain. "Heidi allowed to ride with Tyler? Is Uncle Brady weakening?" Lynda jibed.

"Kind of readjusting priorities, I reckon."

◆ ◆ ◆

Brady and Lynda spent most of the next hour filling out forms at the emergency room entry desk, scraping mud from boots, and drying off with borrowed hospital towels. Brady sat in the waiting room with a gray blanket draped across his shoulders and a white towel over his head when Lynda returned with two steaming cups of coffee.

She handed him a cup. "Did the doctor come out yet?"

"Nope."

"Are you warming up any?"

"I'm better. How about you, darlin'?"

"Don't worry about me, cowboy. You look about as cold as you did last fall in Holter Lake."

"Yeah." The response came with a dimpled grin under the towel. "I was just thinkin' about that myself. I was ponderin' if I could get you to warm me up the same way you did then."

"Hold that thought, cowboy."

"For how long?"

"Less than four days now." *I think I'd better wear Mexican Moonlight tonight. That'll warm him up.*

"Yes, ma'am."

Lynda scooted in next to him on the couch. They both hovered over their cups of coffee.

"Cindy didn't say anything to you?" She took a sip and burned the tip of her tongue.

"She was out the whole time."

"Did she have a head injury?"

"Not that I could tell. I did check her all over."

Lynda bit her lip and then took a gulp of coffee that burned the back of her throat. *You told me that already, Stoner.* "Something went wrong in Cindy's scheme of things."

Brady pushed the towel off his head. His dark, shaggy hair shot out in several directions. "This time they ambushed her."

"You think the other man—the one in the travel home—could have been Joe Trent?"

"From Wendy's description it sounds like him. The bikers were supposed to meet Trent somewhere. Who knows?" Brady looked down at his boots. "Cindy's just got to be all right. We've spent a week trying to catch up with her and keep her from gettin' hurt. We almost made it, darlin' . . . we almost made it."

◆ ◆ ◆

After a trip to the restroom, the juice machine, and three idle passes by a stack of well-used magazines, Lynda slumped back down next to the blanketed Brady.

"I wish we'd find out something," she sighed.

"You want me to go ask the nurse again?"

"No. She'll get ticked. We've bothered her enough. I guess I'm nervous, not only for Cindy, but for me."

"For you?"

"Look, Brady . . . I'm not real proud of this. But the minute it dawned on me that it was Cindy down in the pit . . ."

"You begin to think, *Oh, no, we won't get to go to the ranch!*"

"How did you know?"

"Because that was my exact thought, too," Brady admitted.

"Really? But you just ran out there and started rescuing Cindy, barking commands like a fire chief."

"Darlin', if I had my way, this trip would have been you and me and one dog. But I got to thinkin' while I was slidin' in the mud down in that pit . . . if it wasn't for Cindy, I wouldn't have gotten to see you until Friday night. We might not have had a perfect week, but we've been together. And being with you, even in a crowd, is a whole lot better than not bein' with you at all."

"That thought has crossed my mind, too."

Brady flopped his head against the back of the orange synthetic leather sofa. "If you had it to live all over again, would you spend this week in New York?"

"No way, cowboy."

They both stared ahead at the antiseptically scrubbed Antique White semigloss wall of the waiting room.

"Brady, she's got to be all right. If the Lord led us through all of this, and I think He has, surely it wasn't merely to show up in time to bury her." Lynda reached over and plucked a tissue from a square blue box on the end table. She wiped the corners of her eyes and then blew her nose.

"She'll be all right, darlin'." Brady slipped his arm out from the blanket and began to rub the back of her neck.

"Only half of these tears are for Cindy. The other half are for you, babe."

"Me?"

"I was petrified when you went down the wall of that pit. I couldn't move; I couldn't talk; I could barely breathe. I think I'm beginning to understand Romeo and Juliet a whole lot better. I realized that I couldn't bear the thought of living without you. I'd go bonkers in a minute. I'd be a basket case the rest of my life."

"How about you and me dumping the others, driving

straight for Jackson, and staying at the lodge until the wedding Saturday?"

Lynda analyzed his teasing brown eyes. "Get behind me, Satan!"

Brady laughed. "I deserved that."

A tall man in a white smock strode out of the emergency room. Brady stood up. The blanket dropped to the couch.

"Are you Ms. LaCoste's brother?"

"Eh . . . yes," Brady asserted.

Lynda scowled and tried to look Brady in the eyes, but he focused on the doctor.

"When I mentioned to Ms. LaCoste that she had visitors, she perked up considerably."

"I'm glad we can be here," Brady said.

"Quite a coincidence to have you drive by after her accident."

"Accident?"

"She said it was totally her fault. She wanted a picture that didn't have a chain-link fence in it, so she broke the lock on the security gate with a rock and leaned out too far."

"That's what she said?"

"I heard her give that report to the policeman."

Brady finally shot a glance at Lynda.

The doctor pulled off his silver-framed glasses and gently rubbed the bridge of his nose. "Well, your sister is going to be fine. We've finished the X-rays and blood tests. Here's the truly amazing news. There seems to be no internal bleeding, no broken bones. She has several severely bruised ribs, a pretty good bump behind her right ear, and badly scratched hands and arms. All and all, that's not bad for tumbling into the pit. I think mud softened the blow and helped her dig in and stop the fall."

"Can we see her?" Brady asked.

"Yes . . . and I presume you're Lynda. She asked for you."

"She did?"

"She said the visitors must be her brother Brady and his wife, Lynda Dawn. Were there others with you?"

"We sent them to a motel."

"That's good. We can only allow immediate family members in the emergency area."

The doctor escorted them into emergency, which turned out to be one large equipment-filled room with five beds, each separated by white cotton curtains that hung from an overhead track. As far as Lynda could tell, Cindy was the only patient.

Cindy's sandy blonde hair was still muddy, but her face and arms had been scrubbed. An intravenous tube was inserted above her right wrist.

Lynda watched Cindy's eyes meet Brady's.

"Hi, lil' sis. . . . Doc says you hurt all over, but nothin's busted too bad."

"Hello, big brother." Cindy tried to grin, but she quickly gave up the effort. "I hear you crawled down there and saved my life."

"The Lord does the savin' or the takin' of lives. You know that. All I did was see to it you got out of the rain and hauled to safety as soon as possible."

Cindy slowly turned her head toward Lynda. Her eyes had a tired, pained expression. "You look pretty, Lynda Dawn Darlin'."

"You look pretty bad, Miss Cindy." Austin reached out and took the injured woman's hand.

"Yeah, well . . . we can't all be glamorous big-city editors." Cindy squeezed Lynda's hand. "I didn't mean that to sound snotty. Really. I can't tell you how great it is that you're here."

Lynda stared into Cindy's tired blue eyes. "I take it the tumble into the mine pit wasn't a part of your plan."

"And," Brady added, "we don't believe for a minute that crock about accidentally falling in while trying to take a picture."

"Hey, you've got to admit that until today I was on a roll."

"That you were." Brady moved to the other side of the bed to hold Cindy's other hand. "Tell us what happened."

"I look horrible, don't I?"

"You look like you tumbled down a cliff. Now tell us what happened," he insisted.

"You're right. This was not my scheme. I knew you were only a few minutes behind me, so I pulled into the parking lot at the Homestake. I thought I'd hide out behind a travel home and let you pass me. But when I saw that bike, I knew it was the last one. So I concocted a hurried plan. I spotted McGhee by himself over at that east observation platform. I was going to coldcock him and drop him into the pit, tied by his feet, or something to that effect."

"You were going to jump the guy by yourself?" Lynda asked.

"They aren't all that tough one at a time. Especially if you can sneak up on them with a baseball bat." A pained smile crept off her lips. "Anyway, my idea was to hogtie him and be standing at the sidewalk when you guys drove by."

"What went wrong?" Lynda asked.

"There were two of them. I didn't see the other guy until he had a knife on me. You'll never guess who."

"Joe Trent?" Brady posed.

Cindy's mouth dropped open. "How did you . . ."

"The guy you left tied to a tree told us they were supposed to meet Trent somewhere."

"Did you cut him loose?"

"Yep."

"I figured you would. Brady, what does Trent have to do with these guys?"

"I don't know, Cindy-girl. He's a Las Vegas scumbag. Maybe he's trying to learn how to be a drug peddler like the others. You sure got those at Rushmore busted."

Lynda noticed a slight gleam in Cindy's eyes.

"Yeah . . . that was so cool. I sat up there in the trees and watched the whole thing go down. I didn't know they were really going to be passin' the stuff there. I just figured they must be carrying some if they planned to summer on the road. Brady, do you think Trent set up those bikers to attack me five years ago?"

"I can't imagine anyone, even Joe Trent, doin' somethin' like that. More than likely it's just a case of low-life types naturally gravitating toward each other," Brady suggested.

"Do you hurt a lot?" Lynda asked, glancing up at the tubes and bottles above the bed. "The doctor told us about the sprains, scrapes, and bruises."

"When I first came to, I felt like a horse had rolled on me. You know, Brady, like when he steps in a hole and somersaults right over the top of you?"

Brady held her hand and gently rubbed her bruised arm. "I know exactly what you mean, Cindy-girl."

She laid her tanned face on the other side of the clean white cotton pillow. "Did Brady tell you about the time he was teaching me to team rope, and the steer cut right in front of my horse? We went down, and the cayuse rolled right over me. The saddle horn missed my chest by not more than a couple inches. I didn't cry, did I, Brady?"

"No, lil' sis, you didn't cry." Brady reached up and stroked her muddy hair. "You never cry."

"I cried that one night. I just don't have any more tears. I don't hurt much now. They pumped me full of painkiller, and I'm sailing off to la-la land."

"I think you should tell the police the truth about what happened," Lynda ventured.

"No police, guys. No police. I'm on my own on this."

"Cindy, this is getting dangerous. Don't take any more chances," Brady warned. "Maybe you should let the police handle it."

"I can't tell them I tried to shanghai the guy and push him into the pit, but they beat me to it." She pulled her arm free, wiped her nose on the back of her hand, and then grabbed Lynda's fingers again.

"Cindy, you can't go on like this," Lynda protested. "The Bible says—"

"Yeah, I know. 'Vengeance is mine, saith the Lord.' Well, vengeance is overreacting. I figure I'm not even forcing justice on them, let alone vengeance. Don't worry, Lynda Dawn Darlin'... I haven't deserted the Lord, and He hasn't deserted me. I've been talkin' to Him about this day and night. This is just something in my life I would regret not doing."

"Cindy, maybe it's time to leave it completely with the Lord then," Lynda advised.

"Not quite. There's one of them left—Lamont McGhee. Then the story will be finished. What do you think—will it sell with the new ending?"

"You can't be doing all of this just to get a book published. It isn't worth risking your life."

"I'll admit I started out on this quest to get your attention. But it does make some sense. Every time I put one of them out of commission, I can forget about him. You should have seen the guy's face when I blew up his bike! My anger for him vanished completely when I saw that look in his eyes."

"Cindy-girl, you're going to be laid up awhile." Brady put his hand against her cheek. "You can't go traipsing after Lamont McGhee. He tried to kill you today. Next time he might succeed."

She raised her blonde-brown eyebrows at Lynda. "That would make a good end to the book, too. Right?"

"No!" Lynda shot back. "That's not right! You do not have the right to number your own days. Only the Lord can do that. It is one of His exclusive and fundamental rights. To try and usurp it is extremely wrong."

"The doctor said I could probably leave in the morning. They want to keep me here overnight for observation. I guess they don't want me suing the mine. They want to make sure I don't have any temperature. But he said I could go home with you tomorrow. I just need to take it easy for a few weeks."

Brady quickly agreed. "That's exactly what you're goin' to do. We'll make sure of that."

Brady, we're getting married in less than four days. Don't invite house guests.

"You're coming with us to the wedding. Then I'll have Heather and the girls swing out to Ely on the way back to St. George. You can recuperate at L. G.'s ranch."

"Brady, I really have to finish this job. It's my therapy. You understand, don't you?"

"You can't finish it all bunged up. Think of it like rodeo. You've got a doctor's release. Besides, we need you at the wedding. Right, darlin'?"

Stoner, don't you do this. Lynda shifted her weight from one foot to the other. "Brady's right. We both wanted you to be in the wedding." *Don't ask me what.*

"We want you to . . ." Brady cleared his throat and then turned to Lynda. "You tell her, babe."

You wimp! "We need you to . . . to, you know, to be the hostess . . . and see that everyone signs the guest register!" *Why did I say that? We aren't even going to have a guest book.*

"Nice try, but you can have anyone do that."

"That's not true, is it, darlin'?" Brady again looked toward Lynda.

"That's right. Just the other day Brady said—" Lynda paused and looked over at him, batting her eyelids. "Tell her what you said the other day, darlin'!" *This is your mess, Stoner. You figure it out.*

"Oh, you mean . . . well . . . see," Brady stammered, "eh, we don't rightly know who all will stop by for the weddin'. Might be a number of guys and gals goin' down the road to their next rodeo who pull in. And Lynda knew that you'd know most of 'em. So she figured if she had you at the door, it would . . . you know, make things go more smoothly."

Cindy tried to raise her head and then slumped back into the pillow. "Who do you two think you're snowing?" Then she stared right at Brady. "Do you want me at your wedding, cowboy?"

Brady gently stroked the top of her hand. "I'd be mighty proud to have you there, Cindy-girl."

Cindy flopped her head toward Lynda. "I never did learn how to say no to this bareback rider. Did you?"

Lynda shook her head.

"I'll be there."

"You're comin' with us as soon as they let you out," Brady insisted.

"Okay, but as soon as the wedding's over, I'm going to come back and finish what I started."

"We'll talk about that later," Brady said. "Now it's time for you to get some sleep and for us to get out of these wet clothes."

"Where will I meet you tomorrow?"

"We'll be right here to pick you up, lil' sis. We'll be here by 8:00 in the morning. Now let's have some prayer."

When he and Lynda finished praying for Cindy, she looked up. "Too bad Brady never had any real sisters. He would make a terrific brother, wouldn't he?"

"Yes, I believe he would," Lynda agreed.

"Cindy-girl, the Lord's in charge of who goes in what families. He has more than one way of bringing us together. As far as I'm concerned, you'll always be my sister."

"Is that all right with you?" Cindy asked Lynda.

"Yes, it is."

"Okay. Then here's the first thing I need for my brother to do. Could you see if they have someone here to wash my hair?"

"You got it, sis." Brady disappeared in the direction of the nurses' station.

"Tell me the truth," Cindy continued. "Isn't my story improved by what's happened over the past week?"

"I can't believe you'd do all of this just for a book. But, to be honest, yes. These events have perked up your book. But it's still not a completed manuscript."

"With Lamont McGhee still on the loose?"

"Yes."

"That's exactly why I need to go find him."

"I have a better idea."

"Oh?"

"Fictionalize it," Lynda suggested. "Make up a just and satisfying end to the story—something with danger, yet the Lord protects you at a crucial time."

"But that would be lying."

"No, we call that fiction."

"Can we do that?"

"It's fiction based on fact. Movie director Oliver Stone has made a fortune with that kind of story. We aren't lying to anyone. They'll know it's fiction. That way we avoid lawsuits over getting the details wrong and all of that."

"But that still doesn't give McGhee what he deserves."

"You and I both know that the Lord will take care of that, Cindy."

"Yeah . . . I know. It's just that I figured He was busy enough with other things, so I'd help Him out."

"Hey, here's the good news and the bad news," Brady blurted out as he barged back to the bedside. "They've got everything you need to wash your hair, without having to get up. But the bad news is, they're short-handed and don't have anyone to help until the 11:00 P.M. shift comes on."

"I'll do it," Lynda offered.

Cindy perked up. "Really?"

"That's great, darlin'," Brady encouraged her. "Listen, Doc Cartier called and said she got rooms for us at the Dakota House. It's right on the highway on the other side of town."

"Did they get the animals stabled?"

"Yeah, but it took them longer than I thought. Now I'll just park out there in the waitin' room under the blanket until you wash Cindy's hair."

"You've got to get dry clothes on," Lynda lectured.

"You two go on. I'll be all right," Cindy offered.

Lynda waved Brady off. "We've got both of Cindy's rigs. You take the Cadillac and leave me the keys to the truck. Go on to the motel and get a hot shower and dry clothes. I'll wash Cindy's hair and be there in an hour."

"I'll wait," he asserted.

"You go get some dry clothes, cowboy," Cindy insisted. "We don't want you with pneumonia on your honeymoon! Me and Lynda Dawn Darlin' want to talk about the book-writing business."

"Are you sure?"

"Get out of here, Stoner," Lynda growled. "Do you honestly think we need you around all the time? Get real."

"And get dry!" Cindy added.

He started to walk away and then turned around. "I can stay if you want me to."

Cindy flashed a frown at Lynda. "Is he always this difficult to get rid of?"

"Yep," Lynda drawled. "I cain't remember how many times I had to chase him out of the room with a manure fork."

Brady raised his hands over his head. "Okay. I'm going." He left the room and returned again. "You need me to bring you anything?"

"Get out of here, Stoner!" Lynda commanded.

"I was just wonderin'—"

Cindy squeezed Lynda's hand. "Perhaps you should call an orderly."

Lynda raised her eyebrows. "You want a cute orderly or a strong orderly?"

A relaxed smile crept across Cindy's face. "How about a cute *and* strong one?"

"You *are* in la-la land."

"I told you I'm feelin' pretty good. I wonder if they sell this stuff by the fifty-five-gallon barrel?"

Lynda turned to Brady. "Are you still here?"

The sound of his heels tapping a fading pattern into the polished linoleum emergency room floor was his only response.

◆ ◆ ◆

It actually took Lynda almost two hours to wash Cindy's hair, help her get moved into an observation room, give her a sponge bath, and splash on a liberal supply of Swedish Romance. Most of the time the conversation centered on Cindy's book, with an ample discussion of weddings, marriage, and trusting God. Cindy was dozing off by the time Lynda left the hospital. It was a little after 9:00 P.M., and stars filled the previously cloudy sky. The parking lot still showed signs of the earlier summer thunderstorm. Puddles reflected in the street lights.

All right, Austin. Can you really find your way across the large town of Lead? 'Course, if you get lost, you can always call Brady to come find you.

No way.

"Okay, city girl. It's a Ford pickup and not a Dodge, but it can't be all that different. Automatic . . . hey, this is a piece of cake."

Lynda had the engine started and was hunting for the seat belt when she picked up Cindy's dark wig.

This is one long braid. I wonder what . . . if I let my . . .

She glanced nervously around the empty, dark parking lot and then leaned her head over and tugged on the tight-fitting wig. She tucked her own hair into the cap of the wig by the halogen glow of the parking lot lights. Scrunching around in the seat, she peered in the rearview mirror and tried to catch a glimpse of the long, single braid flowing down her back.

"Why, it's as purdy as a bronc rein, darlin'," she mimicked in a deep voice.

"Oh, thank you, cowboy. I bet you say that to all the girls."

"Yes, ma'am, I do. And it works ever' time."

"I suppose you're planning on chasing me around the barn?"

"Yep," she growled to herself in a deep voice.

She reached up to yank the wig off, then took one more look in the rearview mirror. *Of course, I could just leave it on.*

She left the wig in place and drove out onto the street. *This rig sure beats that old Cadillac. We've got to get a second car. I'm not going to be able to drive Brady's truck when he's feeding cows or something. Of course, I would like a vehicle that will get me to the ranch during a snowstorm—something sturdy enough not to shake apart on the potholes and boulders and big enough to hold a month's supply of groceries and . . . Maybe I should drive Brady's truck, and he can buy himself something else.*

"Oh, great!" she moaned. "The gas gauge is on empty."

Lynda passed through downtown Lead and then pulled in at The Shaft: Minimart and Genuine Black Hills Gold Jewelry. Brown leather purse over her shoulder, she hiked into the store. A middle-aged man with bushy, graying sideburns smiled at her.

"I want twenty dollars of regular unleaded," she announced.

"You jist pump what you want, darlin', and then come and pay for it. I trust ya."

Right. I knew that. It isn't exactly Manhattan out here.
"Thanks. Is this the road to the Dakota House Motel?"

"Yes, ma'am, a mile down the road to your left just past the Deadwood turnoff."

"Thanks."

"Ma'am, if you don't mind me saying, that is one handsome braid. Reminds me of a girl in high school by the name of Jennifer. 'Course that was twenty-two years ago."

Lynda smiled and headed toward the door.

"Your name ain't Jennifer, is it?"

"No."

"I knew you wasn't the Jennifer I went to school with. You probably weren't even born twenty-two years ago. But I thought I'd ask. Sometimes events in your life seem to repeat themselves—you know what I mean?"

"Eh, vaguely."

"Now my Jennifer . . . that's one event I wouldn't mind repeating, if you catch my drift."

"I need to pump some gas."

"Yes, ma'am. Say, are you travelin' by yourself?"

"No, I'm traveling with a circus."

"No foolin'? What do you do?"

"Walk a tightrope."

"Well, I'll be. I would have taken you for a barrel racer . . . but you are a little pale for outside work."

"I'm on pump number seven," Lynda announced as she walked out the door.

A little pale? I live in the city. I only see the sun at noon and on weekends—if I'm lucky. A barrel racer? Just because of this braid? There are other professions in the world. Why didn't he say, "Oh, you must be a world-renowned trial lawyer . . . or the Nobel prize-winning chemist . . . or an award-winning New York City book editor!"

Mumbling to herself, she had reached the truck before she

looked up and spotted a man on a motorcycle parked across the street from the minimart. She could not tell who it was in the dark.

Not good, Lynda Dawn Darlin', not good. What if that's McGhee? What if he saw us with Cindy and is planning on getting even?

She walked straight for the driver's side and crawled up into the cab.

We can get gas in this rig tomorrow.

She glanced in the rearview mirror. The motorcycle started to ease across the road toward her.

He's coming over here!

She scooted across the seat and locked the passenger side door, then hurried back and locked her own. Her hands shook as she started the pickup.

Relax. Just drive to the motel. There's no problem. Brady will be there. He's coming right at me! Come on, truck. Cindy's truck! Cindy's wig . . . the guy thinks I'm Cindy! Get real, I don't look anything like her. Except on a dark night. Like tonight.

He pulled up alongside her door just as she put it in gear. With her foot on the accelerator, the truck squealed and fishtailed as she sped out of the minimart. Lynda was still fumbling for the headlights when she bounced over the sidewalk and down off the curb. An oncoming car squealed its way to a stop to allow her entry onto the highway.

Just go on into the minimart. Prove me to be a paranoid New Yorker.

She sighted the single headlight of the motorcycle only twenty feet behind her truck.

Oh, man, he is coming after me. Stoner, where are you? I told you to stay with me at the hospital. Well . . . I should have told you to stay with me!

Turn green please. This is a podunk town. They shouldn't even have a traffic light! Turn green!

The light was still red when Lynda barreled through it.

"Excuse me. . . . Sorry, it's an emergency. . . . Trust me."
Where are the cops? Come on, pull me over; give me a ticket. . . .
Where is justice?

"So you're just going to hang back there, are you?" she
shouted. "Well, when I get to that motel, Brady Stoner will
beat you to a pulp! You're history, Mr. Lamont McGhee! You
picked the wrong babe, bucko!" Wiping the tears off her cheek,
Lynda felt perspiration bead her entire forehead.

Oh, great, the tank's on empty. That's what I need—to run out
of gas. Where's that motel? He said it was just across town. How big
a place is this? Dakota . . . Dakota . . . where is it, Stoner?

Lynda glanced in the mirror and didn't see any headlight.
She looked back over her right shoulder. *He's gone? I lost him!*

A loud explosion of crashing glass caused her to jump and
whip her head around. The sideview mirror was shattered.
McGhee cruised just outside her window, a short piece of chain
hanging in his hand.

Lynda felt fear, anger, and terror down the back of her
neck. She clutched the steering wheel so her hands wouldn't
shake. Refusing to look at him, she stepped on the accelerator,
but he kept pace.

He's going to break my window! Lord, this has got to stop.

Lynda jammed on the brakes. The truck wheels locked up.
The engine died. She began to slide sideways across the still-
wet blacktop. *Don't brake in a slide . . . don't brake.*

She let off the brakes as the pickup slid back straight. The
motorcycle rocketed past her. The truck came to a stop in the
middle of the road. Cars with horns blaring sped past her.

He's turning around . . . he's coming back. He's crazy, Lord. He's
high on something. Come on, truck. Start! I don't care if there's no
gas. Start! The starter ground away as the engine sluggishly
turned over and over.

"Start!" Lynda screamed. "I mean it! I'm mad! Do you hear me, truck?"

Suddenly, the engine caught. She continued to grind the starter and then let off the key. She put the rig in gear and began to pick up speed. The single headlight came straight at her.

"What are you doing?" she cried. "Is this suicide? Are you crashing head-on into me? I can't believe this."

The motorcycle kept coming.

"You think you're going to chase me off the road? In your dreams!" She stepped on the accelerator and gripped the steering wheel tight on both sides. *I've got on my seat belt. . . . Does this have an airbag? It's too old. Lord, have mercy!*

Lynda closed her eyes and clutched the steering wheel, and then quickly flipped them back open. *No motorcycle? He missed me! Thank you, Jesus!*

In her rearview mirror she saw the bike and biker sliding across the asphalt, sparks flying.

Yes! Thank you! Thank you! Thank you!

She pulled the truck over in front of a closed used car lot alongside the highway. *I don't want him hurt, Lord. I just want him to stop!*

Okay . . . maybe just a little hurt.

Moderate injuries.

In the hospital for a week or ten.

Lynda waited for traffic to clear and then turned a U in the highway. *I'll make sure someone called an ambulance. It's his own fault.*

Feeling the sweat drip from her chin, she rolled down the window and took deep gulps of the cool Black Hills air. The long braid now flopped over her left shoulder and reached her lap.

Instead of finding a body on the ground next to a wrecked motorcycle, Lynda saw a black-leather-clad man limp toward a motorcycle that lay propped against the curb. There were no cars in sight.

McGhee's up and walking around! He's got to be hurt more than that. . . . I saw him . . . What am I doing back here?

The man looked up at the headlights of her truck.

I could run him over. No one's around. It would just be a traffic accident. A bike loses control on a slick road. . . . This is crazy. Lord, I'm starting to lose it. No . . . wait!

"Turn it around!" she yelled at herself. She slammed on the brakes and cut the truck to the left. The biker vaulted to the sidewalk. She cut way in front of him and turned back around.

I missed you by a mile, dude!

The truck engine died just as she stepped on the gas.

"Oh, man, I wouldn't believe this even if it were a Sandra Bullock movie! Come on, truck! Come on!" Again she ground the starter.

"Lord, You can turn water into wine. How about turning the air in that tank into gasoline? Regular unleaded. . . . just hurry! Oh, man!" The starter continued to grind, and she pumped the accelerator. She could hear the lethargic motor slowing each time it turned over.

The battery's going dead. "Yea, though I walk through the valley of the shadow of death, I will fear no evil. . . .'" She saw the biker climb on his bike. "Deliver me, Lord!" she cried out.

The engine ground over once more, then stopped and just clicked.

"No!" she shouted and turned the key again. The engine started immediately.

"That's cutting it close, Lord!" She stepped on the accelerator, and the truck roared forward. "He's back there! I can't believe it. It's like a never-ending nightmare! I can't lose him! Dakota . . . I'm not stopping until I get to the Dakota!"

Lynda didn't even slow down at the next red light. "I'm

from New York," she yelled. "We don't have to stop at stop-lights!"

Neon flashing lights beyond the next stoplight caught her attention. "Dakota! There it is. Thank You, Lord!" Lynda swerved from lane to lane on the four-lane road, the biker right behind her.

The stoplight turned green as Lynda approached. She was going about thirty-five when she started the left turn. The tires squealed, and the driver's side of the rig lifted into the air. *I'm going to tip over!*

The tires slammed back down on the blacktop as she regained control after the turn, propelling her past the neon lights and a highway sign that read: "Deadwood: 3 miles."

The highway? Where's the motel? I turned too soon!

The motorcycle tried to pass her. She could see the angry, bearded Lamont McGhee swinging the short chain in his right hand. Lynda swerved across the double yellow line, forcing him to drop back behind her.

I'm really going to run out of gas! I've got to turn back.

Twice more McGhee tried to pass. Each time Lynda forced him to drop back. While she was fending him off the second time, a yellow Curve Ahead sign flew by on the right.

A mountainous road? I'm going back. That's it, creep.

When the biker sailed around her on the next try, Lynda pulled sharply to the right and braked. She looked straight ahead to see the headlights of a logging truck round the corner and barrel toward the biker, who had just turned his motorcycle around in the middle of the road.

That truck's going to hit him!

The biker heard the air horn of the truck. He accelerated the motorcycle so quickly that it peeled out toward the guardrail on the far side of the road, the front wheel three feet off the ground. The trucker swerved toward the inside of the road to miss the man.

Lynda braced her arms against the steering wheel. *That truck's going to run over me!*

She shut her eyes. She could hear the roar of the truck and feel Cindy's pickup rock back and forth by the force of the wind from the truck passing so close. The truck's air brakes blasted.

Lynda opened her eyes and stared into darkness.

A fiery explosion from somewhere down the mountain signaled the fate of the motorcycle. A car pulled up and stopped across from her. Then the trucker, carrying a long black flashlight, trotted up to her pickup. The driver of the car hurried over to meet them. Hands shaking, Lynda rolled down the window.

"Are you all right, lady?" the trucker called.

"I th-thought you were going to run over me."

"So did I. I tried to miss that motorcycle in the middle of the road, and the outfit started to slide. I don't know how I missed you. It was like my wheels hit a curb or something." He pushed his Seattle Mariners cap back and scratched his head.

"Did a car go over the edge?" the gray-suited driver asked.

"A motorcycle," Lynda mumbled, still looking straight ahead.

"Did you know the guy?" the trucker asked.

"No."

"I'll try to find him. Chances are, he fell off the bike before it blew up."

"I'll call 911 on my cell-phone," the other man shouted as he ran back to his car.

With both men occupied, Lynda backed the pickup out onto the now-silent highway and turned it back toward Lead. Driving no more than twenty miles an hour, she crept back into town. When she reached the stoplight, she didn't even slow down but turned in front of a white Oldsmobile that skidded to a horn-blasting, tire-squealing stop in the middle of the intersection.

The two-story motel stretched for almost a block along the back of the parking lot. Her engine died as she entered the landscaped parking area. She coasted into a slot between a New Mexico Buick and an Alberta Lexus. She pulled out the key and dropped it into her purse. Then she leaned on the steering wheel and bawled.

It took a couple of minutes for her to realize that the horn that was drowning her sobs was the one she was leaning against. People stared from the balcony. She sat up and tried wiping her eyes with her hands. She ran her dripping nose across the bare skin of her right arm. Lynda was still gulping deep breaths of fresh air when she saw him.

Dry clothes.

Barefoot.

Cowboy hat pushed back.

Dimpled grin.

White teeth.

Square-shouldered.

Twinkle in his brown eyes.

"Hey, hurry up, darlin'," he called as he approached the pickup. "The pizza just got here, and we're startin' a game of Scrabble. Come on, you're on my team!"

"Where were you, Stoner?" she began to sob. "I needed you, and you weren't there!"

"What are you talkin' about? You told me to come to the motel."

"I know what I told you!" she cried.

"I'm here now, darlin'. What happened?"

She crawled out of the truck, dragging her purse behind her.

"Hey!" Brady whooped. "Great-lookin' hair! Is that Cindy's wig? Darlin', it looks—"

She yanked the hair piece off and wrapped the braid around his neck, yanking it up from behind like a noose.

"Stoner, if you say one more word about long hair, I'm going to hang you from the railing in the balcony. Is that understood?"

"Eh, yes, ma'am," he stammered. "Is everything all right with Cindy?"

"Cindy? I've just spent the most terrifying hour of my life trying to keep from being killed by a crazed biker and a runaway logging truck, and you ask about Cindy." She stomped past him.

"You did wha . . . Someone tried to . . . a logging truck?" Brady mumbled.

She took two steps up the outside stairway and then spun around. "What room am I in?"

"You and Doc have 216. There's an elevator in the lobby if you . . . Darlin', what happened?" He climbed to the step below her. Their eyes were now the same height.

"Kiss me," she commanded.

"What? Here?"

Lynda threw her arms around his neck and smashed her tear-salted lips into his pepperoni-flavored ones. Every muscle in her body seemed to relax all at once, and she slumped in his arms. Without ever pulling away from her kiss, Brady lifted her up in his arms and started carrying her up the stairs. Lynda let her head slip to his shoulder. *Lord, when it's my turn to go, this is where I want to be.*

"We're all in the girls' room," Brady whispered. He kissed her ear. Heidi was standing in the doorway of 218. "Is Lynda Dawn Darlin' all right?" she whispered.

"Open Doc and Lynda's door for me," Brady called. "She's just a little tuckered. I'll put her on the bed."

"You're goin' to play Scrabble aren't you, Uncle Brady?"

"I'll be there in a minute, Heidi-girl."

"I hadn't planned on doing this until after Saturday," Brady grinned.

Lynda rolled over on her back on the bed. "Doing what?"

"Carrying you over the threshold." He sat down on the bed next to her. "Now how about telling me what happened?"

"I think I just lived out the last chapter of Cindy's book."

"Okay, take it from the beginning. Tell me everything."

"First . . . first I want to stand in the shower for an hour, wash my hair, put on some clean clothes, and spray myself from head to foot with Prairie Passion."

"That sounds mighty good to me, darlin'. But give me the short version so I'm not worried sick over what happened to you."

"I'll give you the long version after I clean up."

"In that case, go right ahead."

"What?"

"Go ahead and clean up. I'll wait right here."

"You'll do nothing of the kind, Mr. Stoner!"

"Then tell me the short version."

"Then will you leave?"

"Maybe."

"Maybe?"

"I'm still dreamin' about you bein' sprayed from head to foot with perfume."

"I'll tell you the short version. Then I'm going to take a hot shower, and you're going to your room and take a cold one."

◆ ◆ ◆

Debra Jean Cartier rolled out to the balcony to read the newspaper the next morning as Lynda finished getting dressed. "It's a beautiful morning."

Cartier looked up. "Yes, absolutely gorgeous. How are you feeling after that ordeal last night?"

"With a blue sky like this and that clean mountain air, it just seems like a bad dream. A really bad dream."

"The Rapid City paper reported that a motorcyclist

'plunged off the highway near Lead, breaking both legs and receiving multiple contusions on his head.' They took him to a hospital in Rapid City. His name was Harold L. McGhee of Henderson, Nevada."

Lynda leaned on the balcony railing and watched as Brady drove Cindy's Ford pickup into the parking lot directly under them.

"Hey, cowboy, nice shirt!" Lynda called out.

Blue jeans and brown boots. New green cowboy shirt with thundering horses galloping across it. Black felt hat pushed back. Silver buckle and brown eyes sparkling, he glanced up at her. "My oh my, like two angels sittin' on the clouds. I didn't know I was this close to heaven."

Lynda turned to Debra Jean. "Now tell me the truth, Doc, are all cowboys as smooth as Stoner?"

"Nope. You've got the sweetest-talking man west of the Mississippi. Butter would feel like coarse sandpaper compared to Brady."

"You two raggin' on me again?" he called up.

"Maybe, maybe not," Lynda chided. "Where you been?"

"I had to get some gas in the truck. Remember?"

"Was it pretty low? I knew I had run out."

"I put twenty-two gallons into a twenty-one-gallon tank."

"You what?"

"Yeah, darlin', there wasn't one drop of gas in that rig. I don't know how I made it to the station, and I don't know how you made it to the motel last night."

"Thank You, Lord."

"You got that right, darlin'. You were workin' the guardian angels overtime."

"The logger said it was just like his wheels were up against a curb. He couldn't have crashed into me if he wanted to."

Brady leaned against the hood of the Ford. "The Lord's

been very good us, Lynda Dawn Darlin'. Now you two finish gettin' ready, and we'll go get the stock."

"Maybe you and Tyler could load up the animals while we finish up."

"Oh, no. Tyler said it took them an hour to get that bull out of the trailer last night. He kept lookin' for his 'mama.' He won't crawl back in there without you hollerin' at him."

"Okay, we'll hurry. When will we pick up Cindy?"

"Call her and see what time she can leave. That way we'll know how soon to load up."

"How are we going to drive four rigs?"

"You can drive one of Cindy's over to the hospital. We'll check with her about what she wants to do with both rigs. Maybe she'll sell one of them."

"Stoner, I'm riding with you, remember? I don't plan on driving to my wedding alone—you got that?"

"Yes, ma'am."

Lynda turned back to Debra Jean. "Did you ever hear anything quite like a cowboy's 'yes, ma'am'?"

"You mean, the natural veneration that rolls right up from his boots?"

"I guess that's it. There is no man in Manhattan who shows that much respect. It makes me seem somewhere between the queen . . . and his mother."

"Or both?"

"Yeah. I'm going to call Cindy."

Lynda flipped through the phone book and then dialed the hospital.

"Hi, I'd like to talk to Cindy LaCoste, please."

A woman's deep voice boomed, "Checked out."

"Yes, she's checking out today. We're going to come give her a ride, and I need to know what time to pick her up. Could you ring me through to her room?"

"I said, she checked out."

"Oh, is she waiting in the lobby? Is there a phone there? I really do need to talk to her."

"Lady, are you deaf? I said, she checked out. She's not in the room, not in the lobby, not in the hospital, and not in the parking lot. I saw her get in a taxi."

"But—but—where'd she go?"

"Now how in the world would I know that?"

NINE

With square-set jaw and narrow brown eyes, Brady stomped around the corral. Early to Bed and Pedregoso stood motionless while he slapped on headstalls and lead ropes—as if they instinctively knew this was not a good morning to act up. He muttered while loading the two horses into the trailer, "We had this all settled, didn't we? She was goin' with us to the weddin', and then, if she didn't feel like drivin', Heather would give her a lift to Ely where she'd rest up at the ranch. All she had to do was kick back and wait for us to come by this mornin'."

Lynda tried to calm him down. "I suppose she never quite bought into it. I doubt if she knows anything about me and Lamont McGhee last night. Do you think she's out looking for him?"

Brady slammed the trailer door closed with such force that both horses jumped and kicked. "How can she? She's all bunged up. Let me tell you, bruised ribs hurt with ever' step and ever' breath. Besides that, she's on foot. We have both her rigs and all her belongings except for the muddy clothes she was wearin' when they took her to the hospital. And they cut some of those off her when they pulled her out of the pit. What kind of hospital would release a patient wearin' nothin' but a green hospital gown and cowboy boots?"

Lynda rocked back and forth on her toes, her hands jammed into the back pockets of her jeans. "She wanted some clean things, so I brought her in some more clothes from the pickup last night before I left the hospital."

Brady slapped his hand on the front of the silver and black Dodge pickup. "Then she was plannin' all this last night."

"I don't think so. She just felt insecure about not having any of her clothes there." Lynda paused, then leaned close to Brady. "You really think she was stringing us along all the time?"

Brady opened a side compartment at the front of the stock trailer and pulled out a slightly muddy rope. "She wants to finish this book . . . this episode. I think she figured if she didn't do the job now, it wouldn't get done."

"But the job is done now. I should have called her at the hospital last night after I got back to the motel. I just figured she needed the rest." Lynda trailed along after him. "She couldn't have planned to go very far all bruised up like that."

"She knew we would follow her. The gal at the hospital said she took a taxi. She must have gone to Deadwood. Anywhere else would be too expensive." Brady crawled into the pickup but left his door open. "Tyler! Catch that gate for me, partner!" While everyone watched, Brady backed the pickup and trailer to the small corral next to the barn. Leaping out of the truck with a coiled nylon rope over his shoulder, he grabbed Lynda's hand and tugged her to the corral. "Come on, Mama, time to load your bull."

"My bull?" She staggered along reluctantly. "It belongs to you and your brother."

"Girls," Brady called to Heidi and Wendy who stood next to the van, "whose bull is this?"

Clad in a black Professional Bull Riders T-shirt and jeans shorts, Wendy called out, "That's Lynda Dawn Darlin's bull."

"See? They all call him your bull."

"I have a bull?" She flipped her hair back and could feel the turquoise and black feathered earrings brush against her hand.

"Go ahead and load him up. We need to get to Deadwood."

She peeked through the rails of the stout corral. "Is that on our way to the ranch?"

"Eh, no," Brady conceded. "But it's only three miles back down the road."

They climbed into the corral. R-43 stood on the far side and glared at them, a flake of hay crumbling from his mouth.

"Okay, the trailer's open. Do your thing," Brady called.

"I don't think he really wants to get into the trailer."

"Of course he doesn't. It's cramped and smelly. But you're just the one to talk him into it."

Lynda could see Heidi, Wendy, Tyler, and even Dr. Cartier watching.

This can't possibly work again. It was just a fluke before. Is this some sort of initiation, Lord? Do they always make greenhorns load the bull?

She hiked to within fifteen feet of the 2,000-pound animal. "Now listen," Austin bantered, "there's the trailer—get in there. Shoo . . . go on . . . get in there!"

The big-eyed bull just stared and slowly chewed the mouthful of hay.

"Bawl him out, Mama!" Brady shouted.

She turned back to the bull, took a keep breath, and shouted, "Do I have to raise my voice at you? I said, get in the trailer, and get in there now!"

The hay dropped out of R-43's mouth. He stood straight, cocked his head, and glanced at the open gate.

Lynda waved her arms toward the trailer.

The enormous, dehorned brindle bull lumbered into the trailer. Brady slammed the door behind him. Lynda scooped up a handful of hay and walked over and shoved it through the slats of the stock trailer. "That's a good boy," she encouraged him. "But next time I don't want to have to tell you twice." She looked up to see Brady grinning from ear to ear and shaking his head.

He turned to the audience. "Now that, gang, is how you load a bull."

"How does she do that?" Tyler quizzed.

"I told you, it's a gift from the Lord," Brady answered. "Listen up, guys, from now on that bull has a new name."

"What's that, Uncle Brady?" Wendy asked.

"We're goin' to call him Mama's Boy."

"A bull named Mama's Boy? That's kind of wimpy, isn't it?" Tyler argued.

"You want to load him next time?" Brady challenged.

"No, sir," Tyler gulped. "Mama's Boy is a fine name."

"That's what I thought. Come on, load up. Darlin', I'm goin' to need you to drive one of Cindy's rigs into Deadwood. We'll either find her there or sell one of the rigs . . . or something."

"Three miles. That's it, cowboy," Lynda insisted. "I told you I'm not going down the road unless I'm with you."

"Yes, ma'am. Trust me."

The caravan left the corrals at the edge of the pine forest of Lead, South Dakota, aiming for Deadwood. Brady drove the Dodge pickup, the two dogs curled in the front seat, a badgered bull in the stock trailer. Lynda followed in Cindy's Ford pickup, the seat cluttered with clothing, candy bar wrappers, and half a six pack of Dr. Pepper. Behind her came Tyler and Heidi in the green Cadillac. Dr. Cartier and Wendy trailed the group, with two extremely bored horses.

Lynda dug in her purse and pulled out a yellow bottle of Captivating Sunburst. She glanced at herself in the rearview mirror and then dropped it back into the purse. Rummaging with one hand, she pulled out a leather-encased perfume bottle. Holding the steering wheel with her knees, she managed to splash the perfume on her neck and wrists. *The sun's coming up in our eyes. That means we're driving east. Sheridan is west. The ranch is west. Jackson is west. Lord, I don't want to go east. I'm getting married in three days.*

Mrs. Brady Stoner.

Then my life can be like this all year around.

I won't make it.

I'll wear out.

Lord, I'll die young.

But happy.

She glanced again at herself in the mirror and brushed the hair out of her eyes. *You're getting some color in your face, Austin. It looks good. With any luck you'll be one shade darker than your wedding dress. Oh, man . . . I hope Kelly and Nina remembered my dress!*

If there was some way You could speed up the next three days, that would be nice, Lord. I'm starting to panic that the wedding will never happen. I know we've got to try to find Cindy. But I don't know what we're goin' to do if we find her. She's determined to go her own way.

Lord, are there some people we just can't help no matter how much we want to? She said she hasn't given up on You, but, well . . . it doesn't seem to me that she's asking You for much advice.

Thick pines lined both sides of the curving, mountainous road. Lynda drove with both hands on the steering wheel. Even though the sky was perfectly clear and deep blue, the blacktop was still wet from the previous night's storm. Steam slowly rose from the highway.

Of course, Lord, I haven't exactly been asking You for direction this week either. Help me relax. I know You want me to marry Brady. I know it's going to happen Saturday . . . somehow. The single life is a lot simpler.

She glanced up at the rig in front of her and thought about

Brady driving alone. *I really, really want to be up there with my cowboy!*

◆ ◆ ◆

Whitewood Creek Canyon was not wide enough for anyone to build a respectable town there. But in its over 120 years of existence, no one ever accused Deadwood of being respectable. The overflow public parking lot on the west edge of town was almost empty as they pulled in and parked the rigs. Capt. Patch and Margarita disappeared into the brush on the mountain side of the gravel parking lot. Brady gathered everyone around Cartier's van.

"Here's the plan," he announced, as he rolled up the sleeves of his black and green Western shirt. "We're going to hike down main street checking in every joint."

Heidi wrinkled her naturally upturned nose. "It's kind of like playing hide and seek, isn't it?"

"But this is definitely not a game," he insisted. "When we get down to The Deuces, if we haven't found any trace of Cindy by then, I'll, eh . . . I'll see if Joysee Draper is there and—"

"You know Joysee Draper, Uncle Brady?" Heidi's blue eyes widened to De Grazia proportions.

"I met her a few years ago."

"You actually think that Cindy went to talk to her?" Lynda quizzed. "I thought you said they got in a fight the last time they were together."

"A fight? This sounds like a headline in the tabloids!" Heidi yelped.

"I bet she scratches when she fights," Wendy added. "Have you ever seen pictures of her long fingernails?"

"Those are false ones she wears for publicity shots," Brady informed her.

"Oh? We are talking fingernails, aren't we?" Lynda fussed.

Heidi's crisp blue eyes seem to double in size. "What were Cindy and Joysee fighting over?"

Lynda squeezed the bulge of Brady's upper arm muscles. "Over your Uncle Brady. At least, that's one story."

"No kidding? I can't believe this! This is so totally cool!"

"All I'm sayin'," Brady inserted, "is that if we can't find Cindy anyplace else, I'll check with Joysee. Now, Doc, how about you and Wendy taking one side of the street? Me and Lynda Dawn Darlin' will take the other."

"What, exactly, are we looking for?" Cartier probed.

"Cindy . . . or Trent . . . or some sign of either. If she wanted us to follow, she'd leave some clue."

"Do you want me to go with Doc Cartier or you guys?" Heidi asked.

"I need Tyler to stay here with the animals, so I figured you might want to keep him company this time," Brady replied.

"While you guys meet Joysee Draper? No way! I'm going with you."

"It'll be kind of lonesome jist sittin' here by myself," Tyler mumbled, obviously hurt.

"You can read *ProRodeo News* or, you know, practice rop-ing," Heidi offered.

"In that case, Heidi can go with Doc and Wendy," Brady instructed. "Tyler, we'll be back in a couple hours maximum. If Miss Cindy stops by, keep her here."

"How am I going to do that?"

"Ask her to teach you how to throw a hoolihan. She's a real good horse-roper."

"I already know how to toss a hoolihan."

"But Cindy doesn't know that."

"Uncle Brady," Heidi interrupted, "Cindy is old, isn't she?"

"She's about my age," Brady assured her.

Heidi's eyes lit up as she helped Doc disengage the wheel-chair from the van's hydraulic ramp.

◆ ◆ ◆

The slight breeze that blew down the narrow main street was cool in a summer sort of way. Lynda's bare arms bristled a bit, but she was glad to be in the sun.

She was especially glad to have her hand laced into Brady's. Casinos, saloons, antique shops, tourist traps, jewelry stores, and curious people lined both sides of Deadwood's main street. They carefully worked their way through racks of cheap T-shirts and glass cases of expensive jewelry.

Finally, from a street corner they watched a German tour group load up on a mine expedition bus. "We're not having much luck, cowboy."

"At least we're together, darlin'. I didn't like that three-mile drive from Lead. I've spent most of my adult life drivin' down the road by myself. I'm through."

As they walked along the sidewalk, she stood on her tiptoes and kissed his freshly shaven cheek. He smelled of quality spicy aftershave.

"What's that for?" He blushed.

"I'm just practicing."

"Practicin' for what?"

"For after we're married. Then I can legally and biblically embarrass you anytime I want."

"You can?"

"Yes, it's in the vows."

"It is?"

"Sure. Didn't you know that? A wife is entitled to do all sorts of mushy things in public to embarrass her husband. It's in the code."

"Oh, well," he sighed. "If it's in the code. By the way, do you plan on flusterin' me again soon?"

"Not while you're expecting it. I want it to be a surprise."

"I'm not expectin' it right now."

"No pathetic begging. That's not in the code. Besides, we have to find Cindy, remember?"

"I remember. There's The Deuces."

"Have you figured out what to say to Cindy this time?"

"Yep. I'm goin' to say, 'Cindy-girl, here are the keys to your rigs. We're goin' to get married. I wish you well. Don't get yourself hurt.'"

"Really?"

"Darlin', this is as far as I go. To the best of my knowledge, the whole motorcycle gang has felt the wrath of Cindy or Lynda Dawn. Anything more than that is destructive vengeance. I want no part of that. I have no intention of being manipulated like we were this morning. Maybe we can make Billings by evenin', hit the ranch by noon tomorrow, and drive to Jackson on Friday."

"That's when we have the reservations, right?"

"Right. You, Kelly, and Nina will stay at the lodge on Friday night. The rest of us are scattered around. I'm not sure what reservations I made. The plans keep changin'."

"What if we don't find Cindy here in Deadwood?"

"I don't want to think about that."

Though only a two-story hotel and casino, The Deuces stretched for a full city block. Built in 1994, it was patterned after 1880s architecture. The stone block and flat-iron construction gave it the feel of a boisterous gold mining boom town. Brady and Lynda scooted past scores of senior citizens parked in front of slot machines and made their way to the hotel registration desk.

A woman in her early twenties, sporting heavy eye makeup, curly black hair, and a name tag reading "Tiffany" greeted them with a scowl. "We don't normally allow people to check in until after 2:00 P.M. You can wait until then, can't you?"

"Just need a little information, not a room," Brady drawled. "Has a woman named Cindy LaCoste left a message for me?"

"What's your name?"

"I'm Brady . . . darlin'."

She scouted though a stack of papers. "No. There are no messages for Brady Darlin."

"My name's Brady Stoner. I just have a habit of callin' women darlin'."

"Why?"

Lynda clutched his arm. "It's a character flaw."

"Did you say Brady Stoner?"

"Yes, ma'am," he replied with a tip of the hat and an ah-shucks grin on his face.

"I *do* have a note!" she announced. "Ms. Draper is waiting for you. You're to go right up to her gym."

Brady shoved his black hat back and rubbed his chin. "Gym?"

"It's her private gym. Suite G. Here's a key." She handed him a plastic card. "After that big build-up Ms. Draper gave you . . . well, you sure aren't what I expected."

"Sorry to disappoint you."

"I figured someone more . . . Mel Gibson-like." She turned to Lynda and smirked. "Ms. Draper didn't mention anything about you. Honey, are you sure you're with him?"

"You bet your false eyelashes I am, Tiffany darling," Lynda shot back. She whipped around without looking back.

"Nothin' like burnin' our bridges as we go," Brady admonished in a mumble. They proceeded, arm in arm, through a maze of slot machines and blackjack tables. "I hope we don't need to ask Tiffany anything else."

"I should apologize."

"Yep."

Heidi, Wendy, and Debra Jean met them at the elevators. All three wore tan legs and wide smiles.

"We couldn't find any sign of Cindy. How about you?" Cartier asked.

"Not a trace," Brady reported.

"Have you seen Joysee Draper yet, Uncle Brady?" Heidi asked.

"We're just going to her gym." Brady punched the up button.

Wendy helped Debra Jean wheel her chair into the elevator. "Her own private gym? Wow, that's so cool."

"I saw her in a movie this spring," Heidi declared.

"You're allowed to watch Joysee Draper movies?" Lynda challenged.

"Only when Mom doesn't know about it," Wendy tattled.

Heidi shook her head in disgust. "Anyway, in this movie Joysee is being chased by the Swampman, who catches her by the boat dock and . . . Well, eh, then she has the tire iron, and she sort of . . . Anyway, you have to see it. Am I talking too much? I do that when I get nervous."

"I hope Ms. Draper doesn't mind an entourage," Cartier commented as they rode up in the slow-moving, mirror-and-gold-plated elevator.

"I've only got to ask her a couple questions—," Brady began.

"Yes," Lynda inserted, "like why was she expecting you? And why did she leave you a key to her private gym?"

Brady held the door open for the women to exit the elevator. The sign on a wide door read: "Suite G (Private)." He inserted the plastic card in the slot, and the small light blinked green.

Lynda tugged on his arm. "Shouldn't we knock?"

"Why did she give us the card if she wanted us to knock?"

"I believe she gave the cowboy a key, not the whole fan club."

Brady held the door open for them.

"This is one time you go first, buckaroo," Lynda insisted. The others nodded agreement.

He barged into the large, high-ceilinged room filled with exercise equipment. Lynda followed, with the others close behind her. The walls were covered with floor-to-ceiling publicity photographs of Joysee Draper. Most were poses in bikinis, shorts and halters, or tight miniskirts, tall boots, and scoop-necked T-shirts.

"This is kind of . . . weird," Lynda whispered.

"Sort of a personal shrine to yourself," Debra Jean offered in a low voice.

"I feel really, really dorky," Heidi sniveled. "I must be the ugliest girl in the entire world!"

Wendy stepped up between Lynda and Brady. "Are we supposed to be here?" she whispered.

"Joysee?" Brady called out from the base of a stair glide machine.

A rattle of glasses from a side room was followed by a melodious shout that sounded close to a purr. "Cowboy, is that you?"

"Yes, ma'am."

"I'm in the kitchen. Come have a glass of carrot juice with me."

"We'll wait out here!" Brady called.

Suddenly the light from the doorway was blocked by the long-legged, leotard-clad, sculptured form of Joysee Draper. Large, round gold earrings dangled from her ears. Her blonde hair was pulled back in a ponytail that seemed to reach her waist.

"It's her!" Heidi mumbled.

"She's . . . she's beautiful," Wendy whispered.

"We?" Draper called out. "Look at this—you brought others!" She walked right to Brady, threw her arms around his neck, and kissed him on the lips. "And I thought I'd never see you again! Now introduce me to your little groupies."

Brady blushed, pulled his hand from her clutches, and

slipped his arm around Lynda's waist. "Joysee, this is my fiancée, Lynda Dawn Austin. We're gettin' married Saturday."

Draper's professional, straight-toothed smile concealed any emotion. "Oh? And the rest are your harem?"

"This is Wendy and Heidi Martin—sort of like family."

"Brady's kind of like our uncle," Wendy added.

"You're really her! You're really Joysee Draper," Heidi gasped.

"Yes, isn't that amazing? I woke up this morning, looked in a mirror, and there was Joysee."

"Really?" Heidi's mouth dropped open. "Oh, you were kidding me, weren't you? I think I'm going to faint!"

"Please don't," Draper said. "I'm all out of smelling salts."

"And this is a very good friend, Dr. Debra Jean Cartier."

Joysee took the towel from her shoulders, revealing the plunging neckline of her leotard.

Lynda tried not to stare. *Now I feel dorky. It's not fair, Lord. She has everything—in abundance. I feel like an old Plymouth after he's seen a Porsche.*

Joysee Draper wiped her forehead with the towel. "Well, how about me buying everyone an early lunch? Just tell them in the cafe to bill it to me. Brady, I need you to stay up here for a minute and help me . . . eh, adjust some of this equipment."

Lynda jabbed him with her elbow. *I can't believe she's doing this in front of me! I'm marrying the guy in three days, and she's making a pass at him! I ought to rip her lips off right now.*

"Joysee, this is going to sound strange, but have you seen Cindy LaCoste? We're worried about her. She bruised some ribs and got hurt pretty bad. We need to find her before anythin' else happens to her. I had reason to think that she might be headed this way."

"I thought you were marrying this skinny thing overdosed on very expensive perfume, which no one should wear in the daylight anyway. Why are you looking for Cindy?"

"Joysee, stop being so snotty. You're way too smart and talented for that. It's not becoming on you," Brady lectured. "We really care about Cindy. Did you know that a few years back Cindy was abandoned by Joe Trent to a gang of bikers, who raped her and just about beat her to death? She deserves a break."

The glitz instantly drained out of Draper's expression. "I didn't know that," she replied softly. To Lynda's relief, she slung the towel back around her neck and let it blanket her neckline.

"We don't want to take up your time, but have you seen or heard from Cindy?" Brady asked.

"I haven't thought about her in years, and then this morning she calls me up from the lobby. But I didn't invite her up. Why should I? She asked if I had seen Joe Trent lately. I met him one time, Brady. He's a real loser . . . a low-life. And believe me, I've known lots of low-life types from Vegas. But I don't have anything to do with him. That's what I told left-hook Cindy."

"Left-hook Cindy?" Heidi asked.

"That's what she caught me with, right, Brady? We were pretty even on the set. Then she hit me with a big left hook. Who would have thought a right-handed woman would have a left hook?"

"Did she tell you I was coming by?"

"Yes, but she forgot to mention your friends."

Brady's arm was still wrapped around Lynda's waist. "What exactly did you tell her?"

"I told her not to call me again. We had nothing to talk about. But if Joe Trent were in Deadwood, he would undoubtedly be at the Black Aces and Eights Casino."

"Why there?"

"It's being run by Sammy Vecicio. He's sort of the king of Vegas independent scumbags. Look, I really didn't know this thing about Cindy. I wouldn't wish that on anyone. I ought to know."

"How's that?" Brady asked.

Draper looked over at Wendy, "How old are you, honey? About twelve . . . thirteen?"

Wendy looked down at her white socks and white tennis shoes. "I'm sixteen."

"I looked about like her when I was eleven or twelve. Anyway, some neighborhood guys jumped me and . . ." Draper glanced over at the big pictures of herself on the wall. She put her hands on her hips, took a deep breath, and then wiped the corner of her eyes with the towel. "Anyway . . . I've come a long way from some abandoned service station in San Bernardino, haven't I?"

"You sure have, Miss Joysee." Brady tipped his hat and turned to the door. "Thanks for the word about Cindy. We'll check for her at the Aces and Eights."

"Yeah, good luck . . . and thanks for shooting me down again, cowboy."

Lynda looked back at the movie star. Draper lifted her long blonde hair and held it on the top of her head. "There's not much about me that is real, Lynda Dawn. But Brady always seems to reach the real part. The truth of the matter is, he would have turned me down even if you all weren't tagging along. That's the real world. No one lets me spend much time in it anymore."

No one said anything until they exited the hotel and stepped out into the sunlight.

"What did you think of Joysee Draper?" Brady asked Lynda.

"I went in thinking I wouldn't like her . . . hated her at first . . . then left with a touch of sadness for her. It's all a phony game."

"It's tough to be yourself when everyone likes you to be artificial."

"I presume you're going to the Black Aces and Eights?" Cartier asked.

"I think I'll go back and wait with Tyler," Heidi offered. "I can't believe I met Joysee Draper! I want to tell him all about her."

"Don't tell him everything," Wendy cautioned. "You don't want him to get mad because he didn't come with us."

"Hah!" Heidi raised her nose with adolescent superiority. "She's not his type."

"Yeah, I suppose those life-size posters would have bored him to tears," Wendy sneered.

"Girls," Brady scolded.

Wendy put her hands on her hips. "I think I'll go back with you, just to make sure you tell the story right."

"I don't need my kid sister to tag along!"

Brady's voice raised in insistence and volume. "Girls!"

Dr. Cartier rolled on down the sidewalk. "Think I'll head back to the outfit, too. Could be more exciting there than in the Black Aces and Eights."

"Thanks." Brady tipped his hat as the girls fussed their way behind Cartier's wheelchair. When they had turned the corner, Lynda slid her hand into Brady's. "She's a remarkable woman."

"Doc?"

"Yes. You didn't think I meant Joysee Draper, did you?"

"No, I guess not. I knew you'd like Debra Jean."

"She deserves to have a husband."

"I agree with you there."

"I don't know why she doesn't think any man would be interested in her. She's got more going for her than most of the women I know. I think maybe that's my next God-given task."

"What is?"

"Finding Debra a husband."

"Is that the kind of thing you tell her you're doing?"

"No. It's a secret work."

"Well, what's your God-given task at this moment?"

"Marrying you, cowboy—in about seventy-five hours . . . but who's counting?"

"You really think that's what the Lord wants you to do?"

"Positive. How about you, Brady Stoner?"

"It's the most exciting and scary thing I've ever done."

"Is it the right thing?"

"Better than right. It's perfect." Brady raised her hand and kissed her fingers. "Let's go see if we can find Cindy."

"You don't think she actually went to take on Trent in her condition, do you?"

"She's a bulldog, just like one New York City editor I know." Brady held her hand as they jogged across the street between a potato chip truck and a yellow Buick from New Jersey.

"Me? A bulldog?" The bright sunlight felt warm on the back of her arms. She wished she had worn shorts instead of jeans.

"Yep. You both are the type that bite into one thing at a time and don't let go until you've accomplished your purpose. Cindy's determined to finish off the motorcycle gang. She thinks she'll find the last guy with Trent."

"If she thinks there're two of them, she won't take them head on, right?"

"There's the casino." Brady pointed to the corner of the next block. "She's been trying to pick them off one at a time. She must have laid awake all night thinkin' of some new plan."

"And if we barge in asking for Cindy, we might jeopardize her safety," Lynda counseled.

"That could be."

"So . . . Mr. Cowboy Detective, what do we do?"

"Maybe if we can spot Trent, we could just watch him . . . without him seein' us until Cindy makes a move."

"How are we going to find Trent?"

"Knowing Trent, I would suppose he's hanging around the

blackjack tables, since he fancies himself the world's best Twenty-one player. Especially if the table's run by a girl in a skimpy outfit."

Brady and Lynda walked slowly down a double aisle of slot machines positioned on the red and black carpet. Smoke drifted across the dark room. The noise of spinning machines and an occasional tinkle of coins deadened their conversation. She reached over and grabbed his arm. He leaned his ear down to hear her words.

"Brady, chances are Trent knows about the biker. And he undoubtedly thinks that Cindy was driving the Ford and did the guy in. So he won't be out in the open. He'll think she is coming after him and hide out somewhere."

"Unless he's determined to take care of her once and for all. Then he would set a little trap and place himself right out in the open."

"But," Lynda continued, "wouldn't Cindy be suspicious?"

"Not if she figures there're two of them, and they think she's in the hospital in Lead."

"Now I'm really confused. This is beginning to sound like a scene from *The Princess Bride*."

"Ah hah!" Brady triumphed. "Do you think Cindy will use tasteless, odorless Lidocaine and poison Trent?"

"I think—"

Suddenly Brady grabbed her around the shoulders, shoved her between two slot machines, and kissed her wildly on the lips.

She struggled to free herself. "Braaaady," she mumbled.

"Kiss me," he whispered. "Joe Trent's right over there at that blackjack table."

She kissed him, then pulled back. "This isn't some gimmick just to kiss me, is it?"

"I don't need a gimmick for kissing you! Keep your back toward the gaming tables."

"Trent's really over there?"

Brady kissed her again. "Yep."

"Is he alone?"

His narrow, slightly chapped lips danced across hers. "Yeah. Just him and a dealer."

"In a skimpy outfit?"

Brady kissed her neck and her ear. "Yep."

"Isn't there something else we can do to stay inconspicuous?"

"You complainin'?"

"Just a little embarrassed . . . in public."

Brady stopped kissing her but stayed hunkered down. "You got any quarters?"

"Two or three. Why? Do I need to start buying kisses?"

"Just play the slots."

"I don't gamble."

"Neither do I. But it would give us an excuse to hang around this spot and see what happens."

Lynda dug in her jeans pocket and shoved a quarter in a coin slot. "Now what?"

"Pull the handle all the way down and then let it go."

"What will happen?"

"All those pictures will spin around and randomly stop, and you'll lose your quarter."

"That's all there is to it?"

"Yeah, and once you get really good at it, you can lose twenty dollars in less than five minutes."

"How do you know so much about casinos, Mr. Stoner?"

"I was the one back at the bunkhouse when the boys came home after blowin' their paychecks."

Lynda pulled down on the lever and turned loose. The cylinders spun.

"Do you see that guy over at the elevator?" Brady asked.

Lynda peeked around. "The one in the ponytail and black T-shirt?"

"Yeah. He's watchin' Trent's every move. I think he's the back up."

"What do we do?"

"Keep waitin' for Cindy."

"What if nothing happens?"

"Either I start kissin' you again, or you stick another quarter in the machine and look excited."

"Excited? This is the most boring game I've ever played in my life. What happens if Cindy does show up?" Lynda pulled the lever and watched the spinning symbols flash by.

"We'll try to grab her before she makes her play."

"And if we don't?"

"I'll take Trent; you take the guy at the elevator."

"You're kiddin'. Look . . . I've got three lemons. What does that mean?"

With a ring of a bell and loud clink, one quarter dropped into the coin return.

"It means you won a quarter."

"One lousy quarter? I can get more money back when the pop machine malfunctions at Wal-Mart!" she fumed.

"That's it—look excited!"

"You still didn't tell me what I'm supposed to do about the guy at the elevator."

"Distract him. You know—wink, faint, throw a quarter at him . . . something."

"Is there an alternate plan here, buckaroo?"

"Run up to him and scream. It always works on Mama's Boy."

"Funny."

"Put another quarter in the machine."

"Spend all my winnings?"

"Go for it. What kind of clothing did you take to Cindy last night? What will she be wearing?"

"A green and black flannel shirt and blue jeans. . . . Look, I lost my winning quarter."

"Play another one."

"I don't have anymore."

Brady dug into his pocket and sorted out three quarters and handed them to her.

"You had quarters, and you made me gamble away mine?" She shoved in one of the coins and pulled the lever as they huddled close to the spinning cylinders.

"Do you notice anything different about the old lady over there?" Brady nodded his head to a gray-haired woman with a long beige dress playing slot machines about twenty feet from them.

"The one with her back toward us?"

"Yeah."

"Well . . . she sure is pumping quarters in fast. Undoubtedly she's done this before."

"Look at her ankles," Brady whispered.

"Her what?"

"Her ankles and the skin right above them. They're thin and smooth and tanned."

"Stoner, have you been standing here with your arm around my waist checking out old ladies' ankles?"

"Those are not old ladies' ankles! I think she's got jeans rolled up under that dress."

"You think that's Cindy?"

"Shhh!" he cautioned. "I know I've seen those ankles before."

"I'm going to pretend I didn't hear that."

Lynda shoved in another of Brady's quarters and pulled the chrome lever. "What are we going to do now?"

"You slide up to the lady on the right, and I'll take the left. If it's Cindy, we'll each grab an arm and escort her right out the front door."

"If it's not Cindy?"

"Eh . . . put a quarter in the machine and pull the lever. Come on. Don't look at Trent." Brady took her by the arm, and they started toward the gray-haired woman.

Lynda had taken three steps when a siren went off behind them. Loud clanging bells. Something like an airhorn blast. And the rattle of coins in the pay-out tray.

She and Brady spun around.

"What's happened!" she asked.

"Looks like you won big, darlin'!"

"Really?"

"Go over there and scream and yell and collect your winnin's. It will divert their attention. I'll go get Cindy and meet you outside."

Lynda scampered back to her machine. *Collect my winnings? How do I collect my winnings?* She tried catching the overflowing coins in her cupped hands. Other curious gamblers hovered around her.

"Wow! You got the Big Casino!"

"I did?"

"I sat at that machine for thirty hours straight and never made more than minimum wage!" a big lady in a bright orange muu-muu complained. "Didn't I, Leroy?"

"You need a bucket!" a man called.

"A what?"

"Here . . . it's a house bucket. You can use it to tote the quarters over to the pay window."

The machine continued to spew out quarters and make loud clanging noises. "When does it stop?" Lynda held the cardboard bucket under the spewing machine.

"Hopefully, never!" the big lady laughed.

"But—but the bucket's about full, and there are quarters rolling all over the floor and . . ."

"Here, you can have my bucket, too," an older woman

offered. Lynda couldn't see anything beyond the circling crowd.

A woman in a short black skirt and black mesh stockings, sporting a badge on her blouse proclaiming, "I can CHANGE you!" stepped up next to Lynda. "I can give you a hand getting this to the cashier."

"Oh, is that how it's done? I've never won before. I mean, I won a quarter. But that doesn't count. This is my first real pot."

"Either you change it in for some paper money, or we'll give you a Black Aces and Eights Casino duffel bag and let you tote it yourself."

The machine finally stopped clinking out coins. The crowd started to disperse. The attendant bent down to scoop some of Lynda's coins off the carpet.

"Are all of those mine, too?"

"Every one of them—2,500 coins."

Lynda looked over at where the old woman had been standing and didn't see her or Brady. Her eyes glanced around the room. "Eh, how much money is that?"

"$625."

"Wow! That's all right!" *The man at the elevator is gone. Trent's gone. Even the blonde dealer's no longer at her table. What's going on here?*

"Did you want me to help you change these?"

Movement up the stairs caught her eye. She spotted Brady being shoved by the ponytailed man through a door at the top of the stairs. Joe Trent was dragging the gray-haired woman into the same room.

"I need the duffel bag, and I need it right now!" Lynda shouted.

"But that's pretty heavy," the attendant cautioned.

"Hurry! I mean it!"

Within a moment, a black duffel bag appeared, and Lynda

dumped all the coins into it. She zipped it up and then struggled to lift the bag.

"Are you sure . . . ," the attendant began.

"I'm sure." Lynda stalked across the casino, limping from the weight of the duffel bag.

I am not losing that man now. We are going to get married Saturday, and he is not going to be beat up. So help me, they are in big, big trouble! I'm not putting up with this, Lord.

Taking one stair at a time, she lugged the coins to the second story. Lynda approached the unmarked door where she had seen Brady. She quietly turned the cold brass doorknob.

Okay, it's locked. Now what?

She banged with her bare knuckles on the heavy oak door. "Open this door right now!" she screamed.

Lynda backed up to the balcony railing, clutching the heavy duffel bag to her chest. "Open the door now!"

Gaining momentum with each step, she lunged toward the door. Just as her shoulder was about to crash into the thick wooden door, it opened just a crack. A brown eye peeked through the slit. With the added weight of the quarters, she hammered the door into the man's forehead. The result sounded like a baseball bat crashing into a concrete step. The door swung completely open, and the man crumpled to the carpeted floor. The four people in the center of the room all gave her a startled glance.

Joe Trent raised a black handgun at her.

Brady shouted something.

Cindy, wigless but still in the long dress, screamed.

Extending the full length of her arm, Lynda swung the duffel bag at Trent. The centrifugal force of the swing brought her feet off the ground, and the duffel bag caught Trent alongside the head. The gun flew across the room. Trent crashed to the charcoal gray carpet with its two of spades and two of clubs design.

The blackjack dealer dropped the knife she was holding

and backed away from Lynda crying, "Don't hurt me. Please don't hurt me. They said they'd fire me if I didn't go along!"

"Good work, darlin'!" Brady called. "Come on, ladies, let's get out of here!" He grabbed Cindy's and Lynda's hands and tugged them toward the door.

"I can't go fast, Brady," Cindy complained. "I'm hurtin'. I got punched. My ribs are hurting really bad." She pulled the long dress over her head and tossed it to the floor. Her jeans were rolled halfway up to her knees.

The trio shuffled out the door and eased their way down the stairs. Lynda still carried the bag of quarters.

"I can't believe you barged in and did that! I was scared witless, and you whizzed in like Wonder Woman!" Cindy wheezed.

"This is not really happening, right? It's just a bad dream or something?" Lynda mumbled.

"Bad? It's a great dream. We were rescued just in time, weren't we, Cindy-girl?"

"What's in the duffel bag?" Cindy asked.

"Quarters."

They had just reached the floor level when the blackjack dealer ran out on the balcony and shouted, "Security! Security!"

"We better hustle, ladies!"

"I can't . . . I just can't move any faster," Cindy moaned.

When they reached the middle of the casino, Lynda could see people hurrying toward them. She set the duffel on the floor and unzipped it.

"Hey, everyone," she screamed, "play a few turns on Lynda Dawn Darlin'!" She turned the bag over and shook the coins out onto the floor. A frenzy of gamblers clamored toward them as Brady pulled them toward the daylight of the front door.

"How much money was in there?" Cindy asked.

"I think it was $625, but I didn't have time to count."

"And you just threw it away?"

"It wasn't mine, except for seventy-five cents. Besides, no one in that place is going to pay attention to us now."

With a woman on each arm, Brady escorted them across the street, out of the shadows of the Black Aces and Eights into the bright sunlight of South Dakota.

"I don't think I've ever seen a gal as determined as Lynda Dawn busting through that door." Brady leaned over and brushed her cheek with a kiss as they continued along the concrete sidewalk.

"Can we slow down just a tad?" Cindy asked. "My ribs are hurting."

Brady slowed the pace and glanced back over his shoulder.

"Anyone following us?" Lynda quizzed.

"Nope."

Lynda let Brady's arm drop so she could weave between the tourists on the sidewalks. "Now tell me what happened while I was watching quarters plunk out of that slot machine."

Brady caught back up to her. "After the noise began, I turned around, and Cindy was gone."

Cindy LaCoste still clutched Brady's arm. "When I heard the jackpot, I made a move on Trent."

"What kind of move?"

"The knife the dealer had was my knife. I was going to jerk Trent aside and make him tell me where that last biker was."

Lynda could feel her hands trembling. She squeezed Brady's hand. "You took on Trent by yourself?"

"Trent's a worthless wimp when he's by himself. I knew if I aimed the knife at the right body part, he'd tell me anything."

Brady slowed down and looked into Lynda's eyes. "Are you all right, darlin'? You're shakin'."

"I'll be fine. After I vomit. It's just all crashing in on me how stupid I was. I came close to getting us all killed!" Lynda moaned. "Go on. Tell me what happened next."

"Cindy had already reached Trent by the time I got to the blackjack table."

"I still can't believe you knew it was me in the wig and dress even though I had my back toward you."

Lynda pulled off her sunglasses. "It was the ankles."

"Ankles?"

"Brady said he never forgets an ankle."

Cindy raised her sandy blonde eyebrows. "Really?"

"I knew the guy in front of the elevator would be breathing down my back, but I still had hopes of pulling Cindy away before anything happened. But we didn't account for Hope."

"Hope?"

"The blackjack dealer," Cindy added. "Trent wimped out like I thought when I pointed the knife at him. Then Hope jabbed a hard right into my ribs. I cried out with pain, dropped the knife, and started to lose my balance. Suddenly the white knight appeared. Brady was there to catch me."

"Unfortunately, that left me vulnerable to the big guy with the ponytail. All of a sudden we both were shoved up the stairs into that room."

"What were they going to do to you?"

"I honestly don't know. We had just gotten there when Super Editor broke down the door and rescued us. I'd smile, but it hurts too much," Cindy sighed.

"Did you tell her what happened to that last biker?" Lynda asked.

"Happened to him?"

"Hey, Lynda Dawn took care of McGhee last night," Brady announced.

"Really?"

"It's a long story, but the bottom line is, he is in the hospital with some broken bones."

"You're kidding!" Cindy threw her arms around Lynda and

kissed her cheek. Lynda gingerly held Cindy for a minute. "You really did him in?"

"He thought I was you, and he sort of did himself in." Lynda could see a sudden relaxation in Cindy's eyes.

"You've got to tell me the whole story. I'm done. I finished the quest."

"How about Joe Trent?"

"I don't know how he fits in. I don't care," Cindy added. "Of the ten that were there five years ago, two died before this year. And I repaid the other nine."

"Nine and two is eleven."

"Yeah . . . they added a new guy, I think. So I paid him off for a bad choice of friends." This time Cindy smiled, then grimaced. "Now tell me how you finished off the last biker."

"Ride with us, and I'll tell you." Lynda turned to Brady. "Can Cindy ride with us?"

"Sure . . . but that reminds me, Cindy-girl, we've got more rigs than we can drive. Do you plan on selling one of them?"

"Maybe I should drive one."

"You are in no condition to drive."

"But I . . . would like to keep the old Cadillac for old times' sake."

"Sell the truck."

"I just bought it."

"Well, we can't—"

"Stoner! What in Casey Tibb's name are you doin' in Deadwood!" The voice boomed across the street from the wide doorway of a service station.

Brady, Cindy, and Lynda turned to stare as two black-hatted, bowlegged cowboys dodged traffic and scooted across the street.

"Mark and Marvin!" Brady muttered.

"Hey, Stoner, you're supposed to be gettin' hitched on

Saturday, and you're pickin' up beauty queens in South Dakota?"

"What are you guys doin' here?" Brady quizzed.

"I won't tell you nothin', Stoner, until you introduce me to these fine-lookin' women." The grinning cowboy pushed his Resistol back and stared at LaCoste. "Whoa . . . Cindy?"

"Hi, Mark."

"It's good to see you, darlin'. I hardly recognized you. I heard you were back on the circuit. That's the best news I've had since I found out Stoner was retirin'."

"Mark, Marvin, you know Cindy, and this is my fiancée, Lynda Austin."

The shorter of the men reached out and shook her hand. "Finally, we get to meet Brady's famous Lynda Dawn Darlin'. I thought we'd have to wait until Saturday."

"Darlin', this is Mark and Marvin—"

"Mark and Marvin Garner," Lynda interrupted. "You're sitting at fourth and sixth in the standings in bareback riding as of the first of June. Mark, it sounded like you had a great time in Houston, and Marvin has been burning up the California rodeos this spring."

Marvin turned to Brady. "I thought you told me this lady is from New York City."

"She's just tryin' to impress you," Brady teased.

"She did a mighty good job of it."

"Did I hear you say you were coming to our wedding?" Lynda asked.

"We are," Mark replied. "In fact, we were headed that way today. Thought we'd pick up a little spending money at Cody and then head for the weddin'. But the transmission went out just past Spearfish, and we drove up here in second gear. Anyway, they can't get the parts 'til Monday. 'Course, if you've got room in the truck—"

"Shoot," Marvin broke in, "you jist put these two purdy women in the back of the pickup, and we'll ride back there."

"Have I got a deal for you," Brady laughed. "We've got an extra rig. How about you drivin' it to the weddin'?"

"Extra rig?"

"Cindy's got her ribs busted up and can't drive."

"Whoa, you and that pony have a wreck?"

"It's a long story," Cindy told him.

"I've got lots of time," Mark insisted. "I'll drive the rig. . . . You tell me your life story."

"You don't know what you're in for."

"Cindy-girl, anything will be better than listenin' to Marvin's singin'."

The younger Garner brother looked at Lynda and shrugged. "He's jist jealous. I always could sing better than him."

Brady turned to LaCoste. "What do you think, Cindy-girl? Can you handle these two big-talkin' cupcakes?"

"Sure. We can take the Cadillac. That way I can stretch out in the back."

"Grab your gear bags, boys, and meet us at the city parking lot on the west edge of town. You can't miss us—just look for a circus train."

"A what?"

"We've got four rigs, two horse trailers, two horses, two dogs, a 2,000-pound bull, Heather Martin's girls, a young steer wrestler from Grand Junction . . ."

"Sounds like you're goin' into the stock-contractin' business," Marvin teased.

" . . . not to mention the pride of Los Alamos, New Mexico," Brady concluded.

"Doc Cartier?" Marvin asked.

Brady nodded.

"I need to talk to her. I've got this ropin' horse that is drivin' me nuts," Marvin began.

"Since when are you a roper?"

"I'm practicin' up for my old age. Someday I'll be old and decrepit like Mark and Brady."

"He's a whole year younger than we are," Brady revealed.

"I'm ridin' with Miss Debra Jean," Marvin announced. "This is business."

The Garner brothers jogged back across the street.

Lynda glanced at Brady and pulled her sunglasses down to the end of her nose.

"He just wants to talk about horse-trainin'," Brady insisted.

"And if you believe that," Lynda chided, "I've got a bridge to sell you."

"He's not the one, believe me."

"I do not need any help with matchmaking, thank you," Lynda sniffed.

"What are you two mumbling about?" Cindy asked.

"Nothing." Lynda tugged Brady on up the sidewalk.

◆ ◆ ◆

The caravan that left Deadwood headed for Gilette had the look of a traveling Wild West show. The lead outfit was Brady's Dodge pickup with ranch sign firmly attached upside down to the side of the rig. Mama's Boy was content in the trailer. Capt. Patch and Margarita were secure in the back, and Lynda Dawn Austin and her cowboy scrunched together in the front seat.

They were followed by Tyler Adams driving LaCoste's Ford pickup. Sitting close to him was a pouting Heidi Martin. That was mainly because sitting next to her was an equally pouting Wendy Martin. The girls were crammed into the cab of the same pickup by the insistence of their Uncle Brady.

Mark Garner drove the third outfit, LaCoste's old green

Cadillac. Cindy rode, not in the backseat, but comfortably stretched across the worn brown leather upholstery of the front seat.

Dr. Debra Jean Cartier drove her custom-made van and pulled a trailer with two horses. In the other bucket seat was Marvin Garner, carrying on some animated conversation that Lynda assumed was about horses.

"Well, cowboy, how far are we driving today?"

"Let's just drive straight to Jackson and get married tonight," he suggested.

"How long would it take us to get there?"

"If we stop only for meals and exercising the animals?"

"Yes."

"I reckon we'd get there about one or two in the mornin'."

"Do you think we could find a preacher at that hour?"

"Sure. Preachers are used to bein' woke up in the night."

"It's tempting." Lynda smiled. "But I think we'd better wait until Saturday. Our friends and family are traveling quite a distance to see the big event. The way things are going, I figure in another day we'll have the entire wedding party trailing behind us."

"At least we rode out Cindy's escapades. Kind of feels good to have that settled."

"It feels good not to have any of us seriously injured!" Lynda exclaimed. "Now where are we really going?"

"Sheridan."

"Finally. How about tomorrow?"

"That's the day the girls are supposed to meet their mother in Cody. So how about sending everyone across to Cody and you and me swing up to the ranch?"

"Just you and me?"

"And Capt. Patch, Margarita, and Mama's Boy."

"That almost sounds peaceful."

"We could look the place over and then drive on down to

Red Lodge for the night. I've got rodeo friends there who've got a bunkhouse over their garage."

"We're not going to stay overnight at the ranch?"

"Darlin', we're only a few hours away from that weddin', and I've been dreamin' about you ever' night. It would be dangerous to sleep over."

She dug through her purse and pulled out a leather-encased milk glass bottle with silver-plated lid. "Only two more days. After that, it's for real."

"Okay, I haven't seen that one before. What are you wearing now?"

"It's called Dangerous Expression. I had to sign a waiver exempting the company from any liability before I could purchase it."

"Wow! Maybe you shouldn't wear it until after Saturday. You really had to sign a waiver, huh?"

"I made that part up, but I knew you'd be the only man on earth who would believe me."

"Ah, shucks, Miss Lynda Dawn, you're jist takin' advantage of a poor, lonesome cowboy," he drawled.

"Hah! It seems to be a universal opinion that you're the smoothest romeo in the West, so don't give me that ah-shucks line."

"Yes . . . ma'am."

◆ ◆ ◆

They ate lunch in Spearfish, South Dakota, and then exercised the animals at the rodeo grounds in Gilette, Wyoming. The sun was setting on the Big Horn Mountains about the time Brady led the parade into a rest stop overlooking the Powder River.

Brady, Mark, Marvin, and Tyler huddled at the back of Brady's trailer as Lynda and the gals ambled for the ladies' room. When Lynda emerged, only Brady and Tyler were standing by the truck.

"Where are your buddies?" she asked.

"They spotted a couple damsels in distress over there by the picnic tables." Brady motioned toward a white minivan with its hood up and a small U-Haul trailer hooked behind.

"Damsels in distress? But I had them all lined up with Cindy and Debra Jean!"

"So I noticed. Maybe you ought to hustle over there and tell them you have their lives planned out for them."

"Here comes Mark," Tyler motioned.

With worn boots scuffing the blacktop, Mark Garner shuffled back toward them shaking his head. "You got a little crescent wrench, Brady? They got a battery cable that needs tightened, that's all."

"I'll get it for you. Why are you grinning from ear to ear?"

"Me and Marvin walked up to these two gals and asked if we could help. Well, they stared us over from hats to boots. Then the dark-haired one looks me right in the eye and says, 'Do you know Brady Stoner?'"

"What?" Lynda roared.

"And Marvin says, 'We never heard of that no-good, worthless bareback rider.' You should have seen their mouths drop open. Say, do you know any gals from back east named Kelly and Nina?"

TEN

On Tuesday nights the Big Horn Banquet Room at the Buckaroo Cafe and Supper Club in Sheridan, Wyoming, hosts the weekly meeting of the Jim Bridger Lions Club. Every Sunday morning from 9:00 to 11:00 A.M., the same room is filled by the fledgling but enthusiastic congregation of the Grace Bible Church.

It was not Tuesday night.

Nor Sunday morning.

And the conversation in the room ranged wide of either service-club patter or holy devotion. Two long banquet tables had been shoved together, and the Austin-Stoner gang had surrounded the food. The waitresses had closed the double doors to the rest of the supper club and abandoned the group to their own amusements.

Steam rose off the platters and bowls on the polished oak tables. Steaks were piled high, baked potatoes were stacked like cordwood, dinner rolls overflowed baskets, and green salad filled a stainless steel bowl the size of a small stock tank.

The dusty wooden miniblinds were closed, and the dim light from a huge wagon-wheel chandelier kept the ambiance somewhere between the glow of a campfire at high school

Bible camp and a company lunch at an artsy basement cafe on Manhattan's lower east side.

With blue long-sleeved shirt rolled up to his elbows, black felt cowboy hat pushed back, and a wide smile, Mark Garner stood up and waved his hands. "You'll jist have to settle down a minute. I think this event calls for some choice words. And before Brother Brady says the blessing, I thought I should oblige."

Marvin Garner, sitting across the table between Nina DeJong and Dr. Cartier, protested, "Sit down, Mark; the food's gettin' cold."

"Quiet!" Mark roared. "The kid has absolutely no sense of timing. This is a solemn occasion. And since I'm paying for this supper, I believe I'm entitled to say a word or two."

"It's really nice of you to buy us all dinner," Kelly piped up from her seat next to Mark.

Mark tipped his hat at her. "Thank you, ma'am, but I'm not buying your dinner. I'm buyin' supper. You're in Wyomin' now, and in Wyomin' we eat dinner at twelve noon."

"Oh." Kelly blushed.

"Don't let him razz you, Kell," Lynda admonished. "I guarantee you these cowboys will eat steak and potatoes any time of the day, no matter what you call it."

"Now that's not fair," Mark complained. "I'm tryin' to impress these two purdy gals from New York City, and Lynda Dawn Darlin' goes and shoots me down."

"Actually I'm from Wisconsin," Nina interrupted. "I just moved to New York a couple of years ago."

"Really?" Marvin slipped his arm around the back of Nina's chair. "I rodeoed in Wisconsin once."

Nina responded with what Lynda thought was a little too obvious wide-eyed innocence. "You did? Where?"

Lynda glanced down at her empty almond-colored porcelain plate. *If she starts to giggle, I'm out of here!*

"Now wait a minute," Mark huffed. "Let me finish what I'm sayin'."

"This is beginnin' to sound like a rehearsal dinner," Brady laughed.

"Well, I wasn't invited to the rehearsal dinner—"

"Neither was I!" Kelly chimed in.

Lynda glanced over at her fellow Atlantic-Hampton employee. *Kelly sounding nervous? She's never nervous around guys. Wait a minute. . . . Mark is for Doc. Kelly has to find her own . . . oh, man.*

Austin cleared her throat. "Actually the wedding is so small I hadn't planned a rehearsal, let alone a rehearsal dinner."

"Okay," Mark continued. "Let me say what I have to say. Sometime during the National Finals Rodeo next December some yahoo reporter from some big-city newspaper is going to come up to me and say, 'Why in the world do you rodeo for a living? Couldn't you make more money doing something else?'"

"Shoot, you couldn't get a job anywhere else!" Marvin laughed.

"That might be true. 'Course, I did take two years of weldin' in college and could probably make more money doing that. But nights like tonight . . . This is why I rodeo. Let me tell you about the people in this room.

"Now down there at the end are Richard Martin's two girls. It was a couple days before Christmas some years back when those girls were sweet, little things no taller than a yearlin'. I got stuck in the Arizona Strip stone-broke. I didn't have enough gas in my rig to drive home to South Dakota. I didn't know what to do. Brady had finished the roundup and was home in Idaho, but he always said if I needed anything, just stop and see Richard and Heather.

"So I did. They literally reached in the cookie jar and pulled out fifty dollars to give me. Fifty dollars. That was a lot of money for a family of four livin' on workin' cowboy wages. I probably didn't have enough sense at the time to know jist how much it was to them. I had never met 'em before in my life, but they knew I was a friend of Brady's. Heidi and Wendy, I guess you know your daddy was the greatest."

Mark continued, "Then there's young Tyler. Never met him before two hours ago. But I can tell you a lot about him. Ever' night he dreams about gold belt buckles and wrestlin' steers at Thomas and Mack Arena. I've been there, son. Shoot, I'm still there. It don't ever fade. You got it in your bones, don't ya? He's got the try in his eyes that shows he'll bust into the top fifteen in a year or so.

"Now sittin' next to me here is Miss Cindy, and over next to Marvin is Doc Cartier. Some people would look at 'em and say those two women have had some bad breaks in life. But one thing we learn growin' up in the West is that you have to play the hand you're dealt. Now I reckon Doc has the highest I.Q. of any horse-trainer in history. She could make a fortune with clinics, seminars, tapes, and books. Instead she gives it all away free to any cowboy or cowgirl going down the road. And Miss Cindy here . . . Darlin', I knew you were just too tough to let life break you. I sure was glad to see you in Deadwood."

"If I buy my own supper, can I go ahead and eat?" Marvin pleaded.

"Miss Nina, if he pipes up again, would you pour that ice water down the back of his shirt?"

"Really?" she giggled.

Lynda slumped in her oak captain's chair. *Oh, brother!*

"Yes, ma'am. Now as for Miss Nina and Miss Kelly, you are brand-new friends. Goin' down the road, you get to meet new friends all the time. And you two are now officially good friends of mine."

"We are?" Kelly demurred.

"Mark has a tendency to make friends with every purdy girl he meets," Brady laughed.

"That's not completely true—mostly true, but not completely true. And then there's Lynda Dawn Darlin'. She is undoubtedly the most talked-about eastern lady on the whole circuit."

"You don't expect me to believe that," Lynda protested.

"Am I right, little brother?"

Marvin Garner leaned back in his chair with one arm behind Nina and the other behind Doc Cartier. "He's right. Stoner there has babbled incessantly for almost two years about his Lynda Dawn Darlin'. It's drivin' us all nuts! When we found out Brady was gettin' married and goin' into ranchin', the bareback riders of the world rejoiced."

Brady laughed and shook his head. "I vote with Marvin. Let's eat."

"Oh, no, I'm not done." Mark took off his hat, and even in the shadows a tan line could be seen across his forehead. "I want to tell you about Brady Stoner. Marvin lied. He said we rejoiced when we heard Brady was retirin'. That ain't true. When I heard about it, I hiked down to the end of the arena to be by myself and didn't come back until my eyes was dry.

"Let me tell you a couple of things about Brady. First, he ain't the best bareback rider I've ever seen. Shoot, I'm the best. But Brady elevates the sport to a higher standard. He lives by a code the rest of us only dream about bein' able to reach. And I'm not talkin' about the fact that he don't smoke or drink. Man, he don't even chew.

"Lots of young guys, workin' hard to be top rodeo athletes, can make a similar claim. But I'm talkin' about Brady's code of how to treat people. I'm talkin' about a man who respects the good Lord and treats ever' soul with courtesy and dignity.

"Dad gum it, what I'm tryin' to say is that the rest of us buckaroos always end up actin' better when Brady's around.

And man-o-man, we're goin' to miss him." Mark rubbed the back of his hand across his leathered eyes and sniffed. "I don't know how come I'm—"

"That air conditioner's sure stirring up the dust, isn't it?" Lynda broke in.

Mark glanced at her and grinned. "You're right, Lynda Dawn Darlin' . . . it must be the dust. Now I've had my say. It's time for Brother Brady to say his prayer, and then we'll eat."

"Amen!" Marvin added.

Mark sat down, and Brady stood. "I don't know why we're all feelin' so sentimental tonight. But Mark's right. This is what rodeo is all about. The buckles and the broncs—that's just extra." He pulled off his hat, and immediately so did the other three cowboys.

"Lord . . . these are my friends. Most of 'em I've talked to You about before. I'd appreciate Your blessin' on this meal. Keep us safe. Keep us in the arena of Your will. And keep us from the evil one. In Jesus' name, amen."

He sat down and put his hat back on. "Now pass those steaks around, and save the rawest one for me."

Forks scraped.

Knives cut.

Glasses tinkled.

Lips smacked.

And most in the room carried on several conversations at once.

Lynda turned toward a meat-chewing Brady and whispered, "That was quite a compliment Mark gave you."

"Kind of embarrassing."

"I'm really, really proud of you."

"Thanks, darlin', and I'm proud of you."

"Me?"

"When you baled Mark Garner out of admittin' to sheddin' a tear."

"Dust in their eyes—that's what cowboys always say. Remember, I do edit Joaquin Estaban and Anthony Shadowbrook."

Brady leaned over to Nina who sat on the left side of the table from him. "Is it true that trailer you're towing is completely full of Lynda Dawn Darlin's perfume?"

"No, we had to send the perfume in a separate truck," she teased. Then she leaned closer to Brady and asked softly, "How about Marvin? Is he a good guy?"

Lynda strained to hear the conversation.

"Go for it, Nina-girl. I don't know, but you might have some competition." Brady raised his eyebrows in the direction of Dr. Cartier, who had Marvin Garner engrossed in close conversation.

"Uncle Brady," Wendy called out from far across the table, "we're going to meet Mom tomorrow in Cody, right?"

"We'll have to get all that figured out. Me and Lynda Dawn Darlin' are probably goin' up to the ranch."

Cindy looked up. "What did you say?"

"We need to discuss tomorrow's plans," Brady called out.

"I'm going with you and Lynda, right?" Cindy called out.

Lynda's elbow stabbed Brady's side.

"We'll talk about it when it's not so hectic."

Lynda zealously stabbed a carrot. *We are not taking anyone to the ranch. No one. Zero. Zilch. Nada. Absolutely not one soul.*

Kelly pulled a hot yellow pepper out of her salad and began fanning her face with her hand. "Now you've got to tell me how in the world you and Brady picked up such an entourage. What's this about a motorcycle gang?"

"Is it true you're the only one that can handle that bull?" Marvin called across at her.

"You ought to see her," Tyler boomed from the far end of the table. "One look from Lynda Dawn Darlin', and he runs for cover."

"Actually . . . I—," Lynda began.

"Mark asked me if I was writing a book about how I took on the motorcycle gang," Cindy called out. "What shall I tell him, Ms. Editor?"

"Lynda, do you need any clothes out of the trailer? We emptied out your whole condo," Nina offered.

"You got everything in the . . ." Lynda's voice raised to a near shout.

Debra Jean Cartier laughed at something Marvin said and then called out, "Lynda, what did you say was the name of the perfume I borrowed from you?"

Lynda leaned forward across the table and cupped her hands. "It's called—"

"Hey, everyone, listen up! Tyler has a great idea," Heidi shouted. "Why don't we write a book about the past seven days? Each of us can sort of write a chapter. I think I'll call my chapter 'Destiny!' What do you think?"

"I think it stinks," Wendy piped up. "You should call your chapter 'Boy Crazy.'"

"And you could call your chapter 'Nerdette Strikes Out.'"

"Girls!" Brady shouted. "Settle down, or I'll have Tyler stuff a roll in your mouth."

"Really?" Heidi giggled.

"I, for one, like Heidi's title," Kelly put in.

"'Destiny'?" Lynda grimaced.

Kelly turned to Mark Garner and tugged him away from a conversation with Cindy LaCoste. "Mark, do you believe in destiny?"

"In what?"

"Well, this afternoon we were at the rest stop needing help, and all of you came along totally by chance . . . or was it? When two people meet, is it just by chance, or were they destined to meet?"

"What do you think, Miss Lynda?"

"I think you're passing the buck, Mark."

"Yes, ma'am."

"Well, whatever it is," Nina chimed in, "it's so incredible that one minute we were afraid we'd miss the whole wedding, and the next minute we're right here with all of you. Lynda, you have to admit that's pretty wild."

"The whole week has been insane. Brady and I have hardly had time to—"

"Hey, does anyone want pie?" Mark blurted out. "Let's get ourselves an apple pie, a chocolate pie, and a lemon pie."

"What about the rest of us?" Marvin teased.

"Have 'em cut the pie in six pieces. Nothin's sicklier lookin' than a pie cut into eight pieces."

"That's eighteen pieces for only eleven of us," Wendy protested.

"That sounds about right. Why don't one of you purdy little girls go out there and tell the waitress to bring us some pie?"

"Little girls?" Heidi turned to Wendy. "Obviously he's talking about you."

"You're probably right. I did hear him mention pretty," Wendy shot back.

Brady put his hand over his mouth and leaned closer to Lynda. "We are having boys—only boys, right?"

"What makes you think boys are any—"

"Brady!" Mark called out. "What was the name of that bronc that jumped the fence with you ridin' him in Rawlins?"

"Little Red."

"And he didn't stop until you got to the Dairy Queen, right?"

"I think it was the A & W."

"They offered him a re-ride, or they said they'd jist give him the horse!" Marvin hooted.

"You mean you rode a bucking horse into the drive-through?" Nina gasped.

Lynda leaned in front of Brady, toward Nina. "Don't believe everything this gang tells you about rodeo. They love to string you along."

"Nina-girl," Brady said with a grin, "have I ever lied to you?"

"I don't know," she said. "Have you?"

"Lynda, you didn't tell us about the clothes," Kelly broke in. "Do you need anything from the trailer?"

"I think I'll just—"

"Hey, everyone, attention!" Marvin Garner called out. "Me and Doc have a great idea. We think we ought to all go to Cody tomorrow and enter the nightly rodeo. It's nothin' big, but it would be a gas to have us all entered. Doc and Cindy could run the barrels. Me, Mark, and Brady could ride rough stock. Tyler could throw steers."

"What about me and Wendy?" Heidi asked.

"Lil' darlin', you two could team rope."

"We don't know how to rope!" Wendy brooded.

"I guess the rest of ya will just have to sit in the stands and cheer us on."

Brady leaned back in the chair. "Marv, me and Lynda Dawn Darlin' need to—"

Mark shoved his chair back from the table and rested his fists on the knees of his worn Wranglers. "It would be great, wouldn't it? One last ride. Just to give Brady a chance, I'll ride saddle broncs, and Marv can ride bulls."

"Bulls? How come I have to ride bulls?"

"You're the youngest. Your bones will mend faster."

"You ride bulls?" Nina laid her hand on Marvin Garner's shoulder.

He slipped his arm around her waist. "Shucks, for you, Miss Nina, I'd ride a wild white rhinoceros."

"You would?"

Lynda rolled her eyes to the ceiling. *I do not know her. This is totally embarrassing. And she's not even asking him to move his arm.*

"Actually Cody's a small rodeo, and they don't have wild white rhinoceros," Brady laughed.

Nina looked around the room. "Are they teasing me again?"

"Uncle Brady, do Wendy and I have to share a room again tonight?" Heidi whined.

"What about it, Brady? One last rodeo?" Cindy asked. "You don't mind, do you, Lynda Dawn Darlin'?"

"Whoa!" Brady called as he stood to his feet. "You all finish your pie. . . . Go back to the motel. Ever'one's got their rooms lined out. We'll meet at that coffee shop across from the motel at 7:00 A.M."

"I'm not meeting anyone at 7:00 A.M.!" Cindy announced.

"Okay . . . at 8:00 A.M."

"Thank you!"

"And we'll decide what tomorrow looks like." Brady tugged Lynda to her feet. "In the meantime, me and Lynda Dawn Darlin' are going by ourselves to . . . to—"

"To look at a horse," Lynda proclaimed.

"Oooh weeee!" Marvin whooped. "That girl has been around!"

"It's dark," Kelly protested. "How can you see a . . . oh! Oh!"

"And," Brady continued, "if I see one of you in the next three hours, I guarantee you will probably not be invited to come help with the fall roundup. Come on, Lynda Dawn."

"Oh, my," Cartier called out, "I want the perfume that girl is wearing tonight!"

Lynda and Brady left the room to a chorus of hoots and hollers. With her hand laced in his, they walked across the parking lot to the Dodge pickup. Brady coaxed Capt. Patch and Margarita into Cindy's Ford. Then he slid in behind the wheel of his rig. Lynda scooted close.

"Are we actually going to be alone? Totally alone?"

"Yep."

She wrapped her arms around his neck and pulled him close. When her lips pressed against his, Lynda felt herself relax.

Finally Brady caught his breath. "Darlin', I hate to interrupt this—"

"Good!" she murmured and kissed him again, closing her eyes.

After a few more minutes Brady pulled away and whispered, "Babe, I think we should—"

"Shut up and kiss me, Stoner!"

"Yes, ma'am!"

His lips seemed increasingly warm and enthusiastic.

A loud banging on the hood caused them both to jump and pull back. "Hey, if you two don't leave the parking lot, how are the rest of us going to get out of the cafe?" Marvin hollered. "Now go on, get out of here before I turn the fire hose on you!"

Lynda slunk down in the seat. "He was watching!"

"We didn't exactly try to hide anything."

"Drive, Stoner—get us out of here!"

The pickup shot out of the gravel parking lot and into the street as Brady raced down a side street lined with trees, trash cans, and parked pickup trucks.

Lynda sat back up and laid her left arm across Brady's shoulder. "Where are we really going?"

"Cruising."

"In Sheridan, Wyoming?"

"You got a better idea?"

"Nope."

"What about this Cody rodeo thing? If we do that, we can't go to the ranch until after the wedding."

"I know. I was thinking about that." Lynda laid her hand on Brady's knee. "Remember how we've said we'll just bum around Jackson a few days for our honeymoon?"

"Yep."

"I changed my mind."

"And where would the very-soon-to-be Mrs. Stoner like to go for her honeymoon?"

"Home."

"Home?"

"To our home. I just want to go to some isolated place at the end of the earth and hole up with my cowboy."

"We don't exactly have a furnished house waiting for us."

"Do we have a stove, refrigerator, and a bed?"

"Yep."

"It sounds like a honeymoon to me."

"Are you kiddin' me?" Brady squeezed her tight. "You really want to go to the ranch after the wedding."

"Yes. Can we make it Saturday night?"

"Maybe we ought to spend the night in Jackson. There are some people we need to visit with—my folks, my brother, your sis and brother and families, the Gossmans, the Hamptons, and all them."

"Okay . . . okay, but you have to promise me we'll be alone at the ranch on Sunday night."

"It's a promise, darlin'."

"Completely alone, Stoner. The animals have to stay outside, and there's not another human for at least seven miles!"

"Actually our neighbors are about fourteen miles away."

"Good. Maybe if we make a lot of noise, they'll move! Wouldn't it be great to own a whole state and just put locked gates at the border?" Lynda suggested.

"I take it you've had a slight overdose of intense company?"

"You got that right, cowboy."

"Well, Miss Lynda Dawn Darlin', does this mean we're going to Cody tomorrow?"

"Somehow I knew I'd never get to go with you to the ranch."

"Well, how do you want to spend the rest of the evening?"

"I want you to drive. I want to lay my head on your shoulder and have my arms around your neck while we listen to some good music."

"Pick a tape."

"You choose." She closed her eyes and snuggled up even closer to him.

"How about a little 'Wyomin' on My Mind'?"

"Sounds wonderful. Can you set your stereo to play the same song over and over?"

"Yeah. Are you sure that's what you want?"

"Listen, cowboy, what I want is to marry you. But I have to wait almost three more days. So this is second best."

The silver and black Dodge extended cab pickup cruised up and down every street in Sheridan, Wyoming, fourteen times. The tight three-part harmony of the Sons of the San Joaquin singing "Wyomin' on My Mind" repeated fifty-four times, but Lynda lost count after seven.

◆ ◆ ◆

Brady had to wake her up when they finally pulled into the motel. Nina and Kelly met her at the door of their room and almost tugged her out of Brady's arms.

"You had plenty of time for that," Kelly asserted. "We've got to talk to this girl."

Lynda waltzed across the green-carpeted motel room and flopped down on her back, spread eagle on the bed.

"Did he wear you out?" Kelly pressed.

"Brady? Hardly. I'm worn out from running around five Western states with a pack of crazies following me."

"Crazies? You mean that motorcycle gang?"

"No, I mean this 'family.' You saw what it was like tonight at the cafe."

"This was probably one of the most fun nights of my whole life," Nina purred.

"Fun? What did you do after I left?"

"She and good ol' Marvin Garner disappeared for over two hours," Kelly reported.

"He taught me to line dance."

"Where?" Lynda pressed.

"Out behind the motel."

"In the dark?"

"Sort of."

"You were just line dancing? Oh, sure," Kelly scoffed.

"You sound jealous," Lynda teased. Then she glanced over at Nina. "You and Marvin, huh?"

"He was really nice to me," Nina reported. "Really, really nice! Hey, can I borrow some of your perfume?"

"Tonight? It's midnight. You're certainly not going to see him again tonight, are you?"

"No, Mother. I meant in the morning."

"I deserved that. I officially release you to the Lord. No more mothering from me."

"But don't stop praying for me," Nina urged.

"You got it, girl. So Marv the bareback rider is the one. Boy, that was quick. And to think I was trying to line him up with Debra Jean."

"I know it. She told me to go for Marv because he was too young for her."

"Doc Cartier told you that?"

"Yeah. She sure gets around good in that wheelchair. She doesn't let it keep her from anything."

"Except getting serious with a man," Lynda added. "She's consigned herself to the fact that no man would want to spend a lifetime with her."

"You're kidding?" Kelly broke in. "Being around her makes me feel talentless and insecure. That woman is a true inspiration."

STEPHEN BLY

"Maybe she thinks a man will want a lot more than to be inspired."

"She might be right," Kelly mused as she flopped down on the other bed. "What did Mark say? You play with the cards you're dealt?"

"How about you and Mark?" Lynda asked. "Are you moving as fast as Miss Wisconsin?"

"No. I think he has serious intentions of pursuing Cindy."

"That might be a slow process. She's not exactly relaxed around men yet."

"Really? Boy, you couldn't tell that tonight."

"What did the rest of you do while Nina and the cowboy were promenading?"

"Cindy, Doc, Mark, and I spent the evening playing hearts. Do you know how to play hearts? This was my first time," Kelly reported.

"A bareback rider and three lovely ladies. Mark was in cowboy heaven."

"He is about the funniest guy I've ever met," Kelly added. "He kept us laughing all night. Did Brady ever tell you about the time that he, Mark, and Marvin ended up riding bulls at a rodeo in Juarez, Mexico?"

"I don't recall that story."

"Oh. Never mind."

"What?" Lynda sat up on the bed. "What?"

"Have Brady tell you. But I'll bet he leaves out the best part."

"What best part?"

"After the rodeo, when he was dancing with that Mexican girl and took the long-stemmed rose out of her mouth and cut his lip on a thorn."

"He what?"

"Never mind that," Nina inserted. "Tell me everything you know about Marvin Garner."

"I don't know much. He and his brother are longtime friends of Brady's. They started going down the road about the same time and—"

"Doing what?" Nina asked.

"Rodeoing. Marv and his brother live in South Dakota when they're home, which is only two or three weeks in December. That's all I know. I just met them a few hours before you did."

"And what's the NFR?"

"The National Finals Rodeo. Didn't I explain this to you one time in the office?"

"I forgot. It's sort of a big deal, right?"

"It's the championship rodeo of the year. Some guys can make more money in that one week than in all the other rodeos combined. Why? Did Marvin mention it?"

"He said if he made it to the Finals, he wanted me to fly out and watch it."

"You're kidding? All of that in two hours? I can't believe this. You sat back in New York saying, 'If I ever go west, I'm going to grab myself a cowboy.' And you did! It's incredible."

"Yeah, it makes me feel like an old maid," Kelly whimpered. "Are some of Brady's other friends going to be at the wedding?"

"I have no idea. We sent out only twenty invitations. A small intimate wedding. Of course, Brady's been traveling around the West personally inviting everyone he knows. So there's no telling what will happen."

"How about any rich cowboy-banker types?"

"I can guarantee there won't be any of those. Most of Brady's friends are broke."

"Marvin made $82,612 last year," Nina blurted out. "That's not too bad."

"How much of that was for expenses?" Lynda pressed.

"About $75,000, I guess. Did you know that he and Mark

have to fly a lot? That's how he got so many frequent-flyer miles and can give me a ticket to Las Vegas."

"He's flying you out?"

"Yes, isn't that sweet of him?" Nina cooed. "Sweet and strong. Did you notice his muscles? There's hardly an once of fat on his body."

"And just how do you know that?" Kelly demanded.

"You learn a lot about a person when you line dance."

"I'm going to bed," Lynda announced.

Kelly groaned, "And I'm going to puke."

"She's just jealous." Nina smirked.

◆ ◆ ◆

The five-rig, three-trailer, eleven-person, two-dog, two-horse, and one-bull outfit pulled out of Sheridan, Wyoming, at 10:02 A.M. the next morning. A delay in Graybull to get a water pump and fan belt replaced in the old Cadillac meant they arrived in Cody about 3:00 P.M. They drove through town to the rodeo grounds where they paid entry fees and secured lodging for the livestock.

Heidi and Wendy stayed at their Aunt Jean's with their mom, while the rest of the gang checked into the Irma Hotel. The entire troupe reassembled that evening in the front row near the center aisle at the Cody Night Rodeo grounds. With Heather Martin joining them, they now numbered twelve.

"Did everyone get entered in time?" Lynda asked.

Brady slid into the bleachers next to her. "Yep. Doc and Cindy will barrel race, Tyler's bull-doggin' . . . and barebacks for me, saddle broncs for Mark, and bulls for Marvin."

"I thought they were short on bulls," Nina put in.

"Here's the thing," Marvin drawled. "They said I could compete if I brought my own bull, so we decided to use Mama's Boy."

"You what?" Lynda gasped. "You're going to ride my bull?"

"Did you hear that boys? *My* bull?" Brady teased. "What'd I tell you? He belongs to Lynda Dawn."

"Well, Lynda Dawn Darlin'," Marvin probed, "I'd like your permission to ride your bull."

"You won't hurt him?"

"That bull weighs 2,000 pounds. I stand in at 161. Who do you think has the greatest chance of gettin' hurt?"

Brady slipped his arm around Lynda. "It won't hurt the bull, darlin'. But there's no guarantee he'll buck. He might just trot around the arena like a Shetland."

"And that won't bother me one bit," Marvin hooted. "I haven't been on a bull in six years!"

"Oh, all right. But I don't want any of you to get hurt. Especially you, Stoner."

He tipped his black beaver felt hat. "Me and Mark and Marvin will mosey over to the chutes and see how things are linin' up."

"Is this the last time I'm going to watch you rodeo?" Lynda asked.

"That thought crossed my mind, too. What can I say, darlin'?"

"Go on, cowboy. Stick 'em."

The three black-hatted men trotted off toward the chutes.

"Is it always that way?" Kelly asked.

"What way?"

"Those little-boy grins—like they just got a new toy or something?"

"Always," Cindy reported. "They love it. It's in the blood."

"And," Debra Jean Cartier added, "every time they mount, they're just sure they're going to win."

"How about you two?" Nina asked. "Are you sure you're going to win?"

A duet resounded from Cindy and Debra Jean, "Yes!"

"But I'll be satisfied being second," Cartier added.

"I won't," Cindy announced. "Sorry, Doc, but I need the money."

"How much will you win?" Nina asked.

"Maybe $100."

"That's all? I thought you said it cost $20 to enter."

"Welcome to the real world of small rodeos." Doc shrugged. Like Cindy, she had her hair pulled back in a long braid and wore a white straw cowboy hat. A large red and white #68 was pinned to the back of her teal blue blouse.

"This is so exciting!" Nina giggled. "Look at me—boots, Western blouse, cowboy hat—this is a long way from 200 Madison Avenue. Guess what Marv gave me!"

"A hickey?" Kelly challenged.

Nina stuck out her tongue. Then she pointed to her belt. "A belt buckle. Cool, huh?"

"'1995 California Rodeo—Bareback Champion.' Girl, do you have any idea what that's worth?" Cindy queried.

"Not really."

"That is real gold," Doc informed her.

"Does this mean we're going out?" Nina asked.

"It means he's investing in the relationship. Do you have any idea what Marvin's expecting from the deal?" Cindy asked.

"Expecting? You mean . . ."

Lynda reached forward and began to rub the back of Nina's neck. "Relax, girl, you haven't sold your saddle—yet."

"My what?"

"Hey, the rodeo's beginning. I think barebacks are first up." Lynda pointed to the arena.

The whole gang grew quiet as the first chute opened and a cowboy raked the bronc just once before the buckskin gelding deposited the man in the dirt.

"That wasn't Brady, was it?" Kelly asked.

Lynda shook her head.

Nina leaned back and asked no one in particular, "They actually like doing that?"

"Absolutely love it," Doc Cartier reported.

"Maybe it's a mineral deficiency," Kelly suggested. "I hear that affects your memory."

Three rides later the announcer called Brady's name. The horse, a big black mare called Matilda, bucked hard straight out of the chute. She kept up the steady, hard buck out to the middle of the arena and then turned and bucked her way back toward the chute. After the buzzer, Brady leaped from her back in a dramatic flying dismount and tossed his hat high in the air. The crowd cheered enthusiastically.

"Wow, that was good, right?" Kelly asked.

"I think so," Lynda assented. "We'll have to wait for the judges' score."

"He jammed his ankle on the dismount," Doc reported.

"What? I didn't see him," Lynda began, then watched in despair as Brady took two steps and tumbled into the arena dirt.

"What's wrong?" Nina asked.

"Twisted ankle, I would guess," Cindy offered. "He should have waited for the pick-up men."

"The what?" Nina blurted out, spilling her Coke on the empty bleacher in front of her.

"The two riders that come alongside and pick up the cowboy after his ride is completed," Lynda informed her, still staring at the limping Stoner as he was helped out of the arena by Marvin Garner. "I told him not to hurt himself! I'm going to have to borrow your wheelchair, Debra Jean, to get him down the aisle."

"He'll make it. Brady's been hurt worse than that," Cindy assured her.

"Is 81 points good?" Kelly prodded.

"No one at a little rodeo will beat that," Wendy piped up.

Brady hobbled to the chutes and waited for the rest of the bareback riders to finish. Wendy's prediction was correct. Brady finished five points better than the second-place rider.

After the calf-roping and a drill team performance that seemed to last forever, it was time for saddle broncs. Lynda spotted Brady behind the chutes helping Mark Garner with his mount. He was third up, and by the time he cracked out, there were no qualified rides. Mark leaned back in the association saddle and raked the big bay horse with a professional rhythm.

Lynda stared at the thick braided rope he held in his right hand. *Pretty as a bronc rein? It's just a fat piece of rope. I can't for the life of me imagine why that has become the standard for all coiffures.*

Mark Garner scored an 84. It was evident to Lynda and her friends that he was a cut above the other competitors. The next highest score in saddle-bronc riding was a 72.

The steer wrestling was coming up, and Lynda watched as Heidi and Tyler strolled hand in hand toward the timed even boxes. She leaned back on Heather's knees. "Uncle Brady has been riding those two pretty close."

"Oh, I was up half the night hearing all about it—from both girls," Heather sighed. "I knew the day would come when she'd get a crush on some cowboy. It's kind of inevitable, like an incurable disease."

Nina looked back wide-eyed. "Really?"

"Hopefully, we'll survive this week, and the two of them will be limited to phone calls and letters."

Lynda rubbed her nose and yawned. "Do you believe that?"

"Not really. I wish I knew more about young Mister Tyler Adams."

"Brady rodeoed with his uncle and thinks pretty highly of him. Of course, we've only known him a few days. Brady told me he had more than one father-of-the-girl talk with Tyler."

"Yeah . . . that's one area where I just can't pull it off."

Heather brushed her wavy black hair off her ear, revealing red, white, and blue star earrings.

Tyler had borrowed a gray mount and looked determined as he backed the wide-bodied quarter horse into the box.

He nodded.

The steer broke out.

The horse galloped.

Tyler dove.

Boots skidded.

A steer's head turned, and then the animal tumbled.

The flag dropped.

The crowd cheered. Especially blonde-headed Heidi Martin.

By the time she and Tyler walked back to the bleachers, she wore his hat, and he wore a smile that dwarfed Yellowstone Canyon.

"He won, Mom! Did you ever see a better run in your whole life? Uncle Brady said a 4.9 would win in a lot of big rodeos!"

"Great job, Tyler," Heather congratulated him.

Lynda pointed to the far end of the arena. "Barrel racing is next."

A thirteen-year-old girl named Reno St. Clair led off with an 18.1, to the enthusiastic cheering of her grandmother a few rows behind Lynda. By the time it was Cindy's turn, the best time was 17.25.

"Cindy looks good out there," Heather stated.

"It's her realm." Lynda nodded.

"There were years that I never thought I'd see Cindy race again," Heather continued.

"There were some days this week I thought the same thing. Her ribs are so sore she can hardly walk. I don't know how she can do this."

"Cowboy up. Or in this case, cowgirl up."

Cindy carried her leather whip in her mouth the entire run and never once applied it to Early to Bed's rump. But with three very tight turns she finished at 16.98. Lynda watched as Mark Garner helped Cindy off her horse.

Cartier was the last barrel racer. Pedregoso pranced like a horse that had spent too much time in a trailer. Cartier turned him toward the rail until he settled down.

"How does she stay in the saddle?" Nina asked.

"Velcro."

"This is another rodeo joke, right?"

"Nope."

"She is one tough lady," Kelly mused.

"Yep," Lynda agreed.

"Nope? Yep? You're beginning to talk just like them!" Nina laughed.

"I reckon I am, darlin'." Lynda tried to suppress the giggles.

Debra Jean Cartier broke toward the first barrel. Her first two turns were textbook. The horse accelerated quickly on the sprints. When she circled the third barrel, she leaned far into the well.

"She's going to fall!" Nina gasped.

Then Dr. Debra Jean Cartier shocked the crowd by reaching out and knocking the barrel over with her hand.

"That's a five-second penalty," Lynda mumbled.

Cartier spurred the horse across the finish line. Her time would have been 16.44 but ended up at 21.44. When the time was announced, Cartier looked behind the arena and gave a thumbs-up sign to Cindy LaCoste.

"She did it on purpose. She wanted Cindy to win," Heather declared.

"This is a crazy sport," Nina asserted. "People lending horses to their competitors, letting others win, cheering for each other."

Heather leaned her head back and glanced up at the bright arena lights. "Yeah . . . I love it!"

With Cindy at his side, Brady limped back pushing Debra Jean's wheelchair. All three still had their rodeo numbers pinned to their backs.

"Well, cowboy, what did you do this time?" Lynda asked.

"I tried to show off."

"And you sprained your ankle?"

"I came down with my foot bent under."

"Do we need to take you to a doctor?"

"Oh, no, darlin', I've been—"

"Shut up, Stoner, I don't want to hear it! Are you going to be limping down the aisle Saturday?"

"I figure it won't matter 'cause I'll be floatin' on air."

All three settled into the bleachers while the second set of team ropers competed.

"I need to know the story in the barrel racing," Lynda prodded.

"Doc let me win." Cindy patted Cartier's knee lightly.

"I didn't need the money." Doc slipped an arm gingerly around Cindy's shoulder.

"Cindy, why didn't you whip your horse in the straight-away?" Lynda asked. "Wouldn't that have given you a better time?"

Cindy held both hands to her lower ribs. "Because I was afraid I'd scream in pain if I took it out of my mouth. I should have listened to you and not competed. I guess I was trying to show off."

"Cindy-girl, go back to L. G.'s ranch and rest up for a few weeks. That's all there is to it, *comprende?*" Brady ordered.

"Yes, Daddy dear."

"He's right," Lynda lectured.

"Brady's always right."

Brady tugged off his worn brown Justin roper boot to look at his swelling ankle. "I don't think I'll be able to drive."

"No doubt about it, buckaroo," Cindy laughed. "Right after that wedding, I want you to go straight home and don't do a thing but lay around the house for a couple of weeks!"

"All right!" Lynda nodded in agreement.

"She's right, Brady. I should know. After all, I'm a doctor," Debra Jean chuckled.

"What does a degree in—" Brady began to protest.

"It doesn't take a rocket scientist to figure this one," Heather piped up. "Or do you want me to spell it out?"

"Okay, okay . . . I get the picture. Don't say any more, or you'll embarrass Wendy."

"Uncle Brady, even I know what they're talking about!"

"You do?" He gulped and glanced up at Heather. "Mama, I think I'm deliverin' these youngsters back to you just in time. Report back to me in about five years, and tell me how it all turned out."

"Coward!" Heather laughed.

"Look!" Nina pointed across the arena. "The bull-riding has begun. When does Marvin ride?"

Brady gritted his teeth as he yanked his boot back on. "He's up last. They wanted to run Mama's Boy at the end."

"Why?" Lynda asked.

"I guess he's sort of an unknown. They figured to save the surprise for the end."

"You mean, they think he'll be a dud?"

"Yeah . . . well, something like that."

Nine times in a row a cowboy nodded.

A gate swung open.

A bull bucked and spun.

And a black-hatted bull-rider landed in the dirt of the arena.

"The bulls are winning nine to nothing," Kelly announced.

"I think the contractor brought in a fresh pen of bulls that he wanted to buck out before the weekend. Obviously, these boys aren't used to 'em yet."

Nina leaned back against Brady's knees. "So if Marvin gets any points at all, he'll win?"

"Yep."

"Well, come on, Marvin!" she yelled.

"Marvin?" Lynda shouted, "Come on, Mama's Boy! Do me proud!"

Brady shook his head. "Heather, do you believe this lady was once a sophisticated New York City editor?"

"Award-winning editor," Kelly corrected.

"You whipped her into shape, cowboy," Heather laughed.

Marvin nodded his head, and the big brindle bull crashed out of the gate and immediately spun to the left. Marvin held on. When the bull pulled back to the right, the bull-rider's legs came clear off the bull. He regained his position only by the strength of his arm.

"Spur him!" Brady called out.

"What?" Lynda screamed. She stood up and yelled at the top of her voice, "Don't you dare hurt my bull!"

The crowd around her started to laugh.

Mama's Boy instantly stopped bucking and stared over at the stands. Marvin tried spurring, him but the bull stood perfectly still. Then the buzzer sounded. Marvin stepped off the bull and walked away.

Mama's Boy trotted toward the bleachers as the pickup men circled to drive him back to the stock pen.

"How come he only got a 61, Uncle Brady?" Wendy asked.

"Because the bull stopped buckin' as soon as he heard Lynda Dawn's voice."

"He couldn't hear me," she protested.

"Ever'one in the arena heard you."

Kelly and Nina turned around and nodded agreement.

STEPHEN BLY

"I think he's looking for his mama now," Cartier suggested.

Every time one of the mounted pick-up men moved in to round up the bull, he'd lower his head and charge at the horse. Even though the rodeo was over and the speakers blared recorded music into the starlit Wyoming night, most in the stands stayed and watched the helpless cowboys in the arena try to clear out Mama's Boy.

"Brady, they're not treating him nice!" she complained.

"Darlin', he's a bull. That's the way bulls are supposed to be treated."

"Not my bull."

"Well, maybe you ought to go down there and help them out."

"Yes, I will."

"Just wait, darlin'. . . . No, I didn't mean that. Let the pick-up men handle this!"

She hiked down to the enclosure and climbed on the rail of the arena fence.

"Lady, you have to get down from there," a security guard called from the edge of the stands.

"Not until I take care of my bull!" she shouted.

The crowd cheered her on.

"Come here, you big ol' cream puff! Come here!" she screamed.

Mama's Boy trotted right over to the rail next to her. She sucked in a deep breath and then shouted at the top of her voice, "You get out of this arena and back into your pen right now!"

The bull turned to the open gate and began to trot across the arena, as the chagrined pick-up men followed along behind. The crowd behind Lynda roared. She turned to the stands, bowed slightly, and then returned to the others.

"I can't—can't believe that!" Kelly stammered.

Nina scooted up to Lynda's side. "Where did you learn to do that?"

"It's a natural talent," Brady announced.

Mark and Marvin Garner sauntered up through the exiting crowd. "I've got to tell you, this was the most fun rodeo I've been at in a long time," Marvin roared. "And I can tell you one other thing . . . that's my last bull ride. He just about ripped my arm off. I was never so glad to have an animal stop buckin' in my life."

A big man with wide-brimmed silver-belly Resistol cowboy hat and dust-covered full-quill ostrich boots scooted his way into the group. "Excuse me, folks . . . excuse me. I need to talk to this little lady." He approached Lynda and pulled his hat off and held it in his hand. "Ma'am, I run this rodeo, and I'd like to say I've never seen a contract act as good as yours. It's a crowd-pleaser. Tell you what. I'll give you $100 a performance and pay your feed and vet bill if you'll stay in Cody and do that all summer long."

"You want to hire me?"

"You and the bull."

She glanced up at a grinning Brady Stoner. "Sorry, I'm getting married Saturday, and Mama's Boy has some better things to do."

"Now what could be better for him than loungin' around all day and workin' eight seconds ever' evening?"

Brady hobbled over to Lynda and slipped his arm around her waist. "That bull is going to have a pasture full of heifers waitin' for him in Montana."

A wide grin broke across the rodeo producer's leathery face. "Well, ma'am, I reckon you all are right. He does have better things to do. Thanks for puttin' on a show for tonight anyway. Looks like this bunch took home most of the sweets. If you change your mind, give me a call. I've been in this business thirty years, and I ain't never seen anything like that bull act!"

◆ ◆ ◆

Lynda walked slowly hand in hand with Brady out to the contestant parking lot.

"You just might have turned down your best opportunity to be a big-time rodeo performer."

"Lynda Dawn and her trained bull?"

"It has a mighty nice ring to it."

"The only ring I want is that one you're going to slip on my finger about thirty-six hours from now."

"The ring! Oh, no!" Brady groaned.

ELEVEN

The bright summer sun reflected off the Absaroka Range to the west as the Austin-Stoner convoy snaked its way out of Cody, Wyoming. This time it was a six-rig contingent. Again Brady, Lynda, Capt. Patch, Margarita, and Mama's Boy led the way.

"Stoner, why is it that it almost seems natural for me to be driving this rig?"

"Pioneer women always drive pickups."

"Well, I'm not a—"

"You're gettin' a lot closer than you think, darlin'. And might I add, you make a mighty handsome sight behind the wheel."

"I bet when you were a little boy, all the girls in your class called you 'Sweet-talk.'"

"You mean, Sarah Jean?"

"Who's Sarah Jean?"

"The only girl in my class."

"You only had one girl in your class?"

"It was a one-room school, remember? But Sarah Jean didn't call me 'Sweet-talk.' She called me 'Toad.'"

"Toad?"

"I guess I jumped around a lot. Anyway, Sarah Jean's my second cousin. She lives in Minnesota . . . or some state that starts with an M. Mom would know."

"They actually called you 'Toad'?"

"That's a mighty purdy green blouse you're wearin', darlin'."

"Are you changing the subject?"

"Yep. It is a mighty fine blouse."

"This old thing? I've had this since . . . about seven o'clock last night. I got it at that clothing store just across from the hotel. That was a crazy shopping trip. Can you imagine shopping with seven women?"

"Not even in my worst nightmare," Brady groaned.

"Anyway, they were all determined to help me select some new things."

"Were you the only one buyin'?"

"No. Kelly and Nina pushed their charge cards to the max."

When the highway swung near Buffalo Bill Reservoir, Lynda could see the entire parade in her sideview mirror. "Nobody would ever believe this."

"It's quite a weddin' train you're leadin', darlin'."

"Stoner, it was a regular caravan last week. This is absolutely incredible. If this scene were in a book, no one would believe it. I don't believe it. Doesn't anything normal ever happen when we're together?"

"Normal, as in boring?"

"I think boring has gotten bad press. The human spirit needs to be bored now and then, so one can survive the rest of life."

"I tried boring once. . . . Didn't like it."

"When?"

"I think it was in the summer after my first grade at the old Reynolds Creek one-room schoolhouse." Brady scrunched down and leaned his back on the pickup seat. "Yep. That was it. I was bored for three days."

"Then what did you do?"

"I trapped myself a badger and spent the summer trying to raise him for a pet."

"I didn't know badgers make pets."

"They don't. But it took me three months, sixteen stitches, and rabies shots to figure that out."

"That sounds gruesome."

"It wasn't boring."

"Whatever happened to the badger?"

"I still have him."

"What? Where?"

"That's his hide tacked up to my wall over the dresser. I called him Bandit."

"His hide! You mean, you took a gun and—"

"Actually it was Mom who shot him."

"Your mother? I can't imagine her with a gun."

"I think it was the fourth time he broke into her chicken coop. She opened the kitchen window over the sink, stuck her rifle out, and plugged him with a pullet still in his mouth."

"Your sweet, little mother did that?"

"Ranch-raised, darlin'. You ought to go elk huntin' with her sometime."

"Are you funnin' me, cowboy?"

"No, ma'am. You ask her about Bandit."

"It will be nice to see your parents again. I really like them."

"I knew you would."

"And your dad—he treats me like a daughter."

"In his mind you are. You always will be. He'll look after you and Lorraine 'til his dyin' day."

"I like that. Now give me this ring thing again. Brock is driving back to Reynolds Creek to get my wedding ring?"

"Yep. I finally reached him at Lorraine's folks' house. He said he'd drive back home today and get your ring, but they wouldn't make it to Jackson until tomorrow mornin'."

"How long a drive is it?"

"About six hours one way."

"That's a long way to go for a ring."

"Well, he needed to pick up my suit and good boots, too."

"You forgot your suit? You were planning on getting married tomorrow, weren't you?"

"Actually I was plannin' on goin' home for a few days when you flew back to New York. But then we got to gallivanting around, and I plumb forgot."

"You know, I got to thinking about it last night," Lynda continued, "and I decided that you have to marry me Saturday even if there isn't a ring."

"Hey, that would save me some bucks!" Brady laughed.

Lynda considered punching him, but he was now on the far side of the cab. *Why is it when the guys drive, the gals have to sit right next to them, but when the gals drive, the guys get to hide over there against the door?*

The sun glared into her eyes from the sideview mirror. "Could you hand me my sunglasses? They're in my purse."

Brady fumbled in the brown leather bag and pulled out a small black bottle. "This is what you're wearin' today?"

"Just the sunglasses, cowboy."

"It's actually called Hint of Love?"

"Yes. It's new. The sunglasses?"

"It smells really nice."

"Thank you. Now if you'd hand me—"

"It's about empty. What do you mean, it's new? You don't use a whole bottle ever' day, do you?"

"Hand me my sunglasses, buckaroo, before I kick you in the sore ankle."

"Yes, ma'am. . . . Here you go."

"Thank you."

"Now are you going to tell me how a new bottle of perfume got used up in one day?"

"I shared it."

"With whom?"

"Cindy, Debra Jean, Kelly, Nina, Heather, Heidi, and Wendy. They complained that they couldn't compete with my perfume, so Cindy decided we should all wear the same."

"Look out, Wyomin'!" Brady hooted. "Seven single gals with high-powered perfume!"

"One of whom will be Mrs. Brady Stoner in only twenty-seven hours."

Brady began to roll up the sleeves of his green shirt with black galloping horses. "Did I tell you I called the builders last night?"

"How is our house?"

"It's all done."

With both hands firmly on the steering wheel she ventured, "Really?"

"Purtneer."

"Purtneer? What on earth is a 'purtneer-all-done' house?" Lynda groaned. "We do have a roof over our head, right?"

"Yep."

"And electricity?"

"Yep."

"And indoor plumbing. You promised me indoor plumbing."

"It's all hooked up."

"Well, what's missing?"

"The floor coverings aren't in yet."

"The carpet and linoleum?"

"Right. You don't put that in until the walls get painted, and I told them we'd do the painting."

"So what is on the floors?"

"Bare plywood."

"Sounds lovely."

"Oh, it'll sweep up right fine. Anyway, it won't take us long to paint. This way you get to choose the colors for each room."

"So everything's finished but the paint and flooring?"

"And the front door," Brady mumbled.

Lynda peered over the top of her sunglasses at him. "What about the front door?"

"They ordered the wrong size."

"Run that by me again."

"The lumberyard ordered the front door with the little stained-glass window—"

"The one showing the cowboy on the bucking bronc?"

"Yeah, but the door came in at thirty-six inches instead of forty. It's their mistake. They had to send it back and order another."

"How long will that take?"

"Four to six weeks."

"We aren't going to have a front door for over a month?"

"It's summertime, darlin'. A little breeze will be enjoyable."

"You're teasing me again, right? Tell me you're teasing me."

"Well, we don't have a door, but I'll rig us up something temporary. There are plenty of wood scraps around."

"Around where?"

"All around the house. I just had them leave the scraps. I figured we could use them for firewood."

"Don't tell me they didn't get the bed built either."

"Now, Lynda Dawn Darlin', they finished it yesterday. The box springs and mattress were delivered Tuesday. All we need are the linens. Of course, there's . . . but that's no problem."

"What's no problem?"

"Well, they were figurin' we wouldn't be comin' home until next Wednesday, so they'll have to hurry and get three coats of varnish on the bedstead before we get there."

"What's the bottom line here, cowboy?"

"The headboard might be a little sticky for a day or two."

Lynda took a deep breath and held it in. *Lord, couldn't there be just one little thing that goes according to plan? My plan!*

"I don't care," she blurted out. "We'll just put the mattress and box springs on the floor and wait for the bed to dry."

"That's what I told them." Brady grinned.

Lynda glanced over at a sign that read: Yellowstone Park: 32 miles. "You mean I'm actually going to get to see the park in daylight this time?"

"See, I told you we'd be back. You'll like it. It's beautiful."

"We aren't stopping this rig until we get to Jackson, buckaroo. We've got a lifetime to gawk at Yellowstone!"

"Yes, ma'am."

◆ ◆ ◆

As usual, Jackson, Wyoming, was full of tourists.

The sidewalks crowded.

The stores jammed.

The galleries buzzing.

And the motels overbooked.

The horses, bull, and stock trailers had been left in a small set of corrals on the north side of town owned by friends of Brady's parents.

The wedding party gathered in the city park in the middle of town while Brady checked all their motel reservations. They sat around a tree-shaded picnic table near the southwest antler-arched entrance to the park. Lynda was describing their log home without a front door to the hoots and hollers of the crowd when Brady limped over to them.

"I got it set," he announced. "This is good for two nights, but that's it. Ever'one's on their own after that."

"You found rooms for this whole gang?" Lynda asked.

"Oh, yeah. I got rooms. 'Course, we're all goin' to have to buddy up a bit."

"Buddy up?" Nina asked.

"Here's what I got. Heather, Heidi, Wendy, and Doc will

have to bunk together in one room with two queen-sized beds at Coulter's Inn. Is that goin' to work for you ladies?"

"I'm sure we can manage," Cartier assured him.

"Over at the Teton View Lodge, sharing the honeymoon suite for tonight only . . . will be Lynda Dawn Darlin', Miss Cindy, Miss Nina, and Miss Kelly."

"All right! The honeymoon suite," Kelly laughed. "I knew I'd get to stay there someday!"

"But Saturday night you'll be at the Coulter. Now, me, and Mark, Marvin, and Mr. Tyler Adams will be at the Snake River Motel. It's only one room, but it's big, and they have a couple portable beds they'll slide in there. That's the best I could do."

"What do we do now?" Kelly asked. "I'm anxious to look at the art galleries."

"All them pictures is purdy expensive, Miss Kelly," Marvin Garner cautioned.

"Who wants to buy a painting? I just want to cruise among the rich and famous."

"Then I reckon you're on your own," Brady reported. "Me and Lynda Dawn Darlin' will deliver Sissy Mark's pottery. Then we can all meet at seven at the Cowboy Cafe."

"That sounds like a wonderful place," Kelly mused.

Brady nodded agreement. "It does serve a mighty fine chicken-fried steak."

◆ ◆ ◆

At 10:00 P.M. Friday night, Brady and Lynda plopped down in the large, overstuffed love seat in front of a huge fireplace in one corner of the lobby of the Teton View Lodge.

Brady reached over and took her hand. "Well, darlin' . . . we did make it back to our favorite spot."

"There's no fire."

"In the fireplace, you mean?"

She looked in his eyes.

A sparkle.

Two dimples.

Mostly straight teeth.

Always chapped lips.

"I dare you to tease me like that tomorrow night, Mr. Stoner!"

"Wheeweeee, Miss Lynda Dawn, are we really gettin' married tomorrow?"

"You bet your boots, cowboy."

"This evenin's been hectic. I thought we'd never have time alone."

"It helped when most of them decided to go line dance."

"I figured Miss Nina and Miss Kelly would want to kick up their heels, but I thought Cindy-girl might want to rest up."

"She popped in some Advil and took off with the rest. I don't think she wanted Kelly to get too big a lead on roping in Mark Garner."

"Two guys and three gals isn't exactly even."

"They thought about inviting Tyler but figured Heidi would have a cow."

"I reckon they're right. Heather, Doc, the girls, and young Mr. Adams will enjoy Miss Peggy's famous Jackson Theatre Melodrama."

"Which leaves us right here . . . on the eve of our wedding."

"Are you scared, darlin'?"

"Scared? Should I be?"

Brady put his arm around her and pulled her close. "You didn't answer my question. In about fifteen hours from now, you are goin' to be a married woman. Your life will be changed forever. Are you scared?"

"How about you, buckaroo? Are you ready for the gate to swing open and the ride to begin?"

"You know, I was thinkin' about that very same thing. But

the analogy breaks down. When I'm ridin' broncs, I only have to do it for eight seconds at a time. Being a husband is a twenty-four-hours-a-day, seven-days-a-week, fifty-two-weeks-a-year experience."

"Can you hang on that tight, cowboy?"

"I've got to. But another thing I was thinkin' . . . when it comes to ridin' broncs, I know what to expect, and I know what's expected of me. At being married, darlin'—I'm a total rookie. Oh, I've got the huggin' and kissin' down pretty good . . . but all that other stuff scares me."

Lynda slipped her arms around his waist and laid her head on his chest. "What other stuff?"

"Makin' a livin', payin' the bills, learnin' to keep my mouth shut, bein' smart enough to apologize, not trackin' mud in on—"

"The plywood?"

"Yeah. And tryin' not to do too many dumb things."

"Do you do dumb things?" she asked.

"Darlin', you know I do. Like buyin' a ranch in Montana and not tellin' you about it."

"Ah, yes. You do have a point."

"Miss Lynda, I don't spend a lot of time thinkin' things through—weighin' the pros and the cons and doin' the most reasonable thing. You know me—I'm impetuous. I operate on instinct. I do what feels morally, spiritually, physically right. I know there will be times that I aggravate you somethin' terrible."

She squeezed him tight. "With the Lord's help, we'll make it, babe."

"That's the key, isn't it?"

"I think so. A lot of my friends sit around complaining about how many marriages don't make it. Sometimes I'm shocked that any succeed. But you didn't answer me. Are you scared of getting married?"

"Yes, ma'am, I am."

"What scares you most?"

"Disappointing you. I keep thinkin' that someday . . . a week . . . a year . . . ten years from now you'll wake up one mornin' and say to yourself, 'This guy's a real dud! I deserve better than this.'"

"You're kidding me."

"Nope. Miss Lynda Dawn Austin of New York City came west and found herself a cowboy. She's been dreamin' about what it would be like to marry him and live on a ranch. But I don't know if I can live up to her dreams. It scares me."

"You thinkin' about backin' out?"

"Yep."

Lynda sat up and pushed herself away from Brady. Instantly, his strong arms pulled her close again.

"To be honest, I did think maybe I shouldn't do this. I'm sure there's men who could take better care of you than me. And I know there's a whole posse of them that would give anything to have the chance. But the thought only lasted a minute. Then I realized that if I don't marry you by 1:00 P.M. tomorrow, I would just shrivel up and die like a worm on the blacktop after a rain. Darlin', I'm scared spitless. I don't have any idea how to be the kind of husband you need me to be. But I want to marry you and live with you forever so bad ever' bone, ever' muscle, ever' joint in my body aches."

Lynda took a deep breath and laid her head back on his chest.

"Now, Lynda Dawn, tell me not to worry because you've got it all figured out and organized."

"Cowboy, you know for a fact that you are the only thing in the world I have never been able to figure out and organize. I have no idea what married life is going to be like either. I don't even have a clue what we're going to have for breakfast Monday morning nor what kind of perfume blends best with barn smells."

"Strong perfume," Brady proposed.

"But none of that scares me. Somehow we'll bumble through."

"So you're not scared at all?"

"I didn't say that. There's one thing that scares me . . . sort of."

"What's that?"

"I don't think I can talk about it."

"Oh, that!"

She sat up so she could look him in the eyes. "What do you mean, 'Oh, that'?"

"Sex. Isn't that what you mean?"

"Well . . . yes, but how'd you know?"

"I could hear it in your voice."

"This is getting weird, Stoner. You know what's in my mind?"

"Yeah, I reckon we'll get better at it as the years go by."

"Get better at what?"

"At readin' each other's mind."

"Oh, that. I know you're right."

"All right, Lynda Dawn . . . what scares you about sex?"

"It's not that I'm afraid. I'm really looking forward to being able to love you completely. But . . . I'm afraid I won't know enough. I mean . . . What if I'm really boring? I've waited all this time, and what if I'm a failure?"

Brady started to laugh.

She pulled back even farther. "Don't laugh at me, Stoner."

"I'm laughin' at both of us, darlin'."

"Why?"

"'Cause we're both over thirty, and we're stumblin' around like teenagers. We're a pair to draw to, darlin'. Here's the way I figure it. We're goin' to talk to each other and the Lord about ever'thing in our marriage."

"Everything?"

"Ever'thing. As long as we keep talkin', I figure between the three of us, we'll work out any struggles."

Lynda stretched across the leather love seat and laid her head on his leg. "Okay, cowboy. You convinced me. I'll go ahead and marry you tomorrow."

Brady reached out his hand and began to rub her back. "That feels really good, babe," she murmured.

"Do you get the idea that the wedding might be a little bigger than we planned?" he probed.

"You mean, the fact that more people are coming?"

"Yeah. Maybe I'm gettin' too worried about it." Brady continued to rub her back.

"Right now I haven't been this relaxed in a month. You promise me you'll sit with me in the living room every night next week and rub my back?"

"Yep. We'll stretch out on the old plywood floor and glance longingly at an empty woodstove."

"Maybe we could stare out the open doorway at the piles of construction trash in the front yard," she giggled.

"Oh, darlin', you jist said that to make me homesick!"

She slipped her arms around his jeans-covered leg and hugged it to her cheek.

"Are you Cindy LaCoste?"

The authoritarian voice behind the love seat boomed throughout the entire lobby. Red-faced, Lynda sat straight up. Brady jumped to his feet—then sank back to the couch.

"No, she's not Cindy. But Cindy is a good friend of ours."

"I'm Detective Brooks with the JPD." He flashed a leather case with a shining silver badge. "I need to talk to Miss LaCoste. She is not in her room. Do you know where I can find her?"

"Not really," Lynda offered. "She and some friends went out an hour or so ago to find a place to line dance. We don't know where they ended up."

STEPHEN BLY

Brady hobbled around to the officer. "Sir, I'm Brady Stoner, and this is Lynda Dawn Austin. We're gettin' married tomorrow, and Cindy . . . well, Cindy's a part of the weddin'. She's sort of like a sister to us."

"I really do need to talk to her," the lawman repeated.

"We can go try to find her. She's been travelin' with us for several days. She's not in trouble, is she?"

The detective stalked around to the empty fireplace and plopped himself down on the brick hearth. "We hear a lot of rumors during the tourist season. I don't know which ones to believe, but I don't like takin' chances. I don't know this woman, LaCoste, but we got word from a bartender over at the Trap Door that a guy from out of state was trying to hire someone for $5,000 to kill a lady named Cindy LaCoste."

"To kill Cindy?" Brady choked.

"I don't know if this is an ex-boyfriend who's drunk or ex-husband tired of alimony, a pimp who thinks he's been stiffed or just a loony stalking his idol. Maybe the whole thing's made up. I just want to warn her and offer her police protection until the deal goes through."

"What deal?"

"We sent word for the guy to meet an undercover officer in the park about midnight. We'll just see how far he wants to go."

"Is the guy a biker?"

"You mean, leather pants and jacket—one of those?"

"Yeah. Cindy had some trouble with bikers last week."

"Nope. According to our witness, he's a tall guy, big muscles, wears a black T-shirt, and has long, dark hair worn in a ponytail."

"Is he from Las Vegas?"

"How did you know that?"

"We had a run-in with a guy answering that description in Deadwood a couple days ago," Brady answered.

"You seem to have lots of run-ins. Why is that? What exactly is your occupation?"

"Well . . . Lynda Dawn here is an award-winning editor at a New York publishing house, and she's . . . gathering material for a book about Cindy. It just puts us in contact with some interestin' characters."

"Do you know this guy's name?"

"Nope. We weren't introduced."

Lynda scooted to the front of the love seat. "He does hang around with a guy named Joe Trent, also from Las Vegas. In fact, I think he works for Trent."

The detective wrote on a note pad. "Were you two serious about helping me find LaCoste?"

"Yes, sir."

"Most of the dance joints are on the south side leading out to the highway. If you could check those out, I'll go back to the office and make some phone calls."

"What should we do if we find her?"

"Bring her right back to the lodge and call me. I'll send a man over. This whole thing might be a big crock. I hope it is. But I'd sure appreciate having her tucked away safe until we get it figured out."

Both Lynda and Brady were standing when the detective left the lobby.

"I can't believe Trent. Kill her? For $5,000? Why?" Lynda asked.

"I don't know. Maybe it has something to do with Cindy gettin' even with the motorcycle gang."

"We'd better hurry. No telling what would happen if Trent comes across her first."

"If she's with Mark and Marvin, he won't do anything. Trent's strictly a hire-someone-else-to-do-your-dirty-work kind of character."

"Then we don't have to worry until he hires someone."

"But who's to say he didn't already find someone. That's a lot of money. Come on, darlin', let's hurry."

They shoved their way through the wide, rough oak doors and out into the Wyoming night.

"What rig are we taking?"

"They took the Dodge with the jump seat, so that leaves us the minivan still hooked up to your trailer of clothes."

"Or Cindy's Ford pickup," Lynda noted. "I vote on the pickup."

"Can you drive, darlin'? My ankle is still killin' me."

They limped and jogged out to the paved parking lot and climbed into the Ford. Brady handed the keys to Lynda.

"Do we have to drive through that mass of people downtown to get out to the clubs?"

"I know a shortcut." Brady waved his arm. "Take a right at the school and go on to a sharp turn to the left. That will lead us over there."

"Is this a residential section?"

"It's the outskirts of town. I think it was the old truck route before they made the new one on the east side."

Lynda cranked the wheel and ended the turn with an "Oh, no!"

"What's the matter, darlin'?"

"Oh, nothing. I just broke my fingernail on the steering wheel." She swerved to miss a sizable pothole. "This road's kind of rough."

"Probably doesn't get much maintenance anymore. But it sure beats going through downtown. There's not much traffic out here."

"Traffic? There's absolutely no one . . . except that car that just turned in behind us."

"I sure hope we don't take half the night finding Cindy."

"If they all stuck together, it can't be all that tough."

"We can just cruise the parking lots lookin' for my truck."

"That ought to work." Lynda glanced in her rearview mirror. "Looks like that guy behind us is in a hurry. He's catching up real fast." She looked over at Brady. "I don't suppose you could dig in my purse and find my fingernail file."

"You can file your broken nail in the dark?"

"I could do it asleep."

"What a girl!" he teased. "I haven't much experience at diggin' in a gal's purse in the dark . . . yet."

"What do you mean, yet?"

"It's just that I . . . oh, crud!" Brady groaned to the sound of assorted items bouncing on the rubber floor mat. "I just spilt the entire contents of your purse on the floor."

Lynda began to laugh.

"Is it that funny?"

"You want me to find the dome light?" she asked.

"Nah, I'll just scoop it all up in the dark."

As Brady leaned low in the cab, the car behind them drove up close and blinked its lights onto high beam.

"Why did he do that?" she asked.

Brady, still retrieving an evasive lipstick tube, replied, "Who did what?"

"The guy in the rig behind us blinked his lights on high and then dimmed them."

"Maybe he wants to pass us."

"Who's stopping him? Does he want me to pull over?"

"Keep drivin'. As soon as I get this bottle of—"

The back window shattered at the exact same time Lynda heard a blast from the car behind them. Lynda swerved to the right shoulder of the road; then she overcorrected. They were suddenly off the road on the left, plowing down weeds and safety markers.

"Brady!"

He was at her side, clutching the steering wheel. "Hang on, darlin'. We've got to get control!"

"What happened?"

"He shot our back window out!"

Lynda bit her lip. "Who is it?"

"Maybe Trent did hire someone to kill Cindy. This is her rig."

"What are we going to do?" she shouted.

"Pull over quick and trade me places!"

"Pull over? He'll shoot us."

"Pull over, and let me drive."

Lynda jerked the truck to the right side of the road and slammed on the brakes. Brady climbed right over the top of her, and she scooted to the far side of the rig.

"He stopped behind us! He's going to shoot us!"

Brady slouched below the window line. "Stay low!"

Lynda peeked back through the opening that used to be the window. "He's getting out, and he has a gun in his hand!"

"Hang on, darlin'!"

The back tires of Cindy's pickup churned a spray of gravel as he floored the accelerator and bolted down the highway. Lynda heard several shots but couldn't tell where they were aimed. "Did you get hit?"

"Just by flyin' glass. Are you all right?"

"I just got shot at on a dark, abandoned road. Am I all right?"

"Yeah, are you going to cry or anything?"

"I just might," Lynda snapped. Then her voice softened. "I'm fine. . . . Is he following us?"

"Nope."

"Why not?"

"Because we're back in town."

Lynda glanced up as the bright blue neon lights came into view. "Someone was trying to kill us!"

"I figure they were trying to kill Cindy."

"Somehow that's not very comforting."

"There's a phone outside that club. I'll call Detective Brooks."

"Look, Brady! There's your truck! This is where they are!"

"You go get Cindy."

"Just Cindy?"

"She's the only one they're lookin' for. Let the others stay and dance if they want to. Wait with her in the lobby of the club. I'll meet you there. We aren't leavin' this place until the police show up."

Lynda jogged toward the front door of the Western Slope Lounge. *Why do they want to kill Cindy, Lord? I just can't understand. After all she's had to go through. Please protect her . . .*

◆ ◆ ◆

It was a little past 1:30 A.M. when Brady and Lynda had another quiet moment alone. Again they were in the lobby of the Teton View Lodge.

"How's Cindy doin'?" Brady asked as he scooted in next to her on the leather love seat.

"She's kicked back, playing gin rummy with Kenny."

"Kenny?"

"The police officer who's protecting her. They're in the sitting room of the suite. Nina and Kelly are lying in bed fully dressed and wide awake. They just know they'll never live through the night."

"Me and the boys offered to trade motel rooms with all of you."

"I'm not giving up my suite at the Lodge," Lynda insisted. "Besides, you and I both know that Trent won't try much on his own. He's always had thugs around to do the tough part."

Brady took Lynda's hand. "What's the latest report from the police?"

Lynda leaned over and laid her head on Brady's shoulder.

"The detective told Cindy this guy working for Trent—his name is Corky Snyder—just happened to spot us in Cindy's pickup and thought it was Cindy by herself. I guess he decided to do the job and collect the five grand himself. But when he botched the job, he fell back on plan #2—hiring someone. The police taped the whole conversation and arrested him at midnight."

Brady slipped his arm around her waist. "He ought to get a minimum of twenty years for that."

Lynda leaned over and kissed Brady behind the ear. "That's what they told him, and he made a plea bargain."

"What kind of deal did he cut?" Brady lifted her dark, wavy hair and kissed her earlobe, her neck, and her cheek.

Lynda leaned her head back on the leather love seat, and Brady continued to kiss her neck. "They said they'd press to get him five years without parole if he would testify against Joe Trent."

Brady softly tugged her chin down and planted his narrow, chapped lips right upon Lynda's fresh Autumn Rose Blush lipstick. He pulled back about the time she opened her eyes. "Did he agree to that?"

Lynda slipped her arms around his neck and pulled him close for a long and increasingly warm kiss. "I guess good ol' Corky doesn't have too much loyalty. He told them everything."

Pulling her even closer, Brady lightly kissed her chin, her neck, and several inches below her neck. "Exactly what is everything?"

She reached down and pulled his face back up to hers. "Not *that* everything, cowboy." She grinned. "Snyder said that the reason Trent came after Cindy is that he found out she's the one who took apart his marijuana-pushing motorcycle gang and was responsible for the bust at Mt. Rushmore."

"The bust at Rushmore? I thought Gutzon Borglum the sculptor was responsible for those." He winked.

"Very funny!"

She pulled off his cowboy hat and put it on her head. Then she kissed the tan line that ran across his forehead. "What were we talking about?"

"Drug busts."

"Oh, yeah. Are you getting tired?" she asked.

"I was tired three hours ago. Finish your story."

"Well, this drug thing is new for Trent. Some big Vegas underworld kingpin was trying him out. As soon as the guys got arrested in South Dakota, they let Trent know he was a two-bit hustler, and they had no use for him." Lynda leaned her cheek close to him. Brady kissed her softly several times.

"So Trent came on this quest to do away with Cindy and prove to those in Vegas that he was worthy of their slime." Brady's strong arms were now completely around her waist and holding her tight.

"That's how it goes down." Lynda kissed him several times on his neck. "They've alerted the police in Nevada, South Dakota, and Wyoming to be on the lookout for Trent."

Brady turned the other cheek. Lynda continued to kiss. "Well, darlin' . . . I would guess he'll hurry back to Vegas and try to tell 'em it wasn't his fault."

"That's what I've been trying to tell Kelly and Nina. By himself, Trent's just your average jerk." She kissed his chin, his neck, and several inches below his neck.

Brady hugged her tight, then released her with a laugh. "Well, I don't know if Miss Nina or Miss Kelly are in danger, but Miss Lynda Dawn is gettin' mighty close to trouble."

"Time to go home, cowboy?"

"One last time, darlin'."

"You know the schedule tomorrow?"

"Breakfast at 8:00 A.M. with your brother, sister, and their families. I meet my folks and Brock and gang at the motel at 10:00 to get the ring and suit. Be at the chapel by 12:00 noon to greet relatives and guests like the Gossmans and Hamptons." Brady kissed her again on the lips. "How am I doin'?"

"You're doin' jist great, darlin'," Lynda drawled with a deep sigh. "Do you know you're the most handsome, exciting, fun temptation I've ever avoided?"

"Usually you give in, huh?" he teased.

"Never!" she declared. "I'll try to get to the chapel by 12:00 or so. My hair appointment is at 10:00. I shouldn't have any trouble there. I just need them to style it."

Brady stood up and tugged her to her feet. "Okay, darlin', I'll go. But one of these nights you won't be able to get rid of me."

"I'm countin' on it, cowboy!"

◆ ◆ ◆

Saturday morning turned out to be more hectic than Friday night. Lynda woke up late to find Cindy blabbing incessantly about Kenny the cop. Kelly and Nina, who now decided they might have long lives after all, plotted the futures of Marvin and Mark Garner.

Breakfast was mass confusion with nieces and nephews running around the cafe as the adults tried to catch up on a year's worth of news. Lynda was proud of Brady, who entered into every conversation with a laid-back cheerfulness.

Nina and Kelly had her long, tight-skirted, fringed white wedding dress spread across the bed when she got back to the lodge. Lynda was relieved to see the white boots, feathered and laced straw cowgirl hat, and bucking-horse earrings lying alongside.

Kelly and Nina went with her to the hair dresser. Cindy

decided she should lie low until Trent was picked up, but changed her mind when Kenny the cop finished his shift and had to leave. All three sat in the salon and giggled with her as Mr. Bobby styled her hair.

It was 11:10 when she tugged on the long skirt and glanced in the floor-length mirror.

"You look gorgeous, Lynda Dawn Darlin'!" Cindy called out.

"Good, because I can only take tiny steps in this skirt."

"Do you have to kneel?" Kelly asked.

Lynda tried bending her knees. "I'd never get back up."

"Yeah, don't kneel," Nina added, "and don't run, don't hike up stairs, and—"

"May I get married?"

"That you may."

"Hand me my hat."

"I thought we'd just take it to the chapel, and you could put it on there," Kelly offered.

"I told you, they just have a tiny bathroom and no dressing room. I have to be ready when I get there."

"Is this how it goes?" Kelly placed the hat down on Lynda's head. The three-inch-wide white ribbon hung down over her forehead, nose, and mouth.

Lynda started to laugh. "It's tough to kiss the bride this way."

"That way the groom gets a surprise. You could sneak someone else in on him, and he wouldn't know until it's too late," Kelly heckled.

"Come on, it goes this way." Lynda turned the hat around and looked in the mirror.

"How's it look?" Nina asked.

"Oh, the hat's nice . . . but my hair—it sticks out too much under the hat."

"That's the way it's supposed to look. Did you notice how Marvin Garner's hair sticks out even after he pulls his hat off?"

Kelly put her hands on her hips. "None of us have ever seen Marvin with his hat off."

"Oh . . . well, it does!" Nina insisted.

Lynda stalked across the room. "Kell, help me put on my boots. Cindy, call Mr. Bobby, and tell him I'll be by about 11:30 to have him touch up my hair with the hat on."

"You're going to the salon dressed like that?" Nina questioned.

"Yes, I am."

◆ ◆ ◆

It was 11:45 when she reached Mr. Bobby's. She sent the others down to the chapel to see that everything was ready. Over her protests they insisted that they would come back for her when she was finished.

When she entered the shop, Mr. Bobby was on the telephone. Five minutes later, he was still talking. Cindy and an out-of-uniform Kenny the cop entered the shop.

"Are you ready?" Cindy asked.

"He's still on the phone." Lynda waved her hands toward the back of the salon. "Hi, Kenny."

The tall, dark-haired man nodded. "Miss Lynda—"

"Kenny offered to be my bodyguard on his own time," Cindy announced. "Isn't that sweet of him?"

"How are you feeling?" Lynda asked her.

"Much better after that back rub Kenny gave me."

"How are things at the chapel? Is Brady there yet?"

"Oh, yeah. He's pacing around like a badger in a cardboard box. And the chapel's half full already."

Lynda looked at her watch. "But it's not even noon. The wedding doesn't start for over an hour."

"Everyone's from out of town and seems to be enjoying visiting with each other. A number of Brady's rodeo friends have come in."

Mr. Bobby hung up the telephone and sauntered to the front of the shop, motioning with a sweeping gesture for Lynda to sit in the styling chair.

"Look, you go on and greet people at the chapel. You probably know more of Brady's rodeo friends than I do."

Cindy turned toward the door. "You want us to come back for you in ten minutes?"

"No, I'll just walk down."

"You are not walking to your own wedding, Lynda Dawn Darlin'. Kenny and I will walk back to the chapel. We'll leave the rig. Here are the keys. It's parked in back toward the alley." She dropped them on the counter.

"No, really, Cindy, you take the—"

Cindy LaCoste came up close to her. "I want to walk with Kenny. You understand?" she whispered.

"Oh . . . okay. I'll drive down."

"If you aren't at the chapel in fifteen minutes, we send a posse back for you."

"I'll be there in five."

◆ ◆ ◆

It took Mr. Bobby only four minutes to get Lynda's hair looking perfect under the hat. She strolled out of the shop into the bright light of a clear-skied Wyoming noon. Lynda searched through her purse and jammed on her sunglasses.

Cindy was right. It does seem strange walking around in a wedding dress—even if it is Western-cut. Everyone in the parking lot is staring. Which rig did they leave for me?

Lynda's heart sank when she saw the Ford pickup with the back window and a piece of duct-taped cardboard. "Oh, this is real classy," she moaned. "Not exactly a chauffeur-driven limo in Manhattan."

She carefully slid in behind the steering wheel and tugged the door closed. It caught on something, and she turned around to stare into the bruised, glaring face of a short man with a chrome-finished gun in his hand.

"Trent!" she shouted.

"Well, if it isn't Lynda Dawn Darlin', the Cowboy's Love Slave. Scoot over!"

"I-I don't have time for this. I've got to—got to get to my wedding," she stuttered.

He physically shoved her across the seat of the pickup and yanked the keys out of her hand. "Well, now, isn't that too bad? Some days nothin' goes right. Like a business deal at Mt. Rushmore that cost me big bucks. Or even this beautiful bruise on my face when I was blind-sided by fifty pounds of quarters."

"Let me out of here!" she tried to scream, but the words came out more like a whimper. "Please! It's my wedding!"

The cold steel of the short-nosed gun jammed hard into the back of her neck. "Well, it will be a day you won't forget."

He pulled the truck into the back alley and stepped on the accelerator.

"Why are you doing this?"

"Well, I expected to find Cindy LaCoste with this truck, but you'll do. Especially since Stoner will come looking for you."

"You are ruining my wedding!" She tried to take deep breaths and not let tears ruin her eye makeup.

The pickup continued to bounce along down the alleys until they reached the edge of town. Lynda was breathing hard. Her head spun. *This is not happening to me. Not now. Not so close to the wedding. It's almost 12:15! They are going to be looking for me. Brady, hurry . . . hurry, babe.*

She glanced out at the sideview mirror.

"You lookin' for Stoner? He won't save you this time, Lynda Dawn. I have other plans."

"Why? Why are you doing this?" she began to sob, unable to hold back the tears.

"We already discussed that, darlin'!" he growled, prodding her with the barrel of the revolver.

Lord, if I try to jump out at this speed, I'll ruin my dress. I'll break my neck. I'm scared, Lord. I'm really scared.

She fought to hold back the sobs. Tears now dripped on her fringed, long-sleeved white jacket. *Lord, surely You didn't give me all of this and then plan to jerk it away from me right before the wedding. There's got to be a reason.*

They had just reached the north edge of Jackson when Lynda spied the huge barn at a ranch ahead on the right. *That's where our animals are!*

"I've got to stop. I've got to go to the bathroom," she sniffled.

"Hold it in. We aren't stopping."

"I'm not kidding. I'm about to lose it all over this pickup seat."

"Come on, Lynda Dawn, I'm not going to . . ."

Lynda began to sob. "Please, just pull over to that barn. I can use the barn."

She felt the gun barrel pull back from her neck. "Yeah . . . well, that barn just might be the place after all."

Trent didn't slow down but raced the truck around to the back of the big gray building, parking close to the welded steel-pipe corral. Grabbing her by the arm, he yanked her out of the truck on the driver's side.

"Go ahead, darlin', do your tinkle."

"At least, I can go into the barn, can't I?"

"You can't go into the barn! Now get it over with, or I'm shovin' you back into the pickup."

"But . . . have some decency. Let me go into that corral. . . . No, there's a cow in there."

Trent glanced into the large pen. "Cow? Lady, that's a bull!" Then he pushed her closer to the gate. "It's a huge bull. This just might be somehow . . . the irony. The Cowboy's Love Slave gets trampled by a bull." Then he turned and clutched her arm. "You're going in there all right!"

"No!" she screamed. It was much more authentic than she thought she was capable of. *Mama's Boy, you do remember Mama, don't you?*

Trent opened the pipe gate a couple of feet. "This ought to make you forget your bladder. And it's a cinch you're not going to climb the fence in that tight skirt!" Just as she entered the corral, he violently shoved her back with the barrel of his gun. Lynda staggered a couple of steps and fell to her hands and knees.

"My dress! You got my dress dirty!" she screamed.

"That's the least of your worries, Lynda Dawn Darlin'."

Still on her hands and knees, she noticed Mama's Boy had backed into the far corner of the corral. Trent shoved the gun into his back pocket and stood outside the gate, holding it open about a foot.

"This ought to be quite a sight!" he hooted.

"I can't believe you got my dress dirty," she cried. "I bought this in February in Houston. It's been carefully hanging in my closet four months, and you got it dirty. May God have mercy on your soul, Joe Trent, because me and Mama's Boy will show you none!"

"Mama's boy? Who's a mama's boy?"

With dirty hands Lynda hiked the tight skirt above her knees and struggled to her feet. She stomped over to the waiting bull and yelled, "Well, don't just stand there, you big lunk. Go on . . . get through that gate!"

Mama's Boy trotted straight at the startled Trent.

"Run, you big galoot! Run fast!" she screamed.

Trent had just slammed the gate shut when Mama's Boy crashed into it. It sounded like two cars colliding at an intersection. The gate swung violently into Trent, catching him under the chin and flinging him through the air. He landed with an ear-jarring crash on the hood of Cindy's Ford pickup.

Mama's Boy just stood at the open gate and stared out at the ranch yard.

"Good boy!" Lynda yelled. "Good boy. You are the smartest bull in the whole world! Come on back in here!"

Holding the dress above her knees, she jogged past the bull out of the corral and climbed into the pickup. She jumped back out of the truck and ran to the corral, this time closing and locking the gate. "I'll buy you a treat next time I'm at the store, honey!" she called out to Mama's Boy.

What is a bull treat anyway?

She glanced down at her watch. "Quarter 'til . . . I still have fifteen minutes! Hang on, cowboy, I'll be there!" Holding up her dress, she ran back and jumped into the truck and started the engine.

"Trent!" she mumbled. The unconscious man with the bloody face lay on the hood of the pickup. She jumped back out of the truck and ran around to the front.

I'll pull him to the ground and leave him here and tell the police where to find him. She grabbed his booted foot and then dropped it with a crash. *But what if he wakes up before the police get here and runs off? Then he'll hire more goons and come looking for me and Brady again . . . and Cindy—all of us!*

She struggled to lift his legs. *I'll toss him in the back of the pickup and take him to the police.*

"This is not working! I can't even lift his legs! What do I do if he comes to while I'm trying to move him?" She glanced at her watch again. *Ten 'til. I've got to go! I'll . . . I'll drive slowly with him on the hood, and the cops will pull me over, and I'll turn him in! But he might fall off . . . eh, Lord, You're in charge of whether Trent falls off or not.*

Lynda was surprised that on the flat hood of the Ford the body hardly moved at all. *All right, cops, where are you? Pull me over. . . . Everyone's staring. Look, there's a man on your hood! There's a hood on my hood!*

Lynda cruised through two red lights and past a tour bus of senior citizens, many of whom snapped pictures of the unconscious Joe Trent.

She glanced down at her watch. "One minute. . . . There's the chapel. Where am I going to park? Anywhere I want, buckaroo."

She could see several dozen people gathered on the steps outside the chapel. She ran the truck right up onto the sidewalk and slammed on the brakes. Hapless Joe Trent slid off the hood and crashed onto the sidewalk. Brady was at her side by the time her feet hit the concrete.

She collapsed in his arms.

Kenny, the off-duty cop, took Trent into custody.

Lynda gave the stunned crowd a quick explanation of what happened.

Brady, in crisp black shirt with rose pink desert scene, Western-cut charcoal gray suit, black boots, and freshly blocked black felt hat, picked her up, kissed her on the lips, and carried her up the stairs of the chapel to the applause of the audience.

"Talk about a grand entrance!" he whispered.

"Yeah, I wanted us to have something to tell our grand-kids."

"They won't believe it."

She kissed him back. "No, they won't, will they? Nice shirt."

"This old thing?"

"I thought you were going to wear the white one."

"I spilled boot polish on it this mornin'," he admitted. "I about died during this last hour when we couldn't find you."

"You think I'd run off?"

"The thought did cross my mind. Are you ready to marry me, darlin'?"

"I've been ready my whole life, cowboy."

"Good." He set her on her feet in the chapel's entryway.

"But," she blurted out, "give me five minutes to clean up."

"Darlin', you look beautiful all smudged up," he teased.

Lynda looked around at the crowd. "Look, everyone, this might seem bizarre, but Brady and I are used to it. So everyone go back inside and . . . and Brady will introduce you all to each other."

"I will?"

"Brady and, eh, Kelly can introduce everyone. Between the two of you, you should know about everyone. Meanwhile," Lynda glanced through the crowd, "Nina, Cindy, and Heather come with me. I need a quick makeover."

◆ ◆ ◆

It was 1:23 P.M. when Lynda emerged from the small ladies' room at the chapel and took her place at her brother William's side.

Her makeup was refreshed.

Her hair reasonably in control.

Her dress slightly soiled.

Her smile wide.

Her hands started to tremble.

"This is it, lil' sis." Six-foot-four William held his arm out. "You look beautiful. A lot like those pictures of Mom when she and Dad got married."

"I wish she could have been here," Lynda sniffed.

"Come on, Lynda, there's a pretty great cowboy anxious to repeat some vows up front."

"He is great, isn't he?"

"You found a good one, Lynda Dawn." William tugged her forward. "There's our cue. Remember to walk slowly and smile big."

Lynda took a deep breath and let it out quickly. *Thank you, Lord. You're actually going to let me marry Brady.*

With a standing-room-only crowd on their feet, Lynda could feel the stares of the entire audience as she walked down the aisle.

What did I forget? Boots, hat, dress, earrings, makeup, garter . . . "Oh, no!" she moaned aloud. Her brother stopped in his tracks.

"Wait right here!" she hollered. "Everyone wait right here!"

Spinning on the heels of her white boots, she yanked her dress up to her knees and scampered to the back of the chapel where Cindy and Nina stood.

"Give me my purse!" she called out.

Nina handed her the brown leather bag.

"Get down there and marry the cowboy," Cindy chided.

"Not without this!" Lynda pulled out a small white bottle with a gold lid and quickly splashed perfume on her neck and arms. The entire crowd broke out in laughter.

"What's it called?" Nina demanded.

"Once in a Lifetime." Lynda grinned and shoved the bottle into Nina's hand. She jogged back to her brother and resumed the processional.

Instead of offering his arm to her when she reached the front of the chapel, Brady gave her a tight hug. She raised up on her toes and gave him a kiss on the lips.

A blushing Brady Stoner stammered, "I-I think, darlin', you're supposed to wait until later to do that."

"From now on, cowboy, I can kiss you any old time I want—understand?"

Holding his hat in front of him with both hands, he nodded. "Yes, ma'am."

She slipped her arm in his and whispered, "I love you, Brady Stoner."

With their backs to the audience, he leaned his head close enough to her that she could smell his crisp aftershave. "And I really, really love you, Lynda Dawn . . . Darlin'."

The next several minutes of the service flashed by, and Lynda was thinking of a desolate Montana ranch and the softest chapped lips in the world when the reverend pronounced, "You may kiss the bride."

"Yes, sir!" Brady shoved his black hat on his head and put his hands on Lynda's shoulders. "Are you ready, Lynda Dawn Darlin'?"

"Go for it, cowboy."

When their brims collided, both hats tumbled to the chapel floor. As their lips touched, the crowd broke into thunderous cheers and applause.

For a list of other books by
Stephen Bly
or information regarding speaking engagements
write:
Stephen Bly
Winchester, Idaho 83555